Praise for J

"Swashbuc... about: this ... tasy, magic...
—Kari ...

"A fabulou... heroine."

"I should ... this book proves it. *Winterwood* is an easy, compelling read which ticks loads of boxes—pirates, fae, adventure, angst, ghosts, wild magic—whilst managing to surprise you with unexpected plot developments and delight you with its beautifully paced story and believably strange world. A delicious page-turner."
—Jaine Fenn, author of the Hidden Empire novels

"Bedford crafts emotionally complex relationships and interesting secondary characters while carefully building an innovative yet familiar world."
—*RT Book Reviews*

"Swashbuckling adventure collides with mystical mayhem on land and at sea in this rousing historical fantasy series launch set in a magic-infused England in 1800."
—*Publishers Weekly*

"It's like an irresistible smorgasbord of all my favorite themes and fantasy elements all in one place, and a strong, compelling female protagonist was the cherry on top."
—Bibliosanctum

"Pirates, magic, and fae in nineteenth-century England. Yes, please! *Winterwood* marks the start of Jacey Bedford's new Rowankind series, and it's a series I can't wait for more of!"
— No More Grumpy Bookseller

W9-BRM-718

SILVERWOLF

Rowankind: Book Two

JACEY BEDFORD

DAW BOOKS, INC.
DONALD A. WOLLHEIM, FOUNDER
375 Hudson Street, New York, NY 10014

ELIZABETH R. WOLLHEIM
SHEILA E. GILBERT
PUBLISHERS
www.dawbooks.com

.i 121049553

ACKNOWLEDGMENTS

My family: husband, mom, and kids for putting up with me while I'm in writing mode and living inside my head, forgetting to cook, eat, organize, tidy, and otherwise do normal everyday stuff.

My editor: Sheila Gilbert and all at DAW, including Josh Starr and publicist Kayleigh Webb. My agent: Amy Boggs of Donald Maass Literary Agency.

Beta readers: Carl Allery, Tina Anghelatos, Terry Jackman, John and Sara Moran, and Sue Oke. All the writers attending Milford SF Writers' Conference in September 2015: Liz Williams, Kari Sperring, Ben Jeapes, David Clements, David Turnbull, Val Nolan, Jackie Hatton, Tiffani Angus, Chris Butler, Matt Colborn, Pauline Morgan, Heather Lindsley, and Gus Smith. Northwrite SF Writers: Sue Thomason, Ian Creasey, Liz Sourbutt, Tony Ballantyne, and C.J. Jessop. Critique groups of writing peers are invaluable.

My good friend and singing partner in Artisan, Hilary Spencer, whose eagle eye catches a lot of my typos before I make too much of a fool of myself.

Happy Ever Afters

*Deep in the Old Maizy Forest,
Somewhere near Chard, Somerset*

Early Spring 1801

A LARGE SILVER-GRAY SHAPE trotted out of the trees, a grizzled brown hare dangling dead in its jaws. In wolf form, Corwen was almost the height of a small pony, but he had to hold up his head to prevent the hare's legs from dragging on the ground. He dropped it to the side of the path and in one smooth movement changed from wolf to naked man.

Corwen was a superb wolf, but I also appreciated his human form. His mane of silver-gray hair, that color since childhood, made him look older and more distinguished from a distance, but close up he was a young man in his prime, tall and well-muscled with lean flanks, a flat belly, and all the attributes a man needs.

"Good hunting by the looks of it." My voice caught in my throat.

Corwen flashed a smile in my direction before drawing a bucket of water from the barrel and dipping his face and hands into it. Damn him, he knew exactly what effect he had on me. I wanted to reach out and stroke his firm back, but I wouldn't give him the satisfaction. Instead, I bent, grasped a dandelion rosette, and pulled. The soft earth from last night's rainfall allowed the whole thing—root and leaves—to come up in my hand, so rather than toss it on the growing pile of weeds, I dropped it into my basket of edibles.

"Yes, very good," he said, straightening from the bucket and shaking off excess water. "I brought a hare for the pot. There may have been a rabbit involved as well." He grinned, white teeth with a hint of the canines showing. "Just a small snack."

"A snack? You still don't trust my cooking?" I dusted off my hands on the seat of my canvas slops, wide-legged trousers left over from my sailing days, and picked up the basket.

"Let's say it's a good job your Aunt Rosie's notebooks included some recipes. Shall I clean the hare and joint it?"

"Now?" I made a wide-eyed face at him.

"You have something else in mind?"

"I might have."

"You're a wicked woman, Ross Tremayne. Come here."

"Uh, get used to calling me Sumner. I need to leave the name of Tremayne on the quayside."

"Sumner rather than your maiden name?"

"Yes. There's a warrant for Rossalinde Goodliffe in Plymouth. I'll reclaim my mother's family name, I think."

"I don't mind what I'm to call you as long as you come here right now."

"Right now?"

"Right now."

I dropped the basket, walked into his nakedness, and held him tight, feeling the heat of his body through the linen of my shirt. I licked the cool water from his lips and pulled his head down to mine.

As he raised his head from the lingering kiss, I wriggled out of his embrace.

"Going so soon?" he asked.

"You want to eat raw hare for supper?"

"I could—"

I stepped in close and pressed against him, a promise for later.

He said something inarticulate like, "Mmmmnnngg," and kissed me again thoroughly. I was tempted to stay where I was, possibly forever, but the makings of dinner awaited. I pushed one hand against his chest, feeling his heart thumping.

"So—you were saying—about my cooking . . ."

"You haven't killed me with it yet."

"Such kind words. Careful, or you'll turn my head."

To be honest, that was probably as much of a compliment as my cooking deserved.

When I was a girl in Plymouth, I'd watched our rowankind in the kitchen. Ruth and Evy had even let me chop vegetables on occasion, but cooking was largely a mystery to me. When I'd run away to sea with my late husband, Will, Lazy Billy had been ship's cook and we'd eaten with the crew. Now Corwen and I were on our own, and I'd learned more about cooking than I thought possible.

I wondered how households across the country were managing without their rowankind bondservants, but decided it wasn't my problem. I liked the quiet life, undisturbed by visitors, magical creatures, or government agents bent on our destruction. I wanted to put the past behind me.

Corwen grinned and turned away. I watched his naked buttocks as he bent to retrieve the hare and take it round to the back of the cottage.

Sighing, I found the last few winter cabbages hiding behind the skeletons of last autumn's woody weeds, cleared around them, and yanked out one for the pot. Satisfied with my afternoon's labors, I washed my hands and face in the icy water, retrieved the basket, and went indoors.

While I'd been finishing my tasks outside, Corwen had finished dressing. He'd skinned, cleaned, and jointed the hare, and was now setting a pot over the fire with herbs and onions from Aunt Rosie's store. He hummed while he worked, a rich, warm sound in a low register that made me shiver. Since we'd relaxed into a life of domesticity, Corwen had found his voice and I loved listening to him.

Will had not been able to hold a tune in a bucket, though he'd been able to shout out a shanty over the howl of the gale when he'd needed to keep the men working in rhythm aboard the *Heart of Oak*. His crew had always responded as if he were the sweetest singer in the world. I could sing, but I'd never had the vocal power for shanties when I'd captained the *Heart*. I left that to a sailor called Windward, who had lungs on him like bellows and a store of dubious verses.

I'd expected to miss life at sea, but I didn't regret leaving it behind for a moment. This was our happy-ever-after—Corwen's and mine—a well-earned interlude after the freeing of the rowankind, a time to heal and reflect. Aunt Rosie's cottage, empty since Rosie had married Leo, was our safe place, protected by a glamour. The Old Maizy Forest itself was one of those liminal places, half in the real world, but only a few steps away from Iaru, the magical home of the Fae.

We'd found a deep sense of peace here, and time to get to know each other properly: one ex-privateer captain and self-confessed witch and one wolf shapechanger formerly in the employ of the Lady of the Forests. We knew it couldn't last forever and soon we'd have to think about our place in the real world, but for now it was all we wanted.

I peeled three large potatoes from Aunt Rosie's store and sliced them into the pot with the neatly jointed hare. As I cleaned and chopped the cabbage and set it aside to be added later, I sensed Corwen behind me. He put his arms around me, his right hand sliding along my arm until he stretched to clasp my knife hand.

"I make it a rule never to touch a woman in intimate places while she has a knife in her hand, especially when she knows how to use it." His voice was husky and soft.

I let the knife clatter to the table as Corwen's lips touched the side of my neck, his breath coming in puffs of warmth on my skin.

He pulled up the long-tailed shirt I had tucked inside my

slops. There was a lot of shirt, and it gave up its secrets slowly, seeming to take hours until his big warm hand met with the tender skin of my belly. I sank backward into him. He held me steady with one hand while the other joined it beneath the fabric and explored upward. I gave a low moan as it reached my breast and then another of deprivation when it continued upward past the ticklish skin of my underarm, into the folds of my sleeve, to my elbow and thence to my wrist. I pulled my arm through the shirt cuff and freed it.

My other arm followed, and he drew the folds of linen over my head, letting the garment pool at our feet. Undoing a couple of buttons loosed my slops to fall to the floor with the shirt, and I stepped out of them. The warmth from the fire flickered across my naked skin as our supper bubbled in the pot.

I spun to face him.

"Ah, Ross," he murmured, running his hands down my back as I tugged on the open neck of his shirt, kissing the hollow at the base of his throat. I unfastened the two neat rows of buttons on the front of his breeches, and our articles of clothing cuddled together in front of the fire.

He picked me up bodily and carried me to the wide bed. He'd made it with his own hands, his first job after we took over the one-room cottage. One of Corwen's minor arcane talents was being able to magically bind inanimate objects, and he'd taken delight in being able to fashion something practical.

The cool quilt was a shock to my naked back, but it warmed quickly.

Impatiently I pulled him onto the bed and ran my hands over his flesh, feeling the taut muscles beneath silken skin. Unlike my body, Corwen's is remarkably scar-free, since changing from wolf to human and back again heals all but mortal wounds.

I felt shabby in comparison. I have a scar across my ribs, and another on my arm, but the worst is my ear. I lost the top edge of it in an explosion that almost killed me. I felt his fingers trace the line of the scar across my ribs, and I reached down.

"Will stitched that one. He wasn't so good with a needle."

"He did his best."

"It puckers at the end. It's ugly."

"Nothing about you is ugly."

"Even this?" I touched the top of my ear.

"Especially not that. Your hair covers it from the world, and there's no need to cover it from me, ever."

He kissed me on the ear, and then his tongue drew a hot line down my neck to my throat. I stroked his flanks and across the ticklish spot between hip and groin, drawing a gasp from him, or maybe it was a curse.

"Steady, woman, or you'll undo me."

"Undo, indeed." I wriggled my hips and dragged my nails lightly across his flank, then wrapped my legs around him and rubbed the soles of my feet down his legs. He groaned and reached between us, at which point I turned to jelly. "Now, Corwen."

"Now?"

"Yes."

"Sure?"

"Yes, now, damn you."

He laughed delightedly as I rose to meet him.

"Corwen!" A loud shout and a heavy thump on the door sent a shock through both of us. "Corwen!"

My love pulled away suddenly, leaving me bereft and panting as if I'd run a mile.

"Corwen!" Another thump on the door.

Corwen swore like one of my common sailors. It was my turn to say something like, "Nnnngggrrrh."

With my hearing and Corwen's nose, it's hard for anyone to sneak up on us, but preoccupied as we were, someone had.

"Someone's here." I stared hard at the door as if it would reveal what lay beyond.

"That much is obvious." Corwen sniffed. "It's all right. It's Hartington."

"It's not all right. Tell him to go away."

Hartington was Corwen's long-time friend and one-time mentor, the stag shapechanger from the Lady's retinue.

Corwen rolled off me and lurched toward his breeches.

"A social call?" I asked.

He sighed and tossed my shirt onto the bed. "I doubt it."

"Corwen, are you in there?"

"Hartington, one moment."

I fought my sense of loss and dragged on my shirt and slops.

"Have I caught you at a bad time?" Hartington sounded amused on the other side of the door.

Corwen swore again. "His hearing is as keen as mine. He bloody knows he caught us at a bad time."

"In that case, can't he hear what you just said?"

Corwen grinned. "Of course he can. Are you decent?"

"Well, I'm clothed . . ."

◆━━━━◆

By the time Corwen opened the door, I hoped the flush was fading from my face although I suspected it wasn't. Hartington stood on the doorstep, his features schooled into a neutral expression as if this were a casual morning call from a polite society acquaintance.

I wondered if he'd traveled on horseback or in stag form. If the latter, he'd managed to clothe himself since changing to human. Like Corwen, he probably had one of the magical packs that held so much more than they seemed to have room for and then melted into his shape when he changed. A little forethought generally meant shapechangers arrived at their destination with clothing to change into. Mistakes could be embarrassing.

Hartington ignored Corwen's meaningful glare and greeted him warmly. He bowed to me more formally, his sandy hair, gray-streaked at the temples, escaping from its loosely tied ribbon. He had a thin, fine-boned face, an upright, almost haughty carriage, and unexpectedly gentle brown eyes. If I hadn't known he was a stag in his animal form, I might have guessed it anyway from his looks. I wondered at his firm friendship with Corwen: wolf and stag, predator and prey. Lucky that shapechangers retained a measure of their rational humanity when in their animal forms.

I wasn't sure whether to bow or curtsey since I was hardly dressed to receive polite company. Corwen had his shirt open at the neck, long tails hanging outside his breeches, and bare feet.

I settled for holding out my hand and Hartington took it, smiling.

"You both look well. You've had time to heal."

Some scars were invisible, but the physical ones had healed as much as they were going to.

"We have," Corwen said.

"Well rested, I trust?"

His voice was light. It might have been a polite inquiry, but to me the words sounded ominous. It wasn't simply a casual question.

Corwen obviously thought the same. "Why would we need to be well rested? What's happened? Does the Lady of the Forests need us?"

"There is a matter she would like your help with."

"A matter she can't deal with herself?"

"She rules the forests. This concerns the sea."

"The sea?" My stomach lurched. "It's not the *Heart*, is it?"

"We have no news of your ship."

"That's good, I expect." I breathed easy again. My old friend Hookey Garrity and his crew of barely reformed pirates were cruising French waters in my lovely tops'l schooner under letters of marque from Mad King George for prizes of fat merchantmen.

"I should say it's a matter of the seashore," Hartington said. "A water horse, a kelpie, has carried off two children."

I felt slightly sick. It was my fault wild magic had returned to Britain. I didn't know much about kelpies, other than the basics. They were shapechanging demons who looked like ponies. They lured unsuspecting people onto their backs, then galloped into the water and drowned and ate their victims. I shuddered. Did I need to know much else? If a kelpie had taken two children, the poor little mites weren't coming back.

"Where?" Corwen asked.

"South Devon, Bigbury on Sea, not far from Bur Isle."

"Aren't kelpies normally associated with Scotland?" Corwen frowned. "It's way out of its own territory."

"I know it." I interrupted. "Bur Isle, I mean, not the kelpie." Raised in Plymouth, I'd visited the area as a child with my father during one of his homecomings between voyages. "Bur Isle is barely a few hundred yards off the coast. You can walk across at low water, but it's cut off from the mainland at high tide. There's an old inn, I forget its name, and tales of smuggling."

"What about the Mysterium?" Corwen asked. "Are they investigating the disappearances?"

"There's a Mysterium office in Kingsbridge," Hartington said. "It's not as big or as busy as the one in Plymouth, but it's still substantial. At the moment no one is treating this as a magical problem, so neither the Mysterium nor the Kingsmen are involved. We should be safe from them—as safe as anyone ever is—though it's always wise to be vigilant, of course."

"So if they're not treating it as a magical problem, what are they treating it as?" Corwen asked.

"The children were taken on two separate occasions. The first was a farmer's son, taken from the bank of the River Aven. The locals thought he might have run away as he's a troublesome lad. Then the second, the daughter of Reverend Purdy's rowankind housekeeper, disappeared from close to the parsonage. They're taking that more seriously as the child is generally obedient and not much given to pranks."

"The reverend has a rowankind housekeeper? Still?" I asked.

"She's not there under duress, but employed. I suspect the missing child to be only half-rowankind."

"The reverend's bastard?"

"His son's more likely." Hartington sighed. "We don't know the full details. It's sometimes better not to ask. The real problem is the kelpie."

"Of course." I frowned. "What does the Lady want us to do? Capture it? Kill it? Can kelpies even be killed?"

"Oh, yes. They can be killed, but they're devilish tricky, have teeth like a tiger, and their hide is tough. It takes silver to kill them, or hot iron, or possibly fire. You can capture them, but only if you find them without a bridle and put on a halter embossed with a cross." He cleared his throat. "At least that's what the legends say. No one knows for sure, except perhaps the kelpie, and it's not saying."

Corwen set his mouth in a line. "Is one wolf enough to deal with a kelpie?"

"Possibly not, but a summoner, a wolf, and a marksman should be enough."

"You're coming, too?"

Hartington nodded. "While you've been lazing about here, I've been chasing round the country after a number of minor magical eruptions: an infestation of pixies in Cornwall; a hob in Coventry; and a headless horseman riding across Wimbleton Common."

"That's one of the things I was worried about." I frowned. "Wild magic released into the world." I turned to Corwen. "Walsingham was right."

"He's dead now. He can't hurt us."

"They'll appoint another one. There's always a Walsingham working against magic. He's as much a danger to us as the Mysterium—maybe more so because he works in secret. He might be on our trail even now. If I hadn't—"

"It's not your fault." Corwen turned to me.

"Whose fault is it, then? I freed the rowankind."

"We knew there was a possibility—"

"Yes, and we considered it worth the risk. I considered it worth the risk. And now two children are dead because of me."

"And thousands of rowankind are free."

I breathed deeply and swallowed hard. "It's still a damned difficult equation to balance."

"Then let's away to Devon while it's still only two children."

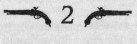

2

The Kelpie

WE SHARED THE HARE WITH HARTINGTON, and we three talked the moon across the sky. At last, our visitor bedded down on the rug in front of the fire. Corwen pulled me to him under the blankets. With Hartington sleeping across the room, all we could do was snuggle together.

We rose at dawn to pack for the trip. Corwen doused the remains of the fire, and I dried and put away the crockery from our meal, leaving everything tidy for when we returned. I hoped it wouldn't be long.

South Devon was a journey of nearly seventy miles, and would have taken us two days even on our Fae-bred horses, but we could cut that journey to little more than a couple of hours if we slipped into and out of Iaru, the Fae's otherworld, accessed via those places in the forests where the walls between worlds had worn thin.

The Fae never said please or thank you, but we'd done them a great service in freeing the rowankind and they didn't like being in anyone's debt. We had permission to traverse Iaru from Larien, one of the seven Lords who formed the Fae council. I could almost claim kinship to him, though I don't think the English language has a term for the father of one's illegitimate Fae half-brother.

Corwen had an instinct for finding his way in and out of the Fae's otherworld at the right points, but I confess my sense of direction was not all that good. I was used to navigating by charts, quadrant and sextant, and by time, the sun, and the stars. Corwen navigated by his nose.

I suspected our Fae-bred horses could navigate Iaru as well, or better than we could.

They were the finest horses I'd ever seen, or ridden, but they must have been protected by a glamour because few people ever remarked on them. Corwen's gray stood sixteen hands high and my bay was only a couple of inches shorter. Both had elegant heads and intelligent eyes. I wasn't altogether sure they weren't sentient in some way, though Corwen assured me they weren't shapechangers, which was a great relief, and would have been so embarrassing to discover.

It had taken us a while to name them. Finally we settled on Timpani for Corwen's gray for the way his hooves drummed the ground at full gallop, and Dancer for my bay, who was altogether lighter on his feet.

Though I'd determined to leave my man's attire at the bottom of my sea chest when I started my new life with Corwen, kelpie hunting didn't sound like an activity I could undertake in a muslin gown, so I once more donned breeches, boots, linen shirt, and a frock coat. It was my Captain Tremayne persona, but with Tremayne now officially dead, I could just as easily go by the name of Ross Sumner.

Rather than change to stag form, Hartington rode double with Corwen as we crossed between worlds. The home of the Fae overlaps our own land yet occupies no space. Our world and Iaru are like two sheets of parchment loosely rolled together. There are places where they touch, and it's possible to step through.

Iaru is a place of lush woodland greenery, of bright glades and deep forests where it's always summer. The Fae live there. Their dwellings are grown and woven from living trees and plants, seeming to be both inside and outside at the same time. They live by magic. I've never seen fields where their food is grown or kitchens where it is cooked. Even their roads are more like deer tracks, mere suggestions of traveled pathways. Our Fae-bred horses picked their way through the landscape instinctively, for which I was grateful.

Iaru is both enchanted and mundane. The April chill that seeped into our bones at home faded as the woodland around us transformed from budding spring to lush summer foliage. We breasted an invisible barrier which manifested only as a kind of physical pressure. Our horses flicked their ears and looked about them as if they recognized home. My bay began to fidget. His stride shortened and his head came up.

Corwen laughed. "I think they're eager to gallop. Hold on." The last instruction to Hartington.

Despite carrying two riders, Timpani set the pace at a hand gallop and Dancer followed eagerly. When they slowed and stood with ears pricked, I thought we must be close to a crossing point. Moving forward more cautiously, I felt the change in temperature as we stepped through, leaving Iaru's summer for a showery English spring.

"We're in the Okewood," Corwen said.

"You recognize it?" I asked, knowing the Okewood was vast.

"I do. I spent the best part of six years running these woods as both man and wolf. There are few parts of it I don't recognize."

The woodland thinned out here. I could smell the tang of the sea blowing in on a coastal breeze. Beyond the trees a country lane lay deeply embedded between overgrown banks. A way marker said we were two miles from Ivybridge which meant we were scarce ten miles from our destination.

A distant church bell chimed nine as we came to Ringmore, where the parsonage stood surrounded by a high wall. Bigbury on Sea itself lay beyond, nothing more than a hamlet with a few fishermen's cottages by the shore, so having stared across the tide-race to Bur Isle, cut off until three in the afternoon, we returned to Ringmore and put up at the New Inn. We were able to secure two rooms, a nooning of bread, cheese, and pickles, washed down with local cider, and some gossip about the missing children.

The first child had been a ten-year-old boy who was something of a rascal, often in trouble with the neighbors, but — as yet — not with the local magistrate. He'd been seen close by the River Aven on the morning of his disappearance, riding a black horse that certainly didn't belong to his parents. They owned only one plow horse, and that a skewbald.

The second child, the eight-year-old half-rowankind girl, was a pleasant, intelligent child, not inclined to wander off alone without permission. Her mother had sent her to gather sea campion, wild daffodil, and sweet cicely to brighten the house. She'd not returned. No horses had been seen in the vicinity.

There had been, the innkeeper said, a grisly find on the beach by Bigbury on Sea, above the high tide mark. Entrails.

"Classic sign of a kelpie at work," Hartington muttered quietly.

"Human?" Corwen asked.

The innkeeper nodded. "But not very big. Mrs. Hampson, the boy's mother, identified a scrap of cloth found with the remains as being from the boy's shirt."

An involuntary cold shiver ran up my spine.

"Should we go and talk to the parents?" I asked. "Maybe the disappearances have something in common that might give us a clue, a time of day, perhaps."

"You and Hartington visit the parents," Corwen said. "I'll go and sniff around on the riverbank and see if I can pick up any clues."

Corwen's nose was good, even in human form, though he'd probably do better after dark when he could transform into a wolf.

I looked at Hartington. "Do you want to visit the farmer or the reverend's housekeeper?"

He shrugged. "Farmer, if that suits you."

A short while later I strolled past the church, pausing to take in the view to the sea at Aymer Cove. The salt tang of the air stirred memories of Will, dead these past four years from a senseless accident aboard the *Heart* in a storm. Vibrant and alive one minute, gone the next, killed by a falling spar. William Redbeard Tremayne had deserved a better death than that. He'd always seemed indestructible. His death had opened up the possibility that anyone I loved could be extinguished at any time by a whim of fate.

The parsonage gate swung open on its hinges, creaking rhythmically in the breeze. I briefly considered trying the kitchen door, but decided on the straightforward approach. I walked to the porticoed front and rattled the lion's head door knocker. I wondered if the housekeeper would be the one to answer, but after a few moments the door opened and the clergyman himself regarded at me quizzically.

"Reverend Purdy?"

The man was rheumy and pale, in his sixties, and of middle height, so I could look him directly in the eyes. He wore a neat gray wig, slightly old-fashioned, but not out of keeping with his age and status.

"I am he." His voice held a question.

"Ross Sumner, sir, at your service." I gave a polite half bow. "I am come about the missing child. My friends and I are conducting an investigation into a child missing in Dawlish and heard about the children here. We came to inquire as to the circumstances." We'd concocted the story between us, and Dawlish was distant enough that our lie couldn't be quickly disproved. We hoped not to be here long.

"A bad business, Mr. Sumner. Will you step inside? I'm sorry to greet you so informally, and without even a kettle on the boil to offer you tea, but my whole household is out searching. Livvy—Olivia—is very dear to us."

I wondered again whether the child was his own daughter, but following him through to his study I spotted a portrait on the wall, a younger man, dressed in a red officer's coat with yellow facings, seated by a window, the light playing on his features. He was a more handsome version of the reverend. Standing next to him, offering a small posy of wild flowers, was a girl child aged four or five with a sweet face and the delicate features of a rowankind.

The reverend saw where I was looking. "My son, Henry." His voice caught in his throat. "He's serving with the 77th Regiment of Foot in India, a lieutenant. Yes, the child is Olivia."

I swallowed the temptation to say she took after her father. The relationship in the portrait was not explicit, and she could easily be passed off as a household servant. Whether the artist had played down the skin coloring of the child or whether she truly lacked the gray wood-grain facial markings of a full-blood rowankind was difficult to tell.

The reverend waved me to a chair.

"When did Olivia disappear?"

"Five days ago."

"During daylight hours?"

"Yes, early afternoon."

"And there's no possibility she's run off? No arguments with anyone? No one she's afraid of?"

"No." He avoided my eyes. "She's . . . like family."

"Indeed. May I speak to the child's mother?"

"I would be grateful if you would."

I must have frowned without realizing it because he began to explain and then ground to a halt. Taking a deep breath, he began again. "Since Olivia disappeared, Charlotte has gone out each morning at sunrise, wrapped herself in a blanket, and sat alone on a rise overlooking the sand bank to Bur Isle. Nothing I can say will dissuade her. You'll find her there, rain or fine."

"Thank you."

I rose to leave.

"Mr. Sumner . . ."

I stopped and turned.

"Have you lost someone, too? A child?"

"Not in this way, Reverend, but, yes, I have."

"Will you come and tell me if you … find anything? Anything at all."

"I will."

I found the rowankind housekeeper, Charlotte, exactly where Reverend Purdy said I would. She looked up as I approached, liquid brown eyes in a heart-shaped face, skin the silvery color of weathered rowan wood with a grain pattern that enhanced her particular beauty. She was younger than I expected, still in her twenties, with dark lustrous hair blowing freely about her face in the breeze.

"You've come to help," she said as I dropped to a sitting position in front of her, crossing my legs.

I recognized the magical aura that clothed her.

"I felt your presence—and two more."

"Corwen and Hartington, shapechangers, a wolf and a stag."

"What are you?"

"A summoner."

"*The* Summoner."

"I was. Now I'm what's left over. I have whatever magic the summoning didn't use up. It's not what it once was, but I'll help if I can."

I knew the clothes didn't fool her for a moment, but she never mentioned my dress or my gender or even asked my name.

"If Livvy were dead, I would know," she said. "I don't know where she is, but she's not dead."

I didn't want to give her false hope. "It's a kelpie," I told her, and watched her face pale visibly.

She knew what that meant. She compressed her mouth into a straight line, took several breaths as if to steady herself, and said, "She's not dead."

Until we learned otherwise, I would trust the mother to know.

"Have you seeking magic?" she asked.

"A little. Do you have anything of your daughter's with you?"

She uncurled her right hand and revealed a lock of soft baby hair, tied around with a sliver of white ribbon.

"May I keep a few strands?"

She held out a small portion of the curl for me to take. "Do you have any seeking magic yourself?" I asked.

She shook her head. "Since we all discovered . . . remembered . . . I found I can work with wind and water, and I have some affinity for growing things."

Wind and water magic. How I missed that ability to call the weather, or still it. I'd lost it in that Great Summoning when I returned magic to the rowankind. I didn't regret it, but still I mourned it.

I closed my own fist around the tiny lock of hair and settled myself. Charlotte reached out and covered my hand with her own, offering to share what magical power she could. Every little helped, and Charlotte burned with a steady magical presence common to all rowankind.

I reached out to search for the child.

Immediately, I understood that she wasn't dead. I found a presence linked to the hair I held, but all around her was darkness. I could call her to me and see if my summoning would bring her forth, but that might be an end of her if she were hiding from something. I tried to get a direction, but I couldn't. I didn't think she was far away, though.

"I told you she wasn't dead." Charlotte's eyes sparkled.

"So all we have to do is find her."

And find the kelpie; otherwise no child would be safe.

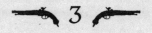

3

Bur Isle

I TUCKED MYSELF INTO A CORNER of the New Inn's front room, close to the window overlooking the street, and waited for Corwen and Hartington. They arrived at the same time from opposite directions.

"Anything?" I asked.

"You first," Corwen said, nursing a mug of spiced cider.

"I don't know about the kelpie, but the girl, Olivia, is still alive, either hiding, or imprisoned somewhere dark. Her mother is rowankind. I'm pretty sure her father is Reverend Purdy's son Henry, who is currently serving in the army."

"Well, that's good news—that she's alive, I mean," Corwen said.

"The boy certainly isn't," Hartington said. "The remains that were found, unidentifiable viscera, mainly, were not large enough to be from a full-grown adult. Reverend Purdy agreed that, given the circumstances, a funeral could be held, and they laid the boy to rest in the churchyard. It's a sad business." He leaned forward and lowered his voice. "The parents believe whatever killed him came from the island."

"Why?" I asked.

"They think the island folk a little strange."

"They're probably involved in the smuggling trade with little liking for strangers."

"There is that," Corwen said. "But there's certainly something by the river—water weed and rotten fish. I can smell it on the shore, too, close to the sand bridge to the island."

"It's a puzzle," Hartington said. "If it's a kelpie, then surely they are creatures of deep lakes and rivers."

"There's a Cornish waterhorse legend associated with the sea," I said. "They don't call it a kelpie, but it is in all but name."

"Whatever it is, if it's taken two children and killed at least one of them, it needs ending." Corwen frowned. "Let's look on the island first."

We walked to the beach. The tide was receding, now, revealing the long, yellow sandbar that formed a causeway joining the mainland to the green dome of Bur Isle. It was already passable, though it would get wider yet. Low tide wasn't until dusk. We had about six hours until the sea flooded in and completely covered the sandbar. Although one might think the depth was not so great that a person couldn't breast the water and cross, the currents were vicious and many foolish strangers had been swept away. The locals knew better than to risk the crossing.

The distance was less than a third of a mile. The recently submerged sand sucked at our feet as we left Bigbury on Sea behind, keeping to the highest and driest part of the smooth causeway, writ anew with each tide. I remembered a few fishermen's cottages on the island and the Pilchard Inn, named for the main occupation of the inhabitants—or maybe the name was merely to fool the excise men, for some of the fisherfolk used their boats for catching more than fish. The smuggling trade with France, despite the enmity of our two governments, went on unabated with wine and brandy the catch of the day.

The few cottages clustered around the shoreline were poor enough, single rooms for the most part, hunched low into the landscape. The island's population obviously didn't prosper greatly either from pilchards or brandy.

The inn almost had its feet in the sea. It was built into the hillside, two stories when viewed from the sea side, but only one from the landward side with a rough track hardly deserving of the name of road rising up on the far side of it. We walked the few yards to the front door and entered the inn's only public room. The thick stone walls had been whitewashed once, but now they were smoke-stained with greasy dark marks at knee height where the landlord's dog, a broad-chested white mongrel, had brushed against them. Locals already occupied three of the four tables. They all looked up as we entered, and the buzz of conversation dropped. A shiver ran down my spine as I slid onto a settle, grateful for the high wooden back behind me.

The landlord was amiable enough, but there was a reserve about him. I wondered whether he had a cellar full of contraband and thought we might be excise men in disguise.

"You'll have heard about the children missing on the mainland," Corwen said conversationally.

There was uncomfortable shifting in their chairs, but the locals said nothing, though one muttered something to his companions.

"Not heard?" Corwen tried again.

"It's a bad business," one whiskered old fellow said in a squeaky voice.

"I ain't lettin' my kids out of the door after dark," another man said.

"The little parsonage girl disappeared in daylight," the whiskery man said.

There was thoughtful silence at that.

The landlord barely gave us time to drink up before he came to collect our empty tankards, whisking them away without asking if we wanted a refill. "You'll be away before dark, I expect," he said. "You being strangers and all, and not used to the causeway. Accidents happen, and it's safest in daylight."

I saw Corwen's shoulders rise and fall in a slight shrug.

This wasn't a place for gossip, not the sort that included outsiders at any rate. We took the hint and left, hearing the sound of conversation rise behind us. The track that began at the beach and led past the front door of the inn dwindled to a couple of ruts farther up the hill, but was easy enough to follow. A few sheep, with lambs at their heels, nibbled the short, tough grass. The occasional *maaa* mingled with the loud calls of gulls and the constant sound of waves on rock.

You could walk across the dome of the island in little more than half an hour, and probably explore the whole place in less than two. It had seemed much larger when I was a child. I recalled tiny coves, hardly more than cracks in the rocky outcrops that passed for cliffs, not enormously high, but the rocks below were jagged and dangerous where the sea dashed against them.

"Do you think there are caves?" I asked. "Olivia was in darkness. It could have been a cave."

"Or it could have been the cellar of that damned inn." Corwen jerked his head toward the Pilchard. "The landlord could do with a lesson in hospitality."

"He certainly didn't want us there," Hartington said.

"Probably got a cellar full of illegal brandy," I said. "We may not be wearing red coats, but we could still be agents of the Excise."

"What's that?" Corwen pointed to a low stone building, bereft of a door, and with a hole where a window had once been.

"The remains of a chapel," I said, remembering my father's stories. "From the monastery that was here hundreds of years ago. It's deconsecrated. The locals use it as a vantage point to see when the huge shoals of pilchards are running in the bay, usually around mid-July. There's fishing all year round, but July's a frenzy. They salt the pilchards and press them for oil, possibly even trade some for contraband."

"Where was the rest of the monastery?" Hartington asked.

"I suspect the stones were robbed to build the cottages. I doubt it was ever such a grand affair as Mont Saint-Michel."

Corwen tested the air. "There's something here that I scented by the river." He reached for his neck cloth and began to pull it off. "I can follow the trail better in my other form."

"What if someone sees you?" I asked. "There probably aren't many wolves native to Bur Isle."

"There's not much choice, especially if we're going to take the landlord's advice and leave while we still have daylight."

He ducked into the remains of the chapel and a few minutes later a huge silver-gray wolf emerged. He quartered the ground, ignored a knot of sheep which ran off in a panic at his scent, and ranged outward, nose down, trotting back and forth across the rough hillside totally absorbed. He began to track in narrower and narrower sweeps as if he'd found something, then he ceased quartering altogether, gave a small yip, and headed directly toward the cliff.

Intent on following him, I didn't see the small group of villagers—five men—until a shout went up and a flintlock discharged with a small puff of smoke and a loud crack. Corwen raced for the cliff edge, hesitating on the brink. The villagers broke into a run. There was another puff of smoke and a crack. Corwen yelped and flung himself over the cliff.

"Stop!" Heart in my mouth, I ran as fast as I could, Hartington close behind. We reached the cliff edge at the same time as the villagers. I peered over, fearful of what I might see. Thirty feet below there was an inlet, hardly more than a cleft in the cliff, filled with a jagged tumble of rocks. Churning waves foamed around them.

There was no sign of Corwen, either as a wolf or a man.

"He won't be stealing no more of our sheep if he's gone over yon rocks," said a self-satisfied voice behind me.

"What do you mean?" Hartington asked, taking their attention from me as I dropped to my knees to look more closely. There was a paw print on the cliff edge, but nothing else.

"Damn big dog's been killing lambs this past three weeks.

Didn't you see him? Near as big as a hoss. Been trying to catch him in daylight, but he's crafty. Reckon we've done for him now, though. Won't be any more guts left on the shoreline."

"Guts?" I heard Hartington say through the fog that had descended on my spinning brain.

I wanted to call out to Corwen, to see if by some chance he'd crawled into a crevice, injured but alive. Had he gone into the deadly water, shot through the heart or the head, or been dashed to pieces on the rocks? I could barely breathe for the tightness in my chest.

I pushed down my panic. It was an old pistol, hardly accurate. It would have been a lucky shot if they'd even winged him at that distance, let alone hit him anywhere vital. Even so, the fall and the ocean could kill him. Wolves don't swim well and the outgoing tide sucked and slurped hungrily at the rocks. I raised my eyes from the cleft and scanned the ocean beyond.

Nothing.

Nothing except angry waves, anyway. This side of the island faced the open sea, choppy and gray on this April day. Oh, if only I still had that magical connection with water.

"They've gone." Hartington knelt by my side.

Something in the back of my brain had registered a conversation taking place above my head, and the self-satisfied noises of men happy with the outcome of their labor, but until Hartington dropped down beside me, I hadn't noticed them leave.

"It's not sheer and his wolf is nimble," Hartington said.

"But he doesn't swim well."

"The wolf may not, but Corwen does. Can you summon him?"

He meant magically *summon* him. I could try, but either I would draw him to me, still living, or—and this is what I dreaded—I would summon Corwen's ghost.

After Will was killed, I mourned him so fiercely that one day I called his ghost into being, drawing him from the spirit world and beginning a period during which he would appear frequently, sometimes when I wanted him and sometimes not. He haunted me, accompanying me into shipboard skirmishes or turning up in the drowsy hours of the night, often professing his love. I'd clung to the remnant of what had been, not realizing that it was my desire preventing him from crossing over to that deeper place. When I finally did let him go, it was as if he'd died all over again.

And now my summoning might draw forth Corwen's ghost, and I would know for certain he was gone from the world.

I couldn't bear it.

Not again. My fear froze me.

"Call him, Ross!" Hartington's voice was sharper this time. "Quickly! Before it's too late. Call him to the surface."

Hartington rapped me lightly across the shoulder.

Of course! Quickly!

I closed my eyes and tried to connect with my magic.

Until the freeing of the rowankind, my greatest magical talent had been manipulating weather, wind, and water—or so I'd thought—but the Fae had taught me that I was, first and foremost, a *summoner*, able to call things to me both in the spirit world and the real world.

In my head and heart, I searched for Corwen's wolf, finding nothing. Then I searched for Corwen the man. There! A flicker of something I recognized. Pray God that it wasn't a ghost. I fastened on to it and pulled. And pulled.

A silver head broke the water. I thought at first it was Corwen's wolf, but he was in man form, naked in the April ocean. If he wasn't drowned, he might be frozen to death.

"Come on, man!" Hartington shouted down. "Climb, for the Lady's sake!"

The treacherous tide began to suck him away from the rocks. I *summoned* and *summoned* again. Whether it was my magic or his innate strength, he dragged himself onto a low rock, dripping water from his naked back and buttocks. From there he scrambled on to a higher rock and up again until he was climbing from foothold to foothold, clinging to cracks in the cliff face.

"Yes, that's it. Climb." Hartington slithered down to a

narrow ledge some ten feet below us, anchored himself to a toothlike needle of rock, and reached down to grasp Corwen's hand. One, or maybe both, grunted with the effort, and then Corwen's head appeared over the edge as Hartington hauled him up, naked and shivering.

He collapsed onto hands and knees and was thoroughly sick, heaving up seawater. I began to take off my jacket to pass it to him, but he solved the problem of clothing. His bare skin grew a downy pelt which lengthened into a thick, bushy, and—thankfully—dry coat of thick fur. He curled himself as close to the cliff face as he could, thumped his tail twice, and tucked his nose between his forepaws.

My head spun. I was delirious with joy.

Corwen changed back, silver fur becoming pink flesh, but now with a healthy glow, not the pallor of the half-drowned and dying of cold.

"Are you hurt?" I called down.

"Nothing serious. Can you get down here, Ross?"

"Why?"

"There's a cave entrance."

4

The Rowankind Child

I HATED CAVES.

    I wriggled over the cliff edge and negotiated the ten-foot climb down to the ledge. I could see what Corwen called a cave entrance, though it was hardly more than a crack between two pillars of rock, barely wide enough for a grown man to squeeze through.

    I looked at it doubtfully. "A waterhorse would never get through there."

    "Not in horse form, no," Corwen said. "But kelpies have human form as well, though I'm not sure they have human reasoning. They aren't like humans who turn into beasts. They are demon-beasts that take on human form. Always hungry. I doubt you can reason with a kelpie. Do you still have the child's hair?"

    I had a few strands wrapped in a kerchief. Enough. I took it from my pocket and held it in my fist, reaching out with my searching magic, trying to find Olivia.

    Darkness and the smell of death surrounded me. I was hungry, so hungry, yet sick to my stomach. I'd kept myself from dying of thirst by licking moisture as it dripped down

*the rock of this dark place. I could no longer feel my feet,
nor even the rough hemp ropes that bound my ankles. The
rope around my wrists had turned my fingers into aching
sausages once the initial pins and needles had subsided. My
clothes were sodden with the dampness of the cave and my
own piss. I wanted to die so that it would be over sooner. I
had seen what she'd done to the rotting and bloated flesh of
the boy. I didn't know why she hadn't killed me, but she
seemed to be waiting for me to die of my own accord.*

I swayed and would have fallen from the ledge, but Corwen steadied me. "You've found something?"

I shuddered. "I was in the little girl's head. She's in there.
Alive, but terrified, and with good cause."

Almost before I'd finished speaking, he was climbing to
the cave entrance.

"Corwen, wait. The child identified her captor as she. I
don't know whether it's a human or a demon-horse in
there, but we should go prepared."

I had the knife I always carried in my privateer captain
days, secured in a sheath behind my waist, but we'd not
come armed, or I thought not, anyway, until Hartington
drew a pistol from beneath his jacket. "Loaded with silver,"
he said. "Base metal won't kill a kelpie, but silver might if I
can hit something vital."

Might. And he had but one shot without a lengthy time
to reload and prime the weapon. Still, it was better than
nothing.

One behind the other, Corwen leading the way, we
squeezed into the narrow cave, traversing sideways through
the gap for what seemed like an age.

I conjured a witchlight, the magic starting deep in my
chest and running up my body and along my right arm to
form a soft glow in the palm of my hand, with barely the
luminosity of a single small candle flame. I tossed it down
to hover low to the ground in front of Corwen, ready to
snuff it out on command if he smelled the kelpie's presence ahead. It was a fine balance between darkness and
stealth.

"The child's in a cave nearby," I whispered, my voice bouncing straight back at me from the rock barely six inches in front of my face.

"It widens out ahead," Corwen said. "I can feel a breeze, and smell it. Seaweed, rotten fish, and decaying flesh."

The passage sloped downward, its sandy floor studded with protruding rocks to snag the unwary. Even with the witchlight, I tripped twice before I got into the rhythm of sliding my feet forward rather than stepping out.

The passage divided, but Corwen scented the air and led us along the righthand fork. When it divided again, we went to the left. There were marks of tools along the walls. Men had widened the natural passage.

"This is a smuggler's cave," I said. "Be careful."

Corwen grunted. "Douse the light."

I did, and we all stood in darkness for a few minutes until our eyes adjusted. Ahead, there was a faint pale glow, hardly a light source, but enough to draw us on. The passage split again and this time there was a set of rough-hewn steps in the stone going upward to where light filtered around the edges of a trapdoor.

"Did you say there had been a monastery here?" Hartington asked.

"So they say. Do we go up?"

"No, it's this way." Corwen led us past the steps and along what was obviously now an excavated tunnel. "Quiet as you can."

I didn't need a warning to soft-foot. I knew Hartington was behind me, but apart from the occasional indrawn breath I heard nothing. Corwen, up ahead, barefoot, was as silent as a hunting wolf. The light source was behind us now, but it was enough to show us a door. Thick planks, stout iron banding, and a lock without a key denied us entrance. Corwen bent and looked through the keyhole, then he sniffed the air current that flowed through it and listened carefully. "This is the place. Can you deal with the lock, Ross?"

Wrapped in a roll of cloth I had my set of lockpicks.

Thieves' charms, Lazy Billy had called them when he taught me how to use them aboard the *Heart of Oak*. My sailors had possessed a variety of skills, and I had made use of their knowledge.

I knelt. It was a simple rim lock, but these types of single-lever locks sometimes used side wardings to protect the mechanism. While Corwen changed into wolf form, I tested my skeleton keys against the gage of the lock, finding one that was close. I'd stripped off all the excess material from the key with a file, leaving only a small piece on the end to activate the mechanism. On the second attempt it turned with a click loud in the silence. I held my breath and listened for any sound of movement from the other side, but all I heard was a slight whimper.

"She's in there," I said. "I don't know if she's alone."

Corwen, in wolf form, had a much more acute sense of smell than in his human form, but no way of communicating other than by body language or with yips and howls. He sat on his haunches looking at the door, like a house dog asking to be let out into the yard. I understood immediately.

"Just the girl?" I asked.

He yipped softly, so I pulled open the door. It creaked for want of oil on the hinges. This was not a door used regularly, maybe not even the only entrance to this place if we were in the cellars of the long-vanished monastery.

"Who's there?" a child's voice called out.

"Friends," I said. "Olivia? Livvy?"

She sobbed. "Yes, oh, yes. That's me."

I put up a witch light and immediately wished I hadn't. The child huddled in a corner, wretched and shivering, her dress stained and torn, still damp. In the center of the cellar a stone trough held human remains: a head with the flesh gnawed from the cheeks and the eyeballs gone; broken bones with the marrow sucked out; a leg, small enough to be a child's, now blackened and putrid; a narrow rib cage still with gobbets of dried flesh clinging to it.

I felt my gorge rise and swallowed hard in an attempt not to part with the recently consumed cider still sloshing around in the pit of my stomach. I tried not to look at the grisly remains while I quickly crossed over to the child and drew my knife to cut her bonds. She held out her hands and then, when the rope dropped away, flung her arms around my neck, clinging in desperation.

I gave her a few moments of comfort before I sat her down and cut through the damp rope around her ankles. Her skin was chafed and bloody. She had one shoe on, but the other had been lost and her exposed foot was blue from the cold. "Can you walk?"

She tried to stand up, but took one look at Corwen's wolf and fell against me.

"Here, let me carry her." Hartington stepped forward. "We're here to take you to your mother, Olivia. Don't be afraid." He scooped her into his arms and nestled her as far as he could beneath his frock coat for warmth.

"She's coming back. The horse lady. She always comes back. She asks me why I didn't drown, why I'm not dead yet, and eats more of . . ." She jerked her head toward the stone trough. "Then she leaves. But she always comes back. She's waiting for me to die."

"Is she a woman or a horse?" I asked.

"A woman, now, but she was a horse before. A black horse, so pretty. I only reached out to stroke her mane, but the strands of it wrapped around my arm and pulled me onto her back by some kind of magic."

"Did she gallop into the sea with you? Try to drown you?"

The girl nodded.

I wondered how she'd survived.

Corwen yipped.

"Explanations later. Let's get out while we can," Hartington said.

"Not with my supper!"

A naked woman stood in the doorway. A rippling mane of long black hair covered her shoulders and draped across her breasts. Her skin was milky white with a startling triangle of darkness below her flat belly. She looked wholly human until she swished her tail in anger.

"Madam, you will eat no more children." Hartington fumbled beneath his coat for his pistol, but Olivia in his arms hampered him. I pulled my knife from the sheath behind my waist and held it in front of me, point up, testing the familiar balance in my hand.

Corwen bounded between me and the kelpie, snarling, ready to leap for her throat.

She startled like a horse, turned, and bolted from the wolf, her natural enemy in the wild. Corwen raced after her and I followed, with Hartington and Olivia close behind. I was barely in time to see her naked buttocks, human except for a horse's tail, disappearing up the carved stone steps, to a square of dusky light. Had we been in the caves so long that it was already getting dark outside?

The trapdoor above closed almost on Corwen's head. He yowled in frustration, changed instantly into a man again, and pushed at the weight of it, shoulder muscles bunching with the effort. It rose and crashed over, and we emerged into the ruined chapel. Halfway down the hillside a black horse galloped at breakneck speed. Corwen dropped to all fours and in silverwolf form streaked after her, scattering panicked sheep, bounding over rough grass and across boulders where she couldn't go. We began to run after, but Corwen swiftly outpaced us. We might as well have been standing still for all the good we could do.

Olivia whimpered in Hartington's arms. "Don't touch her. She'll drag you into the sea."

Corwen caught up with the fleeing kelpie and leaped at her throat. Wolf and horse fell, rolling over each other and scrambling to their feet again almost immediately. Corwen was immune to the charm that had pulled Olivia onto the creature's back, but he wasn't immune to her hooves. She reared and lashed out at him, then wheeled and pounded toward us.

"Here, take the child." Hartington pushed Olivia into my arms and drew out his flintlock pistol, taking steady aim, arm outstretched, the barrel a natural extension of it. He had one chance, one silver ball loaded, the pan primed,

the pistol cocked. He waited as she drew closer and closer
still. Only a head shot would work from this angle, and as
she labored up the hill, her head dipped and rose in a natural rhythm, making it an impossible target. The next best
was a shot to her chest, but a horse's heart is set well back.
A ball into the chest from the front would likely not have
enough momentum to tear through muscle and bone to kill
her stone dead, though it would slow her down, and if it
punctured a lung might do enough damage to kill her
slowly. Silver was poison to her kind.

Hartington stood his ground. I could see a blood vessel
jumping at his temple, but otherwise he showed no sign of
stress as the creature bore down on him. She saw the pistol,
slithered to a wild stop, and turned on her haunches, the
wolf behind, the pistol in front.

And Olivia and I to one side.

She ran at us.

Hartington fired.

I turned to protect the child with my body, but as the
kelpie barged into my side, I felt the magic sweep us onto
her back. They say a kelpie's back is as long as it needs to
be, and that she can carry as many riders as are fool enough
to touch her. Olivia and I had not been foolish, at least not
on purpose, but here we were, astride the glossy black back.
Olivia, in front of me, had the kelpie's bridle rein in her
hand.

I reached around Olivia and took the reins from her.

I could feel the kelpie mare's muscles rippling beneath
me with each stride. If Hartington had struck her with the
silver ball, it hadn't slowed her down. Corwen leaped, but
she shied sideways, a move that would likely have unseated
both of us had we been trying to stay on a bolting horse,
but now it was impossible for us to fall. It was as if we had
been stuck to her back.

She surged past Corwen and down the track to the sea.

He howled in frustration.

Light had almost vanished from the western sky and the
moon had not yet risen, but a glow from the windows of
the Pilchard Inn acted as a beacon. We plummeted down

the hill. I heard a cacophony of shocked voices as we hurtled toward the beach. Someone exclaimed about a blasted wild dog as Corwen shot past.

In the gloom I could see the tide had turned. Waves lapped in from both sides, consuming the wide stretch of sandy causeway. On the far side I could see lanterns moving close to the cluster of fishermen's cottages.

The kelpie tried to veer left from the safety of the causeway into the sea, trying to drown us both. I hauled on the right rein so fiercely that the mare's head came around, but still she galloped on, her hooves in the waves and the water up to her knees. Suddenly she swerved to the right, crossed the causeway in a single bound, and splashed into the sea on the other side. I yanked on the left rein, once more dragging her head around, but it was like trying to stop a sloop with the wind in her sails. She was belly-deep in water now, and my boots were wet. I could feel the pull of the current sucking around my knees, but the kelpie, unconcerned, plunged deeper. I dragged on the rein and hammered her rib cage with my right heel, but she wasn't a horse, trained to the commands of a rider; she was used to being the commander.

She lunged into the waves, lurching from her feet as soon as she was out of her depth, swimming as a horse might, then with a surge she dived beneath the waves and the water closed over our heads.

Or it should have done.

I continued to breathe. A bubble of air surrounded us.

Olivia.

Half-rowankind, the child had wind and water magic which gave her lordship of the air. A bubble had formed around us. That was how the child had survived, and the kelpie had been unable to kill her since the water had not done it for her. Maybe the creature could only eat the flesh of the drowned.

I still had my knife in my hand. I held Olivia around her shoulders, leaned forward, and plunged the knife into the kelpie's neck. The mare bucked beneath us. I drew it out and tried again. I couldn't reach the heart with a short blade, but I could reach the lungs. I drew back my leg, a movement that would have unseated me on a normal horse, and drove the point of my knife home behind Olivia's calf. The mare bucked again and veered to the left. I felt her scrambling for purchase as she once more emerged from the sea, screaming in anger and pain. The water streamed from us as the kelpie galloped on to Bigbury Beach. I thought her stride faltered now. I hoped so anyway.

Suddenly the magic released us. We were catapulted onto soft sand. I landed on top of Olivia and rolled, hoping I hadn't hurt her, though I had more than Olivia to worry about as the beast turned and reared up. A silver-gray shape flung itself at her windpipe and clamped on, lifted clean off his legs as she reared and stumbled backward. Dislodged, Corwen went for her spine, trying to bite anywhere that might disable her. I heard voices. A crowd of fisherfolk, led by Reverend Purdy and Charlotte, charged forward with an assortment of improvised weapons, from shovels to billhooks.

Charlotte dropped her hoe and grabbed Olivia, dragging her to safety.

I flung a bright witchlight into the air so that we could see where the next attack was coming from. The mare tried to dart through the cordon of villagers, still intent upon Olivia, the prey that had escaped her. Corwen leaped for her withers again, but one wolf, strong and determined as he was, couldn't kill a full-grown, angry horse unless he could tear out her throat or bite through her spine—and she was giving him little opportunity to do that.

Hartington staggered up to me. He'd run the third of a mile across the causeway at full pelt and as he raised the pistol, reloaded and cocked, I could see his hand shaking with exhaustion.

"Let me."

He relinquished the pistol to my grasp and I took steady aim.

"Corwen!" I yelled. "Get down!"

The wolf leaped for safety and gave me a clear side shot.

I aimed for the kelpie's heart and pulled the trigger. The pistol cracked and jerked in my hand. The kelpie screamed one last time and fell. As she did so she changed from a raging horse to a naked woman, lying sprawled and ungainly in death, human in appearance except for her mane and tail.

5

Magic Exposed

THERE WERE TOO MANY QUESTIONS to answer, so we answered none, leaving Reverend Purdy to organize the removal of the kelpie's body to the church and to set a watch over her to make sure she stayed dead. With silver in her heart and other injuries from knife and shot, I was pretty sure she was gone forever, but if they wanted to be absolutely certain, that was fine by me. I had no interest in the corpse whatsoever, though I was grateful she had not reverted to looking entirely like a mortal woman as I didn't want to stand trial for murder. The horse's tail left no doubt as to the magical nature of the situation.

A few people looked askance at Corwen, but no one tried to shoot him. He pressed himself to my side as we walked to the rectory, staying in wolf form largely because his clothes were somewhere behind us.

"There's a new Mysterium office in Kingsbridge." Reverend Purdy dropped back to walk with me, keeping his voice low. "Can you expect their help or . . . ?"

"It would be prudent to avoid the Mysterium. Is that a problem for you?" Country folk had always been more tolerant of magicals such as hedge-witches who had no quantifiable power to register with the Mysterium, but were somehow able to charm a wart or ease a colicky baby.

"I wondered if that were the case. I'm afraid they are more active than ever since the rowankind . . . you know." He frowned. "Kingsbridge used to have only one Mysterium officer, but now they have half a dozen and there are both Kingsmen and redcoats at their beck and call."

I put my hand on Corwen's sleek head and felt the low rumble of a growl vibrating through his body. I agreed with him. "We should leave," I said.

"This is a small community, and you've done us a great service. You can stay the night in safety. I offer you the comfort of my own home—in fact, I insist. Rest assured we'll know if the Mysterium approaches, but yes, tomorrow morning you should make all haste."

We agreed to stay, too tired to argue. I said nothing else that might be overheard or misconstrued since we were still surrounded by the fisherfolk, determined to see us safe. The reverend sent two men to the New Inn for our horses and welcomed us at the parsonage, at least for this one night. Soon we were safe behind closed doors and the fisherfolk gone about their business.

Charlotte carried Olivia off immediately.

"Sit, please sit," Reverend Purdy said as he ushered us into his drawing room. "Your dog . . ." He turned to look at Corwen in the lamplight and faltered. "He's not a dog, is he?"

"He isn't. May I borrow a robe or a blanket?"

He sent a maid upstairs, and she returned with a worn but serviceable banyan. He gave it to me, thinking it was to replace my wet clothes, but I tossed it over Corwen. He changed smoothly into man-form, standing and drawing the robe around him. It was a little short and only came to mid-calf, but it covered what needed covering.

"I am, indeed, not a dog, sir, and I thank you for the loan of the robe." Corwen held out his hand. The reverend hesitated, then took it.

"What have I seen this night?" he asked.

"Only something that's been natural to these isles since long before the first Christians built their churches. Nothing that would offend your god, sir."

"Despite what some of my fellow churchmen think, the Lord Almighty is not easily offended. Indeed, as He created everything under the sky, it must be that magical creatures are His as well. Is it not so?"

"I truly hope so," I said.

"But something has changed, and changed recently." The reverend frowned. "The Mysterium . . . the rowankind . . ."

"Wild magic," I said. "It's always been here, but largely unnoticed, because the wild folk kept away, neither interfering with ordinary folk, nor wishing to be interfered with. The rowankind were—are—one such magical race, the lemen and servants of the Fae, called from Iaru over two hundred years ago to aid Good Queen Bess in defeating the Armada."

I didn't tell him it was my ancestor, Martyn the Summoner, who did the calling and who stripped the rowankind of their power for more than two centuries. Neither did I tell him I'd been instrumental in restoring it and thereby the cause of releasing wild magic and so, by default, the cause of the kelpie's presence.

"They were robbed of their power in aid of Britain, so Good Queen Bess was obliged to see the rowankind looked after, and gave them to the care of her subjects, those wealthy enough to absorb them into their households. Within a few generations, however, the rowankind became bondservants, their sacrifice forgotten. Only the Fae remembered. A few months ago, the rowankind regained their power and remembered who they were."

"Ah, it all makes sense, now. Charlotte—"

He didn't get any further. The door opened and Olivia, clean, with dark hair brushed until it gleamed, ran into the room and flung herself into Reverend Purdy's lap with a loud, *Grandpapa!* He hugged the child to him, taking care not to chafe her wrists or ankles, bandaged with linen strips. No one could fail to see the love between them.

Charlotte followed more demurely, but crossed immediately to me and held out both her hands. "Thank you, miss."

"Miss?" Reverend Purdy looked up and noticed my disheveled hair and slender figure. "Bless my soul," he said.

"Strictly within these walls, please, Reverend. Traveling as a man is more convenient for the present. And, strictly speaking, it's Missis." I crossed to Corwen and took his hand, casually forgetting to mention I was not *his* missis. "This is Corwen." Corwen bowed as elegantly as he could while wearing a borrowed banyan. "And this is Hartington." Hartington followed suit.

"We did come to inquire after the missing children, though not from Dawlish, as I told you this morning."

"You are not from the Mysterium, so . . ."

"We are not. The Mysterium isn't equipped to deal with wild magic. It will take those with wild magic to tame it. The rowankind might be prevailed upon, those who have not gone with the Fae." I looked at Charlotte. "I presume you stayed of your own free will."

"I did. I have a husband and a child." She glanced at the reverend.

"It may not be strictly within the law of the land, but God has blessed the union of my son and my daughter Charlotte. I married them myself and entered their names in the parish register before Henry was called away."

"He never wanted to leave us," Charlotte said, retrieving Olivia from the reverend's lap.

"He didn't, indeed." Reverend Purdy frowned. "Henry had—still has, I hope—magic. He was obliged to register with the Mysterium. We expected he would be given a license and allowed to practice as a witch. Three years ago he was offered a commission in the 77th. Using his talent for king and country is the way they phrased it, but it was obvious he couldn't refuse. God willing, when Henry returns from India, he and Charlotte will be able to live openly as man and wife, and not just in secret beneath my roof."

"I hope that may be so."

The reverend frowned. "If the law were not such an ass, they should be able to do that already, but the rowankind have no status in law. Did you know that?"

"I didn't."

"My bishop sits in the House of Lords. He tells me there is not one statute that so much as mentions the rowankind. They don't exist. They're non-persons. It would take a court case, maybe more than one, to make a ruling and set a precedent to give them existence in the eyes of the law, let alone equality. How does that strike you?"

"As more than unfair, sir."

"Even slaves have protection in law. Why, Somersett's case in 1772 found the case for slavery unsupported in common law, yet in the intervening thirty years the rowankind have continued to labor at our command."

Charlotte cleared her throat and looked pointedly at the reverend as he began what was obviously a common diatribe.

"Hmm, yes, sorry," he mumbled. "Forgive me, please, I get carried away."

"There's nothing to forgive," Corwen said. "It's a worthy subject to pursue."

"But maybe not right now, eh?" Reverend Purdy said. "Where do you go next?"

I looked at Hartington. "I suppose it would be too much to ask that we could go home and plant potatoes."

He raised one eyebrow. "The Lady asks that you pay her a courtesy call."

"First I must return to Bur Isle for my clothes," Corwen said. "I can't travel in a borrowed banyan."

"I'll send my man at first light," the reverend offered. "It will be low tide. He is most reliable and can slip across and back quickly. He knows most of the islanders. They're not a bad lot, if a little wary of strangers."

"So we discovered," Corwen said. "I think the problem may have been exacerbated by the loss of a few sheep. The islanders blamed a dog, but it might have been the kelpie before she found her full strength and started hunting human flesh."

"So . . . the Mysterium," the reverend said. "Is it a great danger to you?"

"I can't say it isn't," Corwen said. "The law is harsh and needs to change, but the wheels of government turn exceedingly slowly. We hoped the power of the Mysterium had been broken, or at least chipped at the edges. In Bideford the locals took it upon themselves to burn the Mysterium office. I hoped the unrest might happen in other towns, but it appears it hasn't. The law would hang all three of us for the practice of unlicensed witchcraft if they could, yet none of their registered witches could tackle a kelpie or even a pixie. The country needs new legislation, but with Mr. Pitt out of office and Mr. Addington pursuing peace with the French, it may be some time before that happens unless King George can intervene personally. I do believe he takes an interest in magical affairs."

"Well, well, we live in interesting times," Reverend Purdy said.

Charlotte motioned to Olivia and set her upright, giving her a little push in my direction. The child made a fair curtsey. "Thank you for rescuing me."

"You are welcome, Olivia, but in truth you saved yourself and me, too. You have a great power. You must promise me to always use it for good and not for harm. I'm sure your mother will teach you how." I looked across at Charlotte, who nodded. Olivia would be in good hands.

◆――――◆

We slept well and breakfasted with the reverend, Charlotte, and Olivia early the following morning. I was pleased to see that Charlotte's position as housekeeper appeared to be only for the sake of propriety. The reverend treated Charlotte as a daughter. They had a genuine fondness between them, and supported each other in the absence of Henry Purdy, so far away in India.

Olivia seemed to have recovered surprisingly well from her ordeal. The silvery bloom of her rowankind complexion disguised any paleness, though I fancied there were still dark circles beneath her eyes. Despite her bandaged wrists and ankles, she smiled readily and spoke politely when spoken to, even giggling at something Hartington said to her.

The reverend's man returned early with Corwen's clothes, and we took our leave with all assurances from Reverend Purdy that if anyone asked, the only magic that had been performed was by the kelpie. I was still edgy about the possibility of Mysterium officers turning up, but it felt good to have new friends, and we left them an address where we they could contact us if necessary. Corwen had arranged for letters to find us via an innkeeper whose daughter was a fox shapechanger with access to the Okewood.

The journey to Ivybridge was uneventful, though there was a Mysterium office in the town which Reverend Purdy had warned us about. We crossed the river and made our way along Fore Street. Hartington and Corwen dismounted, as two men riding one horse would be more remarkable than two men walking with one horse. The Mysterium office stood almost opposite the church; its symbol, a triangle open at the top with a small circle balanced in the gap, decorated the door. It was a substantial building, well-proportioned with three stories, each with a bold bay window. I did my best to ignore it as we rode past, thinking that if I did, I would be less likely to attract attention.

No doors opened. No faces appeared at the windows. I thought we were safely past when I saw three soberly dressed men ahead of us. One was approaching middle age, but tall and strong. He wore a periwig and a full-cut frock coat. The other two looked younger, one in his twenties and one in his thirties. Mysterium officers didn't always wear a uniform, except on special occasions, but they were always soberly dressed, a little like clergymen . . . if clergymen wore swords and carried pistols. The two younger ones also wore dark coats, but while the thirty-year-old aped the older man, the younger man's coat was a fashionable cutaway over form-fitting breeches.

These three were exiting what looked like a pie shop. I supposed even officers of the Mysterium had to eat, though

I could have wished they'd chosen a few moments earlier or later to be on the street.

The older man watched us approach, and so the younger ones gave us their attention, too.

"Gentlemen, good day to you." Corwen took the initiative. "Is this the correct road for Ashburton?" He halted, and Timpani stood and stretched his neck out, nosing toward the basket the youngest man carried.

"It is, sir," the older man replied. "You should be there by nightfall if you don't linger."

"Thank you."

"Are you a stranger to these parts, sir?" the older man asked.

"I am."

"Then I would offer you some advice. Don't stray off the road and into the Okewood."

"Miscreants?" Corwen asked.

"Of a sort."

"I thank you for your warning."

We walked on. I imagined I could feel three pairs of eyes boring into my back, but I didn't dare turn around to see. No one shouted. No feet drummed the road behind us. It seemed that we were not remarkable enough to attract attention. I breathed a gentle sigh of relief as we mounted our horses and left the town behind.

From Ivybridge it was a short step into the southern edge of the Okewood, the massive forest that sat in the very center of Devonshire giving rise to legends and tall tales, many of them with more than a grain of truth.

⚓────────⚓

The Green Man and his lady—the Lady of the Forests—dwelled here in the Okewood, the ancient guardians of the forest within a forest that touched all Britain's ancient woodlands. Separate from the Fae's world of Iaru, the Okewood was wholly of our world, and yet only those whom the royal couple allowed could enter safely. Many a woodsman with his ax had run mad from here, but travelers with no ill-intent had passed through safely. This was where I'd first seen Corwen, though then I believed him to be wholly wolf.

Spring had already put a faint sheen of green on the winter-stark trees, and bluebells and wild garlic had pushed through the earth, showing early promise of what was to come. The last time I'd seen the court of the forest folk, it was on the northern edge of the Okewood near Bideford, but the forest lords could appear anywhere, at any time.

As soon as we entered the woodland, Hartington slipped from Timpani's back and disappeared into the dense undergrowth on the tree line, appearing a few minutes later as a magnificent stag with a full rack of antlers. As he bounded off between the trees, we set the horses to follow, trusting that he knew where he was going.

Our horses sprang into a swift trot, then broke into a canter when there was enough space between the tree trunks, jumping small rills and fallen logs in their stride, slithering down into gullies and up again. They avoided tree roots that might have slowed common animals, easily keeping pace with Hartington.

We emerged into a glade near a fast flowing brook. A fallen tree formed a natural bench, and upon it sat the Green Man and the Lady of the Forests. They were a couple living in harmony. His was the magic of growing things, which made him slow in speech, considering each word and movement. His Lady, whose chief concern was the creatures of the forest, was quick and lithe in comparison.

The couple's appearance changed constantly, either with the seasons or on a whim. This time the Lady was dressed in a short tunic of pale spring green. I thought at first she wore a pair of skin-colored leggings, but as we got closer I saw her legs were bare and the skin itself was close furred. Her hair was the light blonde of a faun's underbelly, soft as down, but long and wound around with ivy. Her partner wore brown, a tunic that could either have been tree bark or figured leather, and loose trousers bound about the calves with crossed thongs. He carried an English longbow, though it was not strung, and a quiver of arrows.

The Lady stood as we entered and greeted Hartington

with an approving hand to the side of his neck, then turned to us.

"Welcome Corwen, Rossalinde. Please join us. Release your mounts to roam; they'll not wander far and they'll find forage as they need it."

We quickly stripped the saddles and bridles from Timpani and Dancer. By the time we'd finished, Hartington had changed and dressed.

The Lady motioned the three of us to sit on the mossy ground and with a wave of her hand directed small individuals, tree sprites, I thought, to bring us each a leaf upon which lay an unidentifiable morsel, maybe a mushroom of some kind. Another brought us each a tiny drink in an acorn cap. I had eaten at the Lady's table before. Such food looked barely enough to satisfy a mouse, but if you let it, it would sustain you as much, if not more, than a king's banquet. I ate the tiny mushroom and sipped from the acorn cap and immediately felt replete. I saw Corwen's smile as he did the same. He'd lived with the Lady and her retinue for close to six years. He must have eaten and drunk with her many times, and still it delighted him.

The Lady of the Forests leaned forward. "You have dealt with the kelpie." It was a statement, not a question.

"Yes," Corwen confirmed. "A sorry business, though in the end only one child lost."

"The kelpie, too, of course," the Lady said. "Once a magical creature has enjoyed human flesh they can develop a craving that all but drives them mad for it. I would have liked to have found her before it came to that. I could have offered her refuge."

I hastily revised my opinion of what type of creatures might be inhabiting the Lady's woodland.

"In this case I believe you did the right thing," she said. "A swift end to a dangerous problem is sometimes the right answer."

Corwen cleared his throat. "You have more tasks for us?"

I hoped she didn't, but if she asked, we wouldn't refuse.

To my surprise she declined. "It's true that magical

incursions are troubling the land and there is much need for such skills as you have. I may call on you later, but I think you might have pressing matters of your own."

A sprite came forward and handed Corwen a letter.

"This arrived for you yesterday, carried by the fox-girl from the Westward Inn. In all the years you have served me, Silverwolf, there has been not one missive from your family. If a letter has come it must be important."

She stepped away to give Corwen space to read his letter in private. I sat quietly, wondering whether something terrible had happened.

Corwen's face tightened in the way a man has when trying to hide his feelings. He took a long, slow breath over the paper and sighed it out. "My brother's dead. My oldest brother, Jonathan. I have to go to Yorkshire. I could be some time. It's old news, apparently. It happened before Christmas."

I was shocked. Why hadn't someone contacted him before this?

The same thought might have been running through his mind, too. He raised his head, and there was such an expression of desolation on his face that I put my arms around him, feeling him sag into my embrace.

"I'm so sorry," I said.

"He was the best of brothers, though maybe not always understanding of my wolf. But there's more."

"And your mother has waited until now to write?"

"Not even now. The letter's from my little sister, Lily."

Silently he handed me the letter. I saw his knuckles whiten, and there was a slight tremor in his fingers. I unfolded it. The script was tiny, a woman's hand. It might have been elegant, but in places it wobbled and there was a smudge where the ink had been wet. *A tear?* I wondered.

Dear Corwen, I read.

I turned the letter over and read the addressee: Mr. C. Deverell. I'd never heard him referred to as anything but Corwen Silverwolf, or occasionally Corwen the Gray. I continued reading.

Denby Hall
Second day of February, 1801.

Dear Corwen.

I beg you to come home at once. Mother should have written at Christmas, but Would Not.

I am so very sad to inform you that Our Dear Brother, Jonathan, left us in late December after a short illness, a Rupture of the Appendix which led to a violent infection of the stomach and much Pain. Father fell into an apoplexy at the Funeral and continues frail under the care of Doctor Boucher. Mother will not speak of our Loss, but carries on, determined to be strong for the rest of us.

Freddie has gone up to London, and after one letter to tell us his Lodgings, refuses to answer letters or come Home. You should know that the affliction which caused your split with Father is not yours alone. I became changed by it soon after you left, and Freddie more recently, in his twenty-third year, which has caused him Much Melancholy and swift changes of temper.

The mill is a great concern. It is under the management of Thatcher who is new since your time with us, and I do not like him, nor do I trust him. As I am only Nineteen and a mere Miss, Thatcher will not Speak to me of Business and Mama does not want to Listen.

I know you have no reason to want to help your Family, but if ever we needed you it is Now.

> *I remain, as always, your loving sister,*
> *Lily Caroline Deverell*

I handed it back to him. "When do we leave?"

"You don't have to come with me."

"Yes, I do." I thought of my current appearance, man's attire, hands rough from gardening and domestic chores. "Unless you don't want me."

"Of course I want you. You keep me safe . . . and sane."

"What if I don't fit in? Your father's a landowner, a gentleman of independent means. I'm hardly respectable."

He squeezed me tight. "I thought your family once companied with royalty."

"Until that same royalty tried to have them killed."

"Relax, Ross, you'll probably fit in better than I will after six years. Don't worry."

The Lady of the Forests turned to us. "I wish this were not the only troubling news," she said, "but I have heard another Walsingham has been appointed."

I felt as though my own guts were about to rise and strangle me.

Walsingham was a powerful government agent working in secret for the highest in the land. There had been a Walsingham ever since Good Queen Bess's spymaster, Sir Francis Walsingham, had passed on, leaving his successors to take his name and abandon their own, believing that to give any magical creature knowledge of your true name gave them power over you. The Walsinghams fought magic with darker magic and were above even the upper ranks of the Mysterium.

It had been a Walsingham who had killed my grandparents almost thirty years earlier, and his successor who had nearly killed me only a few months ago, trying to prevent me from setting the rowankind free. I'd killed him instead, in the explosion that took half my ear and almost took my life.

"With all the outbreaks of wild magic, Walsingham will have more to think about than you, Ross." Corwen put an arm around me. "Besides, he's based in London, and we'll be two hundred miles away in Yorkshire."

"I hope you're right." I shuddered.

6

Journey North

IT WAS A LONG JOURNEY from the Okewood to Yorkshire. We chose to eschew public coaches and ride, as we didn't want to leave our Fae horses behind. We decided to go from the Okewood to the Old Maizy Forest, collect whatever we needed from the cottage, and travel on from there.

With Fae-bred horses, and permission to traverse the secret ways through Iaru, we knew we'd be able to reduce the two-hundred-fifty–mile journey to Yorkshire significantly, but we'd still have several days in the saddle. Though Corwen supported me in whatever mode of dress I chose to wear, I couldn't shock his family by arriving in man's attire. Even so, I couldn't face the journey sidesaddle, so I'd compromised, riding astride with breeches and boots beneath my full skirts and redingote. I hated wearing elaborate bonnets, but to leave my head uncovered marked me as a loose woman in many people's eyes. For the sake of propriety, therefore, I adopted a simple bandeau.

Corwen planned our route from the cottage. We'd travel via Bath and take the Fosse Way diagonally across the middle of the country, then turn north toward Warwick, Derby, and Chesterfield. From there, it was only a short journey into Sheffield and the West Riding of Yorkshire, a place I'd never been. Corwen had told me something of his family's home, a house, he said, somewhere close to the edge of the Pennine moors. I had seen the Darkmoor and imagined Corwen's home to be bleak and unwelcoming. Maybe that was one of the reasons he'd stayed away for six years.

He'd avoided talking about his home and family unless I asked him a direct question, perhaps because the scars mine had inflicted on me were still so raw. Corwen managed to convey the fact that he'd had major disagreements with his father, who'd not known how to deal with his son's shapechanging abilities. I could imagine how that had felt. My own mother had given me a hard time when my magic had begun to develop. I resolved not to pester him for information but to wait until he was ready to talk.

We slipped into Iaru for the first leg of our journey, emerging in midafternoon in a small stand of trees close to Midsomer Norton. Corwen squinted toward the sun.

"We can stay here, or push on. We can probably make it as far as Bath before we lose the light, that is, if you're not too tired."

I was bone-achingly tired. My backside had gained far too intimate acquaintance with my saddle. I wanted nothing more than to sit on a cushioned seat and put myself on the outside of a hearty meal, but the letter had worried Corwen more than he had said, so I stretched my back and rose a little in my stirrups to ease my discomfort. "To Bath," I said.

Crossing Pulteney Bridge, we discovered that lodgings in the fashionable part of the city were scarce with the season in full swing, so we found a traveler's inn on the north side. It wasn't fancy, but I didn't care. I could barely keep my nose out of my kidney pie at supper, and it was even an effort to strip off my clothes and fall into bed in my shift.

I was looking forward to the oblivion of sleep as Corwen pulled the covers over me and *tsked* solicitously, dropping his lips to my shoulder. Not even his warm, naked body next to mine was going to keep me conscious. He gave in gracefully and settled for curling at my back, his arm draped around my waist.

And then I lay there ... and lay there ... so exhausted I couldn't sleep. My spine ached and my calves throbbed. I regretted the kidney pie as my stomach roiled.

Eventually I gave in and slipped out of Corwen's embrace to retrieve one of Aunt Rosie's notebooks from our traveling valise, together with my spectacles, and snuggled into bed to recline against my pillow. The lenses did magnify, but that was not why I needed them. I was able to call light so that I could see when I looked through them. It wasn't like daylight, but it was good enough to illuminate the shadows and I could read quite clearly.

Aunt Rosie, my late mother's sister, had spent a lifetime studying magic, experimenting for herself, and learning from the Fae. She'd written things down meticulously and had committed much of it to memory, which was why she'd left the books with me. They held an implicit instruction. Read and learn and when I could, add to the knowledge. There were still empty pages to fill. I would add the information about the kelpie as soon as we reached Yorkshire, while it was still fresh in my mind. For now, I let the book open at random and I read:

"On Spells. My aunt, who was a natural healer, but who had little talent for witchcraft, learned to use two simple spells to help with the lighting and banking of fires. The former enabled her to light a fire without a taper or a phosphor match. In order to do this, she would take a pinch of hot pepper, sprinkle it on the wood and coals and say: 'Fire bright. Fire light.' At that flames would spring up and the wood and coals would ignite. I never saw it fail her."

Hot pepper and: *"Fire light. Fire bright."* That didn't sound too difficult. No, hang on, the other way around: *"Fire bright. Fire light."* It was a pity I had no pepper in my pocket. The fire in the bedroom fireplace would be dead before morning and the room would be icy. I read on.

"To bank a fire at night so it is still alight in the morning, you must get it to slumber. Those with natural fire magic can simply do this by thought, but Aunt Eileen used to do it by rubbing her tired eyes so as to get what children refer to as 'sleep' on her fingertips, then she would blow across them in the direction of a roaring fire and tell it to 'Slumber deep.' The flames would immediately die back and consume no more of the wood and coals until she clapped her hands and commanded it to wake with the words: 'Lazy fire, sleep no more.' The fire would resume as it had been."

That sounded useful. The fire that we had might not be much, but it would be even less by morning. My eyes were gritty enough. I sat up, rubbed them under my spectacle lenses, and blew across my fingers in the direction of the fire. "Slumber deep," I told it, holding my breath to see if this would work for me. The flames died back. I feared I had extinguished it completely, so almost immediately I commanded it, "Lazy fire, sleep no more," and it sprang into flame. I was so fascinated that I did it twice more before finally telling it to sleep and settling down with the notebook and spectacles tucked safely under my pillow.

"Have you finished?" Corwen's voice cracked with tiredness.

"Sorry, I didn't mean to wake you. I thought I was tired, but I found I couldn't sleep."

"Exhaustion takes you like that sometimes."

"Go back to sleep."

"I'm awake now, and since you are, too, it would be a pity to waste the opportunity."

I rolled over to face him, but the shadow-blanketed room, with the fire banked down, was in total darkness. I could feel his breath on my forehead and reached out, finding the warm, smooth skin of his flank within easy reach. I ran my nails down it lightly, knowing him to be ticklish. He juddered involuntarily, grabbed my hand, and placed it in a safer space on his buttock.

"Do you want some light?" I asked, beginning to knead the muscle.

"I think I know you well enough to be able to navigate

in the dark." He chuckled softly as his fingers explored downward. "Ah, here's the harbor."

I threw my leg across him and reached between us. "I'm not sure what I've found here. Is it a frigate or a light-house?"

"That, madam, is a first rate man-o-war."

He gasped as my navigation skills guided him home.

Sated, I lay in his arms, relaxed and boneless, listening to his regular breathing as he drifted into a contented slumber.

I should be able to do the same, now, shouldn't I?

But I didn't. I stared into the thick shadows and stared and stared.

Why wouldn't sleep come?

When it did, I wished it hadn't.

◆————◆

It's one of those dreams where you are aware you are dreaming, but you can't wake.

The sea is dead calm. I am suspended by the wrists from the standing rigging on the Black Hawk, *surrounded by a hundred leering pirates. In the center of them is James Mayo, Gentleman Jim, one of the most fearsome pirate captains to come out of the Dark Islands since Black-beard. He's rigged a swivel gun loaded with sangrenel—sharp pieces of scrap iron. At this distance it will cut me in half, and what is left will look like the product of a meat grinder.*

He stays his hand, quiets his men with a wave, and steps between me and the gun. "It doesn't have to be like this, Ross. Tell me where the winterwood box is, and I'll let you go."

I don't answer him. If I tell him where the box is, Corwen will be his next target.

I should feel pain, my wrists should be scraped raw, my arms should be almost pulled from their sockets, my breathing should be constricted, but my dream self is insulated from the pain. Not from the fear, however. From where I dangle I can see the Heart of Oak, *my ship, safe for now. And she's going to stay that way. Her stout planks protect all*

I hold dear, not only Corwen, but my younger brother David, and my crew.

I concentrate and call a breeze to fill the Heart's *sails, holding it steady. My faithful Hookey will understand the message, seize the advantage, and flee to Bacalao regardless of Corwen's protests. Then I call a second breeze, but this time I feed it into itself and spiral it into a waterspout, spinning faster and faster. I slam it into Mayo's sister ship, the one with her guns trained on the* Heart. *Slam it hard with all I've got.*

As the ship heels over I see Walsingham on her deck with a kelpie. The kelpie lunges for him and they both go into the water, tangled together. The ship heaves herself upright, her rigging shredded.

Mayo curses. "I loved you once, Ross, but you betrayed me."

It's true.

Not long ago, still hot from his bed, I stole back the box, though to be fair he had taken it from me by underhanded means a little earlier. While British ships of the line unleashed their might on Ravenscraig, his stronghold, I escaped with my half-brother David. I'm not proud of that. What can I say? It was before I met Corwen, and I'd newly cast aside my widow's weeds even though the ghost of my husband Will thought we still had unfinished business.

"I'm sorry, Jim. Nothing personal. Maybe if we'd met at a different time . . ."

"It was very personal, Ross." He steps close.

My feet are dangling about a yard above the deck. That puts Mayo's face on a level with my belly. One by one he secures my booted ankles to the rigging so my legs are open. Now he stands in front of me and strokes my inner thigh, his hand warm through my breeches.

"Very personal." His voice is husky. "Don't tell me you didn't feel it."

Maybe I had, once, but not now.

◆─────◆

I woke in a panic, my breathing harsh, my heart hammering. Had I called out? For a moment I didn't know where I was, but common sense reasserted itself as the images began to fade, nightmare versions of what had happened mixed with what might have happened.

It had been six months; I thought I was over the worst, but the business with the kelpie had brought it all back. I tried to relax.

Corwen still slept quietly at my back, his warmth spreading down my spine, nose nuzzling the nape of my neck, one arm draped gently across my waist.

I drew a deep breath and let it out slowly.

"The dream again?" Corwen had that animal instinct that transitioned from sleep to wakefulness without any grogginess.

"Not the same one. Significant differences. This time I was on board James Mayo's ship. He was about to blast me to pieces with a swivel gun at close range and the kelpie was there. She drowned Walsingham, or at least I think she did."

This mishmash of images was something new. My dreams usually forced me to revisit the terrible moments of the last year. They had me leaping from the upper story of a flaming warehouse, clutching my little brother's hand in mine as we fell, or fighting off a frenzied werewolf. Sometimes they took me back to the time we shot through the maelstrom of Thames tidewater beneath London Bridge in a rickety rowboat, barely an oar's length ahead of slavering hellhounds. But the worst dream of all was always pulling the trigger of my pistol with Philip in my sights, killing one brother to save another, seeing the look of utter disbelief in that instant before the light went out of his eyes forever.

The latter was the one that haunted me most.

"Mayo's dead," Corwen said.

"Because of me." Mayo had tried to protect me from Walsingham and had died for it.

"Not entirely," Corwen said. "Mayo was only a gentleman by name. He sold you out before he had a last-minute change of heart."

I wasn't going to defend Jim to Corwen. It was true he was a pirate and a scoundrel with a cruel streak that my dream-self recognized, but I do think he loved me, as much as he was capable of that emotion. Apart from Will, who had finally ceased to haunt me after nearly four years, and Corwen, my love and my lover, Mayo was the only one I'd ever taken to my bed. Maybe I had felt something for him, if only briefly. Lust if not love.

"Ross ..." Corwen's hand, flat on my belly, drew me backward into a closer embrace as he breathed a line of soft kisses along my shoulder.

"Corwen, I ... Not now. I'm still shaking inside."

He didn't let me go, but the intent bled out of him. "Come on, then."

He shuffled backward until he was sitting half upright against the solid oak headboard of the inn's best bed. He opened his legs and pulled me between them to recline with my back against his belly, both arms around me and his knees cradling my hips.

I told the fire to wake and flames leaped up in the grate, flickering cheerfully on the ceiling.

"You are protected," Corwen said.

Yes, here and now, in this bed with my lover, but there were things Corwen couldn't protect me from, no matter how hard he tried, or how much he wanted to.

"Don't think I'm not grateful." I pulled the covers around both of us.

"Not just by me, but the Lady has an interest in your safety."

"I know, and the Fae, though they have a strange way of showing gratitude sometimes." I huffed out a breath. "We are grateful. As a reward you may kiss our collective a—"

"Shh." He put a finger to my lips. "They aren't always as far away as you might think. Better not to offend them."

"I thought Iaru was only accessible via woodland."

Corwen tapped the oak headboard behind him. "It depends on your definition of woodland."

"Ah, right." I clamped my mouth shut and settled into Corwen's warmth.

"Sing to me," I said, implying the *please* with my tone of voice.

He had a rich baritone that fairly rumbled out of his chest in its lower register.

"What shall I sing?"

"Anything. It needn't have words. Hum a tune, something gentle."

He obliged with a melody, haunting and lyrical, soft as a whisper. It may have had an end, but I didn't know because I drifted into a dreamless sleep.

◆——————◆

We continued our journey early the following morning, climbing the hill out of Bath on the Cirencester road. At the summit of the long incline we slipped into Iaru via a small copse of trees.

Timpani raised his head and tasted the air, pricking his ears and stepping out. Dancer's feet had no sooner touched the forest floor than he began to live up to his name.

Corwen laughed. "They're ready to be off."

"Maybe I'm not."

The nighttime terrors and lack of decent coffee at breakfast had left me feeling grumpy. Also, my limbs had stiffened overnight, and I'd discovered muscles I'd forgotten existed.

"I don't think you have much choice." Corwen nudged Timpani's sides and he sprang forward, his hooves pounding the ground rhythmically. Reluctantly, I gave Dancer his head and followed. The horses negotiated the woodland tracks at a hand gallop. If I was entirely honest with myself, their smooth stride didn't tax my aching backside any more than a steady jog might have done, and my spirit lightened with the wind in my face and the joy of a good horse beneath me. I felt myself grin, the bad dreams of the night fading into memory.

When at last we slowed, and the lush summer green of Iaru turned once more to April's new buds of our own world, I felt more at peace. We followed a lively brook to the road. This was a landscape of rolling hills and creamy Cotswold stone farmsteads. A carter, traveling in the opposite direction halted his horses when we asked the way.

"Northleach." He pointed. "Though mind how you go. There's witchery in the district. Soon to be a hanging."

My breath seemed to freeze in my lungs.

"Is this area much troubled by witchcraft?" Corwen asked.

"Not overmuch until the last few months, but there have been three convictions since Christmas. Old Samuel Hitchman saw a Black Shuck on Sunday last and by Tuesday he was dead."

"A Black Shuck?" I heard interest in Corwen's voice. "You're sure?"

"Samuel was. And now he's dead. What more proof do you need?"

"I see, thank you. We shall take care."

"Where are you bound?"

"Warwick and thence north to Derby."

"I haven't been as far as Derby myself, but keep on this road past the House of Correction at Northleach through Bourton-on-the-Water and Moreton-in-the-Marsh. Cross the River Stour at Halford and ask again as the road divides soon after."

We thanked him and continued on.

"You think it's a real Black Shuck?" I asked.

"Could be, or a shapechanger getting careless. There's a white ghost dog sometimes seen on the moors above Penistone, called a padfoot."

"And is that real?"

"Ah, that's the question, isn't it? But though I'm not a betting man, I'll lay odds it hasn't been seen for the last six years."

"Since you left home?"

He raised an eyebrow and tried not to look smug.

Our mood of levity dissipated as we approached Northleach where the house of correction stood, a forbidding place built of stone, standing sentinel at the crossroads. It was nothing like the king's prison on the Darkmoor, but it exuded a gloomy atmosphere, a kind of a chill desperation. I couldn't get past the place fast enough.

"What's wrong?" Corwen asked, nudging Timpani forward to keep pace with Dancer.

"Can't you feel it?" I asked.

He wrinkled his nose. "I can smell it."

He didn't argue when I asked him to find us a way into Iaru, but the land north of the prison had been enclosed and cleared. Where forests and common land had once stood, there were now stone field walls and grazing for sheep. We were forced to continue for some way along the road as it climbed to the high ground again, running remarkably straight.

"The Romans built this road," Corwen said. "That's why it takes such a direct line."

The road may have been straight, but it dipped and rose, dipped and rose between fields and hedgerows, so we could only see the road ahead from the highest points.

As we crested a rise, we saw a vehicle in trouble. Ahead of us a crude box wagon canted crazily to one side, two wheels in the ditch. As we got closer, I could see the wagon had no windows save for one in the rear door, and that was barred with iron. The pair of heavy horses had been unhitched and tied to the hedge where they stood like dull-witted mules, snatching roadside grass and slobbering green slime onto the rings of their bits. Two men, soberly dressed, pushed and pulled ineffectively. One was young with a sharp face like a ferret, the other altogether shorter and more round, with a head as bald as an egg.

"Your assistance, sir?" the eggman asked politely.

Corwen wrinkled his nose and frowned. "You need more than one extra pair of hands to shift a fully laden wagon. Why not let them help?" He jerked his head toward the iron grille of the wagon's only door. "How many prisoners are you carrying?"

"Six, sir, bound for the house of correction."

"It would be easier to right the wagon if it were empty."

"Indeed it would, but they is all dangerous criminals and we dursent let them loose, there bein' only two of us."

I rode closer to the wagon and peered through the bars. I'd seen far more dangerous looking faces in the crew of my ship. These looked poor and downtrodden. Still, six to two, and even the poor and downtrodden will fight back if the odds are right and they perceive a chance to win.

"Please." It was a small female voice from inside the wagon. I looked closer. A pair of large brown eyes stared at me from a rowankind face, her silvery skin delicately marked with the wood-grain pattern.

"You have a rowankind woman in here," I said.

"She's the worst of 'em," Ferret-face said. "Going to be hanged for a witch."

A cold shiver ran through me. "By whose order?"

"Squire Jenkins, the magistrate. Serves on the Mysterium in Sherborne."

I seized on the obvious. "But she's a rowankind," I said. "There's no law says the rowankind must register."

"There's no law says they mustn't," Eggman said.

The Mysterium controlled the use of witchcraft, issuing licenses and regulating those who declared themselves. The penalty for not declaring magical talent was death. If they ever caught me, that would be my fate, too.

7

A Lady's Maid

I LOOKED AT CORWEN. He held my gaze for long enough that I knew he would back me if I attempted to free the rowankind woman. He made no comment and didn't even ride close. Instead, he dismounted and handed his reins to me and made a show of adding his strength to that of the two men, with predictable results. The wagon rocked a little, causing the prisoners to cry out, but settled into the ditch.

Corwen sucked air in through his teeth. "It's no good. The prisoners will have to be brought out. They can't get into much trouble if they're heaving the wagon upright, can they? Besides, don't you have them in fetters?"

Eggman conceded they were, indeed, fettered, so he ordered Ferret-face to unlock the door. One by one, the prisoners emerged into the late afternoon light, blinking. The woman came last. She shocked me. She was younger than I'd first thought, barely eighteen, and she was with child.

While the five men, all with their feet shackled in irons, shuffled off to the ditch, I quickly dismounted and held up a hand to prevent the woman from following. "You surely can't expect a woman in such a delicate condition to strain alongside the men." I made it a statement rather than a question. "I'll watch her. She obviously can't run very fast."

She stumbled over her irons as I led her to the side of the bank opposite the ditch to sit down. Her filthy feet were bare and her ankles chafed by the iron.

"You chose not to flee to Iaru?" I asked her quietly.

Her head snapped up at the sound of that name, and she patted her belly. "I doubt I'd be welcome there with a half-breed babe."

I thought she was wrong, but I said nothing. I pointed to her ankles. She lifted her skirt, and while the men were all distracted I took my lockpicks from my pocket. The shackles yielded quickly, and I eased them off her ankles as quietly as I could. Behind me Corwen yelled, "One, two, HEAVE! And again, boys. Next time we'll have it."

"Can you ride?" I asked.

She nodded.

"Take the bay. He's fleet of foot."

"I'm not a horse thief."

"I didn't say you could keep him."

We stood together, and I kept myself between her and the wagon. She climbed onto Dancer nimbly enough just as the prisoners righted the heavy wagon. It was only when the sound of galloping hooves caught the attention of Eggman and Ferret-face that I yelled for help and promptly fell into what I hoped was a convincing swoon.

Corwen came running across and bent over me while the men shepherded the prisoners into the wagon and slammed the door.

"Well done, Ross," he said quietly, and whistled for Timpani. "Don't worry, gentleman. I'll catch her. My horse is faster than yours."

He leaped into the saddle and pulled me up behind him. We galloped off, following Dancer, ignoring the yells of the men we left behind.

◆──◆

It didn't take long to catch the rowankind girl. Dancer had slowed already, and when I called him, he stopped and waited. His rider slumped forward in the saddle, her fingers curled under the pommel to hold herself in place.

"Quickly. Change horses," Corwen said. "They may follow slowly, but they will follow, and we need to find a route to Iaru before they work out we're not the innocent victims of horse theft."

I slid to the ground and took Dancer's rein as Corwen lifted the girl down. I noticed she shrank away from him as she had not from me, but she said nothing as he perched her on Timpani's solid back and mounted. I yanked my dress around my knees and leaped on to Dancer.

"Find us a route, Corwen, for pity's sake."

It seemed as though we rode on the top of the world, but the landowners who had enclosed the fields had grubbed up trees to make more room for sheep. We'd gone the best part of five miles at a fair clip before we came to a little wood, left for shelter, or perhaps because the ground here was too uneven to turn to plow or pasture. "Can we cross here?" I asked him.

He quested with his nose. "Maybe."

We dismounted. Corwen offered to lift the girl down from Timpani, but she slithered to the ground by herself and avoided his proffered hands. I interpreted a look from him that told me he suspected the babe she carried had not been got willingly. He walked ahead with Timpani, leaving the girl to walk with me and Dancer while he searched out a route through the trees.

"Don't worry. You're safe now." I said it even though I knew it wasn't the case unless Corwen could find the path. The longer we stayed on the exposed road, the more chance we had of being discovered.

"Why would you help me?" Her voice trembled.

"I don't hold with people being hanged for witchcraft."

"Not even if they say I did a murder with it?"

"Did you?" My own hands were hardly clean in that respect.

She looked pensive. "I don't think so, but I might've."

"What happened?"

"I worked at the big house for Squire Jenkins. Mrs. J said no one could pretty her hair as well as me, so I became her personal maid. That's when Mister Hugh started to take notice." She patted her belly. "When the Awakening came . . ."

I'd heard several rowankind refer to it as that. When I returned the magic to the rowankind, it was as if they'd woken from a stupor and suddenly understood they could walk free of their bonded servitude at will, and no one could stop them.

"I walked out of the house. Left everything behind me. I felt the pull of Iaru, we all did. I hadn't been walking long before young Adam, the stable lad, caught up with me and we walked together, talking about the changes we felt. Mister Hugh came riding after us. Said we weren't allowed to leave because his father had our papers. Adam said blow his papers and Mister Hugh flew into a rage. He beat Adam unconscious with his riding crop and dragged me onto his horse. I didn't know how to use the magic, then, though I felt it in me. The sky grew dark, and it began to lash down as we rode. He took shelter in a deserted cottage on the edge of the squire's lands and dragged me inside."

She lapsed into silence.

"He used you ill."

"Not for the first time. Though I determined it would be the last. He had a brandy flask with him, and all those sips added up. He never could hold his liquor. The storm continued into the evening. At length he went out to relieve himself, and a great tree branch came down in the gale and pinned him across the chest. I ran and kept on running. It's funny, the storm didn't touch me. I barely got wet. I looked for Iaru, but I couldn't find the way, and then I realized why." She touched her belly. "I couldn't cross while I carried my shame. The squire's men caught me a few days later. Mister Hugh had died from his injuries, but not before he'd accused me of bringing the tree down on him with witchcraft. They locked me up and condemned me to hang, but not until after the babe is delivered."

"Did you cause the storm?" Rowankind magic worked best with wind and weather.

"I don't know. I . . . might have done, but I haven't done magic since, I swear."

"It doesn't matter to me if you do magic. I used to have weather magic; I know what it's like."

"Used to?"

"I gave it back to the rowankind."

"It was you?"

"It was all my family. The task to return it passed down through the generations and fell to me."

She gave me a sideways look, awe mixed with apprehension.

"It's done now." I sighed. "There's no more to be said about it."

"The world is changed."

"This corner of it that's called England certainly is. Were there many rowankind in the squire's household?"

"Six of us. I don't know what happened to the others. We should all have stayed together. I hope Adam recovered and found Iaru alone."

"What's your name?"

"Alice."

"I'm Rossalinde, though my friends call me Ross. That's Corwen." I pointed to his back.

"He's a werewolf, I can tell."

"I'm not moon-called," Corwen shouted back. He'd obviously been listening.

I smiled. "He's a wolf, yes, but a shapechanger, not a werewolf." I lowered my voice. "You needn't be afraid of him. Corwen's wolf won't rip you to shreds and crack your bones for the marrow, though I don't guarantee the safety of rabbits and I've seen him take down a buck before now. He's a hunter, but not an indiscriminate killer. You can trust him."

"It's here." Corwen halted and turned to us.

The boundary between our world and Iaru was invisible. Sometimes it was hard to tell when you'd actually passed it until the colors changed, became more vibrant and the air smelled subtly different as the trees turned to summer.

"How do I pass through?" Alice asked.

"Walk. It's as easy as that."

"I can't sense anything."

"I'm only just beginning to be able to sense the boundary myself. Corwen's much better at it. Maybe it's his wolf nose."

We walked forward and the spring greenery blossomed into summer between one step and the next. I turned to tell Alice we were here, but she wasn't beside me.

"Corwen!"

He turned.

"Alice."

He frowned and retraced his steps. I turned Dancer around and followed him. We found Alice still in the wood.

"Where were you? You disappeared," she said, eyes as round as saucers.

"Iaru."

Tears ran down her cheeks. "I can't cross. It's the bastard in my belly, isn't it?"

I looked at Corwen. I didn't know, but I suspected the Fae didn't care about half-breed bastards one way or the other.

Back on the road, I heard the rattle of wagon wheels and the steady clop of horse's hooves. The prison wagon, I thought. My hearing is acute, all part of my magic, so we probably had a little time yet, but we needed to get Alice into Iaru as quickly as we could.

"Get on Dancer," I told her. "He's Fae-bred, he'll carry you through."

She refused Corwen's outstretched hand and scrambled into the saddle herself, pulling her skirts down to cover her bare legs. We set off again, but there was a muffled yelp as we passed through, and Dancer was suddenly without a rider.

We returned to the little wood again and found Alice sitting on the ground.

"We need a Fae to bring her through," I said. I could hear the wagon, closer now. "I'm not leaving her."

"Of course not," Corwen said. "Can you summon David?"

And by that he meant *summon* my little brother magically.

"Maybe. I'll try."

I concentrated on David, actually my half-brother as we only shared a mother. I pictured him as I had last seen him, finally restored to his rightful place with the Fae. He'd undergone such a change. I hadn't even known of his existence until a year ago when my mother died. The fourteen-year-old I had taken to be her rowankind bondservant, because that's what he himself thought at the time, turned out to be the son of Larien, a Fae lord who'd seduced my mother, or maybe she'd seduced him, while my father was away at sea. My family is somewhat complicated, but it all came right in the end. I became very fond of my new younger brother, even when he turned out to be the swan in a nest of ducklings. The Fae can sometimes be high-handed with humans, but David's first fourteen years as a rowankind bondservant meant he didn't put on airs and graces.

I recalled his face, delicate features, skin like alabaster. At fifteen he hadn't grown whiskers, and maybe never would. I'd never seen a Fae with stubble. He was slender without being skinny, beautiful without being feminine.

I called him to me.

And again.

The third time was the charm.

"Ross. What's wrong?"

"David!" I hugged him and he hugged me back. In the few months since I'd last seen him he'd grown. He was taller than me now, though not yet as tall as Corwen.

"We need to get Alice into Iaru," I said, indicating the girl who had curtsied deeply, offering respect as most people do on first seeing a Fae lord. "Quickly."

I could still hear the wagon on the road.

"You have my father's permission to cross over."

"But Alice can't cross."

Alice stared at her feet, not speaking.

"She thinks it's because of the baby."

"Why should it? Oh, I see." David grasped the situation straightaway and took Alice's hand. "Walk with me, Alice."

David spoke in low tones and Alice answered him hesitantly. Even with my acute hearing, I couldn't make out what they said, but suddenly Alice giggled, the tension broken. David glanced over his shoulder and jerked his head for us to follow him.

Without Alice even realizing, we crossed into Iaru. The rattle of wagon wheels on the road faded behind us.

Alice stared about her in wide-eyed wonder. "I didn't think . . . It's all so different. It even smells funny."

"You can stay here, Alice," David said. "You'll be safe."

"What about . . . ?" She patted her belly.

"It wasn't your baby prevented you from crossing over. It was your belief you wouldn't be welcome. You are welcome, now or any time. Iaru is the rowankind's home."

"Do I have to stay here?" She looked at me, eyes wide.

I glanced at Corwen who'd hung back knowing he made the girl nervous. His shoulders rose and fell in a shrug I translated as: *Whatever you decide is fine by me.*

"Your life is your own now, Alice," I said. "You can make your own decisions."

"Where are you going to, m'lady?"

"I'm no lady, Alice. I told you my name is Ross. We're going to Yorkshire, to Corwen's family. I don't know how long for."

"I've never been to Yorkshire. Can I come with you? I'm a good lady's maid, and not being too forward, Miss Rossalinde, you look as though you need one."

Corwen cleared his throat gently. "Alice may have a point. My mother will consider the two of us traveling alone the height of impropriety."

I gave him a look as if to say impropriety had never worried him before, but he simply raised one eyebrow and the matter was settled. Without exchanging more than a few words with the girl, he'd taken on the responsibility for her welfare.

My mouth twitched into a smile. "We'll pay you proper

wages, of course, Alice, and when anyone is listening I'm Mrs. Sumner."

"Yes, Mrs. Sumner, ma'am." She bobbed a perfect curtsey.

"We'd better find you some shoes and a respectable dress that doesn't look like it's spent the last few months in a jail cell." I glanced at David.

"Of course. Stay the night, and we'll see you well turned out in the morning."

<hr />

David brought us to one of the Fae's woodland bowers, an indoor-outdoor stand of trees whose canopy provided warmth and shelter. Annie, once a rowankind scullery girl at an inn in Plymouth, and now David's intended, arrived with a basket of provisions, cheerfully handing out bread and cheeses, cold meats and a flagon of a spicy ale, the likes of which I'd never tasted before. She was a sweet girl, gaining in confidence all the time now she had her freedom and David's loyal support.

David, Corwen, Annie, and I chatted over our meal, while Alice, exhausted by her experiences and suddenly freed from the threat of imminent execution, ate quickly, curled up, and slept like one dead already.

Our conversation ranged from Fae politics—so convoluted I could barely follow it—to the situation in France and the state of the privateering trade, a profession I had lately engaged in.

Annie surprised me by having a thorough grasp of dockside gossip about shipping in and out of Plymouth. She grinned at me. "You hear a lot when people treat you like you don't exist."

"I'm sorry for that, Annie. Being treated like nothing, I mean."

"Don't be," she said. "I was content at the time. It was only when the fog lifted from my mind that I understood what other possibilities there might be in the world."

"Does Iaru suit you?"

"Oh, yes." She exchanged a sideways glance with David, and I was reminded that rowankind matured early, as did the Fae. David seemed much older than fifteen. I suspected he would look the same age for the next two or three hundred years, at least.

"How goes it with the *Heart*?" David asked.

My ship, the *Heart of Oak*, the most beautiful tops'l schooner on the seven seas, now sailed under the captaincy of my friend Hookey Garrity.

"I haven't seen her since Bideford. I thought it best to let Hookey settle into being in sole charge without interfering."

"Is it hard to let go?"

Corwen gave me a sideways glance. We'd had this conversation ourselves.

"In some ways," I said. "Yet I know I've made the right decision. I do still check where she is in the world, though." I smiled. "It's a hard habit to break."

My powers of *summoning* extended to the *Heart*, or more likely to the ensorcelled winterwood sliver in her keel. I could find her anywhere in the world and call her to me if I needed her. Mr. Sharpner, the *Heart*'s sailing master, had learned to follow when my little ship ran counter to her course.

David's expression went blank for a moment as if he was concentrating. "She's off the coast of Sussex," he said.

"You can find her, too?" I shouldn't be surprised at that. Though he was every inch a Fae, David was still my mother's son and that meant he'd inherited the ability to *summon*, a talent I was still exploring.

While Corwen, David, and I talked half the night away, Annie curled up with her head in David's lap. At length, her gentle snores drove us all to stretch out and sleep. Annie and David snuggled together, fingers entwined. With no privacy, Corwen and I could only do the same.

The following morning, Annie produced sensible half-boots and a deep green dress for Alice. Though not in the height of fashion, it perfectly suited her new station and accommodated her baby bump remarkably well.

David whistled, and a piebald pony trotted out of the wood, saddled and bridled.

"Alice will need a mount that won't slow you down. Keep him as long as you need him and if you want to send him home, simply tell him and turn him loose."

"Does he have a name?" I asked, remembering how long it had taken us to find names for Timpani and Dancer.

"Brock." David patted the pony. "He's a good fellow, not young but sprightly. I know you'll treat him well."

We said our fond good-byes to David and Annie, not knowing when we'd meet again. Alice was full of curtsies and thank yous.

Dipping in and out of Iaru, we three made our way steadily northward, spending nights in wayside inns of varying quality. Now Corwen took two rooms, one nominally for me and Alice and one for himself, though Alice always slept alone.

I must admit that under her tender ministrations my hair began to look more respectable by the day. Having a maid was a novelty for me. We'd had rowankind in our house when I was growing up, but they were all general servants and not dedicated personal maids. After I ran away with Will, I was a lost cause as far as fashion was concerned, rarely wearing skirts, except when we were in port and he took me somewhere special. After his death, my breeches became my armor.

"I've been thinking," Alice said on the third morning. "If I'm leaving my old life behind I should leave my name, too. I should like to be called Poppy."

"That's probably a good idea, Ali — Poppy," I said. "No one knows your background. It seems to me you can re-write your own history."

So Alice, at her own request, became Poppy Leveret.

8

Blight

W E REACHED CHESTERFIELD in the county of Derbyshire on the evening of the fourth day.

"Not far now," Corwen said as he flung our shared traveling valise on the bed. "We should be home tomorrow unless the weather deteriorates. It's only another thirty miles."

We'd taken rooms at the Royal Oak, an ancient half-timbered building next to a butcher's shop and close to the market. Poppy was already safely installed in one room and had declared her intention to take full advantage of the bed, so I'd arranged for a tray to be taken up for her. Corwen leaned his hands on the windowsill of our room and looked out. His nose twitched.

"What is it?" I asked, my own nose full of wood smoke from the recently lit fire.

"Raw meat. Blood." He licked his lips.

Corwen makes a thing about not being moon-called, and I'm grateful he's not. There's nothing ends a romance faster than being shredded and eaten by your lover. But he is still a predator. He can overcome his wild nature most of the time, but every so often he needs to hunt.

"Maybe the landlord can manage a nice mutton chop for supper," I suggested.

I wasn't sure if the resulting growl came from his throat or his stomach, but less than an hour later we were seated downstairs tucking into mutton chops and mash. I had my chops well-roasted with the skin and fat crisped, Corwen asked for his lightly cooked and running pink. We washed down our food with a locally brewed ale.

Our meal was served by two young women, one with the woodgrain-patterned skin of a rowankind and one not.

"How long have you worked here?" I asked the rowankind girl.

"Four months, ma'am. Me an' Peggy used to work at the Red Lion, but the wages are better here." She jerked her head toward the other girl.

"You didn't want to go to Iaru?"

She started a little at my use of the name, but recovered quickly. "I've got a young man, ma'am. Peggy's brother, Charlie. He's not rowankind. The law may not allow us to get wed proper-like, but as soon as he finishes his 'prenticeship and starts gettin' a decent wage we're jumping the broom together. He works next door for Mr. Burkinshaw, the butcher."

"Would you wed in a church if the law allowed?" I asked.

She stuck her chin out. "When has the law ever allowed rowankind anything?"

She had a point.

⊷——⊶

"Ah, I feel better for that." Corwen flopped onto the bed, fully dressed, when we reached our room.

I pulled a fresh shift from the valise and began to undress quickly in the chill air. "So, tomorrow I meet your family."

I tried to keep my voice casual and light. It was the closest I'd come to prompting him. Corwen had never spoken much about his life before his time in the Okewood, and though I'd been curious, I'd not pushed him on the subject.

He would tell me when he wanted to, but if I was to meet his family tomorrow, I couldn't wait any longer.

"What's left of my family. I can't begin to imagine what we might find when we arrive. Jonnie is—was—the best of brothers. Ten years older than me, he always had a sensible head on his shoulders. He was educated at Eton and Cambridge, but instead of history and philosophy, he came back full of ideas for enclosing the land, animal husbandry, and timber plantations. My father believes the future lies in industry and invention; hence his passion is the woolen mill. He was only ever interested in the land as pasture for his horses, but Jonnie persuaded him to enclose some of the land and use modern methods of farming. The tenants were leery of turnips and clover at first, but they soon saw the sense of it. Father was happy to leave the land to Jonnie's care while he managed his business interests. Jonnie was a . . ." He paused as if choosing his words carefully. "He was a great moderating influence on our father."

"And now Jonnie's dead." I climbed into the cold bed and snuggled close to Corwen, who was still fully dressed and a weight on top of the blankets.

He swallowed. "Father and I left a lot of things unsaid, and said some things which should not have been said."

"I left my own mother with things unresolved."

"Do you regret it?" He put one arm around me.

"Sometimes." I sighed. "I'll always wonder what I could have done to change the way things were between us. If I'd known what she was hiding from me, there may have been a chance, but I didn't and there wasn't." I shrugged. "What about your mother?"

"She was distraught the first time I changed. Her family hadn't prepared her for what might happen. It had skipped a generation, so maybe they thought they were safe. Then she spoke to her aunt who set her straight. After that, it appeared she was determined to make the best of it, though I suspect she felt guilty because I inherited it from her side of the family. She tried to protect me, but my father . . ."

"Thought it was your fault."

"When the change first manifests, it's hard to control.

Father thought I was being disobedient. I recall my parents having blazing rows—though they were always careful to argue where the servants couldn't overhear. They didn't know I could hear. My father wouldn't be swayed, however. There were times when I couldn't sit for a week."

"He beat you?"

"At first."

"What stopped him?"

"My wolf. Even a young wolf has sharp teeth. My father realized beating a boy was one thing, but dealing with a young wolf could be dangerous."

"You bit him?"

"I didn't have to, but I snarled and threatened ... That was when Mother finally got through to him. He never truly understood, though. He always believed I could simply stop being a shapechanger if I wanted to."

"Is that why you left?"

"More or less. There was an incident ..." He raised himself on one elbow to look at me. "Don't worry, I didn't kill anyone."

"I never thought you did." I raised my hand to cup his cheek. "I trust you."

"That's more than Father did. Something had been harrying his horses ..."

"He thought it was you."

"It's not a pretty story. That it escalated into something neither of us could back down from was mostly my fault. Anyhow, Jonnie suggested I pay an extended visit to Emily, my big sister. She's nine years older than me. I doubt you'll meet her. She hardly ever visits. To be honest, I don't know her well. She married young and left home when I was still a boy. Her husband, Charles Marchmont, is well set up. He has five thousand a year and a small estate in Lancashire. He's older than her by fifteen years, and they have, or had when I last saw them, five children. No shapechangers to my knowledge. There may be more than five by now, of course. I only stayed for two days. Emily didn't trust me. She was frightened for her children. She didn't say so, but it was in everything she did."

"Lily's letter mentioned Freddie."

"Ah, yes. He's my twin."

"You never mentioned you had a twin."

"We're not identical twins, though we were close as boys—until I changed. After that he was caught up in Father's treatment of me. Father expected Freddie to be a shining example of what I could be and do if I tried hard enough. For every wrong I did, he had to do something praiseworthy. It took its toll on him in the same way that always being the miscreant took its toll on me. We both had a miserable few years, though for different reasons. He fought shy of responsibility because it was thrust upon him. Father expected too much. Freddie blamed me. I suppose he was right in that. We drifted apart. He was never a good scholar, but I think he was glad to be sent away to school and university. I wasn't allowed to go, of course, since Father never trusted me not to reveal my curse. Freddie's older than me by twenty minutes, so he's the heir, now."

"He wasn't a shapechanger when you left?"

"No. I don't know what might have passed between Freddie and Father after he changed." Corwen swung his legs off the bed and began removing his shirt. "Father always forgave him his indiscretions even though he never applied himself to anything except a wager and the latest fashion. He was always feckless—a bit of a prankster—but there wasn't any malice in him. He had mood swings, though. Sometimes he went from extreme melancholy to frantic activity in almost no time at all. I'm not surprised to hear he's gone up to London. Hiding from his new responsibilities, I expect. Jonnie's are big shoes to fill."

"And you think Freddie will have trouble filling them?"

"It's been six years. Despite his wolf-change, or maybe because of it, he may have grown up. I know I have." Corwen draped his clothes over a chair and slid into bed beside me, naked, radiating heat. "Do we have to talk about my family?"

And that's where our conversation ended.

◆━◆

Coming down to breakfast the following morning, we were surprised to find a couple of stout lads with cudgels guarding the inn's front door.

"What's happening?" Corwen asked the landlord.

"Nothing at the moment, sir. Simply taking precautions."

"Against what?"

"Bread rioters. There's word gone round the street that the baker is planning another ha'penny on the price of his loaves. He says it's because of the price of flour, and the miller says it's because of the price of wheat. And they all say it's because they have to pay their workers now. The people don't like it."

"Can't afford it, more like." The innkeeper's wife came out of the kitchen with a large loaf of freshly baked bread and plonked it on the table. "It's shocking. Almost as bad as five years ago when the poor harvest brought famine to our door."

I had been at sea, and Corwen had been living on the bounty of the Lady of the Forests. He nodded, though. "We had a lot of refugees coming to . . . where I was living. I remember it well. Families who couldn't look after their children; rumors people were hoarding wheat to inflate the price still further."

"And . . ." I prompted.

"We did what we could." He looked to the innkeeper. "You have our sympathies, but we still have a distance to travel and you can understand we would rather not get involved in your difficulties."

"No one will get past my lads at the door."

"Even so, we'll be on our way before the trouble starts. It's hard when people are driven to the streets to protect themselves."

"I'll call Poppy," I said. "Perhaps we could take some of that with us." I pointed to the bread. "It's a pity to waste what so many would be grateful for."

By the time we got into the stable yard, we could hear loud voices in the street. The ostler had saddled our horses and tied them to rings in the yard. Dancer whickered a greeting and nuzzled the outside of the freshly baked loaf, now wrapped in a muslin.

"That's not for you," I said.

He huffed out a breath and snorted as if disappointed.

Corwen boosted Poppy into Brock's saddle and helped her to find her stirrups. I noticed she wasn't so obviously afraid of him, now.

"This way, lads. We'll get some ale by the back door if the bastards won't let us in the front." A rough voice from the alley preceded running footsteps, heavy boots on cobbles. Half a dozen youngsters pounded into the yard, apprentices by the looks of them, using the potential bread riot to cause mischief.

"Oho! A rowankind." One of the young thugs said. "Reckon it's their wages that's causin' prices to go up. Come on then, girls. How are ye goin' to make amends?"

I felt Poppy tense, but it wasn't her he was looking at. The two serving girls from last night were in the back doorway of the inn.

"I know you, Jimmy Beeston," Peggy shouted. "Up to your tricks again. Get out of it, or I shall tell our Charlie. He'll give yer what-for."

"Your Charlie and whose army?" The lead apprentice swaggered. "He can't do nuffink if he ain't 'ere."

Two ostlers ran out to meet them, one with a two-pronged pitchfork, the other with a shovel.

"Leave my Peggy alone, Beeston." The younger of the two ostlers stepped forward.

"Easy up, Bert." The older ostler pulled him back to take a defensive position between the apprentices and the girls. "Get out, boys." The ostler sounded almost conversational, but he braced the end of his pitchfork handle against his stout boot and angled the tines toward the apprentices. "There's no bread in here."

"What's that, then?" One of the apprentices spotted the barely disguised muslin-wrapped loaf, still in my hands, and veered in my direction. I had my pistols under my redingote, but they were hardly an appropriate response to a gang of apprentices.

If it came to a scrap, I could look after myself and so could Corwen. None of the boys was armed; it was only a bit of bravado and some opportunist scavenging.

Then Jimmy Beeston pulled an ugly looking knife, and the temperature of the situation changed in an instant.

I saw Corwen pat Timpani and tell him to stand without taking his eyes off the Beeston boy.

Predator's eyes.

Corwen needed to hunt, and if he couldn't do it as a wolf, he'd do it as a man.

But the boy was a street scrapper and armed with ten inches of steel.

"You want bread? Here!" I tossed the loaf high in the air.

Beeston might have been a scrapper, but he was inexperienced enough to watch the arc of the loaf as it flew through the air, and to raise his knife as if the bread were his enemy. And so it proved, because it gave Corwen an opening. He stepped in close to the blade, grabbed the boy, wrist and shoulder, and turned his hip and leg in to unbalance him. The boy stumbled and the next instant Corwen had the knife and the boy had taken three paces back, pushing the rest of the apprentices outward in a semicircle.

"The rest of you keep away." Corwen tipped the point of the knife toward the boys, then looked Beeston in the eye. "You, boy. Run!"

The boy's nerve broke. He fled. Corwen gave him four paces head start and still had him on the ground before he reached the yard gate. There was a yelp and a voice rising in pitch to a childish: "You cut me!"

Corwen stepped back. The boy rolled over and jumped to his feet, hand to the side of his head and neck, blood pouring between his fingers. I thought for a moment Corwen had sliced into something vital, but he held a small pinch of flesh. Not even a full ear, merely an earlobe, but the blood was very satisfactory and must have terrified the apprentice.

"Next time you pull a knife, remember there's always

someone around who's bigger, faster, and meaner than you." He scowled at the other boys. "Get out."

They stood rooted to the spot.

"Now!"

They ran.

◆————◆

We departed Chesterfield quickly and avoided any further confrontations. Two miles out of the town we found a little wood which enabled us to enter Iaru.

We hadn't gone more than a mile or two before Dancer began to toss his head. Timpani flattened his ears against his skull and snorted. Iaru's perpetual summer always felt fresh, but there was a staleness here, a lingering smell of sulfur and hot metal. The leaves on the trees curled at the edges and looked dry and lifeless.

Dancer felt sluggish under my hands, and Brock sidled in close to us as if for reassurance.

"I wonder if . . ." Corwen didn't finish his sentence but pushed ahead of me, looking for something. "I think we have to leave Iaru now," he said. "I felt something similar when we passed close to Birmingham, but we were several miles from the city and it wasn't as strong."

"But this is Iaru," I said, picking a leaf from the nearest tree. It crumbled to dust. "What's wrong?"

"Think of the rolled parchment. Iaru and our world exist in the same space. There are places where the two worlds almost touch, where things, feelings, humors leech through. I think we're close to Sheffield. Burning ore, melting metal, slag, forge hammers, smog in the air, effluent in the rivers—the steel industry is not friendly to the land."

I only knew Sheffield's reputation for fine cutlery and said so.

"Cutlery, yes, but they've been making crucible steel for nearly sixty years. Sheffield produces thousands of tons a year and the coke-fired forges turn buildings black and clog a man's lungs. Walking through Sheffield at night is like a trip through Hell as they pour molten steel into ingot molds in a temperature that would blister a man's flesh from his bones in seconds, and sometimes does when men get careless."

I shuddered. "And that makes a difference to Iaru?"

"It seems so. Look."

Ahead of us a stand of saplings drooped, leaves scant and sickly. Beyond them was a grove of dead trees, bare branches cracked and decaying.

"This way." Corwen turned around and led us to where the trees were healthy. "We'll find a crossing point here, and travel through Sheffield itself. If we stay in Iaru we'll have to take a wide detour."

I still hadn't worked out how he found the crossing points, but it didn't take long before I felt the chill breeze of an April day and smelled smoke carried on the breeze.

We came out of the little wood, and then I saw it. In a bowl surrounded by seven hills was a smog-filled pit, several miles across, not unlike the common idea of Hades. Dante's Inferno came to mind, for inferno it surely was. The choking stench of sulfur climbed into my nasal passages and sat there like a small demon.

We rode into the town past cramped streets of brick terraced houses, shoved close against cutlers' yards and the blank high walls that surrounded forges. Each street had at least one alehouse. It must be thirsty work forging steel. Our horses' hooves clopped noisily on the cobbled roadway, joining in with the plodding of dray horse hooves and the rumble of cart wheels. I glimpsed an incandescent glow through the half-open gate into an industrial yard. The rhythmic clang of trip-hammers was deafening. Dancer shied so many times from the noise that I finally dismounted and led him. Timpani was less nervous, but Corwen also dismounted and walked with me. Brock followed behind Dancer with Poppy still in the saddle.

Groups of children, some unkempt and barefoot, played on the dusty side streets while careworn women swept their steps or cleaned the grime of the town's smog from small square windowpanes.

"Corwen, I haven't seen any rowankind since we came into the town. Do they—did they—work in the forges?"

"Not in the forges, but there were always plenty around working in other jobs—brewing, carting, working on the canal, in the inns. They unloaded pig iron on the quays, manhandled it to the forges, stoked the fires, tended the water wheels and the steam engines. Some worked for the *Little Mesters*, the independent cutlers with their own yards. I suppose when you freed them, they had a choice of stay or go."

"If I had that choice in this place, I know what I'd do," Poppy chirped behind us.

I agreed.

9

Family

WE LEFT SULFUROUS SHEFFIELD behind with the question of the rowankind unanswered, crossed the River Loxley, and headed north along the River Don. From there, we took a winding road up and over the edge of an escarpment. As we crested the top, we could see the moor stretched out to our left. More used to the granite tors of Devon's Darkmoor, and having become acquainted with Derbyshire's limestone peaks and crags as we passed through, I had envisioned the Yorkshire moors somewhat similar, but was surprised to find them not so much mountainous as a high, bleak plateau bisected by deep valleys and punctuated with gritstone escarpments. Heather grew thick on the hillsides, tough and green, not yet in flower.

The air was clear and sharp, and the cool April sun shone for us.

Beyond the market town of Penistone, we climbed again, and from the hilltop Corwen pointed out a house below us on the lee slope. I don't know what I had been expecting from Corwen's description of Denby Hall. He'd said it was a respectable house, and I'd imagined a solid stone farmhouse, but it was much grander than that. Nestled among land-scaped trees was an elegant country house, three stories at the center with a two-story wing at either side.

"Well?" Corwen asked. "What do you think?"

I frowned at him. "Are you very rich?"

He laughed. "My father is a gentleman of independent means. Though he involves himself in the clothier's trade, he doesn't rely entirely on the income. Jonnie would also have been rich as the oldest son. Freddie, if he comes home to his responsibilities, will be. I, however, as the youngest son, have a modest allowance which I haven't touched for years. A wolf doesn't have much use for currency in the Okewood. Father would have liked to have seen me set-tled, maybe as a vicar with a house and a genteel living from my parish, or perhaps with a commission in the army."

"Hmm, Reverend Corwen Deverell." I tried it out for size. "I'm not sure it suits you. Major Corwen Deverell, however . . . I could see you in a smart red jacket with shiny braid."

He laughed. "I'm not much good at taking orders."

We followed the road down the hillside and turned into the carriage drive that led to the house. The surrounding parkland encompassed an ornamental lake.

Corwen shrugged almost apologetically. "My late grand-father, who was distantly related by marriage to the younger son of an earl, had grand ideas. He dammed the stream to make a lake because he liked fishing, and my mother likes the view."

"Ah, your mother . . ."

He reached over and took my hand. "Don't worry about my mother."

"You're going to tell me she'll like me regardless of the fact that I'm the widow of a privateer who dressed as a man to captain my own ship, who can do magic but isn't registered with the Mysterium, and who shares a conjugal bed with her son without benefit of marriage."

He laughed. "No, she's always been very protective of my privacy. I'm pretty sure she'll see you as a threat and hate you on principle, but she'll come around if you give her the chance. She may seem a bit shallow, but it's an act. There's steel at her core. She never wanted me to marry. She thought it too much of a risk. A wife might not understand, and might never forgive if her children were cursed with wolf blood. She had high hopes for Jonathan, though. She wanted him to marry Dorothea Kaye, the daughter of the most powerful mill-owning family in the area, and a brainless but elegant beauty. Jonathan quietly told her that when he married he would do it for love and not for business. She then turned her matchmaking skills toward Freddie. Freddie, however, never showed the slightest inclination to marry."

He lapsed into silence for a few paces. "Mother's a stickler for propriety." He squeezed my fingers. "But we can solve one problem at least."

"Yes, all right, I promise not to do any magic while I'm here."

"No, that's not it. We can tell them we're betrothed."

"But we're not."

"We could be, if you would consent to it."

"Mr. Deverell, is that a proposal of marriage?"

"Mrs. Sumner, it is."

Behind us, Poppy cleared her throat, and I heard a faint sigh and a soft "Awww . . ."

◆——◆

"Maybe I spoke a little hastily," Corwen said.

"You mean you don't want to marry me?"

"No! I mean I do, but I'm not sure what I have to offer is so very great. My fortune is—well—hardly a fortune at all. I could find us a house, a small one in the country with a few acres, keep you in genteel poverty with a single cow, a few chickens, rows of vegetables in the garden and a maid-of-all-work so elderly she can't get employment anywhere else. There would, of course, be a plentiful supply of rabbits." He raised one eyebrow and gave me a rueful grin. "You don't have to say yes without time to think. Besides all material considerations, I know you loved Will, and if you're not ready—"

"Yes."

"You mean yes, you'll consider it?"

"I mean yes, I'll marry you."

"You will?"

"I love you, Corwen. I promised I'd stay with you. I don't care about my reputation—I don't have one to care about, but if propriety matters to you and to your family, then getting married is the sensible thing to do. I only have one condition."

"Anything."

"Anything? You may regret that." I laughed. "I've lived an unconventional life, so far. Please don't expect me to be a conventional wife."

"Is that all? I'm not likely to be a conventional husband." He cleared his throat and said softly, "I thought you might have qualms about giving birth to a wolf cub or two . . ."

"Well, I presume they're not actually cubs when they are born, and if they change, we . . . we'll deal with that when we get to it, presuming—"

I told him about my son, born on board the *Heart of Oak*, with only Will for a midwife. The poor little thing had come early and had not lived more than a day or two. Since then, I'd taken care not to get with child again, but considering Will's lusty disregard for what time of the month it was, I had been remarkably successful. Maybe I wasn't able to have any more children.

"Children or not, Ross, I love you and want to marry you."

I squeezed his fingers in return. "We should have decided on this earlier. We could have avoided a lot of fuss."

"Fuss is one of the things my mother likes. It puts emphasis on the event and takes it away from the individual. She's always been very good at managing social occasions."

"Oh dear. Now I'm really not looking forward to meeting her."

"Don't worry. She'll be perfectly civil, and Lily will make up for any reserve Mother has. I'm sure you'll love Lily. She's got a good heart."

"You haven't seen her for six years."

"She may have grown a little, but hearts don't change."

I thought about my brother Philip who had betrayed us in the worst way. I was a summoner. My magic could call the spirits of the dead, but he was one spirit I hoped never to encounter.

As we reached the top of the driveway, a small man, wizened and slightly bow-legged, scuttled from the direction of the stables to take our horses. His face lit up when he saw Corwen. "Master Corwen!"

"Hardly Master anymore, Thomas, but good of you to remember me."

"Ah could never forget, sir, as taught thee to ride." He bobbed his head to me and to Poppy, but his eyes were drawn straight to the horses. Here was a man who could see through the glamour to what was underneath. "I'll take thi 'osses. Give 'em a good rub down an' a nice feed."

"Look after them well, Thomas."

"I will, sir. I can see they're a bit special-like, even t'pony."

"They are, indeed. Don't let my father get a good look at them, or he'll be trying to buy them or accidentally letting his mares run with them."

The little man's face clouded. "Mr. Deverell 'asn't been near t'stables since Mr. Jonathan left us, sir. A sad business that was."

"Hasn't he?"

"Not even when Millie 'ad a colt to that Arab." He pronounced it Ay-rab.

To be honest, I was having difficulty following Thomas' broad Yorkshire accent, but I'd caught the gist of the conversation. It sounded as though Corwen's father was more frail than he'd expected. Lily had said he fell into an apoplexy at Jonathan's funeral. That was five months ago. Was he totally incapacitated?

Corwen jerked his head toward the house. "I presume they're at home."

"'Ardly ever go anywhere, now. Samuel upped and left when all t'rowankind disappeared, and t'Missis 'asn't found another butler to suit yet, so it'll be one o' t' girls answerin' t'door. Bit slow sometimes. It's not bolted, though, not at this time o' day."

"Thanks, Thomas. I'll come to the stable later and we'll have a good catch-up."

"Door's allus open, an' t'kettle's allus on—like it used to be."

"I often hid out with Thomas in his loft." Corwen smiled as the little man led away our horses. "Especially when I'd done something stupid, like let the wolf be seen too close to the village. He never asked me what was wrong. Simply made me sit and drink tea so strong you could grease wheels with it." He looked at the front door of the house, guarded by two classical-looking pillars and a portico, and took a deep breath. "Better get this over with."

Corwen tried the bellpull, then got tired of waiting and pushed the front door open as a maid came up the stairs at a run, one hand on her lace cap. She halted and pulled herself together.

"I'm so sorry, sir, who shall I say is calling?" I tried not to laugh. Opposite us in the hallway was a portrait of Corwen with his brothers, an older man, as tall and broad-shouldered as Corwen, but with gray wings to his dark hair despite being—I estimated quickly—about thirty at the time. He must be the recently deceased Jonathan. His portrait showed him as serious, almost stern, but I fancied I saw a hint of amusement in the tilt of his mouth. I wished I'd known him. Freddie, so like Corwen in build, but with softer facial features and mouse-brown hair, sat on a chair, Corwen stood beside Jonathan, hardly changed, his silver hair at odds with his youthful face, and gray eyes dancing with merriment.

If the maid had ever looked at the portrait while she was dusting it, she would have recognized Corwen instantly, but obviously she'd not.

"You may tell Mr. and Mrs. Deverell that their son and his fiancée have come home."

Her jaw dropped slightly. I saw her eyes flick to the painting, and she began to blush. "I'm sorry, Mr. Corwen, sir, I didn't know . . ."

"That's all right. Where are they? I'll announce myself."

"In the drawing room, sir."

"Thank you. It's a little early, but perhaps you could bring some tea and see that Poppy's looked after in the kitchen."

She bobbed a curtsey. "Certainly, sir."

Corwen hooked an arm around my shoulders and shepherded me toward a door. "Tea makes all things better in this household. It's the little rituals that keep everything on an even keel."

He pushed open the door, paused on the threshold, and said, "Hello, Mother."

———◆———◆———

"Corwen!" A tall, stately woman dropped the book she was reading and launched herself out of the chair. I could see immediately where Corwen got his looks from, if not his hair color. Mrs. Deverell's hair was a faded auburn.

She saw me over Corwen's shoulder, and her demeanor changed in an instant. "Oh, my poor nerves. How could you?"

She sank into the chair, fanning herself with a kerchief.

"How could I what? Come home? Am I not welcome?"

"Of course you are!"

A sound like *herrhernn* came from the high-backed leather chair by the window. I had not noticed there was anyone else in the room since the chair was turned so the occupant could see the view across the lake. A young man, a servant by his plain suit, possibly Mr. Deverell's valet, sat on a stool, half hidden by the chair, with a book open on his lap. I thought he might have been reading aloud to Mr. Deverell before we arrived.

"Father!" Corwen crossed the room in three swift strides and made a formal half-bow to the man in the chair. I didn't have to see the occupant to know he was shocked by what he saw. The way he flicked his gaze to me and back again to his father was enough. I hovered in the doorway, unsure of what to do next. Corwen's mother turned her gaze on me. "We have not been introduced," she said, icicles in her voice.

I dropped a polite curtsey. "Rossalinde Sumner, Mrs. Deverell. Pleased to meet you."

She glanced at my left hand where Will's wedding ring still resided.

"I'm sorry, Mother, I forgot myself." Corwen left his father and took my hand. "Please allow me to introduce Mrs. Rossalinde Sumner, my fiancée."

"Fiancée?"

Anything else she might have said was cut short by the arrival of the maid with a tray of tea things: an elegant silver pot on a stand with matching milk jug and sugar bowl, a hot water urn, and a larger bowl for waste. These she placed carefully on a mahogany side table. A second maid brought a tray of teacups, saucers, and plates with a platter of thinly sliced bread and butter.

Corwen's mother immediately snapped into lady-of-the-house mode. She indicated that we should sit and drew some hot water to warm the pot, tipping it into the waste bowl before measuring out leaves from a caddy already sitting in pride of place on the mahogany sideboard, and adding more hot water to brew the tea.

The valet turned Mr. Deverell's chair, which appeared to be on little wheels. I saw for the first time the ruin of a once handsome and vital man. The left side of his face showed what had been. The right side held his present and his future. His features had dropped as if they were trying to slide down his neck, and his right eye was completely closed. His right arm was tucked into his lap as if it didn't belong to him, and he slumped slightly sideways, despite the support of the padded chair.

But the eye on the good side of his face glittered with intelligence.

"This is Rossalinde, Father, Mrs. Sumner."

I made my curtsey. Mr. Deverell was sixty at the most, though by his condition he might well be ninety. How unfair that the Fae were still young after hundreds of years while Corwen's father should succumb to such a debilitating condition.

Corwen's mother was maybe in her mid-to-late fifties. Her face appeared barely wrinkled except for a few lines around her mouth and crinkles at the corners of her eyes which, in happier times, might have been regarded as laughter lines rather than crow's-feet. Her hair was wound on top of her head; she wore a little cap, more decorative than useful, that matched the cream fichu tucked inside the wide, fashionable neckline of her pale green day dress. A Kashmir shawl of the same color was draped elegantly about her shoulders. She must have been a great beauty in her younger days. In many ways she still was.

Corwen's father had been dressed with the same attention to detail, as though his physical condition was something that could be denied if his neck cloth was tied just so, and his coat was wrinkle-free. The valet must be his nursemaid as well.

"*Herrhernn.*" Corwen's father tried to speak.

Mrs. Deverell shook her head. "Sometimes it sounds as if he's trying to say a word, but mostly he makes noises." She turned toward Mr. Deverell and said very loudly and very slowly. "Tea, Arthur? Would you like a nice cup of tea?"

He flinched at the volume of her voice. Nothing wrong with his hearing, then.

She poured milk into a china cup followed by tea, putting it on a small table within reach of Mr. Deverell's left hand. He jerked his hand toward it but made no attempt to grasp the delicate handle. The valet took the cup, poured a little of the tea into an ingenious pottery vessel which was half closed over the top and had a mouthpiece like a short flattened spout. He swirled the tea in the bottom of the cup, presumably to let the heat dissipate and raised the spout to Mr. Deverell's mouth. Even with so much care, some of the tea dribbled down Mr. Deverell's chin, and the valet quickly caught it on a napkin.

"*Herrhernn.*" Again.

"What is he trying to say?" Mrs. Deverell asked. "I

swear I wish I knew. Garden, Arthur? Is that what you want? Drink your tea, and Yeardley will take you outside."

"Perhaps I could take Father to sit in the garden, Mother," Corwen said. "You and Ross get to know each other."

I'd faced hellhounds and pirates, but one glance at Mrs. Deverell and I wanted to beg him not to leave me alone with this woman.

Yeardley brought in a wheeled chair with a woven wicker seat and back. Unlike a Bath-chair which usually had a single steering wheel at the front, this had four wheels, and handles behind for pushing. Yeardley lifted Mr. Deverell into it as though he were no heavier than a child and wrapped his legs in a blanket.

"Let me," Corwen said. He grasped the handles and pushed the chair to the door and out into the hallway with Yeardley following, leaving me smiling inanely and trying not to spill my tea to which Mrs. Deverell had automatically added milk, something I never did. Years aboard a sailing ship without the benefit of a dairy cow had taught me not to soften my drinks with milk. This brew tasted greasy and cloying. I sipped it slowly.

"So, Mrs. Sumner," Corwen's mother said, "you are affianced to my son. Have you known him long?"

Was she asking if I knew he was a shapechanger, or was she trying to work out whether I was after his money?

"Almost a year," I said, which was not far from the truth, though he had been a wolf when I saw him first.

"And where are you from, my dear?"

"My family came from Somersetshire, but I was raised in Plymouth. My father was in shipping."

"Was?"

"He died at sea, eight—no, nine—years ago. My mother died last year, but we were not close. She disapproved of my marriage." That was putting it mildly. "My husband, Will, a sea captain, died four years ago, an accident."

"The sea is a dangerous place. I'm sorry for your loss."

"Thank you."

"Your husband's ship . . ."

"My ship, now. The *Heart of Oak*. She sails under Captain Garrity from her home port of Elizabethtown on the island of Bacalao." That should answer the question she was deliberately trying not to ask. I was not a penniless widow who'd latched onto her son in hopes of improving her situation, but I came from trade, not from the first rank of society. If she didn't inquire too deeply, I might appear respectable enough, though, of course, if she knew my history, she might not want me in her family at all.

"And was your first marriage—it was your first marriage, wasn't it?—blessed with little ones?"

"Sadly, it was not."

"Ah, I expect your husband was away from home a lot."

"No, we traveled together."

"You did?"

"My parents saw each other rarely. I didn't want that kind of marriage. We had a son, but he was born early, on a sea voyage, and didn't survive."

It was a common enough tale. Children were fragile. When I'd been searching for the details of my mother's family, the Sumners, I'd been saddened by the number of dead children in the parish registers.

"Maybe if you had stayed on land . . ." She cleared her throat. "More tea?"

"No, thank you."

I pushed down the urge to tell her not to pass judgment. She knew nothing of my life and circumstances, and with luck never would. We'd stay for a duty visit. Corwen would settle whatever family affairs he could, and then we would leave again. I needn't worry myself about Mrs. Deverell.

"Mama, Corwen's here." A breathless voice came from somewhere in the hallway. "Why didn't you call me? I spotted him out in the garden with Papa. Oh . . . who are you?"

A young woman with a tumble of curly black hair and amber eyes appeared in the doorway in a swirl of skirts and hooked a hand around the door frame to anchor herself. Her cheeks were a healthy pink, and she looked as though she had a laugh waiting to burst forth.

"Lily, how many times must I tell you . . ." Mrs. Deverell frowned. "This is Mrs. Sumner, your brother's fiancée. Come and make your curtsey. Remember your manners."

"Fiancée?" Lily bobbed a polite curtsey to me, and I stood and returned it, wondering whether I was going to have to go through explanations again and whether the daughter would be as icily polite as the mother.

"Oh, how wonderful. Corwen's finally done it."

I saw Mrs. Deverell's mouth compress into a sphincter. I didn't know whether her disapproval was directed at me personally, or whether anyone would have suffered the same scrutiny.

"That's marvelous." Lily stepped forward and took both my hands. "I'll have a sister at last."

"You already have a sister, young lady," Mrs. Deverell said.

"But not here. Never here. Besides, Emily is seventeen years my senior so I hardly know her. And Freddie is never going to present me with a sister. Corwen is an excellent judge of character. I'm sure Mrs. Sumner and I will get along famously."

I smiled at her. "Please, not Mrs. Sumner. My name is Rossalinde, but my friends call me Ross."

"See, Mama, we are friends already. We shall call each other Ross and Lily, like true sisters."

I thought I heard a faint *hurrumph* from Mrs. Deverell, but when I glanced at her, she'd schooled her face into a blank canvas.

"Have you met Papa, yet? Have you seen the garden?" Lily hardly waited for an answer before she asked the next question. "Mama, we should show Ross the garden."

"I need to make arrangements for rooms to be readied and dinner to be prepared." Her implication was that Corwen and I were causing her a lot of trouble, though it would be the servants actually doing the work. "You take Mrs. Sumner outside, and I shall order the household."

Lily let one of my hands drop but firmly held the other and drew me into the hallway and along a corridor to a side door.

"Don't worry about Mama," Lily said. "I didn't tell her I'd written, so Corwen's arrival will be something of a shock."

"And mine even more so."

"Yes, but she will get used to the idea."

"I hope so."

10

Mr. Deverell

BEHIND THE HOUSE the green vista swept down to the lake, punctuated by several stands of ornamental trees, some not yet at full growth, but others already mature. Corwen and his father were nowhere in sight, but Lily led the way along a broad paved path through a formal garden.

"Oh, I do hope they're making up," Lily said.

"Making up?"

"Corwen and Papa were . . . not on very good terms. Corwen surely told you?"

"Not the details. He said he felt there was no place for him here."

She looked at me sideways.

"If you're wondering whether I know Corwen is a wolf shapechanger, I do."

"Ah, good." A look of pure relief flashed across her face. "Papa is much altered. I hope Corwen will let the past go. It's ironic that Father was always comparing Corwen to Freddie. No matter what Corwen accomplished, it was never enough to win Father's approval. He favored Freddie because he didn't have the wolf curse, and then it turned out he did, and so did I, though neither of us knew it while Corwen was still at home. After Corwen stormed out saying he'd never come back, I'm sure Father regretted . . . but it was too late. And now Father can never take his words back."

"Can he really not speak at all?"

"I've made some alphabet cards, but it's slow and laborious. He gets frustrated and angry with himself, and he also tires easily. Sometimes, halfway through spelling a word, he loses concentration or simply falls asleep." Lily turned sideways to face me as she spoke, hop-skipping along. "Yeardley is a wonder at anticipating his needs." She sighed and resumed a normal walking pace, her voice more subdued. "Mama—well, they've always had their differences, caused mostly by how to deal with their wayward children—but now she treats Papa like a child because he can't make his wishes known. I'm sure his understanding exceeds his ability to communicate, though. He squeezes my hand, once for no and twice for yes. Sometimes it's indistinct because his hand trembles, so Mama doesn't always take it into account, especially if it's not the answer she's looking for." She pressed her lips together. There was more, but she wasn't going to trust me with it yet, or maybe she didn't understand the dynamics of her parents' relationship herself.

"That's where they'll be." Lily pointed to a high brick wall festooned in purple wisteria. A door swung open. "I saw them from my bedroom window. There are only a few paths smooth enough for Father's chair. I've been urging Mama to have Shaw make more. Papa loves to be outdoors."

We passed through the gate into a walled garden, neatly laid out with vegetable plots in the center and flowerbeds around the perimeter. The wheeled chair stood on the path while Corwen sat on a low bench facing his father, speaking quietly, his hand resting on the arm of the chair, beneath his father's good left hand. Yeardley had politely taken himself off to the other side of the garden.

"Lily!" Corwen jumped up to greet his sister who flung herself into his arms.

At nineteen, she was slender and pretty, but had puppyish excitability. I wondered whether I'd have thought of her as puppyish if I hadn't known she was a shapechanger. She hugged him and squirmed in his embrace, then slapped him on the shoulder.

"Six years, Corwen Deverell. Six years and not a visit, not a letter. You might have been dead, shot by a hunter in need of a wolf pelt. Mama has been so worried."

She continued her tirade. I looked away, discomforted by this show of sibling affection, for that was what it was. The garden, protected from the Pennine winds, was budding already. Cordons of fruit trees growing against the south-facing wall had begun to pop a few early blossoms. In the far beds winter cabbage still hunkered down low to the soil. Several more beds had been turned over and were ready for spring planting. All the industrious work of the previously mentioned Shaw, I expected, obviously the Deverells' gardener.

"Hsss."

I looked around. Mr. Deverell was regarding me intently with his good eye. I slid onto the bench Corwen had vacated. "Hello, Mr. Deverell."

He waggled the fingers of his left hand and I took them.

"Twice for yes, once for no," Lily said over her shoulder.

He squeezed twice.

"Twice for yes and once for no. Got it."

He squeezed twice again.

"He likes you." Lily turned and smiled.

"How do you know?" I asked as Mr. Deverell squeezed my hand twice.

"He wouldn't talk to you if he didn't."

Corwen sat next to me on the bench, and Lily gave her father a kiss on the good side of his face before sliding onto the bench next to Corwen.

"Father," Lily said, "I know you and Corwen didn't part on the best of terms, but I wrote and asked him to come home because I was worried."

"He says yes," I said, feeling two squeezes.

She turned to Corwen. "We haven't heard from Freddie for almost four months, despite Mama writing to him twice a week. He went up to London last December, wrote us with the address of his lodgings, said he'd met with some old friends from school and had become a regular at Whites. He said he'd won a substantial sum on a horse race; he didn't say how much. We haven't heard from him since."

Corwen frowned. "He hasn't written for more funds?"

"No."

"Freddie was never short of friends," Corwen said.

"He largely withdrew from local society after he changed."

"About that . . ." Corwen said.

"He's a brown wolf. It was a dreadful shock. It happened on his twenty-third birthday. No one should change that late. He was beside himself with pain the first time."

"I remember my own first change," Corwen said. "I was still a child, of course. It hurt like hell, but after the first time or two it got easier."

"I think my change was easy by comparison," Lily said.

"So Freddie is a shapechanger, too. How ironic." Corwen looked sideways at his father and looked away. "Still, that shouldn't make a difference to him in London. He's able to control his changes, yes?"

"He seems to be able to. I ran with him a few times, tried to show him how to be a responsible wolf, how to hide his tracks, how to hunt, and what to hunt. I remembered everything you told me about being a wolf. It made it easier when I changed."

"I learned the hard way." Corwen grinned somewhat ruefully. "Lambs are not for hunting, especially when they belong to your neighbor and he has wolfhounds."

Mr. Deverell squeezed my hand several times. I took it to mean he found the talk of wolves somewhat upsetting.

"Freddie didn't want to run wild," Lily said. "In fact, he didn't want to run at all. Father encouraged him to reject his nature, of course, and after a few changes he simply gave up his wolf."

"That can't be good," I said.

"No, it isn't." Corwen glanced at his father once again. "I imagine it was difficult all round. There's nothing simple about rejecting the wolf. Sooner or later it will emerge—and all the stronger for having been suppressed."

Having lived with Corwen for almost half a year, I knew that too long without running as a wolf and he became edgy and his concentration suffered markedly.

"Damn, you should have written to me sooner," Corwen said.

"How could we? You made it pretty clear you were done with your family."

"Father wanted to see me with a commission in the army. Mother preferred the church. Freddie thought I was an embarrassment and wanted me gone before I ate some unsuspecting neighbor's child and caused a scandal."

"I didn't want you to leave," Lily said.

"You were the only one, sweetling. Even Jonnie never really wanted anything to do with my wolf, but he did understand it was something I had no choice about. I miss him."

"We all do—Mother most of all, though she won't talk about it."

I hadn't realized my expression was so easily read, but Corwen smiled. "You'll come to appreciate Mother in time, Ross. She's got iron in her bones. When I first changed she spent her time protecting me from Father and this family from the world."

Lily nodded. "After you'd gone she sheltered me from outside eyes. When Freddie changed, it started again. You know what this valley is like. Gossip travels faster than a galloping horse. Even though she disliked the Barnsley *ton*, as she called them—those who thought themselves above the rest of us—she kept in everyone's good graces in order to deflect rumors before they began. She understood why you had to go, but she needed to know you were safe. That's all she ever wanted—for us all to be safe: you, me, and Freddie."

Mr. Deverell's hand remained flaccid in mine. He was

not commenting on Corwen's departure. I couldn't tell what he thought by the expression on his face.

"So, should I drop everything and go up to London to bring Freddie back?" Corwen asked. "Or at least get an explanation from him?"

Lily frowned. "Freddie is only one of our problems."

"Tell me everything." Corwen sighed.

"Thatcher."

"The new steward."

"Not so new now. He's been with us for the last two years. Mr. Kaye recommended him when Mr. Roberts became ill. I'm only a silly girl, according to him, so when Thatcher comes here, he still reports to Papa, with Mama in attendance. They forget I'm there, so I listen. Thatcher doesn't *smell* right."

I didn't think she meant that literally, but maybe she did. Wolf noses were sensitive. Even in their human form a shapechanger might be more sensitive to, for instance, the smell of fear that a dishonest man might feel when reporting to his employer.

"Mama says she doesn't understand the ledgers, but I think Thatcher is cheating us. He says there are difficulties at the mill since Father negotiated that the rowankind should have wages." She looked at me. "Are you familiar with the woolen industry, Ross?"

"Not at all."

"Great-grandfather built the first scribbling and fulling mill on the site. In those days he put out all the spinning and weaving to local workers. That was the way of it for many years, even in my grandfather's time, but Father brought in mule frames for spinning and built a weaving shed with looms for broadcloth."

I must have looked puzzled because she gave me the kind of smile you give to children who don't understand something. "Broadcloth is woven in the mill and narrow kerseys are woven by local weaving families on their own looms. That system is what's known as *putting out*. Anyhow, no matter, Thatcher says half the looms in the weaving shed are standing idle and the rowankind work only when they want to. Father had ambitions for a great manufactory, based on the one weaving cotton at Styal Mill, in Cheshire."

"Aren't the rowankind weavers gone to Iaru?" I asked.

"Iaru? Is that what it's called?" She tilted her head to one side. "A few went somewhere, simply disappeared overnight, but not all. Some talked about it, but decided against—or at least they decided not to go straightaway. We've always had a good relationship with our rowankind workers. When they changed—rebelled, awoke—whatever you wish to call it, Papa talked to them and agreed fair wages for those who wished to stay on, and extra for those who would teach their skills to apprentices."

"That makes a lot of sense," Corwen said. "Did they agree?"

"Most of them. They always liked Papa. He treated them well. Respected them. And in turn they respected him. But Thatcher says they've let him down, and the financial returns are poor. I don't know whether it's bad management or whether he's deliberately taking advantage of Papa's condition to cheat us."

"What do you think, Mr. Deverell?" I asked. "Do you trust Mr. Thatcher?"

He squeezed once, hard. "No."

"Very well," Corwen said. "It should be Freddie's responsibility, but in his absence, I'll pay a visit to Mr. Thatcher."

"If Ross has never seen the inside of a mill, how would it be if we took her on a surprise visit since she is come to Yorkshire for the first time?" Lily clapped her hands in delight and then hesitated. "I'm sorry, Ross, I don't mean to make presumptions. Maybe you don't care for business. It's not very ladylike."

I laughed. "I may not understand the manufacture of cloth, but one day, when we know each other a little better, I'll tell you about my former business venture." I heard Corwen snort softly as if suppressing laughter, but I ignored him. "My family was in shipping. I'm from trade, not from gentry."

"Ha! Good!" She grinned at me and turned to her father. "I think Corwen's picked a good match, Papa."

Mr. Deverell squeezed my fingers twice. It seemed I had found favor. I hoped that meant Corwen's differences with his father were resolved.

◆━━━◆

After the interlude in the garden with Mr. Deverell and Lily, I felt better about the prospect of coexisting with Mrs. Deverell for a few days. Like me or not, she'd allocated a pleasant room for my use. A bed with a fat feather mattress dominated one end of it, together with a washstand and a clothes press that must have been over a hundred years old by the design and the state of the wood. The other end of the room had a modern chaise, a small writing desk, and a chair. A fire blazed in the grate, and the chill had already begun to burn off the room. Poppy had laid out my dresses, but they offered little choice for a formal dinner, and I was sure Mrs. Deverell would make this a formal occasion, if only because she could. She was still trying to get my measure, and I hers. Maybe protecting her children from the scrutiny of the outside world had caused her to build a layer of formality as a defense. If that was the case, I admired her for it. It couldn't have been easy raising shapechangers and hiding them from the world while keeping up the appearance of a normal household.

Poppy laid the wine-dark redingote, the rose-pink spencer, and the burgundy pelisse to one side and set out my choices on the bed. There was my walking dress in palest violet, which had suffered a little from being crushed in the valise, my gray linen day dress, similarly creased, and the cream dress that came from the Fae, which thankfully still looked immaculate. Together with the dark green linsey-woolsey traveling dress, that represented the sum total of my wardrobe.

"It's going to have to be the cream one, isn't it?" I said.

"At least it's clean." Poppy held it by the shoulders and examined it closely. "I'll spruce up the gray and the lilac for tomorrow. Come on, sit and let me do your hair."

I stared at my reflection in the mirror. Poppy had wound my dark hair on top of my head though I resisted letting her cut a fringe so she could tease little curls around my face, as it would be more difficult to tie my hair in a cue like a man. Ah . . . realization dawned. Maybe I'd not entirely abandoned my mannish persona. I'd intended to put all that behind me, but the incident with the kelpie made me reluctant to completely abandon my breeches. My man's attire had its uses.

"Poppy what have you done with . . ."

"I left your shirt and breeches with Mr. Corwen." She smiled over my shoulder. "I thought it safer there as any of the maids noticing would assume they were his unless they checked the size against the rest of his clothing."

"Well done." I was beginning to appreciate Poppy's discretion and intelligence. "How is it below stairs? Are you going to be all right?"

"I'll manage."

"Let me know if anyone troubles you. They haven't said anything about your baby?"

"Not a thing, though they've surely noticed. Mrs. Deverell gave me a look, though. You know, like—" She pulled a disapproving face, exaggerating it comically.

An unmarried servant would generally be dismissed without a character reference if she was with child, but Poppy was my responsibility, mine and Corwen's, and his mother had no say in the matter.

Mrs. Deverell was charm itself at dinner. If that had been all I'd seen of her I would have had a completely different opinion, but our encounter in the afternoon had left me with a lingering doubt.

Served at the fashionable time of five o'clock, the table fairly groaned under the weight of beef and lamb, pigeons in white sauce, sautéed mushrooms—far more than we could eat. And when I thought I'd eaten as much as I could possibly find room for, there was another round of serving plates with pastries, jellies, nuts, and candied fruit. I wondered how much of this was to impress me. Surely they didn't eat like this every day.

The same young man, Yeardley, attended Mr. Deverell, assisting him with his food and mopping inevitable spills without making a fuss. I was pretty sure Mr. Deverell was following the conversation as it bounced back and forth across the table.

I knew nothing of Yorkshire. By keeping my ears open and my mouth closed I was able to ascertain there were three or four important families in the area, the Kayes being the foremost. Sir Hubert Kaye was a gentleman with his own mill lower down the Dearne Valley. He had two sons and a daughter, Dorothea, now twenty-four and close to being an old maid. I got the impression that Mrs. Kaye, Mrs. Deverell's dear friend, had been one of the prime movers in the plans to push Dorothea and Freddie together, but I presumed Mrs. Deverell's marriage ambitions had ceased when Freddie's change came upon him.

What were Lily's chances of ever making a suitable match? She was a spirited young woman with a keen intellect and an unladylike, but refreshing interest in the family business. Most nineteen-year-olds would be thinking of suitors and wanting to attend the season in London or Bath, but Lily seemed uninterested in the marriage market. If she ever married, she would have to find a husband who was either too dim to notice his wife's tendency to slip out of bed in the middle of the night to run wild as a wolf, or fully aware of the family he was marrying into.

After dinner we retired to the small sitting room which held a pianoforte. Mrs. Deverell invited me to play, instantly confirming my lack of ladylike skills. I'd been subjected to lessons as a child, but my lack of practice had left me without even a party piece. She asked if I would prefer to sing. Ah, sadly, that was another skill I lacked. I glanced at Corwen who looked amused. The songs I'd lately known on board ship were hardly suitable for a polite evening with one's future family. They probably wouldn't appreciate my unladylike renditions of "Fire Down Below," "The Maid of Amsterdam," or "Round the Corner, Sally."

"I'll play." Lily jumped to her feet and crossed to the

piano, playing a lively tune which I didn't recognize. She beckoned Corwen over. "Remember this one?"

She sang a tuneful version of "The North Country Maid," and Corwen joined her on each chorus:

> *Where the oak and the ash and the bonny ivy tree*
> *All flourish and bloom in my north country*

I applauded when they'd finished, and Corwen went on to sing a creditable version of "The Three Ravens" before Mr. Deverell retired into the care of Yeardley and Mrs. Deverell suggested we play cards. She looked at me as if to ascertain I was not lacking in skills in that direction, but I was not, for there's little to do on the rolling ocean when not on watch.

"Loo, vingt-et-un, or a rubber of whist?" Lily asked.

"Whist, if it pleases everyone else," Corwen said, and we settled around a card table drawn up for the purpose. I had never played whist with Corwen as a partner. All our games at the cottage had been two player games of necessity, but we were well-matched, winning the first round easily. Seeing how Mrs. Deverell watched me, I contrived to be a little clumsy on the shuffle, and I let Lily finess my ace of hearts when she led with her jack, losing that round by one trick. Corwen raised an eyebrow at me for that mistake, so I gave no quarter in the third round. We won the first rubber, Lily and Mrs. Deverell the second, and Corwen and I the third. I didn't react to Mrs. Deverell's comment that I played like a man, but I saw a smile flicker briefly across Corwen's face.

"Well done, Ross." He squeezed my hand briefly as we mounted the stairs, watched by his mother. Was she checking that we were each retiring to our own room?

"The game, or my performance as a polite daughter-in-law?"

He chuckled. "Both. It will get easier."

"I hope so."

We parted with a kiss, lingering but chaste.

 11

The Mill

MAYBE IT WAS BECAUSE I was sleeping alone that dreams disturbed my night.

I dreamed of the sea again.

In my dream I am on deck. The Heart of Oak *is the only ship that doesn't make me seasick. In the laying of her keel is a sliver of winterwood, ensorcelled oak with magical properties. Corwen says she's a forest upon the ocean. Perhaps that's why she suits me so well.*

Then my dream changes. We've boarded a French barquentine. The fighting is fierce. I see Will's ghost, cutlass and pistol in hand. He points and draws my attention to where Walsingham is standing, pistol raised, pointing it at Corwen. Walsingham might have been handsome in his youth, but his powerful frame is running a little to fat. His features are too large for his face, and his skin is pockmarked.

I don't hesitate. I aim the pistol already in my own hand and shoot Walsingham dead.

The dream changes once more. I am in a forest, standing by an open grave. In the grave is a shrouded figure. I hear a cracked laugh and Walsingham is standing behind me, pale as death. "You killed one Walsingham, but the man is not important. The role goes on. You can't outrun the Walsinghams, and you can't outlive them. They will find you."

I raise my pistol and kill him again.

I lay in my bed, shaking. *A dream, it was only a dream,* I told myself, but still my whole body trembled. What did it mean?

The memory of Walsingham still sat like a cold stone in my stomach. I'd thought myself safe in Yorkshire, but safety was an illusion.

Walsingham had failed. We'd freed the rowankind from their servitude. Whether that was a good or a bad thing for the realm remained to be seen, but it was a good thing for the rowankind, so I couldn't regret that. What need for more Walsinghams? Revenge? Surely not. Hookey had reported Redbeard Tremayne and his wife, Rossalinde, dead when he took over as captain of the *Heart of Oak.* I had become Rossalinde Sumner. Surely I was free of pursuit.

Wasn't I?

I swallowed hard, knowing the dream had revealed what my mind didn't want to recognize. I pulled my knees tight to my stomach and curled up as small as I could under the covers.

There would always be another Walsingham. I would never be free.

❖───❖

Eventually I must have slept, but I was awake the following morning before a maid crept into my room to light the fire.

"It's all right, I'm awake already."

I startled the poor girl, who rattled her bucket of coal onto the hearth tiles.

"Sorry, ma'am, I didn't mean to disturb you."

"You didn't. Don't worry. What's your name?"

"Meg, if it pleases you, ma'am."

I wanted to ask what her name might be if Meg didn't please me, but that would be mean. It was lucky I hadn't magically banked the fire the night before. The maid would certainly have noticed something was wrong, and no one gossips more than servants in a household like this. "Thank you, Meg. Please send up water for washing."

She bobbed a curtsey and I got my jug of hot water quickly and efficiently. By the time Poppy arrived, still blinking sleep from her eyes, I had washed and laced myself into my stays.

Poppy looked me up and down. "I could lace those a little tighter."

"They're fine like this. I quite enjoy breathing."

"As you wish. I cleaned and pressed your lilac and your gray, though if you're riding today I'm guessing you'll want the green. I did my best to brush off the mud. You should probably have a riding habit, though I—"

"What?"

"Well, I know I'm only your maid so it's not my place to tell you what to spend your money on. I don't even know if you have any...money I mean. I can see Mr. Corwen comes from a good family, but I don't know...I'm sorry. It's none of my business."

I smiled. "Well, if you want to know if I have enough to pay your wages, the answer is yes. And I can have a riding habit made, too, and any number of dresses, though I don't have anywhere to keep them. Until six months ago I lived on board my ship, and after that Corwen and I stayed in my Aunt Rosie's cottage, somewhat isolated, taking our time to readjust to the idea of joining the world."

"It was you caused the Awakening, wasn't it?"

"I'm afraid so."

"Don't be afraid. It was the best thing you ever could have done for my kind. It's like everything that went before is hidden in a fog. I can recall it, but it seems like a half-life now. Whatever happens in the future, you did the right thing." She squeezed my shoulder briefly and brought me the dark green linsey-woolsey traveling dress.

Breakfast was a cup of bitter hot chocolate and a bread roll with pale golden butter. Corwen and Lily arrived together, but Mrs. Deverell, I was assured, was rarely out of her bed at this hour. I resolved to rise early every morning. While Lily joined me in a bread roll and hot chocolate, Corwen applied himself assiduously to a thick slice of gammon and three eggs.

None of us lingered over breakfast. The stable was our first port of call, a neat, clean, quadrangle, accessed through an archway, with stalls on two sides, a carriage house on the third, and looseboxes on the archway side. Thomas presided over a staff of four stable lads: an orphaned boy of fourteen, two young men in their twenties, and John Mallinson, a strapping man in his thirties who also drove the carriage when the family needed it.

Timpani and Dancer, well turned out, seemed happy.

"I hope they behaved themselves," Corwen said.

"Like gentlemen," Thomas said. "Shall I have them saddled for you?"

I was going to say I could do it myself, but that wouldn't be appropriate.

"Would you prefer a sidesaddle like Miss Lily?" Thomas asked. "I have one that would fit your Dancer a treat."

I preferred to ride astride, but the mill was only a couple of miles up the valley, so I gave in gracefully, hoping Dancer wouldn't object to a sidesaddle. I needn't have worried. He stood as steady as a rock when Corwen boosted me onto his back and I hooked my leg over the cupped pommel and found the stirrup with my left foot, taking care to distribute my weight evenly. Thomas handed me a cane for administering signals on the side with the missing leg. I had learned how to ride sidesaddle when I was a girl in Plymouth, but I was out of practice.

Lily's horse, an elegant bay mare with a pert head, whickered and sidled around to look at the two newcomers to the stable yard. Dancer tossed his head and whickered back.

"Flirt!" I told him, and he nodded his head as if to agree with me.

"That horse has more than a look of Templeman," Corwen said to Lily as she mounted from the mounting block.

"His granddaughter. Speedwell by Sandman out of

Corinna. Papa can trace her bloodlines back to Eclipse and thus to both the Godolphin Arabian and the Darley Arabian."

"I remember Corinna. Father had high hopes for a good foal."

"This is the one. Isn't she gorgeous? We had a filly foal from her last year."

The day was fresh, with a playful breeze from the west. Good sailing weather if we'd been on the ocean. I reached into the wind with my magical senses, but my mastery over wind and water had—if not vanished altogether—diminished. The best I could do was to feel the air currents gently slipping over each other.

As we rode up the valley along a road notched into the steep hillside, Corwen and Lily delved into the mysteries of Mr. Deverell's stud book. Corwen had told me his father's hobby had been horse breeding, and several of the foals he'd bred had gone on to win races at Epsom Downs and at Doncaster.

Water gurgled and gushed below us, more than a stream, but not yet a full-grown river.

"The Dearne," Corwen said. "It rises on the edge of the moor and is dammed above the mill. It turns the waterwheel which powers the hammers in the fulling stocks."

"Father was talking about powering the spinning mules with water when he . . . when Jonnie . . ." Lily lapsed into silence.

Corwen nudged Timpani alongside and took her hand. "Don't think that because I haven't spoken about him that I am not affected by Jonnie's passing, Lily. The house doesn't feel so alive without him, and in everything Mother says I hear her deliberately not mentioning him. If it's her way of dealing with his loss, I'll respect that, but I would be so pleased if you would talk about him."

She shot him a grateful look, and for the rest of the journey Corwen and Lily laid Jonnie's ghost to rest between them.

◆——◆

The road leveled out where the headwaters of the Dearne ran into a dam which, with a series of sluices and a channeled watercourse, ran into a second dam by a long, stone building. A breast-shot waterwheel turned steadily, the rushing of the water and the creaking of the wood-and-iron wheel carrying up to us together with the rhythmic pounding from inside the building.

We crossed over an arched stone bridge with low parapets. I had expected a single mill, but I was surprised by a collection of solid buildings set around a cobbled yard.

Six men unloaded raw fleeces from a wagon. They stopped and looked up. One called over a small boy and sent him scuttling away through the door of what might be an office.

"There's the fulling mill." Lily pointed to the building that sat hunched below the mill dam. "It's where the woven cloth is washed and pounded with fuller's earth to compact and strengthen the fibers. The waterwheel drives a series of tappit wheels on a shaft that, in turn, drives the hammers. When the cloth has been fulled, it's stretched out on the frames in the tenter croft to dry."

"You know a lot about the mill," Corwen said.

"Well, someone had to take an interest. Jonnie was busy managing the land and Freddie, frankly, didn't care a fig. I used to come here with Father and stand around looking like a spare part. It's surprising how much you can learn when no one takes you seriously. Come on, I'll show you around. I think I'm as good a guide as any, and since Thatcher hasn't put in an appearance yet, we could start with the spinning mules."

Lily led us to a low stone shed which held four strange contraptions, looking vaguely like empty bed frames with reels at each end. Forty threads to a frame, Lily said. A winding handle powered each mule, and the ends of the frames rolled outward, drawing threads from one set of bobbins to another. The spinners working the frames, a winder and two boys, glanced sideways at us, but didn't stop what they were doing. My throat began to itch from the stink of raw wool and the mist of floating fibers in the air. Small children darted about the frames, dashing in to mend the inevitable broken threads or cleaning out the accumulation of fluff with tiny fingers operating at heart-stopping closeness to wheels and spinning rollers.

"How old are they?" I asked.

Lily frowned. "Papa wouldn't employ them until they were eight, but some of these look younger to me. Corwen must ask Thatcher. He won't answer my questions."

I couldn't tell if some of them were girls or boys since they were all dressed in raggedy trousers and grubby shirts. With my limited knowledge I couldn't discern what was happening, but Lily pointed out that one set of bobbins contained slivers of carded but unspun wool, and the drawing out of the slivers and the twist turned the soft slivers into strong thread.

"Though we have looms on the premises as well, the mill still puts out," Lily said. "That is, raw wool is sent to the weaver families who spin it and weave it and return it, to be paid by the piece. Most of them have weaving shops upstairs in their own cottages. Take note as you ride by. You can recognize weavers' cottages by the gallery windows that let in more light and extend the working day. The cloth they weave is fulled here." She jerked her head toward the fulling mill. "Then it's sent to be finished down the valley where the cropper lads raise the nap and shear it. That's highly skilled and heavy work, and the croppers are known for being rowdy, so it's best they keep to themselves."

"I don't see many rowankind," Corwen said. "I thought Father agreed to pay them a premium if they stayed to train their successors."

"He did," Lily said. "Maybe most of them are in the weaving shed." She led us out into the yard where I was glad to breathe fresh air again.

"Can I help you, sir, ma'am?" A thickset man of middle years crossed the yard toward us, wearing a sensible woolen coat and dark breeches. His iron-gray hair was tied in a cue, and he carried a stout blackthorn stick by the shaft. "Miss Lily." He acknowledged Corwen's sister, but he paid more attention to Corwen.

"Mr. Thatcher, I presume." Corwen had the advantage of height.

"I am, sir, and you might be?"

"Deverell, sir. Corwen Deverell."

"I see." Thatcher half-bowed, and I saw from his face that he did see, and that seeing didn't sit easily with him.

"We are come to show my fiancée the mill and its workings," Corwen said.

"Of course, sir, of course."

"The weaving shed being next."

Thatcher led the way. Thirty handlooms weaving broadcloth, Lily had said, but by my count well over half of them stood idle; in some cases, they looked as if the person operating them had simply set down his tools and left. Others were not even threaded ready for weaving, whatever that process was called: warping? dressing? I heard terms bandied about but had little understanding of them. It reminded me of the feeling I had during my first few days on a sailing ship when everything had seemed so confusing and I hadn't known a bowsprit from a belaying pin. How long had it been before the inner workings of the *Heart of Oak* were second nature to me? A mill was simply another puzzle to work out. Different systems, but not impossible to learn.

"Where are all the weavers?" Lily asked.

Thatcher looked to Corwen.

"It's a fair question," Corwen said. "You may assume, Mr. Thatcher, that when Miss Deverell or Mrs. Sumner asks a question, they are asking on my behalf, and I would expect your answer to be as forthcoming to them as it would be to me."

"Of course, sir." Thatcher directed his answer to Corwen rather than to Lily. "The rowankind didn't stick to their agreement once your father became ill. And skilled labor is difficult to find now. Other mills in the area are taking on, too. There's competition for good men."

"Have the rowankind gone to Iaru?" I asked.

"To where?"

"Never mind. Where have they gone?"

"I don't know how or where they've gone. Gone is gone. Some have taken work at Kaye's Mill; others are idling at home."

"It's a sorry situation," Corwen said. "What have you done to resolve it?"

Thatcher had no answer to that, so Corwen changed tack. "Perhaps we could see the ledgers now."

"The l-ledgers? That would not be possible, sir, not right away. They are in use, you see, and the day's totals not ... tallied."

"You misunderstand, Mr. Thatcher. It wasn't a request." Corwen turned to his sister. "Lead the way to the counting house, Lily."

Thatcher looked as though he was about to protest, but he closed his mouth on whatever he'd been going to say. He led the way into what had once been the mill manager's house but was now converted into offices with the counting house and Thatcher's own office on the upper floor.

"I think I should look at the ledgers," Lily said.

Thatcher's face went pink; whether from anger or embarrassment was difficult to tell. "It's not appropriate for a young lady," he said.

"My sister may be young and female, but she's very capable." Corwen stared him down. "I also remind you of what I said before. Miss Lily and Mrs. Sumner speak with my voice and are to be given every courtesy."

"Every courtesy, of course, Mr. Corwen, sir. Baines will provide everything the young lady needs in the counting house."

"How often did Mr. Frederick come to the mill?" Corwen asked.

"Once or twice, with Mr. Deverell, but he never concerned himself with matters here."

"Hmm, perhaps that's the problem."

"Pardon, sir?"

"Nothing, Mr. Thatcher. Please don't let us disturb you further. I'm sure you have lots to do."

Corwen ushered us into the counting house where an elderly clerk with ink-stained fingers sat by the window, to get maximum benefit from the daylight as he made careful entries in a leather-bound ledger. He looked surprised when Corwen explained what we wanted, but set about lifting ledgers from a shelf and opening them on a table for our perusal.

Corwen muttered something about checking on the rowankind weavers.

"I hope you know what you're looking at," I said to Lily. "I can add a column of figures as neat as you like, but double-entry bookkeeping is a mystery to me."

"I cut my teeth on it. Father made sure I could understand accounting as well as geometry." She grinned at me. "But you don't have to stay and hold my hand."

"Really?"

"Really. Go and find something more interesting to do."

With a profound sense of relief I left Lily leaning over the large tomes. I found Corwen in the weaving shed with a frown on his face.

"What's wrong?"

"There was someone I expected to find here—a rowankind called Topping who always seemed to know what was going on in the mill. I'd like to talk to him."

We poked our noses into odd corners, checking out the warehouse where raw fleeces—a lot of them—waited to be dealt with. We sampled the delights of the scribbling mill where the raw wool was carded to make the fibers all lie in the same direction, and walked among the tenter frames where women grappled with long lengths of wet cloth to stretch them onto hooks.

Corwen took it all in. "I know from the demeanor of the workers that all's not well here, but I don't know enough about the business to pinpoint exactly what's wrong. Lily's going to be hours in that office, I have a small trip up the valley in mind. I hope Topping might be there, and he can probably tell me what I want to know."

12

Rowankind

"WHERE TO?" I asked as Corwen turned Timpani onto the road up the valley.

"My grandfather built some cottages to house his rowankind workers when the business was little more than a few fulling stocks and an undershot wheel. Topping lives there—if he didn't go to Iaru, that is."

We passed a farmstead which had a small two-story house attached to a barn in what I was beginning to recognize as the Yorkshire longhouse style. The upper floor of the house had a series of long, mullioned windows.

"That's a weaver's cottage." Corwen pointed out. "It belongs to the Denby estate. The whole family makes its living by spinning and weaving in the upper room. Weaving is a man's trade, but his wife spins and the children work, too, learning the trade as they grow. Spinning used to be done on a single wheel, but they probably have a small spinning jenny now. Most families do. That's a smaller version of the mule you saw in the mill earlier."

"They farm as well?"

"In a small way. They run a few animals and grow vegetables to supplement their income. It's pretty much what a lot of the families do around here. My great-grandfather was a gentleman clothier with a good name but not much money. He was an enterprising chap by all accounts. He made an advantageous marriage, but kept the business going, starting by putting out weaving. Then my grandfather, who also made a good marriage, built the fulling mill and the scribbling mill. Father added the weaving shed. Until recently, the family has done well from it. But it's not only profit that matters. The mill provides employment for over a hundred men, women, and children."

"How come your father has so many rowankind?"

"My grandmother was an only child. When her parents died, their rowankind came to my grandfather along with a substantial inheritance. The rowankind took to the weaving trade. Some rowankind families still live independently and weave as outworkers. I don't know how many stayed and how many went to Iaru. It's time to find out."

"Isn't it going to make a huge difference to the profitability of the business without the rowankind's free labor?"

"You know, I've been working it out and I don't think it will. Rowankind labor was never really free because they had to be provided with homes, food, and clothing. If they get a wage, they have to pay rent for their homes and buy their own food and clothing. When you take that into account, all that's changed is that the rowankind have a choice about going or staying, about who they work for, and what work they do. If we offer them a fair wage for their labor, it's up to them to decide whether to take it. In many ways that means it's up to us to make the offer attractive. It's a different way of doing things, but I'm sure we can reach an accommodation. I hope so anyway."

Around the next bend we came upon a long row of ten neat stone cottages, set back a little way from the road. Behind them, the valley side sloped gently upward, and I could see narrow strips of land set aside for kitchen gardens.

At the sound of our horses' hooves on the road, a rowankind man stepped out of his front door and stood waiting for us to arrive, muscular arms folded across his broad chest. He was dressed as many of the workers I'd seen earlier, in straight-legged trousers, a linen shirt, and a waistcoat. On his feet were stout clogs and on his graying hair a cloth cap. His face was dark for a rowankind, though still with a grayish cast, and his forehead and cheeks were handsomely patterned with grain marks like polished wood.

"You'll be Mr. Corwen Deverell, then," the man said without smiling.

"Word travels fast." Corwen dismounted, handed his rein to me, and offered a hand to the man who didn't take it. "I hoped to find you." Corwen dropped his hand to his side. "Mr. Topping, isn't it?"

"It is."

"My father always said if he wanted to know what was happening among the rowankind weavers, he came to talk to you."

"I didn't think you took any interest." The man's tone was accusatory.

"I have been an absentee son, I admit, but my father's condition—"

"How is Mr. Deverell?"

"Frail. Thank you for your concern. He's worried about the mill."

"And so he should be."

"Looms are standing idle."

"That's no surprise."

"Isn't it? Can we talk, Mr. Topping? I would know why idle looms are no surprise and I would appreciate some straight answers."

Mr. Topping glanced at me. "If you and the lady would like to come in and share a dish o' tea I'll give you some straight answers, but you might not like it."

I unhooked my right leg from the saddle pommel and slithered to the ground. A skinny rowankind boy of about nine or ten came out and took the reins of both horses. I noticed he was missing half an index finger from his right hand and wondered whether he'd lost it while cleaning machinery at the mill.

"I got 'em, Missis," he said. "Will they stand?"

"They will." I didn't like to tell him they'd stand with or without him. I noticed they both flicked their ears in his direction as he spoke to them softly.

We followed Mr. Topping into his cottage, a single room, crowded with family and furniture. An iron fire-grate had a blackened kettle sitting above the coals on a trivet.

"A mash o' tea, Mother, if you please," Mr. Topping said to a woman who, by her age, was his wife, not his mother, though with five young children in evidence, being a mother was undoubtedly Mrs. Topping's full time occupation. Her face looked gray with tiredness. She was not rowankind, and the younger children were obviously half-and-half, though I fancied the boy holding our horses outside was full rowankind.

Mrs. Topping sat the child she was holding in a cradle in the corner and sent two girls who looked to be about six or seven to take the toddler outside. The toddler broke away from his sisters and stomped over to Corwen proffering a small carved wooden horse.

"It's very fine," Corwen said, examining the toy before giving it back gently. "Does it have a name?"

"Orse," the older sister said, and tugged the toddler sharply away by one hand.

Mrs. Topping bestowed a shy smile on us and proceeded to warm the tinplate teapot and measure out tea leaves before pouring on boiling water.

"We're not very grand, but sit yourselves down, please." Mrs. Topping pointed to four mismatched chairs around a square table and produced three china cups and saucers, obviously her best. Having made the tea, she scooped the baby into her arms and hurried out after the children.

Mr. Topping poured tea without milk into the cups, then taking his own proceeded to delicately slop the scalding drink into the deep saucer, whereupon he blew on the surface to cool it and slurped from the saucer with some enjoyment. I wondered about the etiquette, and waited to see if Corwen followed suit. When he did, so did I, actually preferring the tea to Mrs. Deverell's milky brew.

A shadow darkened the doorway. "Is everything all right, Da?" A deep voice asked.

"Oh, aye," Mr. Topping replied. "Mr. Deverell, here— Mr. Corwen Deverell—has come to inquire what's going on at t'mill and I was about to tell him. Why not come and join us, since you're a part of it all as much as I am." He turned back to us. "This is my Tommy, a weaver in his own right, and a good 'un, too."

There was at least ten or twelve years between Tommy Topping and the boy who was holding our horses, but both of them were full rowankind. The present Mrs. Topping was obviously a second wife. I wondered how many children Mr. Topping had in total. The cottage looked to have no more than one room downstairs and one up.

"It's not only the pay." Tommy sat on the fourth chair. "We all understand that Mr. Deverell . . . that would be your Da, sir, is that right?"

"It is."

"Aye, you have a look of him about the eyes. We all understand he's poorly. Mr. Thatcher has been promising us our wages for nigh on two months, now. Last week he gave us half of what was promised and told us there was no more. We heard that Kaye's Mill was taking on skilled weavers at a reasonable wage—not as much as Mr. Deverell promised, but more than Mr. Thatcher gave us. Some of the lads have big families to feed, you understand, and couldn't afford to ignore the opportunity."

"You said it wasn't only the pay," Corwen prompted. "What else?"

Tommy looked at his father and Mr. Topping gave a slight nod. "It's the children as well, sir. Weaving's good work, spinning nearly as good, but even so, a family with a lot of mouths to feed can't afford to let the little ones be idle. Some clothiers will employ children in their mills as young as six, but Mr. Deverell wouldn't have them until they were eight. It's a long day, you understand, and when they get over-tired there's accidents."

My heart went out to the little mites working in such a dusty, dangerous atmosphere. I knew it happened, but I'd never seen it close up before. The youngest boy we allowed to sign on as ship's crew was twelve.

"Mr. Thatcher has turned off our nippers and bought a dozen workhouse boys from Barnsley to do their jobs."

"Bought children? Rowankind?" I asked.

"No, ma'am, not rowankind; ordinary workhouse boys, some as young as five. They can't do the job. They fall asleep in corners when there's no one to chivvy 'em up, or get a clout or a kick from the spinners and weavers for being too slow. Last week one of them got hit in the head when a shuttle flew out of a loom." He shrugged. "It happens sometimes even to the best weavers. Fly shuttles can be a bit temperamental. Usually someone gets a bruise or a gash. Sometimes a lass gets knocked insensible and someone has to stop work to carry her out. Mr. Thatcher wouldn't let any of the weavers stop this time. He dragged the little lad out and left him lying in the yard in the rain. It's not a right thing to do. Later the boy was gone and he brought another workhouse child to take his place. One little lad, not more than five, got his hand trapped in the spinning mule. Crushed three fingers. We've not seen him since, neither."

"How can anyone buy children?" I asked.

"They're not buying their flesh and bones, ma'am, but their labor." Mr. Topping explained. "The workhouse superintendent, like as not, pockets most of the money, but it's still a cheap option for an employer. The children sleep on the premises wherever they can find to curl up, often among the raw fleeces where it's a bit warmer."

I bit back a comment.

"It's an unhappy place," Mr. Topping said. "Weaving isn't an easy trade, but your father was allus fair and that goes a long way toward keeping people satisfied."

Tommy's hands curled into white-knuckled fists. "We got even more uneasy when repairs to the sluice and the headrace above the waterwheel were skimped. If the sluice gate goes, the folks working below it—that's all of the poor bastards in the fulling mill—stand to get drownded. Like Dad says. It's an unhappy place."

"The workhouse boys and the missing wages started our unease," Mr. Topping said. "Then Mr. Thatcher laid off some of the women who work in the tenter croft. Their families rely on their wages. That's when some of us downed tools and walked out, though I'm not sure we didn't play into his hands. The situation's likely to drive the rest of the rowankind to Iaru, even though most of us can't see how we might fit into that place when all we know is weaving." Mr. Topping scrubbed his face with the heels of both hands. "I've even been thinking about it myself, but I've worked at the weaving trade all my life and I reckon I'm too old to try something new. Besides, my wife is not rowankind, though she's a good woman."

Corwen frowned. "Have you seen any evidence of cloth being produced that's been sent out to sell in the country rather than the Cloth Hall in Penistone or Huddersfield? Cloth that might not have been accounted for?"

"I wouldn't know about that, for I don't have sight of the ledgers or any knowledge of the way sales are conducted. There's cloth gets made and cloth goes to market. There's fewer and fewer pieces being woven each week, but there's still unsold cloth in the warehouse and more raw wool being brought in than is being used."

"If I were to pay the missing wages at the rate my father agreed, would the weavers come back from Kaye's Mill?"

"That depends on whether they believe things are going to change."

"I promise you they will."

"Then, yes, I think they'll come back."

"Good. Please pass the word. Tell them to come to Deverell's Mill on Thursday. I'll not let them down."

This time when Corwen stood and offered his hand, Mr. Topping took it.

"I think that was productive," Corwen said on the way back to the mill. "Topping seems like a straightforward sort."

"But you're no nearer to finding out if Thatcher is cheating the family."

"We'll see what Lily says. I need to pay a visit to Barnsley tomorrow and ascertain the true state of the family finances and investments. Beckett's Bank, and Joseph Platt, my father's solicitor, are both in the town. It's Wednesday, market day. Would you care to come with me?"

"A shopping expedition? Why not? Soon you'll have me behaving like a real lady. Even my mother never managed that."

"We'll take the carriage. Poppy can come, too."

"I'm sure Lily would enjoy the trip."

"I'm sure she would, but she's likely to be at the mill. One of us has to be."

"She'll be disappointed." I was trying to avoid the obvious next idea, but I felt mean. "We should invite your mother."

He smiled. "That would be a kind gesture, but I didn't want to suggest it. I know she makes you uncomfortable."

"Oh, we'll get used to each other," I said, hoping we would.

❖——❖

We collected Lily as promised. She sneezed as she emerged into the open air from the dusty counting house, and she had one ledger under her arm.

"I'm going to work on this one tonight and spend tomorrow at the mill," she said. "Mr. Baines has been very helpful. He's worked in the counting house for forty years and remembers Grandfather."

Arriving home, Lily took the ledger into what had been her father's study and continued her reading until her mother called her for dinner, earning a harsh look for turning up to the table with a dirty face where she had rubbed her eyes with dusty fingers. She was eager to impart what she'd learned from her examination of the ledgers.

"Papa, would you like to hear about the mill?" Lily asked him, moving her chair so she could reach his good hand with hers. He squeezed it twice. "He says he would. And I think we might need his sage advice as to what to do next."

"You found a problem?" Corwen asked.

"The ledgers I've seen so far are in immaculate order," Lily said. "Not a figure out of place and everything adds up perfectly, just like Thatcher has said on his visits to report to Papa, but the problem is that he hasn't been giving us an accurate overall picture. The plain fact is the mill is over-stocked and undersold."

I saw Mr. Deverell was listening intently.

"Thatcher has brought in fleeces from the south of England, good fleeces, but they are stacked high and unused. Half the looms have been idle, but that's not the worst of it—the warehouse is brimming with unsold cloth. Even with half the looms idle, we're either making more than we can sell, or we're not selling as much as we should. If we re-engage the weavers and return to full production, we have to sell more finished cloth."

At that, Mr. Deverell squeezed Lily's hand many times in agitation. There was something he wanted to say, if only he could say it.

"We'll find a way," Lily promised him. "I know you want to tell us something."

"So what's the upshot?" Corwen asked.

"The mill will be out of business within the year unless we pour family money into it, or unless we increase sales."

⸺◆⸺

Corwen had confided that he needed to hunt. It had been several days since he'd last changed and run as a wolf and he was getting edgy, probably not helped by the fact that he and I were kept apart by propriety. There are those who discount a woman's need for intimate relations, but I was feeling the separation as well. Unfortunately, I didn't have the option of shedding one skin for another and running until I was physically exhausted, so I made my excuses soon after dinner and retired to my room to read more of Aunt Rosie's notebooks.

Lily said she needed some exercise after a day in the counting house and had offered to run with Corwen, so once the house had gone quiet I wasn't surprised to hear low voices on the landing and the creak of the stairs.

I tried to lose myself in the notebook and not worry about two perfectly competent wolves, but I noted the clock in the hallway struck eight shortly after their departure and every time the clock chimed the quarter hour I glanced up and wondered how they were faring.

It wasn't as if the notebook was boring. In fact, I'd happened upon a section that talked about wild magic, and the magical creatures of the British Isles from tiny pixies, fairies, water sprites, and tree sprites to hobs, trolls, and other such creatures—some benign, others definitely not. There was a section on hauntings, headless horsemen, and gray ladies.

I shuddered as I read it, and the clock striking eleven made me jump.

Corwen and Lily had been gone for three hours.

I put the notebook on one side and blew out the candles. My window looked out on the sweep of open grassland that ran to the lake. The moon was up, but not yet full and hidden by scudding clouds. I put on my spectacles and called light into them, but though I could see well enough, there was no sign of a pair of wolves.

I'd sent Poppy off to bed early, and so I stripped off my clothes and hopped into bed in my shift, wondering whether I should add lawn for a nightdress to my shopping list for tomorrow. The clock had struck midnight before I finally heard Corwen and Lily come in. They spoke quietly, but I caught Lily's girlish giggle.

I got up and opened my door a crack. Corwen carried a single candle in a flat holder and held it while Lily said good night and vanished into the recesses of her bedroom.

"Good run?" I asked him.

"Spectacular. I'd forgotten how wild the moor is at night." He stepped close and pulled me to him with one hand around my back, the heat from it eating through my shift. His mouth covered mine, and I returned the kisses fervently. His blood was up, and I wondered whether I could drag him into my bedroom.

"Corwen?" His mother's voice drenched my ardor.

"Yes, Mother?" He stepped back in case her door should open.

"Is Lily home safe?"

"Yes, Mother. Good night."

"Good night."

He kissed me again, and I pressed myself close.

"Corwen?" The matriarch again.

Once more I bottled up my passion.

"Yes, Mother?"

"It's good to have you home again." There was genuine warmth in her voice.

"It's good to be home." He sighed and kissed me on the cheek. "When in Home, do as the Homans do. Goodnight, sweet lady. Here's to our coming marriage. May it be soon."

I returned to my over-large bed with the word *soon* in my ears and the feel of him on my lips.

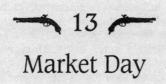

13

Market Day

MARKET DAY DAWNED BRIGHT AND CLEAR. We rose with the light and breakfasted at seven. Lily came and went in a whirl of activity, snatching a bread roll and a cup of chocolate before rushing out to the stable to mount up and head for the mill.

After hesitating, Mrs. Deverell had accepted our invitation to join us, and she expressed herself pleased by the prospect of a trip to market, carrying on light conversation over the hot chocolate, rolls, and butter.

The family carriage, drawn by four well-matched bays, was a sturdy, practical affair as befitted Yorkshire roads and Yorkshire weather. John Mallinson, the coachman, dressed respectably in a caped greatcoat, saw us all installed comfortably with cushions and rugs and then climbed onto the driving seat. He set the horses off down the drive at a steady pace, over the stone bridge and left toward the town some five miles away. He knew his business. Despite having to negotiate ruts and potholes, the journey was smooth enough. It took us little more than an hour to cover the distance.

Mrs. Deverell continued her amiable chatter, though managing to completely ignore Poppy as being beneath her dignity. A servant, unmarried and with child, her dismissive expression said.

The road into Barnsley wound through fields and climbed a long hill, passing a glassworks close to the newly opened canal which skirted the lofty eminence upon which the town stood. The road crested a rise and came into the town by the Parish Church of St. Mary, with the manor house adjacent and the grammar school opposite. The town was chiefly famous for its heavy linen manufacture and a number of collieries, but also had some wire-drawing workshops, which may have been what accounted for the pall of sooty air that I could taste on the back of my tongue.

John turned our coach into the busy yard at the White Bear, almost opposite the town's moot hall at the top of Market Hill. Two ostlers rushed forward to hold the horses while we alighted.

"Get yourself some refreshment while you're waiting, John." Corwen handed over some coins. "It's likely we'll not return before noon, so we'll probably eat here before starting for home."

We split up—Corwen to see the banker and the family solicitor while Mrs. Deverell and I, with Poppy walking a pace behind us, wandered down Market Hill, past wooden stalls arrayed in rows, toward May Day Green and Cheapside. Mrs. Deverell gave me a running commentary and pointed out the town's streets and features as we went. The town was bustling with market traders: pots and pans, poultry of all kinds in cages, fresh produce, used clothing, and domestic wares. People were picking over goods, looking for bargains, and the streets were alive with traders' calls and friendly banter.

If I was going to be riding sidesaddle I needed a proper riding habit. When I mentioned this, Mrs. Deverell took a sudden interest in getting me outfitted. She knew of an excellent seamstress, she said, if we could find cloth to suit. There were a couple of drapers' shops she favored. While I would have settled for a dark green superfine in the first one, Mrs. Deverell said it would not do and led us to a second shop where a deep chestnut wool caught her eye. I had to admit she had good taste. I glanced at Poppy, who nodded to me, and we decided upon it. Poppy's eye strayed to a bolt of black velvet, and she gave me a pointed look.

"This for facings and trim?" I asked Mrs. Deverell. She gave me the first genuine smile I'd seen.

"Perfect," she said, and asked the draper to lift it from the shelf where we could see the quality.

Poppy cleared her throat and jerked her head toward the linens, cottons, and muslins, reminding me we could both use a new shift and that the drawers I favored for protecting my tender parts when riding astride were turning into a raggedy disgrace. Drawers were considered fast, but propriety could go hang, it was comfort I looked to.

"How is your needlework, Poppy?" I asked.

"Very neat, ma'am."

That was a relief. My own sewing skills were almost nonexistent. I retained a little knowledge of embroidery from my wholly traditional upbringing, and I'd made and mended shirts for Will—mended and mended again, for Will was very hard on his shirts. I bought enough muslin for two summer-weight shifts and linen for drawers, making sure I was generous enough with the yardage that there would be some left over for Poppy to begin making baby garments.

We gave orders for our purchases to be sent to the White Bear to await our return and then spent a pleasant hour taking in the sights, sounds, and curiosities of the market before making our way up the hill to meet Corwen. We hadn't long to wait for him. I couldn't tell from his expression what he'd discovered and knew he wouldn't discuss it in the crowded coffee room in case we were overheard. Neither would he discuss it on the return journey in front of Poppy.

◆────◆

"Well?" I asked as we alighted from the coach at the front door of Denby Hall. I dawdled while Mrs. Deverell went inside, calling for tea, and Poppy scuttled downstairs to the kitchen.

"An interesting day," Corwen said. "Let's wait for Lily to come home from the mill."

Lily wasn't far behind us, and we gathered in the small parlor together with Mr. and Mrs. Deverell. Yeardley settled Mr. Deverell and left us.

"Interesting visits, both of them," Corwen said. "The good news is that the family's investments are sound and we are far from penniless. The bad news is that if the mill were our only source of income, we would be bankrupt. There is enough to pay the weavers' wages; however, since Father's illness things have been going steadily downhill."

"Thatcher?" I asked.

"I believe so, though whether it's criminality or sheer incompetence is difficult to tell."

"Whichever it is, you should dismiss him," I said.

"And who would run the mill then?"

He was the only obvious candidate, though I knew it was the last thing he wanted.

He shrugged. "We need to bring Freddie home from London. Then we can get rid of Thatcher and see if we can make a go of the mill."

"We?"

"Freddie, me, Lily." He gave his sister a long, level look. "Freddie's the heir. It's his responsibility."

"Freddie never cared a fig for it," Lily said.

"I can't say I know much about it, or ever thought to turn myself into an industrialist, but I dare say I shall learn, and I'll do what I can," Corwen said. "We can't afford to keep Thatcher on, but someone with more knowledge of textiles than I have has to run the place. You have as good a grasp of the mill as anyone, Lily."

"And yet I am a female and not supposed to be fit to understand business or invention." She cleared her throat. "I have an idea. Hear me out before you object."

"Why should we object?" Corwen asked.

"Because my solution is radical. I want to run the mill myself."

"No!" Lily's mother said. "It would be totally unsuitable. You'd never be able to hold up your head in polite society again."

"What do you think, Papa?" Lily asked.

I reached out and put my hand under his. "Yes," Mr. Deverell squeezed.

"Mr. Deverell says yes. Why not hear her out like she asked?"

"Thank you, Ross. I thought you might be on my side, having captained your own ship."

Mrs. Deverell turned to look at me, surprise written in every line of her face, but whatever questions she had were for another time.

"So, this is the way I see it," Lily said. "Corwen has got the authority, but not the knowledge. I have the knowledge, but not the authority—not yet anyway. Corwen needs to go and meet the wool buyers and try to sell some of our stock. While he's away, I'll manage things in his name."

"You'll need someone in the mill yard as an undermanager," Corwen said.

"You can't seriously be considering this foolish scheme?" Mrs. Deverell said, glaring at Corwen. "Your sister will be a laughing stock."

"I appreciate there may be some social disadvantages, Mother," Corwen said, "but Lily knows the business better than anyone. I have an idea about an undermanager. What about one of the weavers' own—Mr. Topping. He's a fair man. He knows the trade inside and out, and he's respected by all the workers. Who better?"

I felt Mr. Deverell squeeze my hand again. "Your father says it's a good idea," I said.

"But Lily . . ." Mrs. Deverell wore a worried frown. "Among all those men . . ."

"I shall have Mallinson drive me there and bring me home again," Lily said. "And as for all the men, well, there are women working there, too. And if women can handle sodden lengths of cloth and stretch them out on tenter frames, I'm sure I can handle a pen and a few decisions."

From what I'd seen of Lily, I thought she could, too.

Mr. Deverell began to squeeze my hand repeatedly.

"I think your father might want to say something," I said. "Have you got your alphabet cards?"

We gathered around his chair while Mr. Deverell slowly eased himself into the world of communication. Very hesitantly, he squeezed numbers for letters. It took the best part of an hour, but at length we had a message: A.R.M.Y. C.O.N.T.R.A.C.T.8.6.R.U.T.L.A.N.D.

"Eighty-six Rutland?" Corwen frowned. "Do you mean the Rutland Regiment?"

Mr. Deverell squeezed twice.

"There was nothing in the records to indicate any kind of contract to supply cloth to the army," Lily said after Mr. Deverell had been taken to bed by the redoubtable Yeardley. "Though I remember Father making enquiries via his man of business in London, Mr. Wiggins. It's the regimental colonels, or more properly their agents, who arrange for the manufacture of uniforms for the rank and file. There's a chain of supply and money to be skimmed at every stage, but even so, supplying cloth for even one regiment would make all the difference to our situation." She looked at Corwen. "You still intend to give Thatcher notice?"

"I do, but first we'll question him about the 86th Regiment of Foot."

At the top of the stairs, on our way to our separate rooms, Corwen took my hand. "I know you weren't expecting all this, Ross. I don't relish the idea of getting involved in the mill, but if you could bear to stay here until we've sorted it out, I promise I'll disentangle myself from it as soon as I can. Freddie must face up to his responsibilities."

"What if he doesn't like the textile trade any more than you do?"

Corwen shrugged. "We'll deal with that when we come to it. In the meantime, will you stay?"

"I said I'd stay with you, and I will. We knew we'd have to live in the real world sooner or later. Let's see if we can find a place in it. Your family is important. I lost mine. You should cherish yours."

He leaned over and kissed me thoroughly, then stepped back with a sigh. "I'll see the vicar and arrange for a marriage license."

"Good. My bed is too big for one."

❦

On Thursday morning, following a night devoid of dreams, I rose before dawn to take breakfast with Corwen and Lily before they set off to the mill. Lily was in high spirits. Corwen looked more thoughtful. They breakfasted quickly, and with Corwen's warning not to expect their return in time for dinner, they set off in the gray half-light of a drizzle-laden morning, riding Timpani and Speedwell. Corwen had the silver to pay the wages in his saddlebag, and though he didn't expect trouble, he sensibly carried a brace of primed pistols.

I had no worries for Corwen's safety. This was, after all, the English countryside, not the high seas where wind and weather, reefs and rocks, fever, chance accident, or even pirates could snatch away a life in the blink of an eye. I was, therefore astounded by a clamor through the servants' quarters which rose into the hallway barely twenty minutes after I'd returned to the breakfast table to take a second cup of hot chocolate.

"Mrs. Sumner!" Thomas came up the servants' stairs into the hallway as I dashed out of the breakfast room. "Mr. Corwen's horse has come home by himself, all in a lather, snorting and whinnying and making a racket fit to wake the dead."

Corwen was not a man to easily part from his saddle.

What had happened? A fall? Robbery?

"Saddle Dancer, Thomas, please. A man's saddle, not a sidesaddle. I'd be obliged if you and John Mallinson would come with me. Do you have pistols?"

"Locked in the tack room."

"Prime them. I'll meet you in the stable yard."

I ran upstairs for my own pistols, surprising Poppy who first asked if she should come with me and when I said no, produced my redingote while I pulled on my breeches under my dress and loaded and primed my pistols. Dressed warmly, I ran downstairs.

Mrs. Deverell, woken by the disturbance, appeared in the hallway in a dressing robe.

"What's happened?" she asked.

I explained briefly. I didn't want to worry her unnecessarily. Corwen was more than capable of looking after himself.

That's what you thought about Will. A treacherous thought surfaced, but I pushed it down.

"I should come, too," Mrs. Deverell said.

"We're ready to go now, and shouldn't dawdle," I said.

She nodded briskly. "Quite right, too. Take one of the stable lads so you can send a message if you need anything. God speed."

I'd been expecting histrionics, but there was no sign of anything except practical good sense.

Dancer was waiting when I arrived in the stable yard, and Thomas and John were both ready, with horses saddled. Thomas had also thought about taking a messenger, so one of the stable boys was mounted on the ever-sensible Brock. I didn't wait for a boost into the saddle, but hitched up my skirt and mounted like a man. We four clattered out of the yard and down the lane at a fair clip, John leading Timpani, whose saddlebag still contained the silver. If there had been a robbery attempt, it had been unsuccessful.

Below the mill, we rounded a bend where trees, already in spring leaf, overhung the road, shading it and causing a natural tunnel beneath close-knit branches. Two figures were on the ground, one supine, the other hunched over. Lily's mare, Speedwell, stood, legs splayed, head hanging down, sidesaddle half off, a short distance beyond.

"Corwen!"

The hunched figure raised one arm to acknowledge our presence, but the supine figure didn't stir.

"Ross, come quick."

Lily lay on the ground with Corwen's greatcoat over her and his jacket beneath her head. He was holding a kerchief to her forehead with steady pressure, but head wounds bleed fearsomely and her face was streaked with blood.

Blood was good. Dead people didn't bleed.

Speedwell tried to hobble toward her stable mates and made the kind of sound I never want to hear from a horse again.

I knelt by Lily and checked her pulse. Fast but not thready. "What happened?"

"Some bastard set a rope across the road to trip us. I assume it was meant for me. Maybe someone after the silver. I was ahead as we came to the trees. Timpani saw it and jumped the hazard, but it brought Speedwell down. Lily cracked her head as she fell. I sent Timpani home to raise the alarm."

"You saw no one?"

"No, though I drew a pistol, so if someone was intending to come at me, it changed their mind. I couldn't leave Lily's side. There was so much blood, but I knew you'd come as soon as Timpani turned up."

"He galloped into the stable yard braying like a donkey according to Thomas."

"I didn't want to move Lily, and without a horse . . ." He nodded toward Speedwell. "The mare looks bad, even from this distance, but Lily's head was bleeding too fiercely for me to let go."

John had the mare in hand now and Thomas was examining her leg. I heard him swear. Language he wouldn't have used in front of me if he'd known how acute my hearing was, but I'd heard worse at sea.

Lily blinked, groaned, and tried to sit up. I pushed her gently back down.

"You've had an accident. Keep still."

She made a couple of unintelligible sounds and tried to sit up again. "Sick," she said, raised herself on one elbow and promptly threw up. The movement served to tell me her neck and spine were intact. I helped her to sit up and examined the gash on her forehead, gently feeling for swellings or a depression. There was a soft swelling around the gash.

"I think your head is harder than the road," I said. "The bleeding has slowed, but let me hold this over it. The wound is open."

"Owww!"

"I'm sorry. I'll try to be gentle. That better?"

"A little. I can't see. My eye . . ."

"I've got Corwen's kerchief over it, but the gash is above your eyebrow. Your eye is fine, or will be once the swelling has gone down. You may have a shiner, though."

"I'll tell anyone who asks that they should have seen the other fellow." She half-smiled and winced.

"Brave girl."

"Mr. Corwen." Thomas called Corwen over to the mare and I heard him say, "Broken."

"Speedwell . . ." Lily said.

"Not good."

She tried to look, but screwed her eyes up. "Everything's fuzzy out of the other eye, too."

"You've had a bang on the head. It will be fuzzy for a while, but it will get better."

Corwen returned to Lily's side, looked at me, looked at the mare and shook his head. Ah, that was the way of it.

"Come on, Lily, let's get you home," he said, and dispatched the lad with a message to tell his mother Miss Lily had been hurt and was on her way.

"No." Lily reached up, took the kerchief from her head again, and squinted at it. The bleeding had slowed. "I'll go home with Ross. You need to be at the mill to pay the weavers when they arrive. Don't let them down."

He was plainly torn between concern for his sister and acknowledgment of her common sense.

"We'll manage, Corwen," I said. "Maybe this was a robbery attempt, maybe not, but if you want your weavers back at work, you need to be there to pay them."

"All right, if you're sure."

"Speedwell . . ." Lily asked.

"Broken leg." Corwen's mouth compressed into a tight line. There was nothing more to be said.

Lily's eyes overflowed with tears. "Don't let her suffer."

"I won't."

We mounted our horses. Corwen lifted Lily into John's capable arms and at a steady walking pace we headed toward Denby Hall, leaving Corwen and Thomas behind with Timpani and the injured mare. We'd barely rounded the bend before we heard a single pistol shot. Lily whimpered into the front of John's coat.

❖————❖

John handed Lily over to Yeardley at the front door of Denby Hall. Yeardley, being used to carrying Mr. Deverell, conveyed Lily to her room with practiced ease.

"Thank you, John," I said.

"Ma'am, please tell Miss Lily I'll take the flat wagon back for Speedwell with all the grooms and see her buried in the meadow. She'll not go to the hounds. I think the young lady would like it that way."

"Very thoughtful, John. Thank you. I'll tell her."

I hurried up the stair after Yeardley.

Mrs. Deverell took immediate charge of sending for boiled water, salves, and dressings. Any pretense of the superficial society lady was gone. She was calm and practical, and for the first time I thought I was seeing the real person.

I waited until Poppy and Sarah had gone off in opposite directions to bring the items required and put my hand on her arm. "I think Lily may need to change," I said with a meaningful look. "You know . . . *change*. Corwen heals as he makes the change."

Her face paled.

"You have the keeping of Corwen's secret—and Lily's, too."

"And Freddie's," I said. "And I swear no harm shall come to them because of it."

There was the longest pause as she regarded me.

"You can trust me," I said.

She looked at me warily and nodded. "I believe I can. I've never trusted an outsider before. It's a novel experience."

"Do the servants know?" I asked.

"Not the house servants. Our old nurse knew, but she's gone to her rest. Only Thomas knows now. Does Poppy?"

"She knows—rowankind have a sense of magic now, you know—but she's not seen a change."

"You've seen—"

"Corwen's change is beautiful. I haven't seen Lily's, but—"

"Stop talking about me as though I'm not here," Lily said. "My head feels like thunder, and I think I've sprained my wrist."

The door creaked as Sarah and Poppy returned. Mrs. Deverell took the hot water and linens from Sarah and ushered her out again. I directed Poppy to wait outside the door and make sure no one came in. Between us, Mrs. Deverell and I helped Lily out of her layers of clothing and into her bed where we covered her with a single sheet. Mrs. Deverell washed the blood from Lily's face, but wisely didn't touch the head wound in case it bled again.

"Roll on to your side, Lily," I said. "Change as soon as you can." I held her hands.

"You've done this before," Mrs. Deverell said.

"Yes."

"For my son?"

"He's the only other wolf shapechanger I know."

I didn't tell her the injuries Corwen had suffered on my behalf, and I didn't complicate things by telling her about Hartington, the Lady of the Forests, and her retinue of creatures who might or might not be all kinds of shapechangers.

"And you don't . . . mind?" Mrs. Deverell asked. "It's not abhorrent to you?"

"Mrs. Deverell, I've seen much worse than shape-changing. No, it's not abhorrent to me. It's Corwen's nature."

Lily began to change. Under my hands, her fingers became clawed toes and her palms became pads. Where Lily had been, a beautiful, curly-coated black wolf lay, half covered by the sheet. She rolled over, wobbled to her feet, turned three times to trample a nest in the feather bed and sank down with her nose on her paws for all the world like a big, shaggy dog.

Mrs. Deverell kissed her fingertips and touched Lily's head. "I'll go and tell Arthur she's going to be all right. He'll be worried. May I leave you to . . . ?"

"I'll do whatever's necessary, Mrs. Deverell."

"Please, if you're going to marry my son, I should like it if you would call me Mama, if I may call you Rossalinde."

"Rossalinde is fine, or Ross. My friends call me Ross."

"Ross, then, for surely we are friends now."

"I believe we are."

For now, at least. Whether we would remain friends if she found out about my magic remained to be seen.

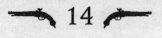 14

Ragamuffins

LILY CHANGED FOUR TIMES during the course of the day. By dinner she was expressing her anger over Speedwell's undeserved fate, cursing whoever set the trip line, and fretting to get out of bed. She was anxious to join the family downstairs, to await Corwen's report of happenings at the mill.

Her mother kept her pinned down only with threats to send for Dr. Boucher combined with promises to send Corwen up to report as soon as he arrived home.

I fashioned a bandage around her temple to hide the fact that the ugly gash was not only healed, but that the scar had already faded to a thin red line. A couple of changes more and it would be gone altogether, which would seem suspicious to anyone who had seen the wound.

I wanted to be downstairs to greet Corwen myself, but I had my dinner on a tray in Lily's room so she wouldn't attempt to get up. Even though the gash had healed, I didn't know whether there was still the chance of a concussion.

"I heard Mama say you've nursed Corwen through an injury like this," Lily said.

"Something like it." Did gashes from a conjured hell-hound count?

"Oh, come on, Ross. I'm bored out of my mind. Tell me how you met my brother. I've already gathered it was no ordinary meeting."

"It was a very ordinary meeting, in the dining room of the Twisted Skein in Plymouth. At least I thought that was the first time I'd met him. It took me a while to realize that this annoying stranger who kept appearing at opportune—and inopportune—moments was, in fact, the counterpart to a silver-gray wolf sent by the Lady of the Forests to guide me to Bideford ahead of a troop of Kingsmen."

"Annoying! Ha! That's Corwen. But you came to love him, right? I mean . . ."

It was complicated.

I gave her an edited version of how I had inherited the winterwood box and the task of freeing the rowankind. I left out the part where we rescued my brother Philip, only to have him turn on us and betray us to Walsingham. That was still too bitter to speak of.

"Oh, how I should love to meet the Fae," Lily said.

"Well, you might and you might not." I told her how several generations of Sumner women had been beguiled into bearing Fae children. Her eyes grew wide, and I had to leave out some aspects of the story to take into account her youth and innocence.

"But you missed the part where you made Corwen change to heal injuries," Lily said. "Surely you haven't told me everything."

So I edited out the hellhound and instead told her about the kelpie, and how freeing the rowankind had released wild magic, and with it magical creatures. She fastened onto the thing that had not become obvious to most people yet.

"The rowankind have magic."

"I think some of them are still discovering it and others are hiding it."

"What about the Mysterium?"

"The townsfolk in Bideford rose and destroyed their

local Mysterium office. I was hoping their hold might be broken, but apparently that was an isolated incident. In the south of Devonshire the Mysterium is busier than ever."

"The regional office is in Sheffield, but there's a Mysterium agent in Barnsley, in the Old Town where there are licensed witches."

I felt like a cold hand had wrapped itself around my spine and was squeezing. Was any part of this country safe for me and mine?

Lily had drifted off to sleep before Corwen returned from a long day. He was tired and somewhat grumpy, but after greeting his mother he came straight upstairs to see for himself that Lily was all right, and also to look in on his father who had retired for the night.

Lily woke as soon as he came into the room and demanded to hear a full account.

"Give me a minute to get my breath." Corwen sat on the edge of the bed and studied Lily's face. "Feeling better?"

"Much." She lifted a corner of the bandage to show it was purely decorative.

"Good."

"Speedwell."

"Taken care of," Corwen said. "It wasn't her fault she fell. If it hadn't been for Timpani spotting the rope, I'd have been spread all over the road, too. The trip line was deliberately set up in the gloom, probably to catch me for the silver. I had let it be known there would be money for wages today, so it was a fair bet someone knew I'd be carrying coins."

"It was a good job Timpani ran home."

"I told him to. He's Fae-bred."

"He understands what you say?"

"Well, I don't say I could carry on a conversation with him, but he understands basic commands."

"Timpani and Dancer are uncannily aware of what we say." I recalled the times when I'd almost had a conversation with Dancer. "Brock, too, probably, though I've spent less time with him. If you don't think a piebald pony is a bit of a comedown after a thoroughbred like Speedwell, you should ride Brock until you get a new mount."

"I don't know that I can replace Speedwell, at least, not until her foal is grown." A tear rolled down Lily's face. "I'm so glad we decided to breed from her." She'd been trying to keep from crying, but now she gave a strangled sob and Corwen folded her into his arms.

"Cry it out," he whispered into her hair. "You'll feel better for it." He let her cry until the sobs subsided into a series of sniffles, whereupon he handed her a linen handkerchief from his pocket and waited while she mopped her tears and blew her nose.

"I'm sorry," she said.

"There's no shame in crying," Corwen said. "Speedwell was worthy of your tears."

"She was, wasn't she?" Lily scowled. "Blasted robbers. If I ever get my paws on them, I'll tear them apart."

"Hush, no, that's no way to talk." Corwen tapped her on the end of her nose with a finger. "I've reported the incident to the magistrate, though I don't know what good it will do. I might go and sniff around later tonight."

He meant he'd go out and let his wolf nose around for clues.

A knock on the door heralded Mary and Sarah with trays of cold ham, capon, and cheeses, which Corwen tore into like a man half-starved, washing it down with a good claret.

"I've been extracting some of the details of your exploits from Ross," Lily said, while Corwen's mouth was too full for him to answer.

He raised one eyebrow at me, and I gave a tiny head shake to indicate that I hadn't told her everything. "Lily wanted to know how we met and how I knew that changing would enable her to heal. I told her about the Twisted Skein and the winterwood box, and about the kelpie."

"Ross says all manner of strange magical creatures may have been released into the land."

Corwen took a slow sip of his drink. "That's true. Some of them dangerous, some not."

"Mary and Sarah say there are stories of the Padfoot returning."

Corwen's mouth quirked up. "The last time that happened, I regret to say it was me, teasing travelers for devilment."

"The ghost dog?" I asked.

"Like a Black Shuck, a devil dog with eyes like glowing red coals, though not always black," Corwen explained. "It used to be thought that it was a harbinger of death, but there are stories of it protecting travelers as well. It's mostly fancy—drunkards weaving homeward being scared out of their wits by someone's sheepdog appearing too suddenly out of the shadows."

"Or a silver wolf," Lily said.

He had the grace to look a little sheepish. "Occasionally."

Lily cleared her throat. "Or sometimes a black one."

Corwen looked at her. "You didn't . . ."

"Only once." She smiled sweetly. "I overheard Papa say the new curate was a little too fond of drink, so I waited among the overgrown graves in the far side of the churchyard after Evensong until all the parishioners had left. When he closed the church door behind him, I howled once and raced past."

"Ah, you need to learn more about your local legends. The Padfoot never makes a sound."

"I'll remember that for next time."

"I hope there won't be a next time." Corwen tried to look stern, but failed.

"I've done enough changing for a while, brother. So, tell me about the mill."

Corwen told of a frustrating day during which the weavers had not turned up. Disappointed, he had ignored Thatcher and busied himself spending time with the workers on each process, trying to understand how everything fitted together. He'd paid special attention to the waterwheel which, he said, was not in the best condition, the headrace and sluice gates needing much attention.

I must have looked puzzled. Corwen explained. "We

control the flow of water down the valley. Our dams are the first on the river, so if we restrict the flow, it affects the level of water in the mill pond at Kaye's Mill below in Denby Dike Side. They, in turn affect the flow of the water to the next mill below them at Lower Putting. None of us takes much water out of the river, but unless we cooperate, we can seriously hamper our neighbor's power source."

"Father has an agreement with Mr. Kaye," Lily said. "A few years ago we had a long hot summer and the river dried to a trickle. That was when Father considered one of Mr. Watt's steam engines. We went to take a look at the beam engine at the colliery in Elsecar which pumps water out of the mine, though that's an atmospheric engine and it uses a huge amount of fuel apparently. There are improvements in the process now, though, and we could install a small engine here."

"To power the fulling mill?" I asked, not sure how a steam pump could be harnessed to power a rotating shaft.

"No, to pump water from the waterwheel's tail race back to the headrace again. It would keep the wheel turning in the driest of summers and give us the capacity to install an additional wheel to power the mules. Steam engines are monstrous, noisy things, but they produce reliable power using water and coal. The principle is sound, and we should modernize."

After dark, I heard the floorboards on the landing creak as Corwen went out, and I heard them creak again as he returned in the deep hours of the morning. I pushed my bedcovers aside and tiptoed to the door, opening it a crack.

He turned as he heard me. I pulled him into my bedroom and into my embrace. I felt him shudder beneath my hands, and he slipped out of the loose banyan. He was naked beneath it.

"Ah, Ross . . ."

I wanted to know what—if anything—he'd found, but once I put my arms around his neck and felt him pressed against me, there was something else I wanted more. He picked me up and carried me to my bed. We made love urgently, in total silence except for our breathing, the wet slap of flesh on flesh, and occasional muffled moan. Afterward, he held me close, and I stretched against him, skin to skin.

"So what did you find out?" I whispered.

"That you make little squeaking noises when you're trying not to scream out loud."

"I do not squeak!" I slapped him lightly on the shoulder. "You know what I mean. Anyway, you grunt when—"

He kissed me, and for a while I forgot what I'd been going to say.

I slid my hand down his belly and curled my fingers in the tangle of his hair. He began to stir beneath my fingers.

He groaned. "You're insatiable, woman."

"I will be once you've told me what you found."

"Ha!" He huffed out a breath as I cupped his tender parts. "I give in. I'll tell you, but stop that for a moment or I won't be able to think. You have me completely at your mercy."

"Good, now talk."

"There were too many scents on the road to be sure, some I knew, some I didn't. I recognized our own people, of course. All the stable hands had been there to remove poor Speedwell. There were mill workers, too, but many of them come up that road each morning to work. Thatcher had been there, but I couldn't tell if that was before or after."

"What about the trip line itself?"

"Unfortunately, Thomas retrieved it and used it to haul Speedwell onto the flat wagon, but I think it came from our mill. It had that tang about it."

"You think it might have been one of our own mill workers?"

"I'm not ruling it out."

"You don't think Thatcher . . ."

"I'm not ruling that out either, but because the man's incompetent doesn't mean he's a villain."

"What if robbery wasn't the motive? What if it was a deliberate attempt to get rid of you? Or Lily? Or both?

What if Thatcher has been embezzling and was trying to cover his crimes? What better way of doing it than to get rid of the people who could expose him?"

"It's something I considered, but I have no proof."

"The sooner we get rid of Thatcher the better."

"My feeling, too."

"Good. Now that's decided . . ."

I began to move my hand and felt him rise to the occasion.

Corwen retrieved his banyan from the floor and crept out of my room as dawn began to break. Neither of us had had much sleep, but we both felt immensely satisfied.

We were both a little bleary-eyed at breakfast. Corwen's knee caught mine beneath the table and we shared a secret smile. Lily arrived, bouncing with energy, and insisted she was well enough to attend the mill with Corwen. She said she'd changed once more during the night and it had cleared any remaining headache and even the slight scar had gone, though she promised to wear a cosmetic bandage for a few more days.

Corwen wouldn't hear of her riding sidesaddle, even on Brock who was as steady a pony as you could wish for. He had the hooded gig harnessed and drove Lily to the mill himself. Brock proved as amenable to drawing the gig as he did to carrying a rider. I went, too, riding alongside on Dancer, my pistols primed. John rode behind on a roman-nosed, big-boned bay gelding. There was, however, no sign of anything untoward on the road.

Thatcher, after a brief greeting, wisely kept out of our way, though I felt an empty ache between my shoulder blades as we walked across the yard and fancied he was watching us from his office window. Whether it was his demeanor or lingering suspicions, I really didn't trust him.

While Lily returned to the counting house, Corwen took off his coat and knelt by the mill dam, sleeves rolled up, examining the sluice gate that regulated water into the headrace and fed the breast-shot wheel.

"What's wrong?" I asked, joining him on the wooden walkway that bridged the sluice.

"Careful where you're putting your feet. Some of these timbers are past needing replacement."

He took my hand and guided me around a suspiciously crumbling plank.

"Can you fix it?"

Corwen's binding magic is a talent he considers not very useful except when he breaks his mother's best teacup or needs to repair a rent in a pair of trousers.

"There's not enough good wood to bind. We'll have to drain the whole dam to effect repairs, which means closing the fulling stocks for however long it takes. I can understand why Thatcher hasn't done it, but it's false economy. If the sluice gate fails it could kill anyone below it. The water pressure could take out half the dam and send a surge down the valley." He frowned. "The fulling mill will be out of action for as long as it takes to rebuild the whole lot. Thatcher says Father told him to leave it a little longer, but that was when there was a schedule for ongoing work. We can't leave repairs on the dam indefinitely."

"How serious is it?"

"Serious enough, but it's not the only problem."

"Lack of weavers."

He nodded. "I wanted to believe Topping. Now Thatcher is giving me looks that say: I told you so. And if the weavers don't come, their children won't come, which leaves the workhouse boys trying to do jobs they're unsuited for. I should take the little ones out of the mill right now before there's another death."

"Another?"

"The boy Topping spoke of, the one who got his fingers crushed in the spinning mule. Apparently, he was sent back to the workhouse where the surgeon cut off his whole hand, but he took a gangrenous infection and died. Five years old."

"What happens if you take the children out?"

"Production slows right down."

"Would that be the worst thing in the world?"

He looked at me. "You're right. It wouldn't, but killing another child would. Come on."

We walked to the mill and, starting with the mule frames, Corwen took the overlooker to one side and called a halt to their machines. Then he did the same to the weavers.

"I want every child from the workhouse in the yard in five minutes," he told them.

One by one the piecers, doffers, scavengers, fetchers, and sweepers trudged out into the yard, blinking in the morning light. They ranged in age from about nine down to one skinny lad who was barely more than four.

"I thought Topping said there were a dozen." I counted heads. "There are only ten here."

"Maybe the two who had accidents weren't replaced."

"Is anyone missing?" Corwen asked the boys.

No one answered.

"You're scaring them. Are they due a meal soon?"

"They are now."

Corwen called an overlooker who sent two girls to bring the children's food. I took one look at it and decided I wouldn't have fed it to pigs, let alone children. There was half a loaf of bread apiece and an onion, but the bread had green mold, and the onions had been in store too long and the tops were sprouting leaves.

Even so, the children fell on the repast eagerly and started munching.

"Is this it?" I asked the overlooker.

"They get lazy if you give them too much," he said.

"What else do they get in a day?"

"Good thick gruel at breakfast and broth with cabbage and potatoes and meat at supper. They get a pint of beer apiece before bedding down. Makes 'em sleep like babies."

"I'll bet it does. There are twelve onions here and only ten children. Who's missing?"

The overlooker counted heads and scowled. "Rat and Weasel. More trouble than all the rest put together. Brothers, or so they say. You can't trust either of 'em. Little bastards, begging your pardon, ma'am. Likely to be hiding in the fleeces. Made a little rat's nest in there where all of the boys sleep. I'll thrash the little—"

"No need. I'll see if I can find them." I left the children eating in the yard and made my way into the fleece shed where the animal stench of unwashed wool was almost overwhelming, but here the constant beat, beat, beat of the fulling hammers was muted, and it was a shade or two warmer.

"You can come out now," I said. "Everyone's in the yard, eating. You're missing out on a meal."

There was no answer, but keen hearing is one of my witch abilities. I stood still and listened. Sure enough, I heard the rasping of breath somewhere above the level of my head on top of the unsteady mountain of piled-up fleeces. I slipped off my half boots, tucked up the skirt of my gray day dress, and began to climb. I knew where I was with rigging on a swelling ocean, but the fleeces shifted and gave beneath my feet. Twice I almost lost my grip, but I made it to the top. The light from the door barely filtered this far, so I saw nothing, but the rasping of breath drew me on. A mottled pile of fleece shook.

"Got you."

I made a dive for the pile, emerging with a child in each hand, wriggling and kicking.

"Want some help with that?" Corwen asked from below.

"Oww! Little bastard kicked me in the . . . never mind. Yes. Here, catch." I dropped the bigger child into Corwen's waiting arms.

The smaller one felt like a rabbit in my grasp, all bone and skin. I wrapped my arms around him and hugged. "Hush. Be still. I'm not going to hurt you." He calmed down, but his breath still rasped.

"This child's ill," I said.

"Come on down. Let's see the problem."

I slithered down with the child in my arms, and Corwen steadied me at the foot of the heap.

"Is there always so much fleece waiting to be spun?" I asked. "Is this what Lily meant by overstocked? Some of it's been here so long it smells as though something's died in it."

"There are lots of things don't smell right about this place."

"Please, sir . . ."

Corwen had set the first boy on the floor but still had firm hold of his wrist.

"What is it?"

"We won't be no more trouble, honest. That mester said he'd send us back if we was trouble."

"You'd rather be here?"

"If you send us back, they'll split us up."

"Why would they do that?"

I took a closer look at the child whose breathing sounded anything but good. "Because his brother is his sister," I said.

So now we had another dilemma. The workhouse children, at least two of them only four years old as we discovered through gentle questioning, were mostly too young to work at the mill, but returning them to the workhouse wasn't a good alternative. Rat and Weasel, whose real names were Robin and Winnifred, were, they said, seven and five years old, respectively, though I thought that might be guesswork.

"What are we to do with them?" Corwen's naturally generous nature would turn Denby Hall into an orphanage if we didn't find a solution.

"Some of them can continue to work here," I said, "only not living like a pack of dogs and sleeping where they can. Perhaps some of the weavers will take them in and feed them, for a price. Pay the children regular wages, and it will cover the cost of their keep. Well-fed and looked after, they'll be better able to work."

We sorted the children out. Six of them were eight or over, but a more ragged, underfed bunch would be hard to find anywhere. Barefoot and filthy, they looked like walking skeletons. I didn't know whether they'd been in that state when they'd arrived from the workhouse, or whether Thatcher's regime of gruel and broth with moldy bread and onions had done it to them.

Corwen sent John to Denby Hall for food, whatever he could find for hungry children. The resulting bounty was bread and a ham from the larder, plus a box of slightly wizened apples that had been in store over the winter. The children fell on them as if they'd never tasted fruit before.

By this time, the working day was so disrupted that the weavers and spinners had downed tools completely and had wandered into the April sunlight to find out what was happening. Corwen called them all together.

"You all know my father wouldn't employ children younger than eight. Some of your own children might have been laid off when these unfortunates came here." He indicated the children, now grouped defensively together. "Those who are eight or more can stay on, but they need homes. I won't have them sleeping where they drop or nesting in the fleeces. I know you have children of your own at home, but if any of you have space, I'm asking you to take them in. Not at your own expense. Their lodgings will be paid for, sixpence a day, and a length of good kerseymere to clothe them."

No one stepped forward.

"And a five-shilling bonus," Corwen added.

"And work for our own children what was laid off?" one woman asked.

"If they're eight years old or over."

"I'll take that one." One of the spinners stepped forward and pointed to the biggest of the boys. "He's a willing worker and he keeps his nose clean. Come on, lad, you're wi' me."

The boy looked a little bemused.

"You don't have to if you'd rather go back to the workhouse," I whispered under my breath.

"No, ma'am, I'd rather not." He went to join the spinner who clapped him on the shoulder in a friendly manner.

"I'll take two." An elderly woman stepped forward. "My bairns are all gone now. It'll be nice to have company, and the coin and cloth, of course. In advance, is it?"

"It is. Come and sign for them."

He turned to see Thatcher watching from the doorway.

"Mr. Thatcher, would you have two men fetch some of those woolen pieces in store. A five-yard length for every child."

"Madness," I heard Thatcher mutter under his breath. He gave instructions and retreated to his office once more.

That left us with the six youngest children.

"I suppose they should go back to the workhouse," Corwen said reluctantly, "but I can't bring myself to do it. I know I can't rescue every child in there, but by bringing them to the mill, Thatcher has made these children my responsibility. The mill has been a nightmare for them. I should like to find them homes, but times are hard for everyone. No one will take them without an incentive, and children too young to work have to be looked after."

"You're not sending Robin and Winnie back?" I phrased it as a question, but it was really a statement.

"No. They can come home with us. I'm sure we'll be able to accommodate them somewhere. Robin looks like a bright lad. He can probably work in the stables when he's a bit bigger."

"Winnie?"

"Let's get her well, first, shall we?"

I smiled at him. "Sometimes I'm reminded very forcefully why I love you so much."

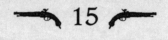

15

Fever

"MR. CORWEN, see who's coming." John looked up from where he was packing the now empty apple box into the gig.

Marching along the road from the village was a procession of rowankind men, women, and children . . . family groups. At their head was Mr. Topping, his son Tommy, and two young women who might have been his daughters. The boy who'd held our horses followed closely behind with another child of about eleven.

"Mr. Topping, good to see you all." Corwen stepped forward.

"Mr. Deverell, the weavers have asked me to speak for them. To be honest, they want to know what your word's worth. I told them you talked a good talk."

"Aye, but is it all talk?" One of the weavers behind Topping shouted out.

"Davey, hold thi gob," Topping said, "unless tha's talking for everyone."

There was some muttering among the men, but Davey said no more.

"He might have spoken out of turn," Topping said, "but it's what everyone's thinking."

"I understand," Corwen said. "I have the wages I promised. Whether the weavers decide to stay or not, they'll get what's owing to them."

Lily stepped into the yard, a bag over one arm and a leather-bound book tucked beneath the other. Baines, huffing and puffing, followed behind her with a small folding table.

"Wages?" she asked brightly, opening her book.

I glanced up at Thatcher's office window and saw him scowling down.

Topping must have noticed the direction of my glance.

"Begging your pardon, Mr. Corwen," Topping said, "but how do we know what's promised now will continue if nothing changes with the management?" He jerked his head upward toward Thatcher's window. "The weavers who leave their place at Kaye's Mill to come back here on a promise won't get taken on there again if things go bad."

"I can't promise I will always be here, Mr. Topping. There may be circumstances beyond my control which call me away, but I can promise you a change of management."

I wondered if Thatcher had heard that. I checked his office window again, but he was no longer watching.

The weavers lined up, and Lily checked each one in the book, working out what each was owed and handing over scrupulously accurate amounts, down to the last farthing, before getting each weaver to make his or her mark next to their name. As each one signed, she gave them an extra half crown, which put a smile on most faces.

Topping was the last in line. "Thank'ee kindly, Miss Lily," he said pocketing the coins.

Corwen raised his voice so all the weavers could hear. "So you've got your wages. Will you stay or will you go?"

The weavers spoke among themselves.

"What about jobs for t'women? Our lass was laid off from t'fullin' mill," one middle-aged rowankind asked.

"If we need more workers in the fulling mill, those who

were laid off will have first refusal," Corwen said. "It stands to reason that more weavers producing more cloth will need more workers in the fulling mill."

"There's more cloth in the warehouse than should be," young Tommy Topping said. "No mill can keep going unless the cloth gets sold."

"There's more raw fleece in the warehouse than there should be, too," Corwen said. "Turn it into cloth before it rots, so it can be sold. I shall be going to London to speak to our man of business there."

"And who will be in charge while you're gone?" Mr. Topping said.

"I will." Lily stood and closed her wages book with a resounding thump. "Can you work for a woman, Mr. Topping?"

"One that pays the wages, aye."

Corwen seized the opportunity. "So who's staying and who's going?" he asked.

"I'll stay." Mr. Topping stepped forward, and his family followed his lead.

There was a heart-stopping pause while no one else volunteered, then the man who'd asked about jobs for the women stepped forward as well, followed by two more. In the end they all signed up.

"What's this, then?" Mr. Topping took note of the excess children sitting around the edges of the mill yard. "The workhouse children?"

"Like you said, some of them were under eight."

"Are you sending them back?"

"I'd rather not."

"Their labor bought and paid for, is it?"

"So I understand, but they're not big enough to work yet. They need homes."

"Well, they don't look as though they'll eat too much. How many are there, six?"

"Four still not found homes," I said. "Two are coming with us."

"Four can come home with me. Our lass can look after 'em."

I presumed by *our lass* he was referring to his wife. "How many children have you got already, Mr. Topping?"

"About a dozen, though some have grown and found places of their own. Four more won't make much of a difference. Look like they need a good scrub down, though, and coats and breeches."

"Will a full piece of good woolen cloth help?" Corwen asked.

"It will, right enough, Mr. Deverell. Thank you."

"Thank you, Mr. Topping. I have an idea for something else that might help, too—something we should discuss. Will you wait here for me?"

"I'll go and take a look around the weaving shed and be hereabouts when you want me."

<hr />

Topping ambled off to the weaving shed, and the rest of the weavers left with orders to present themselves for work on Monday morning. As the yard cleared, Thatcher came to meet us. He didn't look pleased, and he would certainly be less pleased by the time Corwen had finished with him.

"Mr. Thatcher, a word in the office if you would be so good," Corwen said.

"That was ill done," Thatcher said as he led the way up the stairs. "Troublemakers all of them, especially Topping and his brood."

"Papa always spoke highly of the Toppings," Lily said.

"Your father wasn't the one had to stand their meddling."

We reached the landing. Lily turned into the counting house to put the wages book back while Corwen and I followed Thatcher into his office. Standing at his window, I looked into the yard and listened. The ill-fitting old sash window kept out neither drafts nor sounds. If Thatcher had watched the scene unfolding in the mill yard, he probably had a fair idea of what would be coming next.

"Some information if you please, Mr. Thatcher," Corwen said.

"Of course."

"About a contract to supply the army, more precisely the 86th Regiment of Foot, the Rutland Regiment."

Thatcher swallowed, unease showing in his eyes. "I don't believe there ever was—"

"My father says otherwise." Lily stood in the open doorway.

"I thought . . . I mean . . . I don't believe there ever was such a contract actually signed, though your father did mention one had been discussed. That was before his unfortunate collapse. After that I heard no more, and I had no firm details. With the rowankind leaving, though, we lost too many skilled workers to possibly fulfill—"

"Workers who have now agreed to return," Corwen said. "My father and brother agreed to pay them a premium if they would stay on."

"Begging your pardon, but those were wages we simply could not afford."

"That wasn't your decision to make. My sister tells me a sad tale. Overstocked and undersold is unhealthy for any business."

"What does such a slip of a girl know of the wool trade?" Thatcher glanced sideways at Lily.

"She's my father's daughter," Corwen said. "She knows a lot more about the mill than I do. That's why, as of this moment, she will take over management of Deverell's Mill."

"Oh, no, Mr. Corwen, sir. That won't do. I can't work with a woman."

"Luckily, Mr. Thatcher, that was not my intent, but I'm glad to see you tender your resignation willingly."

Corwen dropped a purse onto the desk between them. It clinked softly, the sound of gold guineas. "You've not served this endeavor well, Mr. Thatcher, but in lieu of working a period of notice, I'm paying you the remainder of your year's wages. I'd be obliged if you would clear your belongings out of the Mill House by dusk tomorrow."

Thatcher stared at the purse. "You can't do this."

"Actually, I can." Corwen folded his arms across his chest and tapped his foot on the floorboards. "I'll have the keys now, if you please. Take only your personal belongings from the office."

"You'll regret this." Thatcher dropped the keys between them and snatched the bag, not counting it.

"I don't think so. Good-bye, Mr. Thatcher, and thank you for your service."

"You don't want to cross me. I have contacts in the wool trade. Good contacts."

"Then you should have used them to make more sales."

I thought Thatcher was going to have an apoplectic fit. His face flushed, and he clamped his lips tight on words that were itching to be spoken. He kicked the leg of the desk as he stomped past it and clomped down the wooden stairs.

Corwen took the bunch of keys and locked the office door behind us. Then he went into the counting house across the landing, where Baines sat scratching over his ledgers.

"You probably heard all that, Mr. Baines."

"That depends, sir. Did you want me to hear it?"

Corwen smiled. "I like a man who knows the meaning of the word: discretion. How do you feel about working for a young lady?"

"I like my job, sir, and the young lady knows her ledgers, if you don't mind me saying."

"Good man, Mr. Baines. I suggest you finish early today and come in on Monday morning prepared for some changes."

"I will, sir, thank you, sir."

Baines put down his pen, dipped his head in acknowledgment, and left. Corwen locked the counting house, and we followed down the steps.

A knot of people had gathered in the yard: two carters, a stable boy, two overseers, and five women from the tenter croft, dawdling in expectation of gossip. It was obvious from the way they were all talking together that they knew something major had happened, but as I followed Corwen out of the building, they all peeled away and resumed their work, barely glancing at us.

I got the impression they were not sorry to see Thatcher dismissed.

◈————◈

Topping was waiting for us as Corwen locked the outer office door.

"You wanted me?" he asked Corwen.

"Come walk with us for a few minutes, Mr. Topping." Corwen led the way to the mill dam and around the mill pond on a well-worn track. "Mr. Thatcher is leaving."

"I heard, sir."

"News travels fast."

"Good news faster still."

It had been barely ten minutes; was there anyone in the mill who didn't know already?

"Are the workers displeased, Mr. Topping," I asked.

"No, missis. He's not a popular man."

"Miss Deverell will be taking over," Corwen said.

"That's going to be . . ." Topping paused, seeming to choose his words carefully. "Interesting. She's been her father's shadow ever since she was old enough to ask what a doffer and a piecer did, and to try her hand at it. I think she might do well if she establishes that she'll take no nonsense."

"I think so, too, and to that end I wanted to ask if you'd consider taking on the job of undermanager for her."

"Well, sir, I don't know about that."

"No one knows the mill better, and no one has more respect among the spinners and weavers. My sister has a good grasp of the business, but she'll still need a right-hand man—someone whose advice she values, a practical man who takes pride in his work. Will you do it?"

Mr. Topping blinked at Corwen in surprise, then blew out his cheeks in a silent whistle, staring at the ground in front of his feet. For a moment I thought he was going to refuse, but it seemed as though he was only trying to dislodge the disbelief. When he looked up again, his eyes crinkled in a smile.

"Aye, I will."

"Good man. There will be a fair wage, of course, and if you want it, the Mill House, rent-free. It goes with the job. I dare say Mrs. Topping needs a bit of extra space for those four orphans, and I'm sure one of your sons will be glad to take over your cottage."

"I'm sure our Tommy will."

"Then it's decided. Start right away." Corwen held out his hand and Mr. Topping took it without hesitation.

"Thank you, sir, I'll not let Miss Deverell down."

"I know you won't."

◆━━━━◆

"I'm glad that's over," Corwen said as we rode home.

"Is it? Over, I mean? It seems to me as if it's just beginning. Lily has a lot to prove."

"You mean like you did when you became captain of your own ship?"

"I had a lot of help."

"As will Lily."

"Do you trust Thatcher?" I asked Corwen.

"In what way?"

"I don't know. Can he do any harm? Is he privy to any damaging secrets?"

"Business or personal?"

"Either. Both."

"I doubt he knows about the wolves, and I don't think anything he knows about the business can damage us. We're about as low as it's possible to be and still have a business."

"But would it do for your rivals to know?"

He chewed on his lower lip and frowned. "It's true that rumor can be as damaging as fact, and I dare say Thatcher has more contacts than either Lily or I have, but Father's reputation as a clothier and as a gentleman is impeccable. Damn, we do need Freddie, though. We have to make him see sense and come home. He may have tried to shirk his responsibilities, but he's likely to have been introduced to any number of Father's friends and contacts in the last six years. If Father was intending him to take a position of responsibility, he'd have been training him. Even if Freddie ducked out of a lot of it, some of it is bound to have stuck."

"I thought Jonathan was the heir."

"Jonathan managed the estate. He was happy to leave the mill to Father. I believe he thought of it as Father's hobby." He smiled in remembrance. "In many ways Jonathan could be a little stuffy."

"Stuffy?"

"Proper. He regarded the management of the land a more gentlemanly pastime than commerce. He had it all worked out. He would be the country gentleman, Freddie would be the captain of industry, and if I didn't want to join Freddie, I would be the respectable clergyman or a major in the army. My sisters would do what all proper young ladies did and make good marriages."

"Poor Jonathan. With such high expectations he was bound to be disappointed."

"Only Emily obliged by marrying Marchmont. Our respectable sister, safely away in a respectable marriage to a respectable gentleman."

"There's a question I haven't asked. Who's managing the estate now Jonathan's gone?"

"No one is actively managing. Jonathan was an innovator, and that's gone by the wayside, but a steward sees to the collecting of the quarter day rents and each tenant manages his own land, so the situation is not desperate. I'll deal with it myself once the immediate problem of the mill is solved."

<hr />

We carried the two children home in the gig, each wrapped in a short length of woolen cloth from the pieces handed out to the work house children. I wasn't happy about Winnie's breathing. It was louder and even more wheezy than before. I knew Dr. Boucher was paying a visit to Mr. Deverell the following morning and resolved to ask him to examine the child. In the meantime, I released both children to Poppy's custody with instructions to give them as much food as they wanted to eat, warm baths, and to check them for lice. There were spare rooms in the servants' quarters in the attic, but Poppy said she would keep them both in with her and apply a poultice to Winnie's chest and use camphorated oil to try to ease the congestion in her lungs.

I hadn't been in bed more than an hour and I was still lying awake, resisting sleep in case Walsingham invaded my dreams again, when a gentle knock at my door was followed by Poppy, anxious face illuminated by the candle she held.

"Begging your pardon, but the little girl has taken a fever. I didn't know whether I should wake you, but she's very bad."

"I'll come."

The floor was cold to my toes as I groped around for my slippers in the flickering light from Poppy's candle. I was schooling myself out of putting up a witchlight as a matter of first resort. There were too many people in this household who wouldn't understand, though Poppy wasn't one of them. I pulled on a warm dressing robe, one Lily had lent me, and followed Poppy out.

The floorboards on the landing creaked beneath our feet.

"Is something wrong?" Corwen's door opened, and he peered out.

"Winnie's taken a fever," I said. "Go back to sleep. You have to be at the mill early. I'll deal with it."

He nodded and ducked into his room.

I followed Poppy up a flight of stairs to the attics where the servants' rooms shared space with storage areas. Poppy had a room to herself, though there were two beds in it from when the household had owned several rowankind bondservants. A small fire burned in the grate, a testament to the generosity of the Deverells toward their servants. In the light from its flames I could see Robin sitting cross-legged on one end of the bed in which his sister lay, the blankets pushed down and her sweat-streaked dark hair spread across the pillow. I could hear the rasping of her breathing from the doorway and smell the camphor.

One touch of my knuckles onto Winnie's forehead was

enough to tell me how serious this was. "We need to cool her down quickly," I said. "Does that window open?"

It did, and it let a whirl of fresh air into the room. Cool wet cloths on Winnie's brow and on her wrists helped. Sitting her up propped on pillows eased her breathing a little, but a spasm of coughing left her gasping.

"Is she going to die?" Robin asked, his voice small and frightened.

In truth, I didn't know, and I didn't want to promise that she wouldn't.

"Is there anything I can do to help?" Corwen asked from the doorway.

"I'm not sure you can unless you want to fetch a bucket of clean cold water."

"I'll go." Poppy sprang up.

"No, you look after Robin," Corwen said. "I can carry a bucket of water."

"Maybe some honey, butter, and vinegar to make a syrup," I added.

"Would there be willow bark?" Poppy asked.

"I'll see if I can find some."

Between us, Poppy and I sat Winnie up and rubbed more camphorated oil on her chest and back, but after that we could only wait. Corwen brought the water and the ingredients we'd asked for, but saw there was little else he could do. He dropped a kiss on my head and went back to bed with instructions to wake him if I needed him to ride for Dr. Boucher.

I wondered whether the doctor would come out in the middle of the night for a workhouse child, but in any case I doubted he could do more than we were already doing.

Poppy brewed the syrup of honey, butter, and vinegar in a small pan on a trivet over the fire.

"Willow bark for the little girl."

I jumped at the sound of Mrs. Deverell's voice by the bedroom door. She stood, dressed in what might have been her husband's banyan and wearing a flouncy night cap, proffering a small muslin bag and a pan. "I heard Corwen on the landing. That boy's not as light-footed as he thinks he is. Here, boil this until the water runs pink and let it steep for ten minutes. How is she?"

Poppy took the bag of willow bark and set it to boil in the pan over the fire.

"Not good." I stood to one side so Mrs. Deverell could see.

"Poor little thing looks half-starved, and even in this light she's as pale as a paper moon. Have you made a syrup?"

"It's cooling now," Poppy said. "Honey, butter, and vinegar."

"Honey to heal, butter to soothe, and vinegar to clear. That's a good combination."

Could it be that she actually approved? I saw Poppy's mouth twitch upward at the corner. She'd noticed the venerable Mrs. Deverell thawing as well.

When it had cooled sufficiently, we tried to get Winnie to take the syrup. At first she turned her head away, so Robin took a spoonful, declaring it to be the best thing he'd ever tasted and encouraging Winnie to try. She did, and we coaxed her to drink alternate sips of syrup and willow bark tea.

When Robin began to shiver, Mrs. Deverell frowned. "Here, girl." She pushed Robin into Poppy's arms. "Take him beneath the blankets or we shall have two invalids."

Poppy curled up with Robin in her bed and cuddled him until they both fell asleep. I sat in the low chair and listened to Winnie's wheezing, wondering whether each breath would be her last.

"Would you like me to stay with you?" Mrs. Deverell asked.

"There's no sense us both losing sleep, but thank you for the offer."

"You know she's likely to die, don't you?"

"Yes."

"I'll pray for her."

"Thank you."

Her hand dropped to my shoulder briefly before she left the room, closing the door behind her quietly.

~ 16 ~

Endings and Beginnings

BY THE FOLLOWING MORNING, Winnie had weakened. Her breathing still rasped, but it was shallower now. When I put my hand to her chest, I could feel her rapid heartbeat. She still burned with fever, but now her small frame was wracked with shudders. Whatever we did for her made no difference. Sometimes her eyelids flicked open, but mostly she slept. It was all in God's hands now, and I had no real hope He would be merciful.

Robin, pale-faced, sat on the side of the bed and held her hand, talking to his sister all the time in a low, gentle voice, telling her how he wouldn't let her go back to the workhouse and that he would find them a home where they could both be together forever.

I heard a horse and trap on the driveway. Corwen brought Dr. Boucher straight to the attic. Tall and cadaverous with a slight stoop and a lugubrious expression, he set Robin aside gently and examined Winnie thoroughly, taking her pulse, listening to her chest and searching for swellings or signs of a rash.

"A workhouse child, you say?" he asked.

"From Barnsley. Mr. Thatcher ..." My voice caught in my throat. "He bought their labor. I don't think the child is more than four years old. We've put a stop to it."

"Good. I don't say you should mollycoddle children, but mill work is not appropriate for the very young. They are not strong enough, and their development suffers. If you want to grow healthy workers, you should treat them well, mind and body. Good nourishment and healthy exercise." He looked at Robin. "Been looking after your sister, boy?"

Overawed, Robin simply nodded, mouth slightly agape.

"Well, you've done a good job." He looked at Poppy and me. "All of you have done what you can, but I believe you can't do much more. Her end is near."

Robin gulped down a sob.

Dr. Boucher patted his head gently and gave him his own linen handkerchief. "Do you believe in the Lord, Robin?"

"I says my *Our Fathers*, sir, and *When I Lay Me Down to Sleep*. I taught Winnie that one."

"You're a good boy. And you have one more job to do." He put Winnie's unresisting hand into her brother's. "Sit a while longer and tell her what a marvelous place she's going to. She's never going to be cold or hungry or frightened again."

Robin sniffed up tears. "I want to go with her."

Dr. Boucher looked at me, and for a moment I saw helplessness in his eyes.

"You have to be strong and stay here." I put my arms around the little boy's shoulders. "You have to grow tall and healthy and be the brother Winnie would have wanted you to be."

"And don't worry about that old workhouse," Poppy said. "You're never going back there. Isn't that right, ma'am?" She looked at me pointedly.

I nodded. We'd adopted another stray.

⬥————⬥

Winnie died in the early afternoon, her last breath sliding out of her little body so gently that it was only Robin's small cry that alerted me. Poppy put aside the stitching she'd been busying herself with while we waited for the inevitable. She sighed. "I'll see to the laying out if you take Robin out into the sunshine for a while."

"I want to stay," Robin said.

"No, it's best you come with me." I took his hand. "You can come and say your good-byes soon."

He let me lead him out. Corwen must have heard our footsteps on the stairs. He joined us in the hallway.

"It's over, then?"

"It is," I said. "We're going for a walk. Will you come? Robin and I both need some fresh air."

We walked to the lake in the April sunshine, not saying much on the way there. Corwen pointed out the trout hiding in the shadows, trying to distract Robin a little, but largely we let him grieve in his own way.

"Dr. Boucher was pleased with Father," Corwen said. "He was surprised at Lily's spelling cards, but thought it a good idea and asked that Yeardley work to stretch and exercise his good hand to strengthen it. He thinks if Father can gain some dexterity, he might be able to point out letters, maybe even eventually manage a pen or a slate. It may take some work, but at least it's hopeful."

"I'm glad there's some good news today." I glanced at Robin, quietly walking between us.

Corwen nodded knowingly. "Come on, Robin, I'll race you to the house."

"Hey, not without me." I bunched up my skirts in both hands and set off across the grass, not too fast. Corwen kept pace. We didn't look behind us, but it wasn't long before Robin hurtled past at his top speed. If he didn't quite arrive at the door laughing, at least his cheeks had acquired a healthy glow.

Corwen and I took him to the attic to say good-bye to his sister whom Poppy had washed and dressed in a cut-down shift. The little girl lay in the bed, hands neatly folded across her breast and a small posy of spring flowers tucked beneath them. Apart from the color of her skin and the stillness of her chest, she might have been asleep.

Dinner was a solemn affair. After dinner Corwen and I put on our coats and went for a walk in the garden, enjoying the peace of the sharp April evening under a new moon and a blanket of stars.

"Shall we go to London now to find Freddie?" I asked, twining my fingers with Corwen's.

"As soon as the child is decently buried."

"Robin . . ."

"We'll find employment for him here, in the stables or the garden. Let him grieve and grow."

"I think Poppy's ready to adopt him."

"Well, she can teach him his letters, then. If he proves to be any kind of a scholar, there's the grammar school in Penistone, a venerable institution."

"Did you go there?"

"For a short while." He gave a rueful grimace. "I wasn't the best of scholars, or let's say I didn't apply myself diligently. Father took it upon himself to find me a good tutor instead—not only me but Freddie as well, of course. Mr. Bennett was a fine classical scholar and mathematician who condensed five years of learning into two. Father had plans to send us both to school and to Oxford, but when I continued to run as a wolf, he changed his mind and sent Freddie on his own. Said he couldn't risk me doing something stupid." He huffed out a sharp breath that might have been a laugh. "Freddie got enough education for the both of us, though much good it's done him."

He pulled me closer and kissed me. Under cover of darkness I kissed him back, thoroughly. He wrapped me in his greatcoat, and we stepped into the shadow of a chestnut tree's spreading branches where we were hidden from view should anyone from the house be watching.

Our lips locked and in silence we strained against each other. I felt every contour of his body pressed against mine and thrust my hips toward his. He groaned softly.

"Come to my room tonight," I whispered.

"I swear my mother has a bell that rings by her ear each

time a floorboard creaks," he said. "But I can't take any more of sleeping alone and knowing you are so close. I'll call and see Reverend Donovan tomorrow to arrange for Winnie's funeral and our wedding."

"About time."

"Tuesday for the funeral, Thursday for the wedding. Does that suit?"

"Shall we tell your mother?"

"I'm afraid we have to."

"Will she make a fuss?"

"I expect she will. Perhaps we shouldn't be too harsh. Poor Mother. It's not the wedding she wanted. She'd hoped to arrange Freddie's marriage to Dorothea Kaye. His wolf change must have ended that aspiration."

"I presume Freddie didn't wish to be led to the altar by the nose, anyway."

"I doubt Freddie will ever be led willingly to the altar. Freddie's inclinations are not toward the fairer sex. Oh, he'll flirt and dance and play a good part, but no more than that. While in London I dare say he'll be visiting the molly houses in Moorfields, discreetly, of course. Does that shock you?"

"I lived on a ninety-foot ship with sixty men for seven years. Very little you say can shock me. If there were certain irregularities in the behavior of sailors, Will left matters alone as long as no one was hurt by it. Only once did he ever have to make a point that consent was everything in such matters. He hanged a man for raping a young sailor."

"Would you have done it if it had happened on your watch?"

"I would. I fear I'm not the type of woman your mother would approve of."

"You do what needs doing, and you don't flinch from it. That's only one of the reasons I love you."

"And what are the others?"

"I'll tell you on Thursday night."

The following day was Sunday, a day of rest for the mill workers, but not for Corwen or Lily and therefore not for me. Corwen's mother insisted that before we busied ourselves with tasks wholly unsuitable for the Sabbath, we all go to the morning church service, not only to worship but to see and be seen by the local community.

"It's important," she said. "A family such as ours has so much to hide, so we must always appear to be normal and respectable to allay gossip and rumor. Besides, if there is gossip or rumor, where best to find it than among the ladies of the congregation?"

I began to see what Corwen had told me, but what I had never truly appreciated. His mother had a backbone of iron. She had protected the whole family from scandal and exposure not by shrinking away, but by hiding in plain sight. If Corwen and I had a family, that would be my job, though I would get much more help and support from Corwen than Mr. Deverell ever gave his wife.

Neither Corwen nor I had ever set foot in a church together; however, as he pointed out, we were about to marry in this one on the following Thursday, so it was only polite to attend at least once.

We rode there early and left Dancer and Timpani standing in the shade of an oak tree. Corwen wanted to visit Jonnie's grave and pay his respects. I stood a little behind him as he silently read the headstone, alone with his thoughts.

We said nothing, but he reached for my hand as we threaded our way through the graves to the lych-gate where Yeardley had just drawn up with Mr. Deverell in the gig, the coach with Mrs. Deverell and Lily following close behind. Mr. Deverell didn't come every week, but when he did he arrived early, was kept at a distance, and left early, before the after-service socializing. Mrs. Deverell hoped to mask the fact that he was totally incapacitated. She reminded us to tell anyone who inquired that he continued to improve.

Yeardley transferred Mr. Deverell to his wheeled chair and pushed him into a space by the choir stalls. The rest of us filed into the family pew. The sermon was based around the Prodigal Son, and I wondered whether that was purely coincidental as Reverend Donovan had a slight smile on his face whenever he looked in our direction. Corwen's voice rang out in the hymns, while I mouthed the words, taking sly sideways glances at the congregation who were doing the same to us.

"That's Dorothea Kaye." Lily elbowed my arm and pointed out a young woman of great beauty sitting between a distinguished looking man and a woman in fashionable silks with a spectacular bonnet. I'd neglected to buy suitable head coverings and still wore the bandeau which didn't match my spencer even though Poppy had endeavored to add trimmings. I felt dowdy in comparison to both Kaye women and was glad Corwen's mother had never tried to make a match between him and Dorothea.

"She's beautiful," I whispered back.

"Yes, a very proper lady," Lily said, "but empty-headed. She'd never have suited Freddie, whatever Mother thought."

I felt a little better at that.

As soon as the service finished, Yeardley wheeled Mr. Deverell out to the gig, leaving no opportunity for anyone to approach him socially.

As the rest of us filed out of the church Reverend Donovan greeted us warmly. He had kind words for Robin who had walked to church with Poppy and some of the other servants, clutching Poppy's hand like a lifeline. Corwen's mother was immediately swept up in conversation with a group of ladies of a similar age, her gossip set, I presumed. Lily found a friend and engaged her, arm in arm, to take a turn around the churchyard.

Corwen was hailed by a rotund gentleman in a periwig and frock coat, trailed by two equally rotund ladies. Corwen introduced us. Mr. Josiah Senior, his matronly wife, and elderly mother welcomed me to the area in a friendly manner. Mr. Senior owned the mill at Lower Putting, a somewhat smaller affair than either Deverell's Mill or Kaye's, and seemed keen to engage Corwen in a discussion about the water flow in the Dearne, unusually low for the time of year, apparently. They'd barely begun when the Kaye family bore down upon us through the loitering churchgoers like a frigate cleaving through whitecap waves. I wondered at the Seniors' polite but hasty retreat from our company, especially since, as I understood it, Kaye's Mill stood between Deverell's and Lower Putting, so surely Mr. Kaye would be interested in discussing water levels.

"So the prodigal has returned." Mr. Kaye, balding but impressively tall and broad-shouldered, ignored the departing Seniors and held out his hand to Corwen. "Good to see you again, Corwen. Bad business about your brother. How's your father? He seems to have rushed off."

"A little improved, thank you." Corwen took the proffered hand and gave a polite bow to Mrs. Kaye and Dorothea. "May I introduce my fiancée, Mrs. Sumner?"

I made a polite curtsey to the ladies, and they dipped to me. There may have been some measuring up going on on both sides. I resisted the temptation to brush my skirts. I was sure I didn't compare favorably with Dorothea in either looks or dress. Close up, she was just as beautiful with a flawless complexion, small, white, even teeth, and glossy hair cut short at the back in the latest fashion, with the front pinned in ordered curls. Her dress was cut in the latest fashion, and the spencer she wore for warmth was dark green velvet with a trim of red fox fur to match the muff she carried. I hoped the fox hadn't been anyone Corwen knew.

Mr. Kaye patted his son on the back. "And you remember Martyn? He was barely out of the nursery the last time you saw him, I'll warrant."

"I remember. Hello, Martyn." Corwen shook Martyn Kaye's hand. The boy, slighter than his father, but tall for his age, muttered something polite and lapsed into silence. I noticed he kept looking around at the young ladies Lily had met with and thought his head wasn't in this conversation at all.

Mr. Kaye took my hand and kissed it enthusiastically, leaving behind a smear of dampness that I consciously had to resist wiping on my skirt. There was something about

Mr. Kaye I didn't care for, but I couldn't pin it down. Maybe it was the way his gaze slid away from mine as he was speaking. He was polite enough, but his manners didn't quite disguise his lack of sincerity.

"Fiancée, eh? I had heard."

Was there anyone in this community who didn't know our business? What one lady knew, all knew. It was a tribute to Mrs. Deverell that the family had been able to keep their shapechanging proclivities a secret for so long. I shuddered at the thought of what might happen if that knowledge became public.

"I'm pleased to meet you all," I said.

"You must come to dinner," Mr. Kaye said. "Thursday, perhaps."

Corwen smiled. "Thank you for your kind invitation, but we're to church on Thursday morning and traveling to London immediately afterward."

"Business or pleasure?" He looked at me.

"A little of both."

"Speaking of business, I hear you've let Thatcher go. I hardly like to stick my nose in where it's not wanted, but that's a decision you're going to regret. He knows his business inside out."

Inside out seemed to be the way Thatcher had run the mill, but I said nothing. Mr. Kaye knew a lot about our business, but I supposed it was hardly a secret and proved the power of gossip.

"My father's wishes." Corwen smiled. "We've made other arrangements."

He didn't elaborate, and Mr. Kaye didn't ask. I wondered whether the news that Lily was taking over had spread yet. If so, it might cause a scandal because of both her age and her gender. Mr. Kaye wasn't giving away that he knew, and without Corwen telling him outright couldn't give us the benefit of his advice, which I was sure would be against letting a nineteen-year-old girl take responsibility for the enterprise. Mr. Kaye was fond of his own ideas and also full of his own self-importance. It was in the way he spoke and every move and gesture.

It was a good job Mrs. Deverell hadn't succeeded in making a match between the two families. I couldn't see Mr. Kaye turning a blind eye to any wolf shapechangers in the family. In fact, I suspected he would be hammering on the Mysterium's door to denounce them, even if they were his own grandchildren. I tried to hide a shudder.

"Well, young man, perhaps you might convey my regards to your father. Should his health not prove conducive to business, I would be interested in making an offer for your mill."

I felt Corwen stiffen in surprise, but I doubted Mr. Kaye would have spotted the momentary hesitation. "I will, of course, pass that on to my father, but I think I can speak for him and say the Deverells are not yet ready to quit the clothier's trade."

"That's as may be, but I will leave the offer open. I hear your brother has gone up to London, and I surmise from your long absence that you have little interest in the mill yourself."

"I find it more fascinating with each passing day."

Mr. Kaye actually harrumphed, though whether it was to indicate his disbelief in Corwen's sudden change of heart or in disappointment that his apparently good-natured offer was summarily rejected was difficult to tell. "You know you can always come to me for business advice," he said. "We may be rivals, but we're also neighbors and that counts for a lot. We have to keep the water flowing between us, don't we? Practically, as well as metaphorically."

"Thank you. I'll remember that. And don't worry about the water. There's plenty in the Dearne for everyone."

⬦————⬦

Straight from church we rode to the mill. Although Sunday was a rest day, Corwen wanted to make sure Thatcher was off the premises and everything was in order. We arrived to find two carters loading the last of his trunks and boxes. There seemed a small amount, but the furniture went with the house, so he was only removing personal possessions.

One of the carters produced a cover of oiled cloth to throw over the wagon. "It's looking fair stormy, Mester Corwen." He jerked his head toward the western horizon where gray-green clouds were gathering.

I tried to feel for the weather. I still had a sense of it in my bones. If I'd been at sea, I'd have been taking in sail and battening down hatches. Once Thatcher, all scowls in our direction, was out of the yard, following the wagon on his horse, a sturdy cob with a hogged mane and docked tail, I turned to Corwen. "Unless you want a soaking we should make haste to get back home."

We made it to the stables as the wind started to rise and the first drops of rain blew sideways across the yard. We led our horses into their stalls, two at the end of a row of six. Brock whickered a greeting, which Timpani and Dancer both returned.

"I'll see to them, Mr. Corwen." John appeared from Brock's stall.

I patted Dancer's neck and heard the rattle of shutters and the sting of wind-driven rain on the small panes of glass in the stable window. "I think we may be too late to get to the house while we can still stay dry," I said.

"Have you got a greatcoat, John?" Corwen asked.

"Yes, sir, would you like to borrow it for Mrs. Sumner?"

"No, not at all." He looked at me with a question in his eyes, but I shook my head. "I was thinking you could hurry home and stay dry. We'll see to our horses. It's Sunday, take the rest of the day off. Thomas will be back from visiting his mother in time to do the night rounds, and the other lads are likely to have their feet up already."

"Yes, sir. Thank you . . . If you're sure."

"Go, John. I'm sure your wife will be glad of your company."

I watched him don his coat, a proper coachman's coat with oiled capes. As he left, I raised one eyebrow at Corwen. "Was that entirely for John's benefit?"

He stepped close and kissed me. "Not entirely. Snatching time together when we're not likely to be disturbed is a rarity these days."

I put my hands on each side of his head and pulled his mouth down to meet mine and pressed against him, my hips thrust forward. "It's only four days to our wedding. You can't wait until then?"

He groaned. "I'm not sure I can wait four minutes."

"Not in front of the horses." Sometimes Dancer seemed almost human in his understanding.

Corwen spun me into an empty stall farther along the row and pushed me against the wall, kissing me hard and reaching beneath my skirts.

"Ah." My knees gave as his fingers found my sweet spot. I clung to his shoulders to stay upright and reached for the buttons on his breeches. He laughed and pinned me against the wall to stop me from falling. I hooked one leg around his waist as I felt him firm between my thighs.

"It's a little . . ." He thrust into me. "rough and . . ." He thrust again. "ready."

"I'm ready for a little rough." I wriggled to meet him, heart pounding, giving myself to the rhythm until it took us both.

"All right?" he asked, afterward.

I huffed out a breath. "Oh, yes." I giggled.

"What's the matter?"

"I can't imagine Dorothea Kaye against a wall."

"I've never imagined Dorothea Kaye in any position."

"Well, I'm certainly glad about that. But she is beautiful."

"So is crystal, but it's hard and brittle. Besides, you're beautiful, too."

"I wasn't fishing for compliments. I know I'm not in the same class as Dorothea Kaye."

"No, you're not. You're way above her: bold, clever, capable, and kind."

"I've done many unkind things in my life. Ask the crews of the ships we plundered."

"Did you ever take pleasure in someone else's pain?"

"Not for its own sake. I was glad to see Walsingham dead, though."

"That's different. Self-defense and defense of those you loved."

I might have argued, but Timpani kicked the wooden partition of his stall and whinnied. Dancer joined in and stamped his hooves.

Corwen laughed. "Someone's getting impatient."

"Two someones." I smoothed my skirts. "Stable duty calls. Good job I'm wearing the dress the Fae gave me. It's impervious to stains."

"If I'd remembered that, there wouldn't have been a need to go against the wall."

"Let's take care of the horses and see how much time we have left before Thomas comes back."

17

Water Magic

WE GOT THOROUGHLY SOAKED running be-
tween the stable yard and the house, but I didn't care.
At least it accounted for our state of dishevelment. I in-
dulged myself in a hot bath in front of my bedroom fire
which Poppy prepared on the grounds that it would warm
me up. I hardly needed warming despite the rain, but the
indulgence was a luxury.

Over dinner Corwen and I deliberately didn't catch
each other's gaze because we were both inclined to break
out into smiles, but his knee brushed mine beneath the table and I moved against his touch ... an echo of what had
passed and a promise of more to come.

Corwen's mother retired early, pleading a headache,
sensitive to the thunderheads that I could feel building.
Lily also excused herself, saying she planned to be at the
mill before seven in the morning and wished to get a good
night's sleep.

"Perhaps we should follow suit?" I said, but made no
move to rise from my seat on the sofa in front of the parlor
fire.

"Perhaps we should."

Corwen put his arm around me and we stared into the flames, my head resting against his shoulder. We sat like that for more than an hour, until thunder rumbled outside and squally rain mixed with hail drummed against the windows and pinged down the chimney to hiss into the flaming coals in the hearth.

"It's set in for the night," I said. "But it will blow itself out by dawn."

"Are you sure you don't have some weather magic left?"

"Maybe a little, but even at my best I wouldn't have been able to do anything about a storm on this scale, not without causing something far worse."

We kissed, walked hand in hand up the stairs, and reluctantly parted on the landing. I wasn't sure I would get much sleep, but I must have drifted off despite the torrential downpour because I awoke to a loud banging on the front door and a commotion in the hallway downstairs.

I sprang out of bed, throwing a shawl around my shoulders, and hurried onto the landing.

Corwen was already halfway down the stairs. Topping's son, Tommy, stood in the hallway, water streaming from him. The two maids who had answered the door together gaped as if he were an apparition.

"Mr. Deverell, Da says to come quick, the sluice gate's collapsed and floodwater's starting to pour down the valley. He says it's only a matter of time before the whole dam gives way. It won't hold."

Corwen said something succinct which even his mother didn't reprimand him for as she stumbled onto the landing, rubbing her eyes.

"Go and rouse the grooms, Tommy," Corwen said. "I want every able-bodied man dressed and ready in ten minutes and Dancer and Timpani harnessed to the big cart. Tell Thomas to saddle Brock, too. Are there any injuries?"

"Not at the mill, sir. I don't know about farther down the valley. With all this rain, the water has gone with a fair gush. Dad's doing his best to hold the rest back. He's sent to rouse all the rowankind."

Rowankind. Wind and weather magic. Good, Topping was already taking charge.

"What's happening?" Lily arrived on the landing.

"The sluice gate's given way," I told her. "We're going to see what can be done."

"Not without me. It's my mill now."

"Get dressed quickly, then."

I dashed into Corwen's room for my breeches and shirt from his linen press.

"What do you think you're doing?" he asked as he dodged around me to drag his own clothes on.

"Coming with you—and not dressed in yards of muslin."

I wondered if he might object, but he didn't. "Dress as warmly as you can."

I met Lily on the landing again. She wore an old dress and a heavy coat, with her riding boots beneath them. "Well, look at you," she said. "I wondered what you looked like at sea, Captain Sumner. I wish I had something sensible to wear, but this is the best I can do."

We ran down the stairs as Tommy arrived at the front door.

Yeardley emerged from the back stairs to the attics, muffled in a coat and scarf, with Thorpe close behind him and Poppy close behind them.

"Poppy?" I said, unsure of the advisability of letting a pregnant woman join the party.

"Rowankind," she said. "I won't get in the way, but I might be able to help."

John had Dancer and Timpani harnessed in the shafts of the flat cart. Thomas was on the driver's seat with a huddle of stable boys in the back. "I don't know about this, sir," he said to Corwen. "These two are too fine for this work. Let me harness the Suffolks."

"Trust me, John, Timpani, and Dancer are more than up to the task, and they have the sense for weather such as this."

As he spoke, the sky cracked open, lighting the scene momentarily. Less than a second later, thunder crashed around our ears.

"Holy Mother of God!" someone in the cart exclaimed.

"Steady," Corwen told the horses.

Dancer nodded his head as if he were answering. Timpani just stood rock solid, as if anything as natural as a lightning storm was nothing to be afraid of.

Corwen mounted Brock, his long legs dangling below the pony's girth, but Brock could easily carry a man's weight.

"Be careful," Corwen's mother called from the door.

He waved at her in acknowledgment and led the way down the drive.

<hr />

The journey to the mill was fraught with danger. Any number of times, the Suffolks might have foundered in potholes and flooded dips, but Dancer and Timpani skirted holes and pulled the loaded wagon through mud and flooded ruts without a misstep. They stopped only once, wary of something ahead. I was tempted to put up a witchlight, but there were too many witnesses. I liked my neck as it was and didn't want it stretching, so I let everyone struggle, silently cursing the law of the land that prevented magic being a useful everyday tool.

Keeping out of the Mysterium's clutches had been relatively easy while I made my home on the high seas. It would be less so once I was Mrs. Corwen Deverell and tied to a well-known family. Corwen knew as well as I did what revealing my talents could mean. He didn't ask for magical help; instead, he rode ahead and trusted Brock to find any obstruction.

"There's a tree across the road." Corwen rode back to tell us, since shouting above the tumult of the wind in the trees would have been pointless.

"Let the men see to it," I said to Poppy and Lily as they made to climb out of the wagon with everyone else.

"Shouldn't I be prepared to do whatever the workers are asked to do?" Lily said. "Isn't that what being a good leader is all about?"

"That's one theory, but sometimes you do what you are

best at." I jumped from the wagon and took a carriage lamp.

"You're going," Lily accused.

"Yes, but only to do what I'm best at."

I gathered my magic, feeling it tingle in the small of my back, shiver up my spine, and spread along my right arm to my fingertips. Instead of putting up a witchlight, I brightened the carriage lamp, so the men could see to clear the road. It lit the sheeting rain, turning it almost solid against the black night. Corwen looked at me, and I shrugged. It was better than letting someone get hurt. There was nothing anyone could prove, even if they noticed the lamp was unnaturally bright.

Figures strained to move the tree safely to one side. Lightning flashed again. Thrashing tree branches made shadows whip about like demented snakes. With a final heave and a crash, the men cleared the road.

That same voice said, "Holy Mother of God!" again.

I was soaked right down to my smallclothes. Rivulets of cold water ran inside my shirt which chafed in places I'd rather it didn't. Although it was April, this was hardly spring weather. It was more like the last big blow of winter.

As we rattled into the mill yard, sloshing through puddles, shouts came from the direction of the dam. I could hear water gushing through the mill race, fierce and strong. I took hold of the lantern again and brightened the beam. Water splashed above the deep channel cut for the tailrace, washing through runnels to find its way to the river which was already in danger of breaking its banks and flooding into the tenter croft. The wheel itself, deprived of the water from the headrace, turned with the power of the flood gushing beneath it, creaking and groaning, some of its buckets and paddles stripped away. The river flooded into the fulling mill, sucking and gurgling around the stocks. Full pieces of cloth, each twenty-two yards long, tangled with each other in the swirling waters.

"I hope there was no one in there when the sluice gate went," I said.

"Only old Martha," a voice behind me said, "and she

scrambled out of a window and came to alert me." I turned to find Mr. Topping. "Can you give us some light here?" He pointed to the dam. "That's a powerful light."

"It's only a lamp." I let it fade a little, but not too obviously. People would talk if there was any whiff of magic.

"Of course it is," he said.

With my heart pounding at the near discovery, I made my way to the dam to where Corwen was stripped to his shirt and breeches with a rope tied around his chest, under his arms.

"Corwen, what in hell's name . . . ?" I brightened the lantern to get a better idea of what was going on. "You're not going in there?" The mill dam was only half-drained, and still deep enough to drown a man. A dozen rowankind, all weavers, stood in a huddle, and that's when I saw what they'd done. The sluice gate itself had completely splintered, but a wall of magic held back half the water in the mill dam. They were averting complete disaster. If they let it go, the water could easily cause a monstrous flood that would wash homes away downstream. How long could they hold it?

"It's water magic," Mr. Topping said. "Rowankind magic. There's no requirement for rowankind to register with the Mysterium." He looked at me sideways. "You know about magic, don't you, Mrs. Summoner?"

"Sumner," I said, daring him to call me on my magic.

"Mrs. Sumner, of course." He dipped his head in acknowledgment.

"Mr. Topping, whatever you think you know—you don't."

"If you say so."

I tried to ignore the implied disbelief in his voice. Now was not the time. "So Corwen's going to try and fix planks across from the inside, is that it?" I asked.

"We've knocked together a bulwark out of stout planks. We can lower it down, but someone has to guide it into place. Once it's there, we can nail and lash the top end to the uprights that used to hold the sluice gate. The water pressure will hold the rest of it. It won't be completely watertight, but it will hold back most of the flood."

He waved toward something that looked like a hastily cobbled together raft.

"Canvas and pitch," I said. "It can keep the sea out of a leaking ship, temporarily, so it will help to hold this." There was no magic involved, simply a bit of nautical know-how.

"I'll see what I can find," Mr. Topping said. "There's canvas covers for the wagons and pitch from a roof repair."

He sent off a boy of middle years.

"Corwen, wait." While two of Mr. Topping's seemingly inexhaustible supply of sons gathered the pitch and canvas, I told Corwen the plan to waterproof the bulwark.

"It makes sense," he said, slipping his coat across his naked shoulders, trying to disguise his shivering.

I turned to find Poppy standing close behind me. "Are you part of this working?" I waved toward the rowankind who were holding back the flood.

"No, they started before I got here. What do you need me to do?"

"Form a bubble around Corwen while he's in the water."

"How do you mean?"

I told her how the little girl, Olivia, had survived the kelpie.

"I've never . . ." she swallowed hard. "I'll try, but you have wind and water magic, too."

"I did. Now I'm not sure what's left."

"More than you think, I'll warrant. It'll come when you need it."

◆━━◆

At last the pitch-soaked canvas was wrapped and tied around the wooden bulwark. Corwen shook off his coat again and prepared to jump into the freezing water.

"Mr. Corwen, sir," a voice called out. "That's a job for two." Yeardley stepped forward.

"Are you volunteering?"

"Can't say I like the idea, sir, but I heartily mislike the idea of telling your father you drowned in the mill dam while I stood by."

"Come and welcome, Stephen."

Trust Corwen to know Yeardley's given name, despite no one ever, in my hearing, calling him by it.

Stephen Yeardley shed his coat and shirt, allowed Mr. Topping to tie a rope around him, and teetered on the edge of the dam. "How deep do you think it might be?" he asked.

"It's a bit late for questions like that," Corwen said. "Can you swim?"

"No, sir. I was five years at sea. All the older sailors said not to learn as it only meant it took longer to drown if you went overboard."

"There is that to it, I suppose. Come on, let's find out." Corwen took a deep breath and dropped over the edge of the dam, feet first, straight down. He bobbed up again with an expletive he could barely get out between chattering teeth. Yeardley screwed his eyes up, pinched his nose between thumb and forefinger, and jumped, too.

"Now, Poppy," I said, reaching into the water with my magic senses, feeling for the flow and pressure of it. I felt Poppy's magic working alongside me as she pushed against the surface of the water, molding it, shaping it, forming a depression, lowering the level around the two men until they stood only chest-deep, the water towering above their heads, ready to fall upon them with crushing force.

Mr. Topping looked at me and looked at Poppy, surprised, but took every advantage. Four men lowered the canvas-covered barrier to Corwen and Stephen who pushed it into place against the gap where the sluice gate used to be.

"Hammer and nails, while we have the chance," Corwen called up. Tommy Topping leaned over and handed them down.

Corwen's magical ability to bind inanimate objects might help to fix the barrier into place, but iron nails would be the main magic in use tonight. Yeardley pushed against the contraption while Corwen secured it with a few well-placed nails and set about hammering in more for extra security.

"I can't hold the water for much longer." Poppy's breath came in short snatches between her words. I hadn't realized what a strain I'd placed on her.

"There's something down here," Yeardley shouted up. "Here, under my feet."

"What kind of something?" Corwen asked.

"Metal. Something metal."

"I can't hold it." Poppy squeaked. "Get them out. Oh, get them out. Quick."

"Corwen, Poppy's exhausted," I called. "Get out, now."

"It's here. I can feel it." Yeardley bent and reached into the water, his arm and head disappearing under.

"Leave it, man, whatever it is." Corwen bent to drag him out.

Poppy sank to her knees. The wall of water collapsed and the weight swamped Corwen and Yeardley, covering them completely.

"Get them out!" I yelled to the men on the ropes, who were slower to react than I would have liked.

Without thinking about it, I leaped into the water myself. The all-over shock of the icy water paralyzed my breathing and my rational thought. The next thing I knew I was holding water at bay around the three of us, my lungs bursting with held breath.

Corwen grabbed me around the waist. "Pull, man," I heard him say and I felt myself being drawn upward.

"You can let go, Ross," Corwen said. "Breathe, dammit!"

I breathed, let go of the wall of pressure I was holding, and heard water crash into itself somewhere close to my feet.

"I've got you," Corwen said in my ear. "Relax."

Everything went dark, but that may have been because I let go of the witchlight as well.

By the time I was thinking clearly again, the storm had blown itself out. Dawn etched the eastern sky with violet, and the dam, for now, was secure. I let Corwen lead me away, dizzy with the knowledge that Poppy was right, I still had some water magic in me, buried deep, but still there when I needed it.

I didn't recognize where I was, but I knew the sound of a singing kettle and the smell of tea. Someone had wrapped a blanket around my shoulders and tucked a cushion at my back. My bare shins basked in the warm glow from a kitchen range. Corwen sat, similarly blanket-wrapped, in a second Windsor chair, feet in the hearth. A figure, lit only by the flames from the fire and the single stub of a cheap candle, brewed tea in a tin teapot.

"Welcome to my new home, Mrs. Summoner," Mr. Topping said. "I didn't know who you were at first, but when I felt your magic, I knew who you were and what you'd done."

Damn! It was no use trying to deny my magic. Topping was well aware of what I was. I'd have to pack up and run, leave Corwen behind if he couldn't abandon his family now. Maybe I could call the *Heart* to meet me at Hull or Liverpool, escape to the ocean, settle in Bacalao where I was known as Rossalinde Tremayne. I had money stashed there. I could move on to the Americas where King George and the Mysterium couldn't touch me. Corwen could join me later, if he wanted to. If he had to choose between family duty and me, I didn't know what he would do. He loved me, of that I was sure, but he loved his family as well, and they needed him. I could survive on my own if I had to, and he knew that perfectly well.

"We only came down to make sure that bugger, Thatcher, had left the place in good order." Mr. Topping was still talking about the house. "I thought he was likely to set it on fire out of spite. Good job we did or we might have been too late to do anything about the dam."

"As it was," Corwen reached down and picked up a heavy bundle covered in sacking, "someone—and we can probably all guess who, though we have no proof—gave the sluice gate a few hefty whacks with this." He held a huge iron sledgehammer of the kind navvies use to drive pilings into the ground. "Yeardley found it, or rather his feet did. It had been thrown into the water, or dropped accidentally, maybe."

"Deliberate wrecking," I said. "Thatcher?"

"That's my first guess."

Corwen's knuckles were white on the hammer. If he ever met Thatcher, I hoped he was in human form, because if he was in wolf form, he'd likely rip out the man's throat. A tear escaped my eye and ran down my cheek. I wouldn't be there to hold him in check. I wouldn't be there to help him. Dammit, I was beginning to like Yorkshire, too, and Corwen's family—even his mother.

"You needn't be afeard of us, Mrs. Sumner." Topping went back to using my everyday name. "There's not one of the rowankind would mention the magic that passed here tonight."

"Yeardley, John Mallinson, the lads from the stables, Thorpe, even Lily . . . Where is she, anyway?"

"Gone home in the wagon with everyone else. Lily will say nothing," Corwen said. "You know why."

"But the others . . ."

"It was dark," Mr. Topping said. "Chaotic. The rowankind did magic with water. There's nothing in law that says they can't. No one saw anything else. Who's even going to question it?"

I began to relax. Maybe it would be all right.

⚔ 18 ⚔

Mysterium

W E PLODDED HOME SLOWLY. Corwen and I, bone weary, lapsed into companionable silence. We both rode Brock, grateful that Fae mounts were stronger, hardier, faster, and smarter than any regular horse had a right to be. We were contemplating nothing more than falling innocently into our own beds. The sun was up and the storm already a memory.

Corwen's mother hovered at the door as we arrived. She stared at my breeches. Maybe in the dark and the chaos of last night she hadn't noticed my attire, but it gained the full force of her disapproval now, and I was reminded strongly of my own mother's reaction to my dressing as a counterfeit man. *You're a lady, Rossalinde, not a hoyden!*

"Lily?" Corwen asked.

"Asleep, as is the maid, Poppy. Shall I have Sarah turn down your bed, Ross?"

"I can manage."

"Why didn't you tell me?"

Corwen stiffened at his mother's tone. "Tell you what?" he asked.

"That she's a witch."

I felt the icy fingers of fear clutch at my innards, but Corwen kept his voice even. "What put that idea into your head?"

"Yeardley and Thorpe. It was all the talk in the wagon on the way home, apparently. Yeardley says you saved his life." She turned to me. "Did you?"

"I jumped into the mill dam to help pull him out. Silly of me. Corwen was more than capable. It was rowankind magic that held back the water, though. Poppy's the lifesaver."

"She didn't seem so sure about that when I asked her."

"Probably just exhausted and desperate to get some rest. I'll have a word with her later."

"I'm sure you will."

Corwen put an arm around his mother's shoulders. "We can talk about this in the morning."

"It is morning."

"You know what I mean. Sleep first, talk later. The mill is saved, or most of it, anyway. There's water to pump out of the fulling mill, the wheel to repair, and the sluice to replace, but it could have been worse—a lot worse. It was Mr. Topping's rowankind who saved the situation."

"I worry, Corwen, about you and your sister and Freddie. You know what would happen if anyone found out what you are. Anything that brings magic too close is a danger to the family." She glanced at me again. "I can't always protect you."

"I know. I'll tell the men they were mistaken, make sure they understand."

She seemed satisfied at that, but I wasn't sure how far I could trust her. I peeled off my clothes, still damp, and fell into bed, reveling in the feel of the clean sheets on my skin. I expected sleep to claim me immediately, but I'd seen how fast rumor flew along the valley. Stories of my witchy exploits would spread. Corwen's mother was right. I was a danger to the whole family if I stayed.

Eventually I did fall asleep, but dreams of the Mysterium and Walsingham chased themselves through my slumber, and every scene that played had the shadow of a noose hanging over it.

"Wake up, Ross, Oh, wake up! The Mysterium's here and you're wanted downstairs."

I tried to gather enough spit for speech as I turned over in my feather mattress and sat up, not fully awake, my head throbbing and my eyes gummy and full of grit. *Wanted* and *Mysterium* were the only two words that got through to me.

"Time is it?" was all I could manage.

"It's past noon."

I opened one eye. Poppy's worried face swam into focus as she stood with my shift over one arm and my hairbrush in her hand.

"How come you're awake?"

"I got to bed a full three hours before you did. To be honest, I don't sleep for more than four hours at a stretch." She patted her belly. "This little blighter dances a jig on my bladder every night. Do you want to slip out of the back door?"

I contemplated it, tempted. More than tempted if I'm honest.

"You said the Mysterium, Poppy. How many are down there?"

"One, ma'am, and a gentleman at that."

"If I run away I label myself as guilty from the start. Pass me my shift and set out my cream dress and cashmere shawl."

I'd fallen into bed naked, so now I pulled on my shift and let Poppy lace my short stays on top of it. "I can manage the rest, Poppy, go and wake Corwen. He's likely to be as sleep-fuddled as me."

She did as I asked, but returned in time to twist my hair into the simple style I preferred for daytime.

"There. Do I look respectable?"

"As respectable as ever, ma'am." Poppy caught a stray tendril of hair and pushed it onto the top of my head in one practiced move. "Mr. Corwen said to tell you not to worry."

"Right. This is me, not worrying." I tried to smile, but it probably looked more like a grimace.

I think my knees knocked together as I descended the stairs. There was no one waiting for me at the bottom, and so I let myself into the best parlor, the one with the beautiful vista over the green parkland. Mrs. Deverell sat on a chaise next to Mr. Deverell in his wheeled chair. Perched on the edge of a chair was a gentleman in impeccable buckskin breeches, a plum-colored coat, embroidered yellow silk waistcoat, and a shirt with a neck cloth tied impeccably, bang up to fashion. He didn't look like a typical Mysterium officer. His features were narrow and refined. If I had not immediately thought of him as the enemy, I might have found him moderately handsome. He stood politely as I entered the room, and I saw he was tall and slim, possibly even lanky.

"Ah, Rossalinde, my dear." Mrs. Deverell offered her cheek.

"Mama." I crossed the room and brushed my lips against her powdered skin, smelling her delicate rosewater perfume. She grasped my hand briefly and squeezed. A warning? A gesture of solidarity? Fear? I wasn't sure.

"May I present Mr. Pomeroy, newly come to Barnsley as the town's only officer of the Mysterium, sent from the Sheffield regional office." She told me all I needed to know in one succinct sentence. "Mr. Pomeroy, may I present my soon-to-be daughter, Mrs. Sumner."

"Mrs. Sumner." Mr. Pomeroy made a leg in my direction, a bow so perfect I thought he'd practiced it in places other than Sheffield and Barnsley. It wouldn't have been out of place at court. "Sent from Sheffield, ma'am, but only recently discharged from His Majesty's Navy. I was second lieutenant on board the *Impregnable* until she sank in '99 off Spithead."

He waited for me to sit before resuming his own seat.

"How fascinating, Mr. Pomeroy. Mrs. Sumner has interests in shipping." Mrs. Deverell turned to me, no doubt thinking she was leading the conversation toward safe territory.

"You do?" Pomeroy's voice suddenly became animated.

"A small interest, only. I have a schooner which sails under the captaincy of Henry Garrity out of Elizabethtown on Bacalao Island."

"Her name, ma'am?"

I was tempted to lie, but it would be easy to check. "The *Heart of Oak*."

He looked surprised. "A privateer vessel, I believe."

At that, I got a look of surprise from my new mama. One more black mark against my character.

"Indeed, she is," I said.

"Once belonging to Captain Redbeard Tremayne, as I recall."

I forced myself to laugh. "Tremayne was killed some years ago, but his legend served that little ship well. A small fiction. Keeping his reputation alive saved many a fight and many a life on both sides as I understand it."

The door opened again and Corwen entered, his face slightly flushed as though he'd been rushing, but outwardly his manner was languid. I noticed fresh mud on his boots and caught his glance, receiving a twitch of a smile that seemed to tell me not to worry. I suspected he'd been out to speak to the men in the stable.

Introductions were made again, but when the conversation turned to Mr. Pomeroy's naval experience, Corwen dropped into the chair next to mine and yawned. "I fear I'm a poor sailor, sir, and my fiancée—I'm sure she will not mind me saying—suffers from mal-de-mer out on the open ocean."

That wasn't actually a lie. The only ship I wasn't seasick on was the *Heart*, and that was because of the ensorcelled *winterwood* spliced into her keel.

"Has Mother offered you refreshment, Mr. Pomeroy? Tea, perhaps? Or sherry if you prefer. I'm afraid you catch us unprepared for visitors." Corwen's polite demeanor was only slightly exaggerated into foppishness, but I'd seen him effect it before as a defense against seeming too aggressive or forthright. "There was something of an incident at the mill last night and we were out in the storm trying to minimize the damage. I trust there's been no devastation lower down the valley."

"Not that I have heard, sir, nor seen on my journey here this morning."

"That's a relief. If it had not been for our rowankind weavers I fear it would have been a far different story."

"And why is that, sir?"

"Magic, sir. Magic to save men's lives. I have never seen anything like it. As you well know, since the rowankind's change—may I call it that?—their natural magic has become known, and being not like us, not *people,* as was once ruled in a court of law, they are not subject to registration with your good selves—"

"That may be about to change, but do go on with your tale."

About to change? Was the Mysterium or Parliament trying to bring the rowankind into the system of registration? The practice of licensing witches and limiting them to small magics as prescribed in the Mysterium's own official spell book was, frankly, farcical. Those of us who didn't, for whatever reason, register within six months of our eighteenth birthday were—if caught—subject to severe penalties, usually hanging, but occasionally there were rumors of disappearances. The Walsingham who had pursued me on land and at sea had had several witches working for him who were certainly not limited to the spell book.

Corwen continued. "It appears some rogue took a sledgehammer to our sluice gate at the height of last night's storm with the river running high. I needn't tell you how that might have gone if the whole dam had collapsed, as was surely intended. A wall of water might have rolled down the valley, sweeping away all in its path. Luckily, we employ a number of rowankind weavers and, like all the rowankind, I believe, they have sympathy with wind and water magic. A group of them combined together and held the water in the dam while we made temporary repairs. Held it with the power of their magic, sir, and thus saved lives and property. Why, sir, they should be given medals. Don't you think so?"

"As long as they are not remunerated for their magical services. The law clearly states that no person may be financially rewarded for performing a magical service unless they hold a license from the Mysterium."

"It does, sir." Corwen frowned. "Though according to the Lord Chief Justice, the Earl of Mansfield, in the Plympton case brought in 1771, a rowankind is a non-person with no legal status enshrined in law. This was further supported in Somersett's case the year after when Mansfield specifically excluded rowankind from the ruling because they were neither slaves nor free men. They were, in effect, not persons at all and therefore not covered by the Mysterium's rules. But come, sir, we are splitting hairs. We've not paid the rowankind for their heroic efforts. Is that what you came to ascertain?"

"Not entirely." He glanced at me.

Here it comes, I thought.

"It's alleged Mrs. Sumner also performed magic last night, and you cannot argue that she, begging your pardon for speaking plainly, is a non-person."

I tried not to look worried or guilty. I aimed my features at *puzzled with a hint of offense*, but left it to Corwen to deny it rather than defending myself, which I felt I might do with unseemly vigor.

Corwen looked Pomeroy straight in the eye and laughed with such an open and hearty laugh that I might have joined in myself, except I feared anything I might say or do at this point would do me no good.

"Alleged?" Cowen said, finally. "Who would say such a thing, not anyone working at the mill, surely?"

"Not a worker, but a gentleman." He took out a sheet of paper covered with cramped writing. "A Mr. Thatcher, who observed the events from a position on the roadside and reported it with this, his sworn statement to me, first thing this morning."

Corwen's face was suddenly serious. "Are you aware that Mr. Thatcher was dismissed from my service on Friday? Isn't it suspicious that on Sunday night a person or persons unknown destroyed the sluice gate at the mill, causing the loss of the fulling stocks, the flooding of the fulling mill, and potentially endangering life and limb—deaths for which Deverell's Mill would be blamed? Not only that, but if Mr. Thatcher is innocent in this matter, why would he position himself on the road at the dead of night, in such vile weather, to observe? What was he expecting to observe but an incident he knew was about to happen? And the danger at the mill, having been contained by unexpected magic, what better way to cause further damage to me and mine, than by insinuating that my bride-to-be is an unlicensed witch?"

Mr. Pomeroy frowned. "I see. Do you intend to bring a charge against him?"

"I have no evidence other than conjecture, but you must agree it's suspicious."

"Quite so." Mr. Pomeroy turned to me. "You do admit, however, to attending the event dressed in breeches, Mrs. Sumner?"

"Is that evidence of witchery?" I asked. "Have you ever stepped out in a violent storm in a dress, Mr. Pomeroy? You're a navy man. Imagine being wrapped in a wet sail from head to toe and trying to stay upright on deck in a gale. Would you not prefer to wear something less likely to get you swept off your feet?"

"But it's true that you, a lady, albeit dressed in man's clothing, leaped into the freezing waters of the mill dam and held back those waters to protect Mr. Deverell and another man?"

"I confess I did, indeed, jump into the dam, knowing Yeardley didn't swim, but as to holding the waters back, I believe we only have the rowankind to thank for that."

Mr. Deverell, who had witnessed the whole conversation, sitting still and silent in his chair, made a noise that meant he wished to communicate. I put my hand beneath his, and he dragged his finger across my knuckles, a short-cut symbol which meant he required Yeardley to perform some service for him. In this case I was pretty sure he meant we should summon Yeardley and ask him the direct question as to what he'd observed last night. That probably wasn't a good idea unless Corwen had already managed to have a word with him. I was tempted to deliberately misunderstand, but Corwen squeezed my shoulder.

"He's asking for Yeardley," I said.

"A good idea, Father." Corwen rang the bell that summoned Yeardley.

The man appeared within a few minutes, looking none the worse for almost being drowned. I had never noticed, beneath his neat attire, how well muscled he was until last night. This quiet man, who had been in the navy and who now carried Mr. Deverell about as if he were a featherweight, and who volunteered to enter freezing water in a roaring storm was more than he seemed on the surface. I hoped he wasn't about to condemn me.

"Yeardley, is it?" Pomeroy asked.

"Yes, sir."

"Also a navy man," I said.

"Four years aboard *HMS Pickle*, sir, and a year on the *Alice*." He didn't salute, but stood to attention.

Pomeroy acknowledged his deference with a small nod. "I believe you are to be commended on your efforts last night."

"I did what any man would do."

"And woman, too." Pomeroy looked at me. "Is it true you can't swim?"

"Yes, sir. I can't, sir."

"So you put your trust in magic to keep from drowning?"

"I put my trust in Mr. Corwen, sir, and a stout rope. I know nothing of magic."

"But you do know when something is running contrary to nature." He paused. "Well, man?"

"Sorry, sir, was that a question? I do, sir. And I saw the rowankind magicking the water. Mr. Corwen was willing, sir, and it looked like an extra pair of hands was needed. I know what it's like to be up to my neck in water in a gale, struggling to plug a leak. It seemed this was not very different, so in I jumped."

"And Mrs. Sumner jumped in, too."

"Not straightaway, sir, but when we were swamped, she

jumped in to help. I'd bent down in the water, you see, sir. I'd trod on something strange, something lying on top of the mud beneath my bare feet, and I thought it might be important, but the only way I could get it was to bob under the water. I felt someone grab one arm and someone else grabbed the other. Mr. Corwen and Mrs. Sumner both heaved me out of the water, and I brought up a great sledgehammer that had likely been used to smash the sluice with. There was no rust on it, sir. It hadn't been in the water long."

"And did Mrs. Sumner hold back the water with magic?"

"I don't rightly see how she could have done, sir, nor why she would have needed to with all the rowankind magicking the water like they did."

Pomeroy nodded. "Thank you, Yeardley. That's all for now."

Yeardley gave a small bow, turned to kneel by Mr. Deverell's chair, and slipped his hand under that of the old man. "Do you need me for anything more, sir?" He was as quiet as a good servant should be, and I wondered at his transformation from sailor to servant. There was a story there. Mr. Deverell obviously asked to go to his room. Yeardley made his bow to us and wheeled out the old man.

"You must excuse my husband, Mr. Pomeroy," Mrs. Deverell said. "He is frail and tires easily."

Pomeroy acknowledged her with a small bow. "I completely understand."

Corwen's hand brushed against mine behind the folds of my dress. "Well, Mr. Pomeroy, if you've found out all you need to know, are you sure you'll not take sherry before you leave?"

"I thank you kindly for your offer, but I must be on my way. I have an appointment at the office in Sheffield."

Relief at settling the matter so simply emboldened me. "Mr. Pomeroy, before you go, might I ask you what you meant when you said things might change for the rowankind? There are thousands of them, and still more have gone away to wherever they have gone. Surely the Mysterium isn't going to try to trace them all and make them register?"

"That's not for me to say, but there is talk that Mr. Walsingham—"

"Walsingham?" I suddenly felt queasy.

"The new head of the Mysterium, a royal appointment as I understand it. There's talk that Mr. Walsingham has influence in Parliament."

"You know much of Parliament?" Corwen asked.

"I have connections. Family." He hesitated. "My grandfather—the Earl of Stratford—sits in the House of Lords. The old gentleman is interested in magical matters. It's one of the reasons he encouraged me out of the navy and into the Mysterium."

Had Pomeroy been happy with that change? Since he had no title of his own, he was likely the younger son of a younger son. He might not have a title, but doubtless he still had obligations. With rumors of a settlement with France, the navy had more officers than it needed and a diminished opportunity for advancement. Perhaps Pomeroy had seen better opportunities in the Mysterium as a younger son obliged to earn his own living while retaining the status of gentleman.

He took his leave of us politely. Corwen walked Pomeroy to the door. I was sure it was more to make sure he left the premises without delay than to be courteous. I sank into a chair.

19

Practical Magic

"MY DEAR, you look as though you're about to pass out. You're as white as a sheet," Mrs. Deverell said once Pomeroy was safely outside. "Do you need smelling salts?"

"No, Mama." I still found it strange to call her that. "I'm fine, thank you. Though I admit that was an interview I could have done without. I'll pack my things and be on my way before Mr. Pomeroy changes his mind and returns with a troop of redcoats."

"You'll do no such thing." Corwen's mother drew herself to her full height. "We've lived in fear of the Mysterium and discovery since Corwen's first change. Now it seems as though there's too much magic in the world for them to handle, and that's all to the good. It means less trouble for us if they're out chasing other things. I'll admit I was shocked at first by what I heard last night, but I should have suspected Corwen would not give his heart to someone inexperienced in magic. I will not have the Mysterium driving guests from my door, or indeed, family, which you very nearly are."

"That's kind of you, but I confess I am a witch, and a privateer, too. I'm sorry if you don't approve. I've led an unconventional life. If you're hoping for a conventional daughter-in-law, then I'm not she."

My new mama huffed out a breath that might have been a laugh or a heavy sigh. "Maybe it's time for the truth between us. Cards on the table."

I wondered where to start, but she beat me to it.

"Do you know what it's like to have children?" She didn't wait for an answer. "I've had eight. Six pregnancies, two of them being twins. Jonnie came first, a lusty strong boy, his father's pride and joy and my true darling. Emily was born two years later, a little princess of a child. After that came a boy, William. He died of the croup when he was seven months old. We almost lost Emily, too, but she recovered, though it took some months to regain her strength."

I could see her eyes brimming with unshed tears, but she blinked them away and continued. "Corwen and Freddie arrived three years later. Jonnie was ten years old and had barely had a day of illness in his life. He was a charmed child. Charmed and charming. There was a girl next. I would have called her Elizabeth after my mother, but she was born early and never breathed. I didn't want any more disappointments, but it was not to be. Four years later I discovered I was carrying again, and this time it was twins. Lily survived; her brother did not, and even though I had not wanted another child, I loved her as did her father."

She glanced at the corner where Mr. Deverell habitually sat. "Arthur was a good father, if strict. He tried not to show favoritism, but you could see he doted on Lily. We were such a happy family despite our losses. Then it all changed. Corwen changed."

She left a long silence, and I could tell she was working up to something.

"There were no more children after that. Arthur blamed me. I blamed Arthur. We barely spoke to each other for . . . oh, I don't know . . . months. Arthur distanced himself from Corwen altogether, couldn't bear to be near him. Then he decided that Corwen himself was to blame. He got it into his head the boy could cease to be a wolf if he tried hard enough. I said he was strict, didn't I? Once, after he'd beaten Corwen, I ran away. I couldn't bear it any longer. I took Corwen and went to visit my eldest sister Eugenie, who never married and kept a small house in the country. It was quiet there. I thought we might have some respite. I told Eugie. I had to confide in someone. To my surprise, she was neither shocked nor disgusted. She told me that my father, whom I never knew because he died when I was three years old, had been a shapechanger, too. My mother remarried. I called the man who brought us up Father, and I loved him, but he wasn't my blood. Eugie knew more because she was twelve when our father died. She said the wolf-change happened sometimes in our family. She said we never spoke of it and dealt with it by keeping it secret, but Corwen wasn't the first and would likely not be the last. I had to teach him to guard his secret, and I had to guard it for him until he was old enough to control his wolf."

"Did things change for Corwen after that?" I asked. "At home, I mean, with his father?"

She rubbed her temple as if driving away an incipient headache. "Arthur never really understood, but Corwen learned to master his changes. We couldn't send him away to school, of course, so Freddie got the education and Corwen got the run of the library and a tutor and then a few years at Penistone Grammar School as a day-boy. I don't think that suited Freddie; it was as if he suddenly had to carry the weight of expectations for both of them. Emily was married by then. I worry about her children, but so far they are all . . . unencumbered by family traits. Eugie said it sometimes skips a generation, or even two."

I tried to pick my words carefully. "Corwen told me he had one argument too many with his father and left."

"That's right. And barely two months after Corwen left, Lily changed for the first time. She was thirteen and on the point of womanhood. She'd always been Arthur's favorite, and finally he developed some forgiveness in his soul. I think he was shocked to have lost Corwen. He never thought he would drive the boy away. It wasn't as though he didn't love him. He simply thought he could make him normal again—and he couldn't."

She wiped a tear away with the heel of her hand. "I'd had to be strong for Corwen, then for Lily. I didn't expect to have to do it again, but when Freddie changed, it was terrible. I wasn't sure I had that kind of strength anymore. It broke Arthur's heart, but Freddie was already a young man and couldn't be beaten and locked in his room. Freddie's change was brutal. Maybe he'd been fighting it off for years. He'd witnessed Arthur's treatment of Corwen and decided he could do like his father wanted and stop the changes by willpower alone. I could see how his nature was fighting with his determination, but he suppressed the wolf. Sadly, it didn't improve the balance of his mind."

"You should have sent for Corwen."

"Arthur wouldn't hear of it, and I'm sorry to say I abided by his decision."

"So you carried the weight all by yourself. You're a strong woman, Mama. I take my hat off to you." I hugged her. "My story is mild in comparison." I told her about my magic coming on and how my mother wouldn't accept it, my escape with Will, the death of our child, and—later— the accident that took Will from me.

"I became a privateer in his stead," I said. "Does that shock you?"

"My dear, nothing can shock me now."

"Well said, Mother." Corwen had returned with Lily dogging his heels.

"What did I miss?" she asked. "Corwen told me to warn Yeardley to be circumspect and said I should stay out of the way until the Mysterium man had gone. I heard a little of it through the door, but not enough, and then I came face-to-face with him in the hallway. He's younger than I expected. Are we discovered?"

"It was a close thing, but Mr. Pomeroy seemed reasonable about it all," Corwen said. "Whether his masters in Sheffield will see things the same way, I don't know."

"Did you hear what Pomeroy said about the new head

of the Mysterium?" I turned to Corwen. "Walsingham. It can't be a coincidence?"

"Someone you know?" Corwen's mother asked.

"Not the exact person." I shuddered. "Walsingham—in this case, anyway—isn't a family name. It's a title. There's a government organization so secret it doesn't have a name. Only the monarch and his spymaster know about it. It's existed for two hundred years, and the head of it is always called Walsingham. Each time a new Walsingham is appointed, he sheds his real name so it can't be used against him magically. The organization fights magic that they believe to be a direct threat to the realm. It has carte blanche from the Crown to demand assistance—no questions asked—from the army, navy, or Mysterium.

"If Walsingham has been openly put in charge of the Mysterium, that's a bad sign. It brings together the two organizations that suppress magic, and not in a good way."

"And there's a new Walsingham now?" Lily asked.

"There is. I killed the last two. Self-defense, I assure you." I swallowed hard. "One of them was my brother."

Some of it Lily knew already, but I told the whole story of the winterwood box and the freeing of the rowankind, how Corwen and I met, how Philip betrayed us, and how I had another brother who was a Fae lord. Corwen came and sat next to me while I related the whole tale, his thigh warm and reassuring against mine, especially when I faltered over the account of Philip. I couldn't look anyone in the eye when I got to that part, so I didn't see their expressions, but no one commented. I believe they could see how hard it was for me to tell it all, yet I felt that by getting it out into the open I removed the last barriers between myself and the Deverells. They were my family now, as well as Corwen's.

"The Fae do exist, then?" Corwen's mother fanned herself, looking flushed.

"They do, though they prefer to keep separate from the world of men, and who can blame them?"

Corwen cleared his throat. "Except if the Mysterium tries to interfere with the rowankind in any way, I believe they might take radical action, and that wouldn't be good for anyone who got in their way."

"Corwen's right," I said. "They agreed that the rowankind would be free from interference of any kind, to stay in the world or cross through into Iaru as they wished. As long as the rowankind are allowed to live in peace and freedom, they've promised not to interfere. If those freedoms are curtailed, I don't know what might happen. The Fae have a literal way of regarding their promises."

"And the Fae are powerful?" Lily asked.

"More than you can imagine."

My belly gurgled impolitely.

"Breakfast." Corwen grinned at me and patted his stomach. Damn, his hearing was good.

Lily followed us both as we looked for what breakfast might be left. "I've been up since dawn," she said. "I need to go to the mill now."

Corwen sighed. "We didn't fall into our beds until dawn, Lily. Give us time to catch our breath before we spring back into action." He looked across at me. "How are you?"

"Apart from my heart still racing after facing Mr. Pomeroy, and admitting all my crimes to your family, surprisingly all right. You?"

He wriggled his shoulders. "The bruising has almost gone."

"All right, I get it," Lily said. "You two are heroes and I did nothing but stand by uselessly last night, yet I can be useful today—as long as I'm actually there. I'd get Mallinson to take me, but all of the stable hands are walking around in a daze."

"Go easy on them. They had a hard night, too," Corwen said.

"I can't believe anyone would damage the sluice deliberately," Lily said. "Imagine if the whole front of the dam had gone and water had washed away some of the cottages at Dike Side or ripped Kaye's water wheel off its mounting, or flooded the mill at Lower Putting."

"Pomeroy saw no damage down the valley," Corwen said.

"The servants are saying the same." Lily sat at the table with us and reached for a bread roll, shredding it with her fingers rather than eating it. "It could have been far worse."

This time the news had flown up the valley as fast as it usually traveled down, to our advantage for a change.

Corwen swirled the last of the coffee in his cup and downed it in one swallow. "All right, let's go. I'll take you to the mill, and then I shall find Mr. Thatcher."

"You won't do anything rash, will you? Should I come with you?"

"Will you be protecting him from me, or will I be protecting him from you?"

"Fair point."

Though the gale had abated, there was still a brisk breeze whipping stinging sleet into our faces. It slapped at me as we made our way to the stable yard. After her fall, Lily vowed not to ride sidesaddle again and had asked my advice on suitable undergarments for riding astride. Mrs. Deverell was scandalized by the idea of breeches, even worn under a dress. She couldn't prevent me from doing as I pleased, she said, but she was not going to have her nineteen-year-old daughter showing her legs in man's clothes. The idea of riding astride made her shudder—maybe she feared a maiden could lose her virginity to a saddle—but I backed up Lily when she said how dangerous a sidesaddle could be.

Lily glanced briefly at Speedwell's empty stall, and I thought I saw her blink back tears, but she acquainted herself with Brock, and though she said he had a common head, he had a kindly eye. He endeared himself to her by rubbing his nose against her arm and making a gentle whickering sound, at which Lily stroked his neck and pronounced herself pleased with him as a temporary mount. Brock, for his part, behaved like a perfect gentleman while Lily turned down Thomas' offer of a boost, pulled her skirt above her shins—modesty saved by her long boots—and mounted using her stirrup. The whole operation was possible because of

Brock's pony stature. Dancer being fully two hands taller than Brock, I gave in gracefully and allowed Corwen to grasp my bent knee and ankle, and boost me on board. I could mount by myself if I had to, but skirts hampered me.

We arrived at the mill to find only half the looms working. Mr. Topping had sent all the rowankind to the mill dam. The sleet had abated, and though there was still a touch of dampness in the air and the clouds were gray, I thought the day might be brightening a little.

"How goes it, Mr. Topping?" Lily asked, handing Brock over to one of the stable boys who had come running.

"Well, we can see the problem, now it's daylight, Miss Lily." Mr. Topping walked to the dam with us and stared glumly at the damaged breast-shot wheel and the ruined headrace, half of which had been washed away when the sluice was shattered.

"There's standing water in the fulling mill. We can't see if there's any damage to the stocks until that's pumped out. The level of the dam itself is a worry. We lost half the volume of water, and that's a concern. The storm should have topped up the levels, but now we have even less than before. It being April already means we're going into the spring and summer with precious little in reserve. If there's a dry spell, the water level might be too low to operate the wheel effectively, even presuming we can get a foundry to make repairs in a timely manner."

"I shall write to Atkinsons within the hour to order what's needed," Lily said. "Please have a rider deliver the letter. Now, as to the standing water, I've seen what your rowankind can do. Of course we can't pay for their magical help since paying anyone without a license for magical services is illegal, but there may be another way. If the water in the fulling mill were to magically empty itself into the tailrace and thus into the river, or even back into the dam, it might be that there would be some pieces of cloth revealed in there that would be perfectly usable if some enterprising fellows took them home and dried them out."

Mr. Topping gave a knowing smile. "I think I might find

you a few volunteers, men who will do it out of the goodness of their hearts, though the cloth won't go amiss."

"Mr. Topping," Corwen said. "We had a visit from Mr. Pomeroy this morning."

"Oh, aye. Mysterium man from Barnsley," Mr. Topping said. "He called here and asked a few questions."

"You didn't by any chance tell him the truth, did you?"

Mr. Topping gave Corwen a look that said he wasn't likely to do that. "I told him no more than he needed to hear. That the rowankind who work here had all banded together to save their livelihood."

"Did he ask about me?" I asked.

"I told him I thought you'd got too close to the edge and fallen into the dam. It looked to me like Mr. Corwen had to pull you out, but it was dark and I couldn't see much, you understand."

"I understand perfectly. Thank you, Mr. Topping."

"You're welcome, ma'am."

Corwen nudged my leg. "I think the mill is in safe hands between Lily and Mr. Topping's rowankind. Let's leave her to her new kingdom for a few hours and collect her in time for dinner. We'll go down the valley and ask after Thatcher."

"I believe he put up at the White Hart when he left here," Mr. Topping said. "That was certainly his intention, though I'd be surprised if he was still there, especially if he's responsible for the sluice gate."

Mr. Topping returned to supervising the cleanup. He was right. If I was Thatcher and I had taken a hammer to the sluice, I'd have been running for my life by now, heading for the nearest port or losing myself in a busy city where no one knew my name. Even so, that was no reason to ignore the possibility of finding him.

20

A Wedding

AS WE TURNED ON TO THE ROAD to Denby Dike Side, Corwen said, "I need a run."

I knew what kind of run he meant. "It's daylight, is it safe?"

"Safe enough if I stick to the wood. Do you mind?"

"Of course not."

I rode through the wood on one of the paths that wound between the trees and ran roughly parallel to the river, leading Timpani and carrying Corwen's clothes wrapped in a bundle. I kept seeing flashes of silver gray out of the corner of my eye and sometimes turned to catch sight of Corwen's wolf as he disappeared into the undergrowth. Twice he splashed through the river where it ran shallow over rocky steps and once he disappeared for fully thirty minutes before padding back and sitting in the path facing me. I pulled up.

"Ready for your clothes?"

He yipped and I dropped them to the ground between the two horses, providing some measure of shelter as he changed from wolf to naked man in an instant. He dragged his clothes and boots on quickly, shivering in the April afternoon.

"I quartered the ground to see if I could pick up Thatcher's trail," he said. "But the rain has washed it away. Let's head for Denby Dike Side and check at the White Hart. Also I'd like to ride by Kaye's Mill and see how they fared in the storm."

The wood filled the river valley from below Deverell's Mill all the way to the village of Denby Dike Side where Kaye's Mill straddled the river. There was a corn mill in the village, a baker, a grocer, two butchers, three public houses and two nonconformist chapels. Rows of narrow stone cottages clung to the steep valley sides, built into the hill.

Corwen pulled up Timpani. "Kaye's mill dam; does anything look strange to you?"

"Well, it's full, which is more than I can say for ours."

"It's not only full, but the level is considerably higher than usual. It's almost as if they had their own sluice gates set to catch the runoff as the extra water flooded down the valley."

"You think Kaye knew?"

"I don't know, but it's advantageous, isn't it?"

The White Hart stood on the corner of the junction where the road forked. A stable boy came out, and Corwen gave him a penny to hold the horses since we were only going to be a few minutes.

The interior of the inn was dim. The gray day outside seemed to have invaded here, too, and though a fire burned in the hearth, it was half-hearted.

"Spencely, isn't it?" Corwen addressed the landlord.

"It is, Mr. Deverell, sir. I'd heard you'd returned. What can I get you and the lady?"

I saw Corwen about to refuse a drink, but I was already chilled from the ride. Corwen never seemed to feel the cold, but I wasn't so hardy. "Sherry would be nice," I said, "and a few minutes by the fire."

"My best sherry coming up," Spencely said.

"And some information, if you please," Corwen said. "I understand Mr. Thatcher was here. Is he still?"

"He paid me for three nights in advance, but left yesterday."

"Did he by any chance say where he was going?"

"Hired a horse and paid for his bags to be carried to the Market Inn in Barnsley. Said something about catching the mail coach, but I don't know which direction he was traveling in."

I finished my sherry, feeling the warmth in my throat. Corwen thanked Spencely, and we left.

"Barnsley?" I said as we mounted our horses.

"There's no need for you to come with me," Corwen said. "It's going to be a long ride there and back, and you're already chilled."

"I'll come."

He didn't argue with me. We crossed the Dearne and rode up Miller Hill, joining the Barnsley road at Upper Denby. After yesterday's rain the rutted road was muddy. No paved turnpike, this road twisted and turned, uphill and down. In places it showed signs of having been mended, probably by the local farmers filling the worst holes with a jumble of stones. On lesser horses we'd have been forced to a slow pace to protect their legs and our necks, but Timpani and Dancer ate the miles between Denby and Cawthorne at a ground-eating canter. We gentled our pace only to pass a few rumbling wagons and the occasional pedestrian. We slowed to a trot through Cawthorne village itself and from there the road into Barnsley widened out and showed signs of having been surfaced.

It was late in the afternoon when we rode into the town. The Market Inn was not the most salubrious of establishments, and Corwen insisted I wait outside with the horses while he made enquiries. It was probably as well he did. Two rough-looking women stumbled out of the front door, much the worse for drink and holding each other up.

"What you lookin' at?" One of the women lurched toward me but tripped and fell into the gutter. The second woman began to heave her to her feet, but when Corwen emerged from the inn, dropped her again and sidled up to him. "You lookin' for a good time, mister?"

Corwen avoided her outstretched arm and swung himself on to Timpani. "Thank you, ladies, but I'm otherwise engaged."

A stream of invective followed us as we rode up Market Hill to the White Bear. Thatcher's goods had arrived at the Market Inn apparently, but the man himself had not, leaving the landlord wondering what to do.

"I doubt he'll find it much of a problem. Come next market day, Thatcher's remaining possessions will be out on a stall for as much as he can make out of them," Corwen said.

At the White Bear we were lucky to find the agent from the Post Office supervising the postal bags as he waited for the mail coach to arrive. The results of our inquiry didn't help much, however. Mr. Thatcher had taken the morning mail coach to London.

"We've lost him," Corwen said. "I'll see if Father's man of business can initiate a search for him, but in a city the size of London he could be anywhere."

"Or he could pass straight through the city and take ship for anywhere in the world," I said.

We rode home at a steadier pace, arriving tired and dispirited some two hours after dinner was over. We made do with leftover roast lamb, and then Corwen went to write to Mr. Wiggins, the Deverells' man of business in London. It was the best we could do. Thatcher was a loose end we might never be able to tie up. If he was the culprit, and neither Corwen nor I had much doubt about that, what was his motive? Had he been embezzling, somehow, but hiding his tracks well? Was it revenge for Corwen dismissing him? He might have lost his job, but Corwen had at least given him a generous severance payment in lieu of notice. That was more than he deserved.

The only small consolation was that he had fled and was unlikely to return to cause more mischief if he knew what was good for him.

⬧━━━⬧

Tuesday morning dawned fair for Winnie's funeral. The wind had died away, and the procession that escorted the

small coffin to the church in Denby was a somber affair.
Robin, clutching Poppy's hand, had said good-bye to his
sister before her pale form was covered, bravely trying not
to cry until Poppy knelt in front of him and told him tears
were quite proper under the circumstances. He howled
into Poppy's waist when the lid was nailed into place, and
she held him close. She'd spent all the day before stitching
him a simple jacket and trousers so he wouldn't attend the
funeral in rags, and Corwen had found him a length of
black silk for an arm band.

No one had known Winnie—she'd come and gone so
quickly that there hadn't been time to form an opinion of
her—but everyone felt sorry for Robin, so Winnie didn't
lack for mourners. Corwen and I walked behind Robin and
Poppy. Lily drove her mother in the gig with a black blanket over Brock's pied rump. Thomas and John followed at
a respectful distance with the coach to bring us all home
again. Mr. Deverell and Yeardley watched from the front
door, bareheaded, as we set off. At the church, Mr. Topping
and those mill hands not needed at the looms stood to pay
their respects to the little girl.

It was a short service, but Reverend Donovan said all
the right things as we laid Winnie to rest decently. We sent
Poppy and Robin home in the gig with Thomas while John
settled Mrs. Deverell in the coach with a blanket around
her knees.

Mr. Topping waved to attract our attention, so we joined
him by the lych-gate.

"Archie the Packman brought news from over the bor-
der in Cheshire."

"Yes?" Corwen said.

"Styal Mill has closed its pumping engine, and there's a
team of rowankind working round the clock to raise water
from the millwheel's tailrace to its headrace, using the
same water over and over and over again. And . . . they're
being paid for it. The Mysterium is turning a blind eye, or
at least, they've brought no charges yet."

"Interesting. Thank you."

"Do you think it means we might be in the clear to use

our magic?" Mr. Topping said. "It seems to me that water power with rowankind help might be very efficient."

"Would you not find it tiring, Mr. Topping?" I asked. "Raising the same water time and time again, I mean." I'd mostly worked with wind and weather; I'd never tried to raise a volume of water against gravity for an extended period.

"Lord love, you. No, ma'am. Not everyone has the same skill in the same way, but working water is easy for most of us. I'd be more worried about the Mysterium." He looked at Corwen. "Is it time for changes in the law, sir?"

"It's beyond time, Mr. Topping, but sadly I fear that when changes come, they'll not be for the better."

◆━━◆

Corwen and I went to church on Thursday morning to make our vows.

I wore my best cream dress and traveled in the coach accompanied by Lily, my bridesmaiden, and my soon-to-be new mama and papa. Yeardley had carefully lifted Mr. Deverell in, and securely wrapped him in blankets. Now he followed closely in the gig with Poppy. They had Robin squashed between them looking more cheerful than I'd seen him since the funeral. Corwen rode separately with Thomas who had agreed to be his groomsman since Freddie had not responded to Corwen's letter.

My last wedding had been a riotous affair. Will and I were attended by our crew. It was before we rescued Mr. Rafiq from the slaver and before Hookey deserted Gentleman Jim to join us, so Will's groomsman had been Mr. Sharpner, and instead of a bridesmaiden I had Nick Padder, who was then only twelve years old, as a page boy. Afterward, we retired to the inn across the road for a wedding breakfast which consisted, mainly, of a large amount of rum for the men and spiced wine for me.

This time, Corwen and I made our vows more quietly before family and servants, Corwen's mother having acceded to our request not to invite the whole neighborhood.

Standing in front of the altar with this man, I reflected

on how lucky I was to have found not one love in my life, but two. I'd loved Will with all my heart and yet, here was Corwen and I loved him, too. Was my second love any different from my first? I thought it was. Different but no less sincere. Loving Corwen didn't take away the love I'd had for Will, and my memory of Will didn't stand between me and Corwen.

I felt an echo of a breath on the nape of my neck. *Be happy,* Will's ghost told me. I thought he'd moved on. Maybe it was only my imagination.

When we'd exchanged rings, and Reverend Donovan had finally pronounced us man and wife, Corwen and I surfaced from our first married kiss and turned to find, sitting in the back pew of the church, David, Annie, Larien, Aunt Rosie, Leo, and Rosie's daughter, Margann. Standing behind them, could it be? Yes! I blinked away a sudden rush of tears. Hookey Garrity, Mr. Sharpner, Mr. Rafiq, Nick Padder, Lazy Billy, Crayfish Jake, Windward, and the Greek. Only Hartington was missing, but I guessed the Lady was keeping him too busy to attend weddings.

Corwen and I almost sprinted down the aisle to greet everyone. Now my family was here, too, actual blood relatives in the case of David, Aunt Rosie, and Margann, and adopted family from the crew of the *Heart of Oak.* All of a sudden we were laughing together and hugging. Even Larien, a Fae lord not endowed with much of a sense of humor, had thawed his usual cool demeanor. I wondered how Corwen's parents, now truly my mama and papa, would take to these visitors, evidence of my less-than-ladylike past. Mama surprised me once again. She was politeness itself, even to the Greek, whose grasp of English consisted largely of profanities. She invited everyone to share the wedding breakfast. I wondered if the food would stretch to an extra fourteen people, but I needn't have feared. When we arrived at Denby Hall a huge spread was laid out. Among the delicacies on the table I recognized some that could only have come from the Fae.

How thoughtful.

Or did they want something?

There were far too many of us to sit at formal table so a buffet board had been set out. Aunt Rosie, my mother's twin sister, and much more understanding of me and my magic than my mother had ever been, hugged me close and took me to one side.

"You're not going to give me that wedding talk for new brides, are you?" I asked her.

She patted her graying hair. "My dear, if you don't know what goes where by now there's no hope for you at all." She laughed. "No, I wanted to ask if you have my note-books with you."

"I do. Do you want them back?"

"No, I wanted to tell you to read them thoroughly. Have you tried weather-working yet?"

I hesitated. "I tried after—you know—and couldn't raise the lightest of breezes."

"And have you tried since?"

"Not with weather, but once, with water." I told her about the mill dam.

"Some things are only truly lost if you believe they are. I have a theory—it's like a pendulum. You pulled the magic from all of us Sumners with one huge swing of the pendulum, but it's still swinging back and forth, back and forth, a little less each time. Slowly it will find a resting point. There may be times when the magic is yours again, and times when it isn't. Stronger and weaker. Stronger and weaker. Not until the pendulum finally comes to rest will we know what's left. Read the notebooks, Ross. Learn. You may need to know." She gave me a hug and looked around her at the fine surroundings. "This is a bit more elegant than my cottage. Who'd have thought that your silverwolf was gentry? Someone said there was going to be dancing later. I hope so. I can still step lively. In the meantime, I must find Leo so we can pay our respects to your new father-in-law."

The crew of the *Heart* may not have had the best table manners I've ever seen, but they knew how to appreciate food. Mr. Rafiq's fine manners were the exception, and my new mama seemed to take a shine to the tall, cultured black man. Mr. Rafiq, for his part, was as comfortable in polite society as he was on the deck of a ship, yet he wasn't coy about his origins. I overheard him telling her about his background as a slave, being educated for high office in the household of some Eastern potentate, but escaping before he was old enough to be turned into a eunuch. She looked a little pale at that, but the rest of his adventures certainly entertained her through the meal and afterward, too, when we all moved into the best parlor which overlooked the vista down to the lake.

While Corwen introduced his father to one after the other of my relatives and friends, I sought out Hookey. He took my hand and gave me a big kiss on the cheek. He looked in fine form with his new steel hook and a smart velvet frock coat, cut with a swing. It may have been a little behind the fashion, but it suited him. Since he'd shaved off his bushy beard, he presented a dashing figure, every inch a sea captain, though more than a little piratical. "Mr. Rafiq has some papers for you." He raised one eyebrow and grinned. "Our last voyage was very successful. We took one of Boney's supply ships off Calais, and brought her to London for the prize money. We're in Wapping. Usual berth."

I took it that the *Heart* was anchored off Wapping Old Stairs, close to the Town of Ramsgate public house, which served good rump steak—always Hookey's favorite when he was ashore.

"We've got another reason to be in London," Hookey said. "We're looking to take on a weather witch. We miss your talents. Your weather-working gave us a fine edge and kept us out of trouble. Sure you don't fancy a few more trips on the briny?"

"I barely own any weather-working, now, Hookey." I didn't tell him about Aunt Rosie's theory or that I'd worked water at the mill. That might have been a lucky result of the pendulum swing. "All my powers went to the rowankind."

"Aye, and those folks are not suited to the sea at all. Pity."

It was true the rowankind were so utterly seasick that

they were likely to die on a long sea voyage. It was one of the reasons why rowankind, as far as I knew, were not common outside of Britain.

"If you're looking for a licensed, legitimate weather witch, you might try the Mysterium offices," I said. "In fact, if you do, please listen out for the name Walsingham."

Hookey cursed, luckily not loudly enough for my new mama to hear. "I thought you'd killed that godless bastard," he said.

"Yes, but there's another one, and this one has been put in charge of the Mysterium."

"If I hear anything, I'll get Mr. Rafiq to write you a letter."

Hookey wasn't illiterate, but Mr. Rafiq wrote an elegant hand and tended to be the ship's official scribe.

"We're coming to London, Hookey. We have business on behalf of the mill, and Corwen needs to find his brother, Freddie, who's shirking his obligations."

"Brothers!" Hookey huffed out a breath. "I'd say you were better off without 'em. Look at me, I never had brothers, or if I did, I never knowed 'em." Hookey had grown up on the streets and had thrown himself into the arms of a press gang at the age of twelve, serving six years in His Majesty's Navy until they turned him off with a few shillings after losing his hand. "Still, you didn't do so bad with young Davey, there." He jerked his head toward my little brother, who had sailed on the *Heart* for a short while before we discovered he was Fae. "He's done well for himself."

I still wondered how David was adapting to living with the Fae when he'd grown up believing himself a rowankind bondservant—so many changes in such a short lifetime— but outwardly he seemed to have settled. Larien had finally become his real father, in practice, not merely by blood.

Today David looked elegant and there was nothing left of the rowankind skin-tone and grain that he'd had for the first fourteen years of his life, a glamour conferred on him by his hidden Fae heritage, I supposed. In this light he looked wholly Fae, which is to say, like a very elegant human. He didn't have the gawkiness of most fifteen-year-old boys. The last few months in his new life had built his confidence and given him the grace of a dancer. He wore a form-fitting dark suit and silk waistcoat with his neck cloth tied neatly if not ostentatiously. I'd never yet seen a Fae look shabby or unkempt. It was as if regular dirt wouldn't dare stick to them.

"How did you even know about the wedding?" I asked David when I managed a few minutes alone with my brother. "Not that I'm not pleased to see you. And I suppose I have you to thank for bringing Hookey and the crew?"

"Aunt Rosie came and told us. Did you know she keeps an eye on us all by scrying? I know how much the crew means to you. I *searched* and knew the *Heart* was in London, so Annie and I paid the ship a visit and brought your friends to Richmond Park to meet my father. He guided them through Iaru. Margann brought Aunt Rosie and Leo. They're all looking well, aren't they?"

"Yes, very. Aunt Rosie and Leo, too." Aunt Rosie had regained her former plumpness after her hardships, and white-haired Leo, a blacksmith by trade, looked strong and sprightly for his fifty-some years. "Marriage suits them. I hope they're making up for lost time."

"As it will surely suit you." David hugged me. "I am truly glad to be at your wedding, Ross, but I fear my father may have had an ulterior motive for attending."

I sighed. Somehow I wasn't surprised. "Larien seems to think we're at his beck and call, as does the Lady of the Forests."

"The kelpie hunt, you mean?"

"If we hadn't been called away to Yorkshire, I think she might have had a list of strange occurrences and eruptions of magic for us to deal with. As it is, I'm sure Hartington is doing his best."

"It's true that wild magic is seeping into the land."

"Can't the Fae do something about that?"

"My father might. He's spent time in the human world

and has a little more understanding of it, but the Fae Council is reluctant to interfere."

"So what does Larien want of us? I thought we'd discharged our obligations to the Fae when we freed the rowankind."

"I'll let him tell you himself."

21

London

DAVID LED ME OVER TO LARIEN, who'd managed to blend in with all the humans. Those who remember the existence of the Fae speak of them in hushed tones as the Shining Ones for a good reason, but today Larien simply looked like an extremely handsome and imposing man in the prime of life. Anyone meeting him for the first time would assume he was no more than thirty-five, but I knew for a fact he was over two hundred and fifty years old. How much over I might never find out.

"Lord Larien, how kind of you to bring my family."

"Mrs. Deverell." He made a leg as politely as any human gentleman, and I bobbed a curtsey back.

"So formal," I said, knowing that if Larien had been wearing his usual Fae persona everyone in the room would have been bowing so deeply their foreheads would have grazed the floor. "David tells me you want something. Let's walk out in the garden. Should I call Corwen?"

Larien inclined his head. "I believe he's already on his way to join us."

I saw Corwen had handed his father over to Yeardley. Without appearing rude to anyone, my new husband accepted congratulations and felicitations as he made his way through the room to join us on the terrace. Down toward the lake I saw Poppy and Margann playing catch with Robin. Not wishing to disturb them, we turned toward the gardens at the side of the house.

"Your family is delightful," Larien told Corwen. "I hadn't realized your sister was a shapechanger, too. Such a pretty girl."

"Don't get any ideas about Lily," Corwen said. "She's under my protection." The Fae had a habit of winning away pretty humans into Iaru to bear their children, hence Rosie's long separation from Leo, and Rosie's daughter, Margann, being Fae.

Larien's expression asked what could one wolf shapechanger do against a Fae lord, but he acquiesced politely. "Of course, and therefore she's under my protection, too."

"Thank you. Besides, Lily has a mind of her own. She aims to be an industrialist. She's more interested in machines than magic."

"Machines are bringing decay to Iaru," Larien said.

"We noticed the blight around Sheffield. Is it serious?"

"We thought it was contained, but it's spreading. Birmingham is badly affected, and London, of course, but now there are individual spots where steam engines are being installed. The Fae want none of it. We can't even enter your industrialized cities anymore without protective magic."

"David went to London to bring the *Heart*'s crew," I pointed out.

"Yes, he seems almost immune so far. Probably because he grew up in Plymouth."

"Is that what you wanted to talk to us about?" I asked. "Because we can't do anything about the progress of the machines."

He sighed. "I know. It may be that we have to retreat farther into Iaru. We have many options, but it's the rowankind's position in your world that concerns me. We promised they could make their own decisions once they were free, that they need not come to Iaru to serve us."

That had been one of my stipulations when I agreed to free the rowankind from the spell my ancestor had used to draw their power from them.

"But it has come to our attention that your government intends to enslave them again."

"Enslave them?"

He might not be wrong. Things were changing. If the rowankind were forced into registering their magical abilities with the Mysterium, they'd be subject to restrictions and control. I could see how that would look like slavery to the Fae.

I said as much.

"I don't see what we can do about it," Corwen said.

"You can speak to your king," Larien said.

"It doesn't work like that." Corwen held his hands wide. "Even if we could get close to the king, how could we possibly make him listen? And presuming he does, he's mad. Why would his ministers in Parliament take any notice of him?"

"Because they must."

"Larien, even if your High Council has no knowledge of British politics, you lived in our world once. You know it's not as easy as that."

"Easier for you than for us, and better for your people. If we have to treat with humans, we are not likely to be gentle. There are those on the council who would choose a show of strength and an ultimatum. My brother Dantin, for example . . ."

I knew how Dantin regarded humans. He wouldn't hesitate to squash them like insects beneath his boot, and he had the power to do it.

"Is Dantin the only one?"

Larien's expression told me he was not. "There are those," he said, "who would reclaim the power we had over humans in the elder times."

"But you wouldn't?" Corwen asked.

Larien shrugged slightly, a very human gesture. "As you say, I've lived among humans, albeit briefly. I believe they would make troublesome subjects. I have no desire to spend the next two centuries quelling annoying rebellions or providing for those who proved incapable of providing for themselves."

"So what would you have us do?" I asked.

"Find a way. Open the door to a gentler negotiation."

"I wouldn't know where to start," I said.

"I might," Corwen said. "I make no promises, but Freddie has some good contacts courtesy of his Oxford education. He might have paid little attention to his studies, but some of his fellow students were the sons of lords."

Larien inclined his head. "Then go and seek your brother."

"How long have we got?" I asked.

"Time is flexible in Iaru," Larien said, "but should something happen to disadvantage the rowankind, I can promise you that Dantin's voice will not be the only one calling for action."

"You've set us a difficult task."

"You have proved equal to difficult tasks in the past."

"So the reward for succeeding is being given a more difficult task."

"Correct."

I wondered if the Fae understood the concept of irony.

◆————◆

Larien offered to transport us through Iaru to Richmond Park, but we'd arranged for places on the overnight mail coach and would have had a lot of explaining to do if we'd simply disappeared into the nearest patch of woodland with the Fae.

With much amusement, Larien wished us well of sixteen uncomfortable hours in a swaying, bouncing coach and bade us farewell, taking our guests with him.

Poppy met me wide-eyed at my bedroom door. "The young lady, Margann, said it was all a wedding gift and not to worry, they would all look after themselves. I think she meant they were all like your cream dress and couldn't be got dirty if you rolled in a midden in them."

I looked past Poppy to see half a dozen fashionable dresses, a riding habit, a traveling cloak, a redingote, three spencers, and two pelisses of different lengths. There were a couple of bonnets and a top hat for riding.

"She said if the fashions changed, they'd remake themselves. Can you believe it? There's even a new pair of boots and a set of gentleman's clothes in your size, which is lucky because I doubt I shall ever be able to get your old breeches truly clean again."

I stared at the bounty.

"Oh, and she said they'd fit in here." Poppy held a new valise.

"Well, then, we'd better pack."

She was correct. Everything fitted into the one bag, even the top hat which would normally have needed a bag to itself. I pushed Aunt Rosie's notebooks in with the clothes and added my pistols.

"Are you sure you won't let me come along? How will you manage without me to do your hair?"

"I can manage my hair, Poppy, and the clothes will look after themselves. You heard what Margann said. Besides . . ." I inclined my head toward her belly. "You don't know when your baby's due. It could be soon by the look of you, and I don't think sixteen hours in a mail coach would be good. You'll be all right here with Mrs. Deverell, and besides, Robin needs you."

"I suppose so."

"We'll be back soon."

"Ma'am, while you're away . . ."

"Yes?"

"Would you have any objection to me walking out with Mr. Yeardley?"

"Good heavens, of course not. Walk out with whomever you please, as long as he's someone you trust."

"Mr. Yeardley is trustworthy, don't you think?"

"From what I've seen of him, he's very trustworthy." I smiled. "I like him. Have you taken a shine to him?"

"I think I have. And him to me, despite this." She patted her belly. "He likes Robin, too."

I gave her a hug. "Take every chance for happiness that comes your way, Poppy. You deserve it."

We bade farewell to the Deverells at dusk. John drove us to Barnsley in the coach. It was the first time we'd had a moment alone since Corwen had slipped the wedding band on my finger, my old ring now being on the third finger of my right hand.

"Come here, Mrs. Deverell." Corwen held out one arm, and I leaned into him.

"It's not going to be much of a wedding night," I said. "This may be the only privacy we get between here and London. Even so . . ." I was acutely aware that only the thin shell of the coach separated us from our coachman.

"I gave John half a guinea not to disturb us on the journey." Corwen's eyes crinkled with mischief.

"Half a guinea? You must want your privacy very badly indeed. Perhaps I should ride on the box with John." I rolled away from him and he grabbed my shoulders and drew me down, covering my mouth with his own. I kissed him back hard. He pulled my lace fichu away from my throat and slipped his hand inside the low-cut neck of my dress. His lips traced a warm line to kiss what was exposed, and tease what wasn't.

I wriggled around to face him, and he pulled up the folds of my dress, his hands warm against my stockings and hot against my bare thigh.

He laughed with delight. "No pantalettes!"

"Well, it is our wedding night. John's done well out of us."

"You didn't . . ."

I grinned. "Half a guinea."

"We'd better make it worthwhile, or I shall ask him for some change."

I let the curtains drop across the carriage windows, then turned and straddled him. "I was thinking the same."

An hour later we pulled into the yard of the White Bear in Barnsley, our clothing rearranged and the Fae fabrics already proving their worth. Maybe my hair was a little mussed and my cheeks a little more pink than usual, but our clothes were still immaculate.

"Thank you, John," I said as he helped me from the coach.

"You're welcome, Mrs. Deverell, ma'am," he said with a perfectly straight face.

"Thank you, John," Corwen said as he took our two small valises from the coachman.

"You're welcome, Mr. Deverell. Have a safe journey, sir."

"I'll bet he's laughing all the way home," I whispered to Corwen as he handed me into the mail coach.

"I don't care a fig!"

◆――――◆

It was barely seven months since my last visit to the capital. Then I had been totally focused on rescuing my brother Philip from Walsingham, and I'd barely moved from the river, confining myself to the area between Wapping and Vauxhall. There were some things I would rather forget and others that would haunt my memory forever: the weirdness of Vauxhall Gardens all closed up out of season; Walsingham's hellhounds; shooting the torrent beneath London Bridge in a rowboat.

Now, as we approached the Strand in the mail coach, my backside was numb from nearly twenty hours of jolting in the badly sprung vehicle. It should only have taken sixteen, but one of our horses had gone lame and we'd had to wait while the postilion led it back and fetched a sound one. We pulled up with a clatter, four hours late, and London assailed all my senses—the clamor of street sounds in my ears, the stink of the gutters in my nose, and all the hustle and bustle in my eyes.

It was dusk already as we descended from the coach into a damp smog smelling of acrid coal smoke. Oil lamps lit the streets, each one acquiring a misty halo and casting its light only as far as the mouths of narrow alleyways. The street was awash with people, the gentry rubbing coattails with all classes and trades. Shops glowed like palaces, still doing business at this hour behind large bow-fronted windows composed of many small panes of glass. Adding to the general hubbub, coaches, wagons, and a couple of smart phaetons competed for the narrow space between a brewer's dray and a stack of crates. The drayman cursed the phaeton creatively, but to no effect.

The falling sun barely touched the tumble of roofs above our heads, and the sucking mud and horse muck in the street threatened to splatter us to the knees. Print shops, book stalls, coffee houses, hawkers and harlots, watchmen and the occasional drunk all grabbed my attention in quick succession until I felt that alcohol had nothing to do with inebriation. I could easily get bosky on the city itself.

"Twelve pence a peck of oysters," came the cry from an oyster seller, a man remarkable for his pockmarked face and hare lip.

"Buy my fat chickens!" A portly man swung past us with a pole over his shoulder and a basket dangling from each end of it, filled with live birds, all squawk and panic.

"Four for sixpence, mackerel." An old woman with fish tied around her waist by their tails, their dead eyes glazed, cleared her own path by the stench surrounding her. I stepped away quickly.

"Father's man of business is expecting us." Corwen took my elbow. "He has chambers on Gray's Inn Lane. It's not too far to walk, and my bones could do with a little relief."

"You, too?" I smiled ruefully. "I may never want to sit down again. I'm glad we didn't bring Poppy. All that jolting might have shaken the baby loose. I think I'd make a poor midwife. God, that cleric stank of rubbing liniment. I don't think I'll ever get the memory of it out of my nose."

"His wife—no I'm not going to say."

Corwen's wolf nose was a lot more sensitive than mine.

"Perhaps we should have taken Larien's offer."

"Maybe, but leaving magic behind us for a while is no bad thing. Let's start as we mean to go on and not attract attention."

Arm in arm we walked, or rather pushed our way through crowds. Corwen knew where he was going, so I followed his lead, trying not to step on anyone's heels.

The row of four-story houses, most now businesses, either shops or public houses, looked as though it had been standing since Good Queen Bess ruled England. Each floor cantilevered crazily outward from the floor below it. A brass plate proclaiming the offices of Foster and Wiggins told us we'd arrived, and Mr. Wiggins was, indeed, expecting us. A young clerk led us up a twisted staircase, no one step of which aligned sensibly with its neighbor. Mr. Wiggins' chamber on the first floor was brown and smelled of pipe tobacco. Wood-paneled walls supported bookcases almost black with age, while the ceiling, which might once have been lime-washed, was yellowed by years of tobacco smoke. The room was made cozy by a cheerful fire, and a sooty kettle simmered its welcome on an iron trivet. Mr. Wiggins was a man whose features were too large for his face. As if to make room, they kept on the move constantly. His eyebrow movements punctuated every sentence and his mouth opened twice as far as was necessary to enunciate words. Altogether, it made him appear very lively even though his body movements were economical.

He was bald on top, but he didn't cover his head with a wig. Rather, he cut his hair short and brushed it upward.

"Mr. Deverell, good to make your acquaintance again. How long has it been?"

"I was last here with my father and my brother seven years ago."

"Goodness, is it so long? It seems like yesterday. And this must be Mrs. Deverell."

I held out my hand. "Pleased to meet you, Mr. Wiggins."

"My felicitations to the both of you. Please sit and have some tea."

I managed to sit without wincing, and noticed Corwen did the same. Mr. Wiggins handed each of us a china cup and saucer. "It's my own blend, made for me with oil of Seville oranges. How do you like it?"

"Very fragrant." I sniffed at the infusion, offered without milk, which suited me well.

"You'll be tired, I'm sure. Sleeping on a coach is no easy thing. I've done as you asked and rented a small house for you. It's in Wimpole Street, not the best address, but by no means the worst if you wish to enjoy the season."

I assured him the season wasn't the reason for our visit, and we wouldn't be seeking admission to Almack's or even a box at the theater. The Ton held no interest for either of us.

"Has my brother been to see you?" Corwen asked.

"Mr. Frederick Deverell called several months ago to establish a line of credit drawn on family funds."

Corwen groaned. "How much is his debt?"

"Well, that's just it. He drew twenty guineas on first arrival and after that never drew against it again."

"Did he give you an address?"

"Yes, he has bachelor's rooms in Duke Street."

"That's the same address as he gave us, but he's not answered letters. You've heard nothing else?"

Mr. Wiggins shook his head. "Nothing at all."

"And the other matters?"

"I have several people looking, but so far they have found no trace of your Mr. Thatcher, I'm afraid. It's a big city and it's easy for someone to lose themselves if they wish to, even supposing he stayed here."

"And the cloth for the army?"

"That may take some time to plumb the depths, but I am hopeful. The matter of supply is often about making the right contacts and greasing the right palms. I'm working on finding out who is the new agent for the 86th Regiment of Foot. Colonel Carter is in charge, but it's usually the agent who deals with practical matters. The 86th only boasts one battalion, nominally a thousand men, though rumor has it they are under strength since their return from India. My sources tell me they are recruiting, and new recruits need new coats. The agent will have contracted with one or maybe more than one tailor to make the uniforms, and it's the master tailors themselves who source the cloth."

"Let me know as soon as you discover anything."

"Of course. Let my clerk call you a carriage to take you to Wimpole Street. I've engaged staff on your behalf, a reliable couple called Pirt who recently worked for Lady Osterley until she returned to the country. They come highly recommended. They're expecting you. I told them to prepare dinner."

I yawned, prompted by the fire and the tea. "Food be damned. I simply want a bed that isn't rattling beneath me."

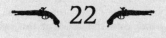 22

Freddie

THE HOUSE IN WIMPOLE STREET Mr. Wiggins had found for us was a typical stucco-fronted town house, narrow but tall, with a front door and two windows at street level and a servants' area below in the basement accessed by steps off the street leading to a yard area protected by spiked iron railings. The front door, up half a dozen steps, had a small portico flanked by two classical columns. Corwen rat-tatted on the knocker.

"Mr. and Mrs. Deverell?" A short, wiry man of middle age and neat appearance answered the door.

"Mr. Pirt." Corwen stepped into the entrance hall as the manservant stepped back. Mrs. Pirt, tall and muscular, of copious girth and a florid complexion that spoke of too much time in front of a hot kitchen stove, hovered at the far end of the hall with a maid of all work, introduced as Ruth. Ruth looked to be about eighteen and had a pockmarked but otherwise pretty face and flyaway, straw-colored hair escaping from her lace cap.

Mr. Wiggins had described the Pirts as respectable and reliable, and so they appeared.

"Would you like to see around the house first, or would you like some supper?" Mrs. Pirt asked. "Mr. Wiggins said you'd likely be hungry, but with not knowing what time you were arriving I've prepared cold ham. There are potatoes in their jackets sitting in the oven, and a pot of pea soup."

"That sounds like the very thing, Mrs. Pirt," Corwen said. "We've been bouncing around in a mail coach for the best part of a day, and the food at the last coaching inn wasn't very sustaining."

"Though I would like to see the house," I added. "Perhaps we can have a quick look around while you're finishing off in the kitchen. Let's keep it simple. Food and then sleep. We'll discuss the finer points of the household tomorrow."

"As you like, ma'am." She nodded to her husband. "Pirt can show you around."

"That's all right," Corwen said. "I doubt we can get lost."

"Would you prefer to take supper in the dining room upstairs, or the morning room?" She indicated a door.

The entrance hallway ran the full length of the house and incorporated a stair. There were two main rooms on the ground floor. I opened the first door and stuck my head in to discover a comfortable morning room, or maybe an all-purpose parlor, not large but with two tall sashed windows, shuttered against the darkness. The walls were hung with paper printed in a trellis pattern, neat but not too showy. The furnishings, chairs and a sofa with a small table, were not new, but they'd been fashionable in their day and were still tidy. A fire burned in the grate set into an arched cast-iron surround.

"We'll eat in here, Mrs. Pirt," I said. "It looks very welcoming."

Corwen, in the meantime, had taken an oil lamp and was checking the second door which opened into a smaller room, done out as a study with mahogany wainscoting which matched the ornate desk and breakfront bookcase. It bore the marks of a man's room, but peeking over his shoulder I decided it was one I could happily spend some time in.

"Shall I take your bags up?" Pirt asked, eyeing our small valises, no doubt wondering when our luggage would arrive.

"If you don't have your own maid, would you like Ruth to unpack for you?" Mrs. Pirt asked.

I wondered how we would explain the Fae bags. "No, it's all right."

"There are two rooms prepared," she said.

"One will do, thank you."

"Of course."

I smiled at her expression. "We were married yesterday, Mrs. Pirt."

"Oh!" That expression held a world of understanding. "I'll bring your supper in ten minutes."

"Thank you."

The oil lamp threw shadows into corners, but it was enough for us to get an idea of what the house was like, so I didn't brighten it with magic. We could take a closer look in daylight. At the front of the house on the first floor was an elegant drawing room with three sashed windows looking out onto the street. A fire flickered in the grate, but the room wasn't exactly warm. The furniture here was more fashionable and less practical. It almost looked fragile compared to the pieces in the morning room below.

At the rear of the house was a dining room, wainscoted and painted green. The table in the dining room was a relic of a bygone age, heavy dark oak with monstrously thick turned legs. It might have been new when Oliver Cromwell was a lad, and it had seen a lot of service, but since we didn't intend to entertain visitors here, it was perfectly adequate.

The main bedrooms were on the next floor up, one as large as the drawing room and occupying the whole front of the house. Corwen placed our valises on the large blanket box at the foot of the bed and bounced on the feather mattress. "This will do. I'm almost tempted to skip food." He raised one eyebrow.

I leaned over and kissed him.

"I'm not used to having staff. Let's not antagonize them

on the first day. Besides, I'm starving, and food sounds better than sex to me right now."

He sighed theatrically.

I kissed him again. "After supper, I may change my mind."

We continued our exploration. Three smaller bedrooms occupied the top floor, and above them there were attic rooms for servants, one of them belonging to Ruth. The Pirts would have rooms in the basement, probably a bedroom and a little parlor, but that was their domain and, unless invited, we wouldn't venture to intrude.

We arrived in the morning room as Mrs. Pirt delivered a tureen of soup.

Hot pea soup, fresh bread, cold ham, and hot potatoes with butter dripping down the skins tasted like a meal fit for a lord. The Pirts had thought of everything, and had even spent threepence on that day's copy of the Times. I scanned the Foreign Intelligence column which dwelled on the action and capture of the Spanish Xebeque frigate, *El Gamo*, by the much smaller 14 gun *HMS Speedy* under the command of Thomas, Lord Cochrane. *Speedy* had a crew of only fifty-four men, while *El Gamo* carried three hundred and nineteen. I smiled at the report and made a mental note to warn Hookey never to engage the *Speedy* with Cochrane on board.

Then I noticed a smaller article. There was now a regular front page column headed *Mysterium Notes*. The article announced the reopening of a Mysterium office in Bideford, following the unfortunate fire which destroyed the old office. There was no mention of the riot. The office had been opened by the new head of the Mysterium, a Mr. Walsingham. A chill shivered down my spine as I read an extract from the speech he'd given:

"The good people of Bideford, and indeed the whole of our blessed country, may rest easy in the knowledge that the number of officers of the Mysterium has been doubled in order to suppress outbreaks of unlicensed magic. We will deal with miscreants swiftly and harshly for the benefit of all. To this end, I give you my personal pledge."

I passed it over to Corwen who read it in silence.

"This new Walsingham sounds as though he's throwing himself into the job wholeheartedly."

I shuddered. "I wonder if he's completely new or whether he was trained by the old Walsingham."

"I don't know, but it seems odd that even though he's now head of the Mysterium and therefore much more visible, and presumably much more accountable than the secret Walsingham ever was, he's adopted the name and presumably left his own identity behind."

"When was the opening of the new Bideford office?"

"The seventh of April."

"So he could be back in London by now."

Corwen turned the page. "It's likely, but London's a big place. The Mysterium can't watch it all. Oh, hang on . . ." He frowned as he read. "There's an announcement, a series of public meetings to educate the populace in the ways in which a person performing magic illegally may be recognized."

"What? Let me see."

I grabbed the newspaper from him and looked at where he was pointing. "The first one is two days from now at the West Street Chapel near Seven Dials at the hour of six. Corwen, we should go."

"Are you mad?"

"We might learn something."

"And we might walk into a Mysterium trap, even presuming we could get in and out of Seven Dials without getting our throats cut and our purses plucked. It's no place for a lady."

I looked at him and raised one eyebrow.

"You know what I mean."

"But wouldn't it help to know which parts of the city they're watching?"

Corwen didn't exactly say no, so I took it as a yes.

"Let's worry about that later, Mrs. Deverell." He put his hand over mine. "May I remind you this is our proper wedding night and we did talk about after-supper activities."

"If you can get me upstairs and into bed before I'm fast

asleep, we might possibly have a wedding night. I make no promises." I grinned at him.

He laughed and picked me up bodily. "That's a challenge I'm not going to fail."

"Good." I kissed him.

<hr/>

We did have a wedding night after all, and so both Corwen and I were slow to wake on Saturday morning. Someone had been in and lit the bedroom fire while we slept, and the room was warm. There was a jug of hot water outside our bedroom door and I wondered how many times Ruth had had to replace the cooling jug with a fresh one.

We headed downstairs. The morning room was light and airy, the window shutters open wide. Mrs. Pirt appeared as if by magic asking what she could bring us for breakfast. I'd been used to hot chocolate and a bread roll at Denby Hall, but my old craving for strong coffee reasserted itself. Corwen requested eggs and ham, which sounded good to me.

Freddie's address in Duke Street was barely half a mile away, so by eleven we were on our way, hoping to catch him before he breakfasted, since young gentlemen of leisure were likely to be roistering into the wee small hours of the night and therefore not presenting their face to the world before noon. The streets had dried considerably since our arrival yesterday. What had been mud was now dried mud, rapidly turning itself into dust between the granite sets of the paving. We walked briskly along Wimpole Street, turned right on Wigmore Street, and threaded our way between pedestrians of all classes from parties of well-dressed gentlefolk to tradesmen going about their business. We crossed the road to avoid gangs of builders, stonemasons, carpenters, and laborers working on a terrace of half-finished houses to the inevitable tune of hammering, sawing, and banging. Following Pirt's sound directions, we found Duke Street on the left.

There were several establishments where young, single gentlemen had sets of rooms. We located Freddie's address easily. By the quality of the building, it appeared he'd not stinted on his accommodation. At this time in the morning the place was predictably lacking in activity except for one gentleman, who looked slightly hungover, departing from the front door as we arrived.

"We're looking for Freddie Deverell," Corwen said.

The departee looked puzzled for a moment and then tried a cautious smile, wincing slightly. "You'll have to excuse me. Haven't been here long myself. There's a chap who keeps himself to himself on the first floor. Never see him about much, though. Come to think of it, haven't seen him for weeks. Up there. Help yourself. If I have to be out and about at this frightful time of a morning, don't see why everyone else shouldn't be disturbed, too. Good day to you, sir, ma'am."

He inclined his head and was gone, having invited us into the hallway with its balustraded stairway curling upward.

"Come on, then." Corwen led the way. There was only one set on the first floor, so Corwen rapped on the door in a businesslike manner. There was no answer. He tried the door, but it was locked.

I glanced up the stairs. There were other sets of rooms above us.

"Good idea," Corwen said as if reading my mind.

We ascended to the next landing. Here were two doors. Corwen knocked on the closest. It opened to reveal a manservant, muscular but short.

"I'm looking for Mr. Freddie Deverell," Corwen said.

Before the manservant could reply a voice from inside called out, "Who is it, Simpson?"

"A gentleman and a lady enquiring for Mr. Freddie Deverell, sir."

"Show them in. Show them in. I've told you before about leaving callers on the doorstep."

The manservant opened the door to reveal a neat bachelor apartment, soberly furnished with a sofa and a single armchair, a desk and a small dining table. Rising from the desk to meet us was a young man with straw-fair hair and blue eyes, slight of stature, but wiry, with a very upright posture. His neck cloth was tied in such a complex knot that I doubted he could bend his head at all.

"Danvers. Edwin Danvers." He bowed at just the right angle, for the correct length of time.

"Corwen Deverell at your service, sir, and this is my wife. I'm sorry to trouble, you but I'm looking for my brother, Freddie. I tried the rooms below but there's no answer."

"You won't get an answer, I'm afraid."

"He's moved away?"

"Only in a manner of speaking. He vanished about three weeks ago. Strangest damned thing—begging your pardon for the language, Mrs. Deverell, ma'am—his door was open, all his things left like he was coming home at any moment, but he never showed up. At length, the landlord's man of business locked the door. I believe it's his intent to sell the contents if Deverell hasn't returned by the time the rent is due."

I could see several layers of worry running through Corwen. I had questions myself.

"Did he mention any plans to visit anyone?" Corwen asked.

"Not to me, but though we were on speaking terms, we weren't close associates."

He placed some emphasis on the word close, and in that one phrase he was both admitting to knowing, and also denying any involvement in, Freddie's sexual practices.

"Do you know if any of the other tenants here were Freddie's particular friends?" Corwen asked.

"Not that I know of. Mr. Deverell had his own circle. I never met them."

"Did Freddie have a manservant?" I asked Mr. Danvers, but looked toward Simpson for an answer.

"Well, Simpson?" Mr. Danvers asked.

"Not so far as I know, sir."

"Thank you," Corwen said. "We shouldn't trouble you further."

"Well, I wish you the best of luck in finding Mr. Deverell."

"Thank you. I expect he'll turn up when he's ready."

Corwen gave the impression he wasn't worried, but as we left the house I heard him say, "Damn!" under his breath.

"You're worried," I said.

"I really don't want to contemplate this, but I may have to visit the Bow Street Runners to see if there have been any unidentified bodies that match Freddie's description in the last three weeks."

"This is London."

"Yes, I know. There are probably hundreds."

"Does Freddie have any distinguishing marks?"

"He does." He pointed to the side of his neck below his right ear. "A birthmark, deep red and about the size of a guinea."

Early the following morning, despite tossing and turning throughout most of the night, Corwen set out for Bow Street to try and discover if there was a central record of unidentified corpses, a depressing job in itself, even if you weren't looking for a missing twin brother.

He decided not to take a hackney coach and said the walk would do him good, help to clear his head. I suspected what he really wanted was to fling off his clothes and run and run as a wolf until he exhausted himself, but he wasn't going to get that opportunity in London. I kissed him good-bye, held him tight, and said I hoped he found nothing. He departed with steely determination.

Left to myself, I spent the day with Aunt Rosie's notebooks, learning more about spellcraft. Five o'clock came and went, and Corwen still hadn't returned. The daylight was fading fast, helped by black clouds rolling in from the west. Mrs. Pirt came up to see what she should do about dinner, since it was almost ready. Did I want mine now or would I wait for Mr. Deverell?

I told her I'd wait and continued reading, putting on my spectacles and calling light into them. What I saw through the lenses was day-bright, yet from the outside they looked like a normal pair of spectacles. I thought this might be closely akin to Rosie's description of filtering magic into the everyday. Instead of putting up a witchlight which would be obvious to everyone, I could call light into spectacles, or even into lamps to brighten them beyond the capability of oil and wick.

Then the door opened again and admitted Mrs. Pirt to ask the same question about dinner now it was seven o'clock.

"Good heavens, Mrs. Deverell. Trying to read in the dark, you'll ruin your eyesight."

Next time I'd have to remember to light a lamp or a candle as a token gesture.

"Not reading, Mrs. Pirt. I'm afraid I'd dozed off. I'm sorry if dinner is ruined by trying to keep it warm, but Mr. Deverell didn't say when he'd be back. I expected him sooner than this, I admit."

Right at that moment a sharp knock resounded on the front door and Pirt, who had closed the shutters and bolted all the doors with the coming of darkness, shouted to see who it was. I heard Corwen's voice and jumped up to run downstairs with only one question, one that I didn't need to ask.

Corwen looked haggard. "Nothing, though I've read through more descriptions of people done to death or died of natural causes than I needed to see in a lifetime." He took off his overcoat, the top cape damp from the drizzle outside, and sank into a chair in the downstairs parlor. "The Bow Street Runners have some records, but they're not complete. Sometimes if an unidentified body is found, say perished from cold in the street, it may be buried in a pauper's grave by the parish, and there are over a hundred parishes. It would take an army of investigators to check everywhere."

I shoved a large brandy into his hand and dropped a kiss onto the top of his head. "I'm sorry you've had such a bloody day."

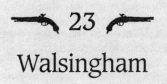

23

Walsingham

THE FOLLOWING AFTERNOON Corwen decided to go to White's Club, close by, on St. James Street. He and Freddie had both been admitted to the membership some years ago, largely thanks to their father's good standing. Corwen had rarely crossed the doorstep, but it seemed likely Freddie had been a frequent visitor, especially because of his admission of a generous win on a horse race. There was the famous leather-bound betting book at White's which might hold a clue to his associates, who in turn might know of his current whereabouts. Or maybe the Master of the House might recall something useful.

I reminded Corwen about the Mysterium's public meeting later that evening, and he promised to be back in time for it, knowing full well that I would go without him if he wasn't. I stayed at home that afternoon, ordering the house with Mrs. Pirt. I arranged menus—simple food, well cooked—and though Mrs. Pirt mentioned she'd once cooked much more elaborate meals for a duchess, she was amenable to making plain food. I mentioned that Corwen liked his meat lightly cooked, which didn't faze her at all.

Later, I ghosted through the house, checking rooms we were unlikely to use. Everything was in order. I expected nothing less. Then I was stuck. Being used to life at sea, or the necessary day-to-day activity of living in a cottage in the woods, or the constant bustle of Denby Hall and the mill where something was always happening, I found London boring or, more specifically, I found being in the Wimpole Street house boring. The street outside was not a major thoroughfare and there was only so much entertainment to be had from watching passersby. Life at sea might have had its quiet periods, but living at close quarters with sixty assorted sailors, from the cultured Mr. Rafiq to the youngest gutter-ràt powder monkey, was, in itself, a recipe for lively interest—and now those sixty sailors were close at hand. I resisted the temptation to get Mr. Pirt to call me a hackney carriage to take me to Wapping where the *Heart* was lying at anchor in the Thames.

Corwen returned from White's Club at four in a filthy mood. Freddie had been there four weeks earlier and had laid a wager of a hundred guineas that it would rain before midnight, but after that there was no further record of him. He'd lost the bet and not turned up to pay his debt, which was out of character according to the Master of the House.

Corwen dropped his coat over a chair and untied his neck cloth. "I settled his debt. I checked the betting book. He'd bet on anything, but there was no pattern to it. He rarely wagered against the same person twice."

He bit back whatever else he'd been going to say as Pirt entered with the soup. We sat at the table and began to eat in silence.

"How could he?" Corwen thumped the dinner table with his fist, causing the soup tureen to rattle and his spoon to bounce on to the floor.

"No, it's all right," he said to Pirt who moved to retrieve it. "My apologies. It's totally my fault. The dinner is excellent. Please give Mrs. Pirt my compliments. We'll call when we're finished."

Pirt took the hint and left us in private.

"How could who do what?" I asked.

"Freddie's gambling was excessive and erratic. He bet twenty thousand on the outcome of a single race."

"Did he win?"

Corwen pressed his fingers against tight muscles in the side of his neck. "Yes, but that's not the point. He didn't have twenty thousand. It would have fallen to the family to pay off his debt if he'd lost."

"And after that?"

"A series of smaller bets, some lost, some won. He lost ten thousand on the turn of a card and won five of it back again before the night was out."

"So is he in debt?"

I pushed back my chair and went to stand behind him, swatting his hand away and digging the tips of my fingers into the tense muscles of his shoulders through the linen of his shirt.

He sighed and let his head droop forward. "Apart from the last wager, I don't believe he is, though only by the greatest of luck."

"Sometimes they say of sea captains and soldiers that any amount of skill will do them no good unless luck is with them."

"But luck will do them little good if they throw their ships recklessly at the rocks or their troops at the enemy artillery."

"True. So are we any nearer to knowing where he is?"

"No, though the Master of the House does recall Freddie in his cups one night saying as how there were opportunities for a man of substance in the Americas."

"You think he might have taken off without letting anyone know and without so much as packing his clothes?"

"I doubt it. He's as seasick as the rowankind, and mortally afraid of water. I can't see him taking ship to anywhere." He shrugged. "I simply don't know. It doesn't seem sensible, but Freddie was always impulsive as a child, and this late change to a wolf may not have helped."

"You think he might be unstable?"

"It had crossed my mind."

"So what next?"

"Can you search for Freddie?" He lowered his voice. "Magically, I mean."

"Not without some possession of his, something that was personal to him."

"We need access to his rooms."

"That's a place to start. We'll go early in the morning before the young men are awake, and I'll bring my lock-picks."

"Did I ever tell you you're a wonderful woman?" Corwen said.

"You can tell me later, when we're private."

❦

We finished our dinner without lingering and warned the Pirts that we would likely be out until nine. I contemplated wearing my breeches, but decided it would not make me any safer, so I dressed in my plainest walking gown with a fichu tucked demurely into the neckline, wore my old red-ingote on top, and finished off the respectable but unremarkable outfit with a light capote bonnet. Corwen looked me over and pulled the bonnet brim forward to partially hide my face.

"You'll do," he said, swinging his arms into a well-worn and totally forgettable overcoat he'd borrowed from Mr. Pirt.

Mr. Pirt had secured us a hackney carriage for the journey.

"Don't look so worried," I said as our coach rattled along through busy streets.

"Hmm, let's see . . . It's Seven Dials, possibly the poorest, chanciest neighborhood in London, and we're going to a meeting held by the Mysterium about unlicensed magic. What could possibly go wrong?"

"I promise I won't draw attention to us, and if it looks too dangerous, we'll leave straightaway."

"With any luck, it will be so crowded we can't get in."

But it wasn't crowded at all. It seemed the people of Seven Dials were ambivalent about the magic threat. I guess they had more immediate things to worry about, such as feeding their families. We arrived a quarter hour before the meeting was due to start and chose to ascend to the chapel's horseshoe-shaped gallery. We sat on a bench along the side overlooking the pulpit, trying not to draw attention to ourselves. The audience for the meeting was composed of a wide cross-section of London's inhabitants. I suspected some of the poorest were only here for a respite from the persistent drizzle that had set in around midafternoon, or perhaps a little peace and quiet from the tumult of raising a family of eight children in a one-room basement in the Rookery. Others looked shabby but respectable, London's working class: laborers, artisans, and threadbare clerks. Somewhat higher up the social scale were merchants and professional types. I was surprised to see a little knot of licensed witches, most of them female; all were wearing a red armband stitched around their left sleeve to comply with local regulations.

I nudged Corwen with my elbow and twitched my head toward the witches who were sitting downstairs, toward the rear of the room.

"I suppose we should have expected it," he said. "Seven Dials is known for its witches and quack healers, plus those who claim to be in touch with recently deceased spirits."

As one who could summon spirits, I knew most of those in the business were fakes, though my late brother Philip had once told me he'd made money out of gullible widows. In his case, I knew his talent for summoning to be real, but I doubted he'd actually used it most of the time. Summoning spirits could be tricky. Not all of them were cooperative, and holding them for any length of time was exhausting, both mentally and physically.

There was a slight commotion downstairs as a party of individuals marched down the central aisle and took places in the front pews. I'd assumed the front was empty because most people's natural inclination was to sit toward the back of the room rather than attract the attention of the speaker, but it appeared that the front seats had been reserved for guests of quality, the like of which usually avoided Seven Dials. I counted heads: a dozen people varying in age from maybe nineteen or twenty to an elderly gentleman with a goatee beard and monocle dressed in a smart cutaway coat and top hat which he did not remove. He could have been the grandfather of the youngest member of the party, a bright-eyed miss wearing a burgundy pelisse and a bandeau. She looked excited and linked arms with the elderly gentleman, her cheerful chatter lost in the general hubbub.

"Is that Frankland?" Corwen asked.

"Lord Frankland?"

"I believe it is. I was introduced to him once at Whites, with Father. Opinionated gentleman, as I recall. He's some relation to Mr. Addington."

"The Prime Minister—that Mr. Addington?"

"The very same." He pressed his lips together. "I would have thought this an odd event for such a gentleman to attend. And as for the young lady—"

Corwen swallowed whatever he'd been going to say as the doors downstairs closed with a heavy thump and the audience, expectant, turned toward the pulpit. Six Kingsmen in dress uniforms, midnight with gold frogging, entered from the rear of the pulpit and took up positions, three on each side of it, eyes forward.

A rotund gentleman of middle years, slightly old-fashioned in his mode of dress, stepped in front of the pulpit and began to speak. As he did so, I noticed the man still in the shadow of the doorway, waiting to make his entrance. He was hidden from most of the audience by a carved screen, but being in the gallery and to one side, I could see over it. The man was tall and well-favored, with a fine head of dark curls cut short at the nape of his neck. He was elegantly dressed, a dandy in the refined style of Mr. Brummel with a black cutaway coat and narrow black trousers. As he was waiting for his introduction, he swept his gaze around the balcony. For a moment our lines of sight intersected. I blinked to break the contact and just caught the last words of the speaker: *Please welcome Sir Edward Walsingham.*

Walsingham!

I'd grabbed Corwen's hand and was squeezing the blood from his fingers.

"Do you want to leave?" he whispered.

"No." I was horribly aware that sitting on the side balcony had brought us closer to the pulpit. "We'll attract too much attention if we move now."

We sat, trying to disappear into the rest of the audience, applauding when they did, uttering low sounds of approval or disapproval as they did and generally trying to blend in. Corwen could disguise us with a glamour, but we didn't know whether this Walsingham had magic like the last one. If he did, he might be able to sense a glamour. Even if he didn't, there were the witches in the auditorium who probably could.

I gradually became aware of what Walsingham was saying. His voice was mellow—the kind of voice you instinctively trust—and instead of ranting, he was speaking rationally about the recent occurrence of a mermaid spotted in the Thames at Deptford and the sudden snap of icy weather which had seen snow falling on London at Easter. He spoke about pixies in Cornwall souring milk, opening gates to let sheep out into the lanes, and swapping babies from two adjacent households in their cradles. He assured the audience that the fine body of men of the Mysterium, together with the Kingsmen and the redcoats, were here to protect them, and that any strange occurrences could be safely reported direct to the Mysterium itself, or at the nearest magistrate's office.

There were no histrionics, no tub-thumping, just sound and reasonable common sense and an assurance that the Mysterium was working for them. He acknowledged the witches with a glance and a half-smile, and reassured the audience that magic users licensed by the Mysterium could be safely engaged for approved workings.

I found myself relaxing. I couldn't imagine the old Walsingham setting an audience at its ease quite so well, or even wanting to. This Walsingham was completely self-assured. As he finished his speech, his eyes strayed to Lord Frankland and his party of gentlefolk. He exchanged a nod with Frankland and looked toward the young miss who gazed at him with nothing less than complete adoration.

For an instant I saw his expression crack, and the two of them shared an intimate glance that cut out the rest of the room completely.

That's what the party of gentlefolk were doing there. Unless I was severely mistaken, Walsingham was in love, and that sentiment was returned by the young lady.

Then Walsingham dropped in the information that I suspected this evening was all about. "As from Monday next, for your safety, the Mysterium will be deploying a militia whose function will be to search out illicit magic and to protect the residents of this fair and industrious city. For your own safety your absolute cooperation will be required at all times. The first two militia companies will be assigned to Westminster and here in Seven Dials, but within the year every parish will be protected. Thank you. God save the King."

A militia to protect against magic. I felt as though my blood was freezing in my veins.

"So, Westminster and Seven Dials are the places to avoid," Corwen said under his breath. He sounded so calm.

I swallowed hard. "For the time being," I said. "Pretty soon the whole of London will be dangerous for the likes of us. And maybe they'll extend it to the other major cities."

"How are they funding it?" Corwen asked.

"How do you mean?"

"When the previous Walsingham was in charge of a secret organization, there were only a few of them. Their budget must have been relatively insignificant, but the Mysterium is funded by the government. Employing a militia is going to be expensive. Someone is taking the magic threat very seriously."

We hurried from the building and walked briskly toward the nearest hackney carriage stand, not speaking to each other until we were safely in a coach and trotting toward Wimpole Street in the deepening dusk.

"He didn't mention the rowankind," Corwen said. "Was that deliberate, do you think?"

"I don't know, but I do know Mr. Pomeroy was right

when he said that New Walsingham had connections in
Parliament."

"How do you mean?"

"Didn't you see?"

"See what?"

"The look that passed between Walsingham and the
pretty young miss in the company of Lord Frankland. I'll
wager there's a wedding in the offing. Walsingham is marrying into a family with at least one member in the House
of Lords and a connection to the prime minister himself."

"Marriage would be remarkable—for a Walsingham,"
Corwen said.

The previous Walsingham had been dedicated to root-
ing out magic considered dangerous to the Crown to the
exclusion of everything else. He'd renounced family, wife,
and children—and even his name—to take the position of
Walsingham. To my knowledge he'd been simply Walsingham, without title or Christian name. Sir Edward Walsingham had both. Of course his name was unlikely to be the
one he'd been born with. That would be securely protected
in case anyone magical used it against him.

"In general, what did you make of the new Walsingham?" Corwen asked.

"If I hadn't known who he was, I might have liked him.
He's a good speaker and seems sincere."

"Yes, I thought that, too—not at all like the previous
Walsingham."

"That doesn't mean he isn't dangerous, though."

"Indeed."

◆────◆

We were awake and breakfasting by seven the following
morning. At seven thirty a boy delivered a note from Mr.
Wiggins asking if Corwen could call to see him as he had
some important news.

"Some news from the army, do you think?" I asked.

"Maybe. We should go to Duke Street on the way."

"Good idea."

I packed my lockpicks in my reticule, such a delicate

container for such a businesslike set of tools. Shortly after eight we walked down Duke Street.

"What if the front door is locked?" Corwen asked. "Can you deal with that lock, too?"

"Yes, as long as it's not bolted on the inside, but it will look suspicious. Let's hope it's open. Some of the young men may not even have returned home yet."

As we approached, a hackney carriage halted outside the house and the same young man that we met on the doorstep previously lurched out of it unsteadily.

"Our luck is in." Corwen hurried forward and took the young man by the elbow. "Let me help you, sir."

"Sverra kind 'vyou. Don't I know you?"

"Indeed you do. We met here, the day before yesterday."

"Oi, that's a shillin' owin'," the cabbie said.

Corwen reached into a pocket and tossed the man a florin. "You were never here."

"That's right, sir. Somewhere else entirely." The cabbie drove off with a clatter while Corwen took the young man's front door key and assisted him to unlock it, guiding him through and leaving the door unlocked behind us.

"Which are your rooms?"

"Right there." He staggered a few paces toward a door on the ground floor.

Corwen used the keys again, and the man tottered to the nearest chair and started to sit down.

"Come on, old chap, far better to sleep it off." Corwen grasped the drunkard's elbow and guided him to the bed. "When you wake, we'll be nothing more than a dream."

"Sweet dreams."

"I'm sure they will be." Corwen took off the man's shoes and dropped a cover over his shoulders.

We exited into the hallway, and I pulled the door closed behind us. Corwen set the young man's keys onto the hall table where he would find them.

We took a few minutes to listen for any indication that the residents were up and about, but the house was silent.

Up on the first floor landing I took out my lockpicks and knelt by Freddie's door. The lock was a simple lever mechanism, and I dealt with it in less than a minute. Still listening for sounds of stirring, we opened the door and let ourselves in.

The first thing that greeted us was a whiff of sour milk congealed in a pan close to the cold ashes of a fire as if put by ready to heat on the trivet.

"It looks like he was intending to come back," I said.

The room was comfortably furnished, a book open on the table by an armchair, a stub of a candle snuffed out, not burned right down, and some moldy bread slowly crumbling to green dust on a plate on the table. The shutters were closed as if Freddie had left after dark.

Corwen opened the shutters. Early morning sun streamed in, lighting disturbed dust motes. I followed him through to the bedroom where the bed lay, messily unmade, clothes discarded on the footboard. Corwen picked up the shirt and inhaled its scent. Even in human form Corwen's nose was particularly keen.

"Definitely Freddie. Something else, too." He leaned over the bed and sniffed. "I think the last time he was in this bed he was in wolf form."

"You don't think he went out as a wolf from here, do you?"

"It's possible, but from what Lily said, he resisted changing. He might have fought off the change for too long. If that happens, sometimes the body takes over and the change happens during sleep—an involuntary reaction."

"So he might have left here on all fours, which would explain why the door was swinging open."

"Lord, I hope not."

"Can you find me something personal of Freddie's? Something I can use to search with."

"His clothes?"

"Better than nothing, but something that holds meaning for him would be better."

Corwen began to open drawers and check the contents.

"He brought this! Well, it's the last thing I would have expected." He held a small wooden horse about the size of his hand. "Jonnie carved one for each of us for our eighth birthday. Freddie took his to bed with him and wouldn't let it out of his sight. I suppose it holds special memories of our brother."

"Perhaps Freddie cares about family more than he's willing to say."

"Perhaps he does. What can have driven him to cut himself off?"

"You cut yourself off."

"I suppose I did, but they always knew how to find me if they needed me." He frowned. "Anyway, will the horse do? Is it personal enough?"

"I believe it is. Let's go before the house wakes up."

We let ourselves out of the rooms on to the landing and pulled the door closed behind us. At the top of the house I could hear a door opening, a voice, and footsteps coming down from the attic.

"Quick!"

We made it down the stairs and out into the street. By the time the front door opened again, we were strolling arm in arm along Duke Street, but this time I had the little wooden horse tucked into my reticule along with my lockpicks.

Success!

24

Goblins

WE FOUND A HACKNEY CARRIAGE at a stand around the corner and we were on our way to Gray's Inn within ten minutes, rattling along the road at a respectable pace for such a crowded city. The streets seemed a little quieter this morning. I wondered whether it was just the fact that I was getting used to them. I barely noticed the smell now, the raw sewage combined with the sulfurous stench of coal burning in the fireplaces, factories, and forges, and to support the myriad steam-powered engines. Even here, in the polite west end of the city, the smell was noticeable.

Mr. Wiggins greeted us warmly once more, but once the pleasantries were over, he got down to business.

"I have a contact at Horseguards, a Mr. Sparks, who keeps the regimental records for a Mr. Charles, the recently appointed civilian agent for the 86th Regiment of Foot under Colonel Carter."

"The man responsible for buying new uniforms?"

"Precisely. He will have dealt with a tailoring firm and the tailoring firm is responsible for sourcing cloth and having the garments made up, largely by women and children working in their own rooms, though I have heard that some tailors have set up manufacturing workshops."

"So all we need to know is which tailor had an agreement with Deverell's."

"Indeed. Mr. Sparks is not only approachable, but has been approached, and for a consideration has checked the list of tailors."

I wondered when Mr. Wiggins was going to get to the point, but he seemed to take pleasure in drawing out the story. Corwen, however, was impatient. "So you've found the one?"

"In a manner of speaking."

Corwen tilted his head waiting for Mr. Wiggins to elaborate. When the pause grew too long, he cleared his throat pointedly and said, "What manner of speaking would that be?"

"The tailor's name is Mr. Tingle. I sent a man to his place of business, but he reports it is abandoned. Says it looks as though no one has been near it for years."

"Yet the agreement must have been made some time shortly before Father's illness, so no more than six or seven months at most."

Mr. Wiggins shrugged. "A puzzle."

Corwen frowned. "Did your man ask around to see if the locals knew anything?"

"I'm afraid not. Whitechapel isn't always a friendly neighborhood."

It looked as though we had one more call to make before returning home so that I could try my luck with Freddie's horse.

◆────◆

Whitechapel was one of those places that made you wish you had eyes in the back of your head. I'd spent some time in Wapping, which was rough and ready, full of boatmen, stevedores, warehouses, public houses, and houses of ill repute, but Wapping had a purpose to it, to serve the great river. Whitechapel's purpose seemed to be to house the largest number of persons in the smallest possible space amidst manufactories small and large. Corwen's nose twitched at the strong smell of hops from Bullocks' brewery as our coach pulled up at the narrow entrance to George Yard, a passage connecting Whitechapel with Spitalfields between the high brick walls of buildings whose purpose was hidden behind inelegant blank facades. Any windows were so filthy I wondered how they could possibly allow light to enter.

Mr. Tingle's place of business was supposed to be halfway along the yard on the left hand side. As Mr. Wiggins had said, it was derelict, in such bad repair that anyone braving the boarded-up doorway and entering the premises might risk it all falling on their head.

A shiver ran down my spine and I felt slightly queasy, the feeling increasing as we got closer. In fact, looking at it made me not want to look at it, or anywhere near it. My scalp prickled and I swallowed a slimy lump in my throat. There was something odd about the whole building. "I can see why Mr. Wiggins' man didn't stay around here to ask questions."

"Huh?" Corwen sounded surprised. "I've seen more prosperous places, but I'd hardly call it a ruin."

I wondered what state a building had to be in before Corwen did call it a ruin.

He approached the door with obvious intent.

"Corwen!" I hung back.

"What's the matter?"

"You're not going in there?"

He frowned at me as if I was being particularly stupid. "Why not?"

"It feels . . . wrong."

His frown deepened. "What do you see?"

"A ruin . . . but there's something odd about it. It shifts when I'm not looking at it."

He took my hand and pulled me close. "Look again. What's underneath?"

"I told you . . . Oh!" For a moment the boarded-up doorway disappeared and I saw a normal door in its place. Then the ruin was back again.

"It's a glamour," he said.

Corwen has some small skill to create glamours, though not on the scale that would allow him to disguise a whole building as something it's not. I'd read about glamours in Aunt Rosie's notebooks, but never tried to create one, nor, until now, had I ever tried to see through one so strong.

"What do you see?" I asked.

"Tall building, high-sided, built of brick. Windows above head height. Door with a knocker. There's a smell, too. People, all close together; cloth, cotton, wool, some linen. And there's a privy that needs emptying." He stiffened. "I can also smell something . . . not human."

"Not human?"

"There's a whiff of magic about him."

"Him?"

"Definitely."

Corwen's nose is a thing of beauty. How he gets so much information from sniffing the air is beyond me, but if that's what his nose tells him, then that's what there is.

"You're just going to knock on the door?" The back of my neck prickled.

"You guessed my clever plan."

Without waiting for more objections Corwen did exactly that. The door swung inward. I saw nothing but darkness, but Corwen stepped confidently across the threshold, drawing me with him. Once the door closed behind us, my feeling of queasiness eased. We entered a short corridor with two doors to our left and a larger double-door at the end. To the right was a long slit of a window divided into small panes. It ran the length of the corridor. Through it I could see a large room, well lit by high windows, in which forty or fifty women of all ages aided by boys and girls as young as eight or nine, stitched with needles and thread, some at tables and others hunched over their laps. At the far end was a long table over which three men labored with shears, cutting patterns from crimson cloth.

"It looks like we're in the right place," Corwen said.

"Are you?" A voice said behind us. "I'm wondering why."

I whirled around, my hand going to the solid lump in my hidden pocket that was one of Mr. Bunney's gold-barreled pistols, but it was not primed, so not much use unless I threw it at him. The *him* turned out to be a neatly respectable young man, pale-skinned, but handsome in a sharp-featured kind of way. The only slightly odd thing about him was his nose, hawkish and hooked with slit nostrils.

Corwen turned more slowly, his face not showing any of the consternation that I felt. "Mr. Tingle?" he said.

"Who would like to know?"

When he spoke, there was a flash of pointed teeth—not only his canines, but all of his incisors.

"Deverell. Corwen Deverell." Corwen kept his voice light and non-threatening. "Here on business to speak with Mr. Tingle."

"Business?"

"Just business."

"Show him in, Barnaby." An older voice bellowed from behind the second door.

The young man blinked, closed his lips over his teeth, and drew a long breath that caused those slit nostrils to widen and close again. "My grandfather will see you now."

He opened the office door and we stepped through. I felt Corwen hesitate and wondered what he could see. I saw an elderly gentleman in a periwig, stout of girth but wearing well-cut clothes, fine enough for any dandy. His country-fresh face with rosy cheeks and shrewd blue eyes set beneath bushy white brows now beamed at us. He looked like everyone's favorite grandfather. And again I felt that when I wasn't looking at him he was something different. Another glamour? I thought so, but I couldn't see through it. What was it Aunt Rosie's notebooks had said about countering a glamour?

"Come in, my dears, come in. So who have we here?"

He took my hand and bowed his head over it, not quite kissing it, but inhaling deeply. He offered his hand to Corwen, who refused it somewhat rudely.

"Drop the glamour," he said abruptly.

"Ah, it's you, then, and not the witch. I wondered which of you could see through it."

◆———————◆

Abruptly the old man was gone and a white-skinned creature stood before us. The only things similar were his height and his immaculate suit. The portly belly had gone in favor of an emaciated body with an over-large, hairless head with the same hooked nose and slit nostrils as his grandson. His fingers were long and slender with three joints instead of two. He wiggled the fingers of his right hand in a repeating pattern as if he were stopping himself from reaching for something. He smiled, at least I think he meant it to be a smile, but it was no longer benign. Now it displayed a double row of jagged teeth.

I stiffened and stepped back.

"Mr. Tingle is a goblin," Corwen said. "Though I doubt he's a danger to us." He scowled at the goblin. "Are you?"

"Are you a danger to us?" The grandson, Barnaby, closed the door behind us and leaned against it. It appeared he didn't have a glamour. The nose was all he'd inherited from his grandsire. Half goblin? Quarter goblin? I didn't know goblins could interbreed with humans, but it was obvious the young man was not full blood. I revised what I thought I knew about them, going over Aunt Rosie's notebooks in my head. Magical creatures, not of the Fae realms, but wholly of this world, living deep underground; hence the pale countenance.

Were they dangerous? Aunt Rosie had had little to say on that score. I'm not sure she'd ever met one.

The older goblin's nose slits vibrated and he looked at Corwen. "You smell of the Lady of the Forests. What are you? Stag? Pony?"

"Wolf," Corwen said, letting his teeth show. "And yes, I'm in her service when she needs me."

"I hear she's taken an interest in ridding the land of magical creatures."

"Only those who are making their presence felt, harming humans."

"I heard about the kelpie and the pixies in Cornwall."

"The kelpie murdered a child and would have gone on killing."

"The pixies surely weren't dangerous."

"They were becoming noticeable, souring milk, riding sheep to the point of exhaustion, swapping babies in their cradles, doing the kind of thing pixies are noted for. I believe they were offered the choice of abandoning their mischief or finding an alternative home away from humans."

Corwen jerked his head in the direction of the workshop. "What about your humans?"

"All my workers are under my protection. They're under no enchantment. I don't work them until their fingers bleed and fall off, or they forget their homes and their children. They're simply workers. I pay them. They sew. It's an arrangement that seems to work. This is a legitimate business operation."

"Run by goblins."

"Even goblins have to live. If there's a good deal to be had, there's a goblin involved somewhere in the chain. I can trace my family back for centuries. This city runs deep underground. The Romans built the first tunnels. Now most of the city is built upon cellars. Some might say humans encroach into our territory, so we don't hold off from encroaching into theirs. Some of us have lost our taste for sewers. It only takes a little glamour and . . ." He transformed briefly into the beaming grandfather and back again to his own true self. "I'm a gentleman when I need to be." He looked at Barnaby, who had not moved from his position guarding the door. I took it that his grandson didn't have the ability to cast a glamour.

"Do we have a problem?" the old goblin said. "If so, what will it take to make it go away? I have resources."

"The Lady didn't send us," Corwen said.

"Then why are you here?" the grandson growled.

"Business," Corwen said. "You had a contract with Deverell's Mill in Yorkshire—woolen cloth for army uniforms for the 86th Regiment of Foot."

"I did. You're that Mr. Deverell?" He looked surprised. "I understood you were not long for this world."

"My father's ill, but his business is now safe in family hands; however, I've recently had cause to replace his man of business in Yorkshire. During investigations, I discovered a missing contract."

"Canceled by your father," Mr. Tingle said. He crossed to the shelf behind his desk and pulled off a leather-bound volume. "Ah, yes, here it is. Canceled in January. I was relying on that cloth. Caused me a few problems until your father's man of business—"

"Thatcher?"

"Yes, Mr. Thatcher—suggested an alternative supplier."

"And who might that be?"

"Mr. Deverell, your father let me down. I'm not obliged to give you confidential information about my business."

I put my hand on Corwen's arm and turned to the goblin. "You certainly aren't obliged, Mr. Tingle, but it seems to me that an increase in magical creatures in the capital is bad for business. Magic—wild magic—is on the rise."

"So I've noticed."

"Wouldn't it be prudent to cooperate with each other on matters magical and mundane? What do you know about a man called Walsingham?"

The grandson, behind me, made the kind of sound that let me know I'd hit home.

Mr. Tingle frowned. "The new head of the Mysterium. Has a small army of thugs on the street, looking for anything unusual, and there are spells that alert him to magical occurrences. My grandson and his sister barely escaped his men a few weeks ago."

Barnaby cleared his throat. "Had to take to the sewers to get away." He drew himself up. "We are not sewer goblins anymore."

I took it that was a point of pride for his family, and that there were still other goblins in the sewers of London.

"We have a common enemy," I said. "The Mysterium is a danger to all magical creatures."

Mr. Tingle inclined his head.

"I would be happy to convey your regards to the Lady,"

Corwen said, "and assure her of your goodwill and that your interaction with human society is entirely beneficial."

"That would be acceptable."

"And in return you could pinpoint any wild magic which may draw public attention."

"I have my contacts."

"As you say, your family has been in the city a long time." Corwen offered his hand this time, and the goblin took it.

"And the other, the wool supplier?" Mr. Tingle said.

"I would take that as a kindness." Corwen pressed so gently that Mr. Tingle yielded without further protest.

"Kaye's Mill," he said. "A neighbor of yours, I believe."

I felt Corwen's surprise, but he covered it well.

"Thank you. It might interest you to know that in January my father was too ill to cancel any contract, but Thatcher was probably being paid by Kaye for services rendered. Deverell's Mill had the stock then, and has the stock now. In fact, we can supply you immediately, and at a good price, especially if you have a way to finagle yourself out of any agreement with Kaye. Might I ask if you would be interested in discussing the matter further?"

"I'm always interested in quality goods at an advantageous price, Mr. Deverell, and I have a good lawyer, a third cousin."

"Good, I'll get my sister to write to you."

"Your sister?"

"A very astute young woman."

"Is she a wolf as well?"

Corwen simply smiled.

"You're not that brown wolf that's been seen on Hampstead Heath, are you?"

Corwen stiffened. Freddie was a brown wolf.

"No."

"Good, only I heard there was a hunting party out after the brown one, and I would hate to lose an ally so soon."

"Hunting party?"

"Mysterium."

"Thanks for the warning."

Our driver, despite instructions to wait for us, had gone. Whitechapel wasn't a good area to hail a passing carriage and there wasn't a hackney stand nearby. Few of the inhabitants of this part of the city could afford to hire a carriage, and the street traffic consisted largely of people on foot, costermongers' carts, or brewery drays pulled by muscular carthorses, in teams of four.

We attracted a few sideways glances; as Corwen took my hand I felt his own magic at work, casting a glamour over both of us until we attracted no more attention than the people we passed among.

Corwen walked silently.

"What are you thinking about?" I asked. "Brown wolf or Kaye's Mill?"

"Both."

"You think Freddie would be incautious enough to let himself be seen on Hampstead Heath?"

"I hope not."

"But you think he might?"

"If he's been repressing his wolf so much that his body forced an involuntary change, he might not have been thinking rationally. He'd be thinking mostly like a wolf. In that case he'd be likely to find the wildest stretch of land that presented itself."

"Hampstead Heath?"

"It's not far as the wolf runs. His nose could have taken him there."

"I suppose so. The Mysterium?"

"If the wolf got sloppy, used the same place on a regular basis . . ." He shrugged. "I don't know. I hope not. I hope it was some big dog mistaken for a wolf. Let's go back to Wimpole Street and you can use the toy horse to search for him."

"And Kaye's Mill?"

"The final piece of the puzzle. Kaye suggested Thatcher in the first place. Coupled with the smashing of the mill dam, and the leet at Kaye's Mill being advantageously open, this

last bit of information is enough for me. Our friends the
Kayes are not, in fact, our friends at all. Exactly the opposite."

"You'll tell Lily?"

"Oh yes. I'll write immediately."

"And she'll do what, exactly?"

"Be prepared."

We arrived at our own cozy house in Wimpole Street at
noon. Before settling down to magically search for Freddie,
I insisted on lunching on cold chicken and a salad of potatoes.

"You can think about your stomach?" Corwen asked.

"Better to eat now, before I start. It takes a lot of energy
to search for someone or to summon them. You do realize . . ." I raised my head from my plate.

"What?"

"That it's a fine line between *searching* for someone and
summoning them. If Freddie is . . ."

"Dead. You can say the word."

"If Freddie is dead, I could summon his spirit instead of
locating his body."

Corwen kissed my hair. "If Freddie is dead, at least we'll
know. All this running around feels useless. I could check
every police office in London and still never find a trace.
Then what? Search the Americas? Advertise in the newspapers or the *Gentleman's Magazine*? Post a reward for the
recovery of a lost brother, as if he's no more than a favorite
pocket watch?" He covered my hand with his. "And this is
all presuming he wants to be found, that he's using his real
name, and that he isn't determined to get away from Yorkshire, the mill, and his family. Maybe he's in funds and has
run off to the country with his particular gentleman friend."

"You're sure he's a molly? Some men swing both ways."

There was a long silence. "I haven't seen him for six
years, but though he did his social duty and danced with all
the daughters of gentlefolk, he never formed an attach-
ment and I never heard him mooning after a female the

way he talked about some of the boys at school or the young men at Oxford. We never discussed it. He didn't confide in me. Probably thought I would be horrified or ashamed. Poor Freddie. There's scarce a country in the civilized world that wouldn't hang him for his preferences."

"Do you think less of him?"

"Good Lord, no. He's a wolf shapechanger. Being a molly is the least of his troubles!"

25

Wapping

AFTER I'D STUFFED MYSELF with chicken and potatoes, Corwen and I retired to our bedroom. Let the Pirts think what they liked about a newly married couple taking time for each other in the afternoon. At least they wouldn't disturb us for any reason short of the house burning down.

I took the carved wooden horse from my reticule and settled myself, cross-legged in the center of the bed.

"What do you need me to do?" Corwen asked.

"Nothing except watch. Make sure I don't lose myself."

"How will I know?"

"You'll know."

"If you summon Freddie's spirit . . ."

"You'll see him. You could always see Will when no one else could, except me."

Corwen sat at the foot of the bed, one leg curved on the counterpane, the other on the floor. I smiled briefly and he returned it, somewhat tight lipped.

Wasting no more time, I closed my eyes and held Freddie's horse to my breast, allowing myself to connect with it and therefore with Freddie. I only had the portrait in the hallway at Denby Hall to go on, and what Corwen had told me about his brother. Now, connecting with the toy, I was able to try and ascertain who Freddie Deverell really was.

The first thing I got was uncertainty. Freddie liked everyone to believe he was confident, but nothing could have been further from the truth. He was like a frightened little boy trying to do what the world wanted while his instincts took him in other directions. His mother had once pushed him toward Dorothea Kaye while he'd already been in love with a young man called Roland, a university chum. His father had pushed him toward business, which he felt he had no head for at all. And then had come the worst betrayal of all, that of his own body. His wolf began to break free. How he'd fought, but to no avail. The one advantage he'd had over his twin had vanished in an instant.

In that instant I was tied to Freddie with sympathy, understanding, and a degree of pity. I let my mind range out across the city searching for the troubled man he'd become. Out and out my mind roamed, finding nothing. It was as if he had never been.

I opened my eyes and blinked at Corwen.

"Nothing?" he asked.

"Nothing."

I tried again, this time searching the spirit world as well. The plane of the newly dead echoes our world, furnished by the last thoughts of those who frequented it, those waiting for passage to some other after-life or those who, for some reason, were stuck without being able to pass over. Will had inhabited this plane for more than three years until I'd finally let him go.

I didn't know anyone who had passed recently enough to be there.

Even as I thought that, Winnie materialized. I saw Corwen jump.

"Where's Robin?" the spirit asked.

"With Poppy. He's well looked after and we promise to take care of him."

"What is this place?"

She didn't mean our Wimpole Street bedroom, she meant her new plane of existence.

"It's the place where you wait to go to heaven."

"Is heaven beautiful?"

"I'm sure it is."

"I'd like that."

She faded away with a serene smile on her little face.

"Winnie," Corwen said.

"She looked peaceful, didn't she?"

"She did. But no Freddie?"

"No."

"Does that mean he's still alive?"

"I think so."

"But you can't locate him."

"No . . . I wonder . . ."

"What?"

"When David and I were trying to hide the winterwood box from Walsingham, we paid a witch to cover it with a shield, one that deflected magic and made it invisible to all types of scrying. I don't know if you can do that to a person, but it could be that we won't be able to find Freddie if the Mysterium has him."

"I need to go to Hampstead Heath, see if I can sniff out any kind of trail."

"It's too dangerous."

"I won't go as a wolf, not unless there's no other option."

"Let's both go. We can hire horses. I have my riding habit now."

"Agreed."

⸺◆⸺◆⸺

Mr. Pirt directed us to the nearest livery stable where, for a modest sum, we were able to hire two riding horses. I resigned myself to having to ride sidesaddle. My mare was nappy, so it took me a while to calm her down. Corwen's gelding was solid and unflappable, and set a good example. After a couple of miles my mare settled reluctantly.

The heath itself bordered the small town of Hampstead and was comprised of some three hundred acres, give or take a few enclosures. Its summit was a sandy ridge, and there were many springs and swampy hollows with patches of ancient woodland and more recent plantations. From the highest point we could see London stretched out before us, swathed in its industrial smoggy haze. On the heath's east side were a series of reservoirs and an ancient windmill on a mound. The tiny hamlet once known as Hatchett's Bottom and recently renamed the Vale of Health, lay completely surrounded by heathland, like an oasis in the desert. I thought its renaming to be the most optimistic piece of foolishness I had heard in a long time. Slough of Despond might be closer to the truth.

I followed Corwen, who rode where his nose took him.

"Anything?" I asked.

"No. My wolf can track a lot better than my human nose."

"It's too dangerous."

"It won't be after dark."

"Corwen . . ."

"Can you think of a better idea?"

I admitted I couldn't.

We returned our horses to the livery stable and pretended to be having a normal night at home while the Pirts went about their business. With an hour to go before midnight, and the Pirts safely abed, Corwen took the small bag that magically held his clothes, and quietly let himself out of the front door, leaving me to bolt it behind him, the taste of his farewell kiss on my lips.

I should have gone to bed, but I didn't know how long it would be before he returned home, so I wrapped myself in my cashmere shawl and curled up in the chair in the front parlor where the fire still glowed gently. I may have slept, but mostly I remember the long night, waking and dozing, waking and dozing. Sometime in the early hours, I put a few more coals on the fire to keep it burning and dozed again until a scratching at the front door brought me fully alert.

I ran and unbolted the door as quickly as I could. A silver wolf almost fell on top of me. He slithered to the floor and there he changed into a naked man, his shoulder streaked with blood. I knelt by him and padded my shawl against what looked like a bullet wound. I didn't waste time on words, but locked and bolted the door and helped him to his feet and up the stairs to the bedroom.

"It's not as bad as it looks," he muttered through chattering teeth, "but I couldn't change back."

"You ran here as a wolf?"

"Not straightaway. I led them a merry dance across the heath first and through enough pools that I lost their trackers."

"Trackers! They were waiting for you?"

"For someone. I almost walked straight into them right after I'd changed. They had the whole heath under surveillance."

"The Mysterium?"

"I think so."

"Are you sure they didn't track you here?"

"I'm sure they didn't follow me physically. Whether they have any way of tracking me magically, from a distance, I don't know. We have to get out of here."

"Agreed."

"Now."

"You aren't going anywhere like that. Let me examine the wound."

It was high on his left arm, a gouge rather than a hole. "You're lucky, the bullet just nicked you, but you need to change to heal it. Change and change again."

He rolled over onto the bed, already beginning to sprout sliver gray hair on the backs of his hands while his fingers curled into claws. My cashmere shawl was a gift from the Fae and would clean itself, but how was I going to account for the bloody mess on the hall floor. I left Corwen, now well into his change, and went to clean away the blood so that I didn't have to explain anything to the Pirts.

❖──────❖

I gave Corwen another hour to change to human, while I packed both our bags. By the time Corwen was a man again, the wound looked a week old. It had closed and scabbed over and was showing no signs of infection. I helped him into his shirt and masterfully refrained from saying *I told you it was dangerous* every time he winced.

By five of the clock I was hammering on the Pirts' door, rousing them as I'd roused Ruth a few moments earlier.

"Ask no questions, Mrs. Pirt. We have to leave right now, and you must do the same. Apply to Mr. Wiggins, and he will pay you three months' wages and a good reference in lieu of notice."

"What's wrong?"

"I said ask no questions. Suffice it to say there may be people arriving soon whom we would rather avoid."

"Bow Street Runners?"

"No—a private matter. Just pack your bags and leave. I suggest within the hour."

I ran upstairs into the front hallway and helped Corwen into his greatcoat. We left without looking over our shoulders, walked to the end of the road, and turned left along Wigmore Street. If anyone was tracking Corwen, it made sense for us to lead them away from the house. We didn't want to be responsible for them finding the Pirts and Ruth at home and accuse them of hiding us.

At the nearest hackney carriage stand we hailed a sleepy-eyed driver resting inside his cab, his horse dozing, hipshot, with its lower lip drooping.

"Go straight to the *Heart*," Corwen said. "They won't be tracking you."

"We'll go together, take a boat at Westminster, and approach by river."

"Do that. Be safe."

"What about you?"

"I'm going to double back to the house and check that the Pirts and Ruth have departed safely, then leave in the opposite direction and spend the rest of the morning riding around London in twenty different hackneys, crossing and recrossing the river by boat until I'm sure they can't follow. I'll join you by nightfall. I won't lead them to you, my love."

"You think they have Freddie?"

"I'm pretty sure they do. I think they were on the heath looking for any companions. Use the horse again. See if you can locate him."

"I will."

He gave me a swift kiss and was gone into the morning haze.

I threw our bags into the carriage. "The Strand," I told the driver.

In the Strand I took another carriage to St. Paul's and from St. Paul's to Westminster where I took a boat to Wapping. It was slack water, so passing under London Bridge was easy, not like the last time I'd done it, chased by Walsingham's hellhounds with the river flowing fast enough to turn the water between the bridge's piers into a six-foot waterfall. I knew we were nearing Wapping when the pervasive smell of pitch from the shipbuilding trades drifted across the river. We approached the *Heart*, and I called for permission to come aboard.

"Good to see you, gal," Hookey said as he looked over the side. "How's married life?"

"There's been some excitement, but I'm looking forward to being on the *Heart* again."

He had a rope ladder lowered. "Mind how you go."

Climbing a rope ladder in a long dress is not ideal, but I managed. Hookey offered me his hand like a gentleman. I took it like a lady, smiling to myself as I recalled the times I'd clambered up netting, boarded a French merchantman with a sword in one hand and a pistol in the other, and kicked off my shoes to climb the mainmast. What a difference a dress made.

I think the same thought might have been running in Hookey's head because he gave me a rueful smile. "You're getting too grand for the likes of us," he said.

"Never." I hitched up my skirts and climbed over the rail to applause and whistles from my old crew. I let go of Hookey's hand and jumped onto the *Heart*'s deck.

"Hello, lads," I said.

"Hello, Cap'n." Windward grinned at me. "Nice wedding."

"Made better by having unexpected guests. What did you think of your trip through Iaru?"

"Is that where we went? Good job that new fancy house isn't too far to walk in a day, it sure was warmer than I expected."

I didn't tell him he'd traveled the equivalent of two hundred miles in a few hours. Hookey could enlighten him later.

The *Heart of Oak* sat at anchor out in the Thames, off Wapping Old Stairs. Her draft was shallow enough that she could sail this far up the river, but too deep to moor at one of the many ramshackle jetties sticking out from the Thames shoreline like teats on an old sow.

"Are you sailing with us again, Cap'n?" Nick Padder shouted.

"I'm not so tired of my new husband that I'm willing to exchange him for sixty pirates. Not yet, anyway."

There was a general cheer before Hookey sent them all about their business and I was left with Hookey, Mr. Rafiq, and Mr. Sharpner, while Lazy Billy loitered nearby.

"I can make tea, Cap'n," Billy offered. "It won't be as fine as that your new mama serves, but it's hot and wet."

"Billy, I've been missing your tea. Everyone up there serves it with milk out of a china cup so fine you think you might pinch the handle off when you pick it up. It's only the mill hands know how to make a good brew."

"Tea coming up, then. Good to see you again, Cap'n."

I watched Billy disappear down into the galley, shaking my head. "He shouldn't call me Cap'n, now."

"It's a hard habit to break, Captain." Mr. Rafiq smiled.

He was the only person on board who never shortened it to *Cap'n*. It wasn't an affectation; he was always so precise in his pronunciation. I think Mr. Rafiq had availed himself of all the education the rest of us had missed out on. It was his recommendation of books that filled in the gaps in my knowledge, and conversations with him in the long hours at sea that had extended my education beyond what were normally considered fit topics for young ladies. We'd discussed philosophy and science, mathematics, religion, anthropology, natural history, geography, and all topics under the sun.

When I followed my three old friends into what had been my cabin and was now Hookey's, I was pleased to see some of the same books Mr. Rafiq had recommended to me. Hookey had learned his letters in the navy and Will had taught him the finer points of navigation. No one had had to teach him how to fight. He was a natural scrapper, deadly with a blade and a dead shot with one of the newfangled rifles we'd acquired in an underhanded deal from a supply officer at Greenwich whose debts outweighed his pay.

"You've made a few changes," I said, looking around.

The bed I'd shared with Will had gone, replaced by a narrow cot which left more floor space. Clearly, Hookey wasn't intending to entertain ladies in here; it was all business. A cot, a chart table, a stool, and my old armchair liberated from a vessel we'd taken shortly after Will's death constituted all the furniture in the cabin.

I dragged my thoughts away from Will and how I'd felt after his death. If I thought too hard, I feared I might call his ghost back, and that would be cruel and unjust. Will deserved to move on as I had done.

"Is this a social call?" Hookey asked. "We're pleased to see you, of course . . ."

"Not a social call. You know Corwen's brother Freddie wasn't at the wedding."

"Someone might have mentioned it a few times." Hookey pulled at his earlobe.

"Corwen's mother."

"The lady was pretty upset that Corwen had chosen a servant for his groomsman because Mr. Freddie hadn't showed up."

"As well she might be. However, it probably wasn't Freddie's fault. He's disappeared."

"Not another brother taken by Walsingham, I hope," Hookey said. "I'd rather not have a second trip to Vauxhall Gardens and another encounter with those hellhounds."

"Taken by the Mysterium, we think."

I explained what had happened and that Corwen was, at this moment, leading them a merry dance—I hoped—and would join us by nightfall. We'd consider our options after that. If we had to put out to sea to escape them, then that's what we would do. Corwen wouldn't like leaving Freddie behind, but it might be our only option.

⸺◆⸺◆⸺

I had some serious magical work to accomplish, so I needed to get my mind settled in order to be able to do it efficiently. I had to push down the anxiety that was threatening to render my powers completely useless, and concentrate on what I knew I could do.

I wondered where else help might be found, but neither the Lady of the Forests nor the Fae had agency in a city like London. There was only me and my seafaring family.

I didn't want to oust Hookey from his cabin and offered to sling a hammock belowdecks myself. I couldn't think of any safer or more comfortable place than lying alongside sixty sailors, each one protecting me from the others and all of them protecting me from whatever was out there.

Of course, Hookey was too kind to let me sleep with the men, though I wouldn't have minded, so I ended up in the cabin which had once been my home, but was now changed enough to make it unfamiliar. After the feather mattresses in Yorkshire and at Wimpole Street, the cot felt hard and uncomfortable. I was getting soft. It was no different from the bed I'd slept in with Will, just narrower.

My first job was to do as Corwen had asked and search for Freddie again. The lookout platform on top of the main mast was as good a vantage point as any.

I kicked off my half boots and untied my dress, letting it fall in waves around my feet. Layer by layer I peeled away the lady I was trying so hard to become and turned instead to the breeches, shirt, and jacket I'd worn for so long as captain, leaving off only my shoes and stockings. Thus dressed, I went on deck and stared up at the platform atop the mainmast through the smoky haze that hung low over the river. It was too small to call it a crow's nest, but it served our lookout at sea. Had it always been such a long way up? Once upon a time I'd climbed there in rolling seas without a second thought, but now—becalmed and at anchor—it suddenly looked dangerous.

Barefoot, I began to climb, and the worries dropped away.

I climbed steadily, only glancing down once to see Hookey's worried face forty feet below.

"It's all right," I called. "I'm doing what I do best."

He touched his forehead with one finger in a salute of acknowledgment.

I continued to climb, reaching the empty platform and tying myself onto the line that had saved our lookout's life more than once. I sat cross-legged and massaged my bare toes.

From my vantage point, eighty feet in the air, I could see a forest of masts swaying gently on the tidal swell as the great river breathed. Halfway to low water with the afternoon sun obscured by clouds and a thin layer of smog, the stinking mud lined the river. Across the shallows, a collection of ramshackle buildings, some large and some small, dipped their toes in the ooze. The stench was distinctive: rotting vegetation and ordure, washed over by salt. Beneath it lay the city smells of pitch, sulfurous coal, wood smoke, the nearby brewery, tanneries, and livestock living in close proximity to thousands of people.

I took several deep breaths, trying to clear my mind, but pictures of Corwen lying bleeding on the hall floor kept jumping into my head.

I retrieved Freddie's horse from inside my shirt and clasped it tightly in my hands, trying to make a connection. As before, it was as if he'd never existed. I even tried to summon his spirit again, hoping there wouldn't be a new-made ghost waiting for me. At least that hope was fulfilled, but I was no farther on with my search. Finally, I climbed down to wait for Corwen.

Night came, but Corwen didn't.

I waited, not letting myself panic.

And waited.

Hookey paced the deck, the closest he ever came to looking agitated. Eventually, he told me to take his cot in my old cabin and he would let me know as soon as Corwen approached.

Despite having had so little sleep the night before, I lay wide awake listening to the sounds outside. I don't remember going to sleep, but I awoke with the dawn. Still no Corwen. I came on deck, shivering. A thin rime of frost had settled on the deck and rails. The sheets glistened, and the early morning sun burned through the mist and lit icy sparkles.

"What now, lass?" For a big man, Hookey could walk light as a cat. only the clank of his hook against his sword gave him away.

"I should go and look for him, but I don't know where to start. The only place I can think of is Wimpole Street. He was going to double back to the house and lay a false trail. He could be anywhere. But he did say he'd be on board the *Heart* by nightfall, so something must have happened."

"You're not going alone."

"Thank you."

26

Murder

SO I FOUND MYSELF DRESSED as a man and in the
company of Hookey Garrity and Daniel Rafiq, heading
for Wimpole Street in a hackney carriage. We didn't take a
direct route. Windward and the Greek rowed us upriver as
far as London Bridge, and we split our journey into two,
changing carriages at Fleet Street.

The house in Wimpole Street looked untouched at first
glance, but then I looked over the railings into the area below. There was dried blood on the steps, maybe not a mortal amount, but enough to be serious.

"Down here," I said to Hookey and Mr. Rafiq.

The basement door was unlocked. The Pirts would have
locked it as they left. The instant I pushed the door open I
knew what I would find. The smell alone was enough.

"Let me go first, lass." Hookey had smelled death enough
times to recognize it, too, and he drew the sword he always
carried. When I saw it in his hand, I remembered one of his
early lessons. *You can kill one man with a pistol, but if he has
a friend, you're dead. You never have to reload a sword or a
good, sharp knife, though—you just have to be quick.*

Numb, I stood aside and let him enter the basement first. A small vestibule gave way onto a front room, the province of the Pirts. From there a short corridor led to the kitchen.

I'll never forget the stench: ruptured guts mixed with the bitterness of burning pork.

We found Mr. Pirt first, slumped inside the doorway of their neat little parlor, or, at least it had been neat before blood had spattered the walls and gray, rubbery guts had spilled out across the floor. Mr. Pirt's face was a mask of surprise. Whoever had broken in had caught him unawares and had done for him quickly. A slash to the throat had probably killed him before the belly wound, though it was impossible to tell which had been administered first.

I'd seen death before, but this neat, gentle man had not lived by the kill-or-be-killed code of the privateers. He certainly hadn't deserved to die like this.

Hookey and I followed Mr. Rafiq into the kitchen.

Neither man tried to protect me from the horror of what awaited: Mrs. Pirt, sleeves rolled up and flour still on her fingers, lay facedown in the hearth, a broad bloodstain spread out from beneath her body onto the flagstones. She'd flung out her arms as she fell; one hand had landed in the ash pan under the fire-grate where her fingers had slowly cooked in the heat.

It was not, after all, pork that was burning.

I swallowed bile that threatened to choke me.

The door to the stairs was open, and a bloody handprint showed at least one intruder had gone that way. They might even still be in the house.

Where was Ruth?

I made to climb the stairs, but Mr. Rafiq put one hand on my shoulder.

So far we'd said not one word since entering the house, all of us wondering whether we were walking into a trap. Now Hookey took the lead, feet quiet as a cat on the stone steps, his hook lifted away from his sword hilt. I followed with one of my pistols drawn and a razor-sharp carving knife in the other hand. Mr. Rafiq came last with a sword and pistol at the ready. The door at the stair head opened out into the hallway. It was eerily empty of signs of life.

We listened.

No sound except for the street outside and the usual creaks and groans of a house talking to itself.

"Stay together," I mouthed.

"Oh yes," Mr. Rafiq breathed in my ear.

Room by room, we searched the house: parlor, study, drawing room, dining room, main bedroom, three unused bedrooms and up to the attic. There were no signs of a disturbance. It seemed likely the intruders hadn't risen above the ground floor, which meant they'd got what they came for. My stomach churned.

Hookey pushed open the door to the last room and narrowly escaped being brained by a chamber pot being hurled toward his head, followed by a screeching cry.

"Ruth?" I pushed Hookey out of the way. "It's Mrs. Deverell. Are you hurt?"

"Oh, Mrs. Deverell, I didn't know what to do, I was so frightened." The girl flung herself at me, and we both sank to our knees, she sobbing, and me trying to calm her.

At last Hookey grabbed her by the shoulders and sat her on the edge of the narrow cot. "Start from the beginning, gal."

"After Mr. and Mrs. Deverell left, I ran to the attic to fetch my bag and that's when I heard screaming. I was too frit to go below stairs, but I heard men's voices, and it sounded as though Mr. Deverell had come back, and there was fighting and crashing around."

The knot in my belly tightened further. Corwen wouldn't have left the Pirts to fend for themselves; that wasn't his way. Now our two respectable servants were lying in their own blood and gore, and my husband was missing.

"Did I do right? Should I have gone for the Runners, ma'am?" Ruth eventually asked, when she'd gone through every handkerchief we had between us.

"You did right, Ruth. You couldn't know if they'd left anyone downstairs."

"Mr. and Mrs. Pirt?" she asked.

"I'm sorry . . ."
She began to wail again.

◆────────◆

There was nothing more we could do for the Pirts.

Mr. Rafiq secured a hackney carriage, and we sent Ruth to stay with her sister, the wife of a blacksmith in South-wark, where she would be safe and comforted. I would ensure Mr. Wiggins sent her six months' wages. I knew the Pirts had no living family except each other, but I would see them both decently buried. I would also need to inform Mr. Wiggins of what had happened and to ensure that he notified the Bow Street Runners about the murders.

Despite my inward panic, I managed to think logically through the immediate necessities. Worry about the rest later.

"Come on, lass, back to the *Heart*," Hookey said. "There's a carriage waiting."

I nodded numbly, my brain still stuck on Corwen. He'd been their target; there was no other explanation. They'd made no attempt to pillage the house once they'd secured him. If they'd simply wanted to kill him, he'd have been here, still lying in his own blood with the Pirts. Yes, there was blood on the steps, but not a mortal amount. They'd taken him. What did they want with him?

Whatever they wanted, they wanted him alive. I held onto that thought.

Would I know if he were dead? I thought so, but I couldn't search for him without calming myself down. I needed to center myself in order to *search* or *summon*.

Oh, Merciful Lord, what if I summoned him and drew his ghost to me? I'd lost Will. I couldn't bear to lose Cor-wen, too. My heart was pounding heavy as a horse, and my throat felt constricted. No—I definitely couldn't do any-thing magically until I'd calmed myself.

◆────────◆

I barely noticed the road. I let Mr. Rafiq guide me through the change of hackney carriages and into the boat at London Bridge. My mind was racing. Maybe I couldn't find Freddie, but I could damn well search for Corwen. I knew him so well that I didn't need anything of his as a focus.

Had the Mysterium taken Freddie, or was the story of a brown wolf on Hampstead Heath a red herring? Was Freddie in hiding and covering his own tracks? I dismissed the latter thought. Just because my own brother had proved treacherous didn't mean Corwen's brother was. What had he said of Freddie? More concerned about fashion than industry? Well, that was no crime. Feckless? Not a character trait to be proud of, but not necessarily criminal. Perhaps he'd gone off with his lover and was living the high life.

I huffed out a breath. I was overthinking things. First of all, let me see if I could find Corwen magically.

Once back on the *Heart*, I climbed the mast again. I let my thoughts dissipate on the wind and cleared my head of everything except a vision of Corwen: husband, lover, wolf, occasional agent for the Lady of the Forests. I recalled him as I'd first seen him, a silver-gray wolf almost the size of a small pony, with a luxuriant ruff and icy gray eyes. And then as I'd seen him as a man, not realizing he was also the wolf. Tall, confident, charming, he'd walked into the breakfast room at the Twisted Skein in Plymouth as if he owned the place. He'd introduced himself since there was no other in the room to make any kind of formal introduction, then acknowledged David, who was masquerading as my rowankind servant. Later, he'd even drawn a smile from the rowankind serving maid. I hadn't loved him then. In fact, I'd found him nothing less than annoying because everywhere I turned, he seemed to be already there. Even so, I couldn't deny he was attractive.

When I found out who he was and what he was, I'd left him behind, chained belowdecks on this very ship, but he'd escaped and followed me. By that time there was a feeling between us that neither was ready to acknowledge. Yet acknowledge it we did, though it took us a while longer to do something about it. My dead husband had something to do with that.

The memory of Corwen, stark naked and facing off against Will's ghost for possession of me, brought a rueful smile to my lips. What had I said then? I'd told both of them I loved them, and that I had a right to choose. I would always love Will, but he wasn't in the world anymore. I'd clung to his ghost for three years, but now it was time for both of us to move on, and though I would never stop loving Will, I loved Corwen, too, and I wanted him in my life, in my bed, between my legs. But then I told both of them to forget possession. I belonged only to myself.

Did I still?

Yes.

This was me, Rossalinde or Ross: Goodliffe, Tremayne, Sumner, or Deverell. The name didn't matter. In my life I'd been a dutiful daughter, a rebel, a runaway, a bride, a mother, a sea captain, a privateer, a sister, a niece, a kin killer, and now once again I was a wife, but I was still me. And I was, and would always remain, a witch. A powerful witch, I reminded myself. One who could *summon* the spirits of the dead, light the night as if it were day, and even call wind and water. Experimentally, I let my awareness rove into the lazy afternoon, drawing the breeze toward me and letting it whirl twice around the mast before sending it on its way. Aunt Rosie was right. Some things were only truly lost if you believed them so. I knew for sure now that my power over wind and water had lessened, but it had not deserted me completely. When I needed it, it would be there.

I knew what I was, and I knew what I could do.

Thus centered, I let my thoughts range out across the city, searching for Corwen, hampered only by my lack of local knowledge. Even if I found Corwen, how would I recognize the place where he was?

The city was awash with emotion. I saw it in shades of heat and light, akin to colors. Some areas were drenched in despair, punctuated by blazing acts of violence, bruised purple with incandescent reds and oranges; others were the quiet blue of solid citizens going about their business. Occasional patches of bright yellow shone where people gathered socially in coffee houses, taverns, theaters, assemblies, and gentleman's clubs. The city crowded in on me like a wave breaking over my head. How could I hope to sort out one place from another? How could I find one man among close to a million people?

Focus.

I tried to clear all the debris from my mind and refine it to the image of just one person. The more I tried, the harder it became.

The colors faded. A gray fog crowded into my mind, blotting out everything else. It was possible to hide things magically. Theoretically, that included people as well, but it was a complex and draining procedure, requiring a lot of magical energy. The last time I'd done it I'd slept for days afterward.

Was Corwen hidden from me . . . or was he dead? I had to know.

Instead of searching, I *summoned* his spirit, my heart pounding in dread that it would appear and confirm all my fears.

Nothing.

The rhythm of my heartbeat began to settle. I breathed again.

That was good, wasn't it?

I hoped so.   •

Tiredness washed over me, the penalty for using so much magic. I reluctantly climbed down to the deck.

Hookey was there, asking a simple question with one raised eyebrow.

I pressed my lips together and shook my head.

He huffed out a breath and jerked his head in the direction of my old cabin. I stumbled my weary way down the companionway, falling onto the narrow cot fully dressed, feeling sleep take me and dreading the dreams.

I think there were dreams, but I slept for close to fourteen hours, and in the morning all I could recall was a jumble of faces and an underlying sense of urgency.

I have nothing against shipboard food, especially in port when fresh produce is available on the dockside daily, but

Hookey, Mr. Rafiq, and I rowed across and breakfasted at
The Town of Ramsgate.

"Get yourself on the outside of that, gal," Hookey said
as the landlady brought three plates of fried beefsteak and
eggs. "You're going to need your strength."

I looked at the plate and the eggs stared back at me. A
wave of nausea threatened. How could I eat when . . . ?

Mr. Rafiq nudged the plate toward me. "Try it."

I picked up my knife and fork, cut the meat, and dipped
it in the soft egg yolk. He was right. I expected to feel as
though I was chewing on ash, but it tasted wonderful. Once
I'd swallowed the first bite I realized how hungry I was and
finished the whole lot without pausing.

"That's it, gal," Hookey said. "You won't do that wolf of
yours any good if you starve yourself. What are your plans?"

"Same as yesterday," I said. "More magical searching,
but I'd appreciate it if Sim could run an errand for me. He's
got plenty of common sense and a good manner. I need to
let Mr. Wiggins know to contact me here, and I need to
make sure he's taken care of the Pirts' funeral arrangements."

Surely I'd have better luck today.

We rowed across to the *Heart* after breakfast, and I
climbed the mast with more optimism. Alas, optimism was
only another name for false hope. By midafternoon, my
optimism had dwindled to grim determination.

Hookey fetched me down at dusk before I fell down. He
pushed a bowl of Lazy Billy's unnameable stew at me and
bundled me off to bed, but he couldn't force me to sleep. I
was desperate to slip into unconsciousness, but it wouldn't
come. When it did, I wished that it hadn't. My dreams were
fragmented and chaotic, but at the heart of them Corwen
always lay dead.

The next day was no different. By now I was sure someone was magically hiding Corwen from me.

◆———◆

Three days later I finally felt a flicker of something useful
when I went aloft to search.

By that time, I was a wreck—mentally if not physically.

I'd spent every waking hour aloft searching. During that time the weather had changed from mild to blustery. On Wednesday afternoon the wind had abated, the heavens had opened, and rain, sharp and straight as stair rods, had battered me mercilessly. Despite my oiled cape, I was soaked to the smallclothes after a few minutes. When the rain stopped, I continued searching until Hookey climbed up and settled beside me, reminding me I would be no use to Corwen if I died of pneumonia.

Reluctantly, I accepted his common sense advice and climbed down again, only then realizing how stiff my joints were and how cold my toes.

"Get out of them wet clothes, gal," Hookey said and he thumped a bowl of Billy's salmagundi on the chart table in front of me. The hot stew of mixed meat and fish with barley, onions, and vegetables made my belly gurgle with anticipation. It didn't take long to wolf down the lot.

"You're still shivering," Hookey said as I tipped the bowl and drank the last of its contents.

"I should have brought Poppy. She'd have made me a hot mustard footbath by now." With a guilty start I realized if I had brought Poppy, she might have died with the Pirts.

"Ah, well, I ain't no prissy lady's maid." Hookey stomped out of the cabin, and I wondered what I'd said to upset him, but in less than ten minutes he returned with a leather bucket of hot water deep enough to immerse both feet up to the ankle bone. "Billy says you'll have to make do with ginger. He says it's a sovereign remedy for the ague or whatever ails you."

I wasn't sure about the ginger, but the hot water worked a small miracle. By the time the water had started to cool, I was warm enough to roll into the cot in my shirt and fall asleep.

In my dream I was still searching, lifting the corners of the fog and peeking behind as if it were a curtain. I shivered as dampness enveloped me. Corwen! I got the impression of blackness and pain, but I couldn't get a location. All I had was a smell in my nostrils. That made sense. Corwen's nose was sharp. It smelled like shit with the overriding sickliness of hops. A sewer? A cellar? Somewhere close to a brewery, maybe. There were breweries all over London.

The people who specialized in what went on beneath the city were the goblins.

I needed Mr. Tingle.

27

Underground News

I DIDN'T KNOW WHERE THE GOBLINS LIVED, only where their place of business was, so there was little I could do immediately. I tried to sleep, but my dreams delivered the horrors of the Pirts' corpses, Ruth's screams, and the image of blood on the steps.

Not enough blood for the wound to kill him, I kept telling my dream-self. Corwen lives. If he were dead, I would have been able to summon his spirit. I couldn't, so therefore he lived.

Before first light I was awake and dressed. At this time of year, with barely thirteen hours of daylight in every twenty-four, a sweatshop like Mr. Tingle's would have its workers arriving with the dawn, ready to take advantage of the natural light to ply their trade. I would be at Whitechapel with the first workers.

I wasn't desperate enough to go alone. Lazy Billy, Windward, and the Greek would be my escort, a trio tough enough to give anyone second thoughts about interfering with my business. Hookey and Mr. Rafiq both offered to accompany me, but I didn't want to overwhelm the goblins. I needed their willing help.

The hackney carriage Lazy Billy found smelled as though someone had died in it, but I couldn't be picky. The four of us piled inside, and I gave the driver directions to George Yard.

While Lazy Billy stayed with the coach to make sure the driver didn't abscond, Windward and the Greek walked me up the alley, exclaiming at the state of the building. I still saw it as a wreck, but knew that now for a glamour, and so I watched for the first workers to arrive. A group of six women, family members by the look of it, came down the yard from the opposite direction, arm in arm. The youngest one, maybe twelve or thirteen, was barely awake. They passed through what looked to be the boarded-up doorway easily enough. Either they could see through the glamour, or they knew how to ignore it.

I slipped through behind them, doing exactly as they did. Once inside, a fragrant, savory smell assailed my senses.

"Mrs. Deverell," a surprised voice said behind me. "Joining us for breakfast?"

I turned to find the twinkling old gentleman, and even though I knew this wasn't his real appearance, I wanted to smile at him.

"Breakfast?"

"I find I get more and better work from my ladies if they have a warm start to the day. It costs but a few pence for oats, and rewards me much with loyalty and goodwill. How many other employers feed their workers twice a day?"

"Are all your ladies . . . ?"

"Ladies?" He laughed. "Yes they are all ladies, but some of them are goblins. Very nimble-fingered when they wish to be. Of course, that makes them good pickpockets as well." He raised one eyebrow. "I try to keep them honest. I lose fewer that way. The law is not kind to miscreants."

"It certainly isn't."

"Might I inquire as to your business?"

I told him, briefly, what had happened and explained

that I thought Corwen might be in a cellar or sewer, some-where near a brewery. I described the city to him the way I'd seen it, swirls of heat and color, then the fog and my dream.

"It all sounds like a nasty affair. You're asking for my help?"

"I'm begging it."

"In return for?"

"I don't know. What might I have that you need? I can pay."

He thought for a few moments. "An unspecified favor, to be claimed at some future date."

My stomach lurched. How desperate was I? One of the first rules in Aunt Rosie's notebook was never to make an open-ended deal with a magical creature. I took a deep breath. *Sorry, Aunt Rosie.*

"An unspecified favor." I knew I was probably letting myself in for trouble, but I'd deal with that when it happened. "At some future date."

He nodded. "Done. But there are many breweries in the city, and many cellars. I'll set my contacts looking." He shrugged. "It may take some time. Where can I find you?"

I gave him directions to the *Heart.*

"Are you sure you won't join us for breakfast?"

"Thank you, no."

⊹⸺⊹

My stomach grumbled loud enough to make itself heard above the rattle of the carriage wheels over cobbles. I should have taken breakfast with the goblins, but it seemed too mundane a thing to do. I needed to find Corwen, and find him fast.

"It won't do either you or Mr. Corwen any good if you starve yourself," Lazy Billy said as my stomach gurgled loudly. "As soon as we're aboard the *Heart,* you'll get some proper grub inside you."

"Did you boss me about like this when I was captain?"

"Well, you was Cap'n then, Cap'n." He grinned at me.

He was right, I reflected, an hour later. Safe on board the *Heart* and full of pottage and eggs, I felt better.

A little before noon a messenger arrived from Mr. Wiggins with a letter from Lily:

Dear Corwen,

I trust that you will soon be home with Freddie and that you are all well.

I received your letter about our family Friend who is not our Friend after all, and have set a Watch on the Premises as you advised. At the moment the situation is All Quiet.

Mr. Topping is a Treasure. The Mill is dry of Water and I have brought in a team of carpenters to repair the Fulling Stocks, the Headrace, and the Sluice Gate. I am assured the Water Wheel will be fully operational by the middle of next week.

Tell Ross that Poppy and Yeardley are drawn together in Affection. It's sweet, though Yeardley remains as assiduous as ever in his duties toward Papa, who continues to Improve slightly. His hand is Stronger and he has held a pen and made marks on paper, though he has little Coordination yet and it tires him Quickly.

Mother sends her love.

In haste if I am to get this letter to the evening mail coach from Barnsley by John Mallinson's hand.

> *Your loving sister*
> *Lily*

Should I write and tell her what was happening? No. It would be soon enough if and when we found a clue to Corwen's whereabouts. I would go aloft and search again.

Climbing the mast was easy now. Without Corwen, would I return to a life on the ocean? Hookey had been looking for a weather witch. I could slide back into shipboard life without the responsibility of being captain.

Don't think about it!

I couldn't imagine life without Corwen.

A little worm in my brain told me I had never imagined life without Will, either, until it had happened. Losing Will had brought home the reality that life was uncertain. Whomever I loved could be ripped away from me in an instant.

These were not thoughts I wanted to accompany me onto the precarious lookout platform. I concentrated on the climb and tried to forget the rest. Balanced on the platform, line tied securely, I took Freddie's toy horse from my pocket.

"Now, Freddie, where are you?" I spoke aloud to the horse as if it might answer.

The city still roiled in my vision, but I ranged beyond it until it was a concentrated blob at the center of my search, like the yolk in a fried egg. I didn't pay the city any more attention than its environs, but let my mind hover above it all, sampling here and there, looking for a connection between the toy and the man.

There, a flicker! It was not in the city but some miles east. My heart thumped. He was on the water, close to where the Thames emptied itself out into the sea. What had Corwen said about Freddie's fear of water? Surely he hadn't set sail of his own volition. I looked again, trying to sense Freddie himself. All I could perceive was a jumble of fear and pain.

Now I was torn. Freddie was at sea, but still close. We could probably catch him. The *Heart of Oak* was fast, faster than most cumbersome cargo vessels. The only ships that could beat her were the new Baltimore Clippers.

But to go after Freddie now would be to leave the search for Corwen, and I couldn't do that. I would go aloft again in an hour and see where Freddie's vessel lay so I could determine the speed and direction. It should be possible to track him, for a little while at least.

I was on deck when a skiff pulled alongside, a Thames

waterman hunched over the oars. Looking down I saw his
passenger was Barnaby, Mr. Tingle's grandson.

"Permission to come aboard?" Barnaby shouted up.

Hookey looked at me for a nod and then said, "Aye."

Barnaby eyed Hookey with some wariness. I must admit
Hookey's scowl didn't do anything to put the half-goblin at
ease, and Mr. Rafiq, tall, silent, and as black as the goblin
was white, looked intimidating. Mr. Sharpner, however,
patted the newcomer on the shoulder with a jovial, teeth-
rattling slap as he found his footing on the deck and nearly
lost it again under the friendly onslaught.

It took him a few seconds to recognize me, dressed as I
was. "Can we speak?"

"There's nothing you can say that my friends can't hear."

He glanced sideways as Lazy Billy and Windward pretended to find something to do by coiling rope that was already as neat as it could be.

"My grandfather says his contacts found a place. It was
in use, but now it's been emptied."

"What kind of place?"

"A cellar, as you suspected. Beneath a brewhouse rather
than a large brewery. It's not far from Lincoln's Inn. There
may even be a passage."

The Mysterium was situated in Lincoln's Inn. I suppressed a shudder.

"Does your grandfather believe the location to be a coincidence?"

"Not entirely. One of our underground brothers knew
of the place because his son was careless enough to get
caught in daylight without a glamour and ended up there,
briefly. It was not a happy outcome."

I guessed not if the Mysterium had caught themselves a
goblin. The incursion of wild magic must be making them
panic by now. The Mysterium wasn't equipped to deal with
dangerous creatures, or to recognize when a creature
wasn't dangerous. They didn't even know how to deal with
the rowankind who had been living among humans for two
hundred years. Tame rowankind were easy to understand;
free ones, with magic, were much more difficult.

"Might your contacts have any idea as to why the cellar is now empty?"

Barnaby shook his head. "They said it didn't smell of murder this time."

This time? Should I be relieved by that? I took a deep breath. "Thank you. Tell your grandfather I owe him a favor."

"He knows, Mrs. Deverell. He won't forget. Nor about the cloth contract."

He bowed and descended to the waiting boat.

"What now?" Hookey asked softly.

I raised my eyes to the mast again. "Wherever Corwen was, he isn't there now, but it's likely the Mysterium has him. Another search."

◈—————◈

"You're climbing like you used to do," Hookey said as he watched me descend from the tops after barely an hour.

"My feet have gone soft."

"Nothing that won't harden up again, given time."

It was an oblique invitation to return to the *Heart* if all didn't go well, but I'd found something, or thought I had.

"Corwen's at sea," I said. "The estuary, maybe."

Hookey narrowed his eyes and stared downriver as if he could see that far. "And the brother?"

"Freddie hasn't moved. He's still off the mouth of the Thames, but Corwen's position and Freddie's are converging."

"You'll be wanting us to weigh anchor then, gal?"

"I would be much obliged, Captain Garrity." I made it absolutely clear I wasn't trying to take over from Hookey.

"Some of the lads are ashore, but likely they'll not have gone much farther than the nearest alehouse."

"If you're sending a boat for them, I need to write a letter. I'll make it quick."

I jumped down the last few steps of the companionway as I used to when this place was my home. My feet knew the shape of the treads, and I landed nimbly.

In Hookey's cabin I scribbled a note.

Dearest Lily,

There was a distressing break-in at our house in Wimpole Street and I have fled the ugly scene and am currently lodging in my old room with the friends you met at the wedding. You may write via our Man of Business in London.

I fear Corwen has been Pressed to visit M, an old acquaintance, and cannot currently Get Away. Freddie is All At Sea, too. I hope to catch up with both of them soon. My Heart is racing at the thought.

Further to Corwen's last letter about forces close to home, you might inquire of Mr. Tingle if you don't hear from me soon, as he has been most helpful.

I urge you not to make any Changes in your activities. Expect a call from the charming Mr. Pomeroy, I believe his Interest in you to be keen.

> *Your Loving Sister*
> *Rossalinde.*

There, it was a little cryptic but I hoped she would understand. Corwen and Freddie were both missing, and I was on the *Heart*, trying to track them down. Don't change into a wolf under any circumstances as the Mysterium may be watching. I sealed the letter and entrusted it to Lazy Billy to make sure it was sent as a matter of urgency.

Lazy Billy and Sim rowed across to Wapping Old Stairs and in less than an hour had returned with the letter sent on its way, and a boatload of crew in various stages of drunkenness. Hookey hauled them upright, sloshed a bucket of water over two of the worst, and sent them to sober up.

By midafternoon we were underway, with the fast tidal current running at four and a half knots in our favor, and a light breeze from the southwest. The brown, murky river carried us between mud flats, past the Blackwater, complete with its shallow draft barges and oyster fisheries. Mr. Sharpner kept us well clear of the spritsail-rigged barges waiting at anchor for the tide to carry them upriver. Low and flat-bottomed, they could float in three feet of water.

At last we saw the twin lighthouses of South Foreland, the upper and lower lights, both shining out as the sun dropped low, warning of the dangers of the Goodwin Sands where many fine ships had come to grief. The Goodwin Sands were reputed to be haunted by the *Lady Lovibond*, a schooner deliberately driven onto the sands and sunk with all hands due to the jealous rage of the first mate on the occasion of the captain bringing his new bride on board. Two vessels, independently, had reported seeing the specter only three years earlier, and the story, much embellished, had been repeated in several newspapers. It had become the talk of dockside taverns. Sailors were a superstitious lot and loved to spread a good ghost story.

Some of our present crew still believed Will Tremayne haunted the *Heart*. Will had haunted me, which, since I was on the *Heart* most of the time, amounted to the same thing. If Will's ghost had been out in front, leading the boarding party whenever we'd engaged another vessel, the crew felt confident we'd prevail. Though none of them could see him, someone would invariably shout: "Is the old captain there?" The answer was always yes.

It still was. I hadn't told them Will had passed on to wherever spirits go when they're at peace. If Will leading the charge gave them courage, let them believe it for as long as they liked.

Searching for both Corwen and Freddie was considerably easier once we left the city behind. Their paths were converging. I didn't even have to go aloft anymore; there was a steady pull on my senses, and I studied Mr. Sharpner's charts to see if I could pinpoint their location. With only one direction and no way to triangulate, I couldn't tell exactly how far they were, but I could give him the heading.

I couldn't begin to guess the reason for them being at sea. Corwen had been held in a cellar which, according to Barnaby Tingle, didn't smell of murder *this time*, meaning it had probably been the scene of foul deeds in the past. It was way too close to the Mysterium for my liking, and if young Barnaby was right, there were underground passages connecting it far too conveniently with the Mysterium office. If the Mysterium had both Deverell twins, would they investigate the rest of the family?

By the time my mind had tried to envision every possible scenario, I was exhausted. I set my hands to work cleaning and priming my pistols. In the hold, my sea chest, which I had left behind, not thinking I would need it again, held my short sword wrapped in a length of silk. It was smaller than a cutlass, but more suited to my size and strength. I honed it until it was sharp enough to shave the hairs from a rat's arse.

"It makes me nostalgic for the old days," Hookey said as I came on deck. "You're expecting trouble."

"If it's the Mysterium, there will be trouble." I pushed down anger. "I thought I'd done with them, but it appears they're not done with me."

28

Guillaume Tell

I KEPT A MENTAL LINK between the *Heart* and Corwen's location, which had now converged with Freddie's
completely. It told me where they were, but not how they
were, other than the fact they were both alive. I guided Mr.
Sharpner through the early evening gloom as he worked
with his coastal charts to avoid running us aground on
Goodwin Sands like so many ships before us. We sailed
past the North Kent marshes with its wheeling seabirds
and into open water off Deal and the Kentish coast.

"It's close now," I whispered, barely a minute before
Nick Padder, aloft with a glass I had magically enhanced
with light-vision, called *ship ahoy*.

"Is it them?" Hookey asked.

"Unless there's another vessel out there in its shadow
made invisible by a glamour."

If only I had the skill to cast such a glamour, we could
sail right up to the ship, quiet as you please. Unfortunately
we didn't have that option, though we were far enough distant that it was likely they hadn't seen us yet, unless they
too had an ensorcelled glass.

No easy target, the ship was large, a warship of French design, but I'd kept up with the news; if I was correct, this was the *Guillaume Tell*, dismasted and captured by the British off Valetta in March of last year. She'd been repaired but obviously hadn't yet been commissioned as a British ship of the line, so what was she doing at sea with her canvas furled and my husband and his brother on board?

I needed to get close, but I couldn't simply sail the *Heart* alongside and hail her, even in the dark: *Ahoy there, unregistered vessel, I've come for your prisoners., Hand them over, or we'll pitch our eight guns against your eighty.* Imagining that scenario made me wince. The *Guillaume Tell* was a full-rigged ship more than twice our length and beam. Fully armed, she carried eighty guns spread between her lower deck, upper deck, quarter deck, and fo'c'sle. When commissioned, she carried a complement of almost eight hundred. I had no way of knowing whether she was fully crewed and armed.

If Will's ghost had still been at my beck and call, I could simply have sent him to spy and report back, but just because I could summon him, it didn't mean I should. That set me thinking. A recent ghost who'd not yet passed over, one who had good reason to help, might be available. I hadn't known Mr. Pirt that well. As his temporary employer I hadn't known him at all, certainly not as a person with a history, aspirations, and fears. I knew how careful he was to lock doors, shutter windows, and secure the Wimpole Street house from dusk to dawn. He was a quiet man, not given to sudden movement or the appearance of rushing, but he carried out his duties assiduously.

Mrs. Pirt, on the other hand, was louder and more robust, with a way of looking me directly in the eye when making a helpful suggestion about the house which was tantamount to me giving me an order. *Do something different if you dare,* her look seemed to say, while remaining perfectly polite. Since she knew her business far better than I did, I always accepted her suggestions gracefully.

Calling her spirit would take its toll, but I might be able to find her on the other side before she passed to that deeper place. Mrs. Pirt would do nicely. She might not know much about sailing, but she could count the number of crew and tell me where Corwen and Freddie were and what condition they were in.

"I need to call a ghost, Hookey," I said.

"The old captain?"

"No, let him rest. I need a new-made ghost. She may well be angry and confused. It would be better if I used your cabin. No matter what you hear, don't disturb me or let anyone else in."

"Is it dangerous? The old captain was—"

"Will was different. But even though he loved me and loved the *Heart*, there were times when he didn't act in our best interests. When people pass over, their perspective changes. They become a reflection of what they used to be, but the mirror is distorted, so some things are more important to them than others."

"And this spirit you're going to call . . . ?"

"My housekeeper at Wimpole Street."

"The woman with her fingers in the fire? A bad death, that. Are you sure?"

"I have a connection, even though I only knew her for a few days. She died because of us, because of Corwen."

"Nay, lass. Neither you nor Corwen is to blame for the actions of others. You didn't invite those boys into your house to kill the Pirts. Don't take any blame if she tries to dish it out."

"I'll remember." I smiled at him. Hookey may have had a scant education, but he was wise, and it was what I needed to hear. I felt guilty about the Pirts, but he was right. Our only crime was underestimating the lengths to which the Mysterium thugs would go

<hr />

I locked myself into Hookey's cabin. It still didn't feel like mine. Just those few subtle differences were enough for me to feel discomfited, but I couldn't let that interfere with what I had to do next. I settled into my old armchair—the only thing that felt familiar—and closed my eyes.

I fastened on the image of Mrs. Pirt, not as I'd last seen her, splayed on the kitchen floor with floury fingers cooking in the hot ash, but standing before me in the parlor suggesting that we needed to order more coals and to have the chimneys swept as she doubted they'd been done for a year or more. I pictured her neat pepper-and-salt hair firmly pinned beneath a lace cap, her sensible cotton dress, not remotely fashionable, but practical and well-kept. Her name ... what was her given name? I'd never called her anything but Mrs. Pirt, but Mr. Wiggins had given us their references. Elsie—that was it. Elsie and Horace Pirt.

"Elsie Pirt."

As I said her name, I summoned her spirit mentally.

"Elsie Pirt."

The third time was usually the one.

"Elsie Pirt."

I felt as if all the blood was draining out of me. My knees turned to jelly and I doubted I could move from my chair even if I wanted to.

"What do you—? Oh, it's you." The spirit glared at me.

"Yes, it's me. I need your help."

"I'm not your housekeeper now."

She swelled up, larger in death than she had been in life, and loomed over me, her face too close for comfort. I felt myself pushing back into my chair even though I knew she couldn't hurt me except with the power of suggestion.

"Indeed, you're not." I took a deep breath. "I'm sorry for the circumstances of your passing."

She shook her hand and sucked her fingers as if there was residual pain from the burn, but Will had once told me one of the tragedies of being a shade was that he could feel neither physical pleasure nor pain.

"We should have gone when you said, but Ruth wanted to pack her things and took her sweet time. We couldn't leave her. And then the men came—four of them—and Mr. Deverell came back and tried to help, but one of 'em knocked him senseless from behind with a billy club."

"The men who ..." I wasn't sure how to word it. "It was a deliberate and barbarous act, and I'm sorry for it. I'm following Corwen now, and I know where he is, but I need you to spy out the situation for me. Corwen and his brother are on a ship—"

"The men who killed us—Pirt and me—are they on it, too?"

"Possibly. I don't know."

"Bastards, they are. Pure dark bastards. I'd see them dead in a heartbeat. No, not a heartbeat. No beating hearts. No pumping blood. A body's too quiet when its blood's not pumping. No blood. No ears. No body. How does all this work, then? Is this heaven? It's not what I expected. But I didn't expect a knife in the gizzard either."

"I'm sorry, I don't know. I think there's another place . . ."

"Where's Pirt?"

"I don't know that either."

"You're not here. Not real."

I was beginning to feel unreal, weak and tired, but I didn't like to tell her she was the one who was no longer in the real world.

"Please, Mrs. Pirt, I need your help."

"Why?"

"To find Corwen. To find the men who killed you and Pirt."

"A ship, you say."

"Yes, they're on a ship."

"I don't know anything about sailing. I've never been on a ship."

"You're on one now."

"I am?" She looked around the cabin for the first time. "Doesn't seem so bad."

"This is my ship, the *Heart of Oak*. The ship I want you to spy on is called the *Guillaume Tell*, and she's close by, just below the horizon."

"How do I get there?"

"How did you get here? Wish yourself across, I think. You can go where you please. I need to know how Corwen and his brother are, where they're being kept, and whether they're being restrained. And I need to know how many crew are on board and whether there's anyone else there.

In particular, a man called Walsingham. Anything else you can find out which will help me free Corwen will be an advantage."

"And the men who killed us? I want justice."

"If the men are there, I'll set things straight for you and Mr. Pirt."

She gave me a nod and disappeared from sight.

I didn't move. I couldn't. I was breathing as if I'd run a race, my heart pounding.

Will was the only spirit who had ever come to me of his own accord, without draining me of energy completely.

———◆———◆———

It seemed to take forever for Mrs. Pirt to return. In reality, it might have been less than an hour. I'd managed to get to my feet and was staring through the sea-scoured glass at the sparkles of moonlight reflected in the *Heart*'s wake. I felt the temperature in the cabin drop, heard her behind me, and turned.

"What a vessel!" She sank onto the chart table. "Four decks. Plenty of nooks and crannies. They were there, two of them at least."

"Corwen?"

I sat down again before I fell down.

"The men who did this." She placed one hand on her belly and blew on her burned fingers again. "You said you'd square it up with them."

"I did. How will I know them?"

"Mr. Deverell knows them."

She started to fade away.

"Wait? What about the rest? You found Corwen and his brother?"

She became less translucent. "Mr. Deverell, and a lot more besides. There's two levels with guns on them, huge guns. I didn't count them. Does it matter?"

"No."

"I had to keep going down and down," she said. "There's a big space below the gun decks. Cages in it, for animals and the like. Dark it is, and it smells like a sewer. People in

there, not only Mr. Deverell, though he was there, too. I
didn't see any brother, though. Mr. Deverell had a big
brown dog curled at his feet. Chains. Some were in chains,
some in big cages."

"How many others?"

"You didn't ask me to count them, but more than a few.
Some all slumped together in the darkness, others restless.
Some real people, a few rowankind, and some the like of
which I've never seen before. A couple of great big hulking
things, some little itty-bitty things, some with white faces,
noses like beaks and bulging eyes."

"Goblins?"

"There were some creatures I couldn't rightly name.
What is Mr. Deverell? Is he a witch, like you?"

There didn't seem much point in not telling her, after all,
who was she going to tell? "He's a wolf shapechanger."

"A werewolf?"

"He's not moon-called." It was a point of pride with
Corwen. "That dog may have been his brother, a brown
wolf."

"If you say so." She sniffed disapprovingly.

"And how many sailors on board?"

"Close to a hundred, though none of them doing any
sailing. Even I recognize what an anchor chain is for. And
all the sails tied tight on those cross-bars."

"Is that it?"

"A few men—not sailors. Muscles for brains. And some
well-dressed gents giving orders. Mr. Deverell said to tell
you—"

"He saw you? He's uninjured?"

"He did. He's not mortally injured, though I've seen him
looking better. He said to tell you there are two Walsinghams and a witch. And you should know that Olivia is
there, too. Livvy, he called her."

"Livvy? A rowankind child? Aged about eight?"

What was going on?

"A rowankind child, yes."

"Two Walsinghams?"

"That's what he said. There was a man who couldn't see,

but he could see me. I felt him. Had an air about him. Witchy like you, only . . . more so. And another man—gave a lot of orders. He troubled my calm."

Mrs. Pirt began to fade. I didn't have the energy to keep her any longer. "Thank you Mrs. Pirt. Safe journey to you."

Two Walsinghams. How could that be? One had to die, or possibly resign, before the next was appointed and the name passed on. Had they learned their lesson? Did one Walsingham act as a balance to the other? The Walsingham I'd fought and killed had been out of control, using dark magic that was worse than the magic he was trying to eradicate.

But the new Walsinghams weren't the main problem. At least a hundred men stood between me and Corwen. And there were imprisoned magical beings. Would they be a help or a hindrance? There was no way I could lead my crew to board the *Guillaume Tell* and overcome their crew in a fair fight, so what next?

I couldn't leave Olivia behind, so that was three people to rescue now, and what of the rowankind? They would be hopelessly sick on the ocean, maybe even sick enough to die. As for the rest of the magical creatures, some might be dangerous, and I would have to deal with them if they became a problem, but they need not all be.

I was sorely in want of a plan. How was I going to get on board the *Guillaume Tell* quickly and quietly without being seen? We needed a distraction.

What would draw every man jack of the crew's eyes regardless of their duties?

Something beautiful? Something terrifying?

Something beautiful and terrifying.

A ghost ship.

The *Lady Lovibond*, last seen in this area only three years previously, and widely reported.

Could I summon the *Lovibond* herself?

I doubted it.

I didn't know what had been the cause of those sightings, but I'd never been given any reason to suppose ships could have any kind of ethereal existence after being soundly sunk or broken up on a sandbank. If they could, I would have seen some sign before now.

But I could create an illusion.

I had the *Heart*, and I had my ability to make light.

Midnight would be the perfect time.

"You know what to do?"

I assembled Mr. Sharpner and the crew belowdecks.

"Aye Cap'n," they said, almost in unison. They weren't all comfortable with the idea because they were sailors, too, and some of them were as superstitious as the sailors we were trying to fool.

"But what if—" That was as far as one sailor got before Lazy Billy dug him in the ribs. I didn't recognize the man. He was new since my time as captain which meant he'd not been around when I'd created light before. My regular crew had taken it for granted after a while, and my ability to manipulate wind and water had been well known, but little talked about.

"Cap'n's a witch, but she's *our* witch," Lazy Billy hissed. "Why d'you think this is a lucky ship? Hush yer yammerin'." He turned and glared at the assembled crew. "Anyone want to argue has to argue wi' me."

"An' me," Windward said.

"Aye." The Greek stood shoulder to shoulder with them.

Nick Padder stepped forward, together with Crayfish Jake and Sim Fairlow. It was enough to start a wave of support.

Mr. Sharpner nodded. "There'll be no backsliding. We know our part, and we'll play it to the full."

"I know you will. It has to look good, but if the *Guillaume Tell* starts to run out her guns, I'll let the light fade and you need only sail a safe distance and stand off. I'll call if I need the *Heart* to come closer."

"Are you sure you don't need a bigger boarding party, Cap'n?" Crayfish Jake asked.

"This is a sneaky job, Jake, a rescue. We can't get everyone, so I'll be trying to bring out Corwen, his brother, and a little girl called Olivia. If we need the *Heart* to come in with guns roaring, you'll know about it, believe me. I'll send up a flare so bright they'll see it from the Tower of London."

Hookey stood to one side, saying nothing, his face a mask of misery. He'd wanted to be part of my small boarding party, but he understood why I wouldn't include him even though he was one of the best scrappers I've ever known. He was captain now, and it was his duty to stay with the *Heart*. Besides, if we needed rescuing ourselves, there wasn't anyone I'd trust more to do the job.

Mr. Rafiq, Windward, and Lazy Billy were the only ones coming with me in the boat. Mr. Rafiq for his clear head and fighting skills, Windward for his extraordinary strength, and Lazy Billy for his sneakiness and lock-picking ability. He'd taught me everything I knew and probably knew a whole lot more besides. We had loaded pistols, but they were for emergencies only; our blades were much more silent.

⬥━━━⬥

The ship's boat held eight comfortably, twelve at a pinch, and fourteen before she was in danger of riding too low in the water. My priority was to rescue Corwen, Freddie, and Olivia. With the size of the boat, we could rescue four or five additional prisoners if all went well. The four of us took an oar each and pulled toward the *Guillaume Tell*. When we'd covered something over half the distance, we shipped oars and I turned my attention inward to where the seat of my magic lay.

It had always been weaker at sea than on land. I was truly a creature of the forest. It was the source of my power. I clutched the wooden seat beneath me and brought to mind when it had been a living tree. It shuddered beneath my hands as if it remembered. What had been a knot put forth a tiny sprout, budding with a single leaf. I touched the edge of it in wonder. Here was my forest. I drew on the connection and concentrated on pure white light. Creating light had always been one of my ready-magics. It came easily to me. I needed light but not heat. Burning the *Heart* to a cinder wasn't in my plan.

I'd stationed men, dressed all in white, their faces and hair floured like ghosts, to stand along the top yard, high above the deck, arms outstretched. I hoped the safety lines wouldn't be highlighted. The *Heart*'s white sails were all deployed, right up to the t'gallants, but I'd calmed the air to barely a breeze, enough to keep her underway without her canvas flapping. The rest of the crew were dressed in their darkest clothes, hidden from view as much as possible apart from a single white-clad helmsman and one white clad figure on the bowsprit whose job was to point a finger at the *Guillaume Tell*.

Time to put on a show.

I made light. I felt a tingle deep within my torso as the magic shivered out of me. I couldn't afford to have our little boat lit, so the light had to stay on the *Heart* herself.

"There!" Daniel Rafiq breathed out next to me as a flicker of unearthly white light shone up the mainmast. Next I lit the foremast. I let the glow spread to light the ghostly men on the t'gallant yard, standing fingertip to fingertip, the sails billowing beneath them. Then I lit the main and the fore sails, the stays'l, the jib, and the outer jib until the *Heart* was a ghostly apparition skimming the surface of the water.

"Oh, Cap'n, that's a sight to turn white trousers brown," Lazy Billy said.

"Quick, pull for the *Guillaume Tell*," I said. "Let's take advantage of all this distraction. I'm not sure how long I can keep it up."

I could feel the energy use pulling at the edges of my consciousness. It wasn't draining me yet, but it would. Stand with your arms stretched out holding an apple and the apple weighs next to nothing, but try to hold that position for any length of time and the apple gets heavier and heavier.

We bent to our oars again and approached the big warship unobserved, tying onto her stern as quietly as we could and climbing onto the deck, no mean feat in itself.

As I'd hoped, the *Guillaume Tell*'s crew were on deck, gaping at the ghostly apparition. Some were exclaiming in fear, some in wonder, but all eyes were riveted exactly as I'd hoped.

Silently, we slipped down the aft companionway, soft-footed in the shadows.

Following Mrs. Pirt's guidance, we didn't examine anything on the gun decks but ran straight to the hold, meeting no resistance.

A stench met us that I'd last experienced when Will took a slaver off the African coast. Too many bodies, too close together, and not enough sanitation. How many people were crammed in this hold?

"Is that you, Bushy?" A voice spoke from the shadows. "Christ, man, what's happening up there? Come take my place so I can see for myself. I don't want to be the only man without a story to tell."

"I guarantee you'll have a story," Mr. Rafiq said.

"That's not Bushy. Who are you? Have you come to relieve me?"

There was the sound of a sharp knock and a body slumping to the floor.

"You are relieved," Mr. Rafiq said. "Billy, tie him and gag him."

I risked a single witch light, conscious of not depleting the lights I was still holding on the *Heart*.

"God's ballocks!" Windward said. "How many of the bastards are there?"

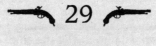

29

Rescue

DOWN THE LENGTH OF THE HOLD, each side of a central aisle, were iron cages which held a variety of magicals, some in chains. Nearest to me, goblins scrambled to their feet and stood, some clutching the bars, regarding us warily.

"Mr. Tingle sent us," I said. Not strictly speaking true, but close enough. "How many here?"

"Twenty-eight of us," the nearest goblin hissed at me. "And some others."

"What kind of others?"

"Many. Hobs, rowankind, brownies, naiads, dryads, trolls, creatures, humans, witches."

"The rowankind must be sick."

"Can't you smell them?"

Vomit was certainly part of the miasma.

"Any of you hurt?" I asked.

"Nothing to stop us from grinding the bones of those who put us here if you free us."

"No bone grinding without my permission. Not yet, anyway."

He grunted at me. "You're not a goblin."

"I'm a witch. I'm going to get you out of here." Damn! Another hasty promise to a magical creature. How was I going to do it? "Have patience. Where's Corwen Deverell?"

I walked along the cages. In the one next to the goblins was a naked woman. Her mane and tail, pure white, told me straightaway what she was. She looked at me, then looked away. Across the aisle was a larger cage with many rowankind crammed into it. The stench of sickness was almost unbearable and most of them were lying or sitting. No use asking how they were; rowankind could die from seasickness very quickly. Some of them might already be too far gone. How long had they been here?

"Corwen?" I raised my voice as I walked between the cages. "Corwen Deverell? Freddie Deverell? Olivia? Livvy?"

"Miss Rossalinde? It is you!"

"Olivia." On the floor of a cage Olivia crouched with her arms around the neck of a large brown wolf. He drew back his lips in a snarl.

"Hello, Freddie," I said as calmly as I could. "I'm your new sister-in-law, Ross. Where's Corwen?"

"He won't change back, miss. He's been a wolf since he got here. Weeks. I've lost count. I wouldn't have known he was anything else until they brought Mr. Corwen."

"Where's Corwen now?"

"They took him in there." She pointed for'ard to where there was a door in a bulkhead. "Nothing good happens there. Sometimes people don't come back."

"Are you sick, Olivia?"

"Sometimes, if it's rough, but not as bad as the full bloods. Some of them have been here for months. Two died yesterday. They . . . they throw the really sick ones overboard. Are you here to rescue us all?"

"Yes," I said. "Billy, start picking the locks on these cages." I raised my voice. "Everyone stay where you are until all the cages are open. Don't run off on your own, or you'll get killed. Not that one." I pointed to the kelpie's door. "She's too dangerous."

She grabbed the bars. "You need me," she said. "If you are going to take this ship, you need me."

"I've nearly been killed by one of your kind."

"And I've nearly been killed by more than one of yours, but I swear no harm to you or your people. When this is over, we can go our separate ways."

"All the people in this hold are mine, for now, at least. They're protected: human, rowankind, goblin, wolf. Especially the wolves."

"Understood."

A wave of light-headedness came over me, and I checked to see if I still had a connection with the *Heart's* ghostly lights. Yes, everything was in order. I closed my eyes briefly and then blinked several times in quick succession to clear my head.

"Set her free, Billy, but if she turns into a horse, don't touch her."

Billy crossed himself before kneeling to pick the lock, and I saw the kelpie sigh and shake her head. Perhaps this one had more human reasoning than the one we dealt with on Bur Isle. People varied in intelligence; why shouldn't kelpies?

Snuffling in another cage were two eight-foot trolls. Lord knows where the Mysterium got them from. It had to be the Mysterium. We were on a Mysterium prison ship, not a hulk for it was still seaworthy, but a floating jail all the same. Where were all these magical creatures being taken? I spotted brownies, hobs, and a smaller cage full of pixies. There were several people who looked human, some imprisoned together, a couple separate.

"Witches?" I asked.

Some said yes, but one man simply stared at me as if I were dirt on his boot. He was not only caged but bound in iron chains. He could stay there until I found Corwen.

"You'll regret that decision," he said as if he could read my thoughts.

"Then tell me who you are and what you intend," I said. "I didn't come here for you, but I'll not leave anyone behind except those I think mean harm."

"Some harm, maybe." He spat. "To those who deserve it. I offer a temporary alliance—like the kelpie."

"Not good enough if you're the one who decides who gets harmed and when the alliance ends. I need more reassurance."

"I give you my word you'll get fair warning."

"We take this ship. With as little bloodshed as we can." I was still forming a plan, working with what I had: three sailors, some goblins eager for a fight, and at least a hundred other magical folks if you counted the pixies.

He grunted. "Agreed."

I nodded to Billy and turned my attention to the door in the bulkhead. It was locked, of course, but I had my own set of lockpicks and Billy had taught me well. It took me a minute, maybe two, before the stout iron gave way.

The room beyond was totally dark, but as I put up a second witchlight, I recognized a voice I had never thought to hear again. "Mrs. Tremayne, I wondered how long it would take you to come for the wolf."

❖━━━━━❖

Walsingham. My nightmare come true.

"I thought you were dead," I said, trying to keep the sudden tremor out of my voice.

"I was—as good as. An explosion will do that to a man."

I brightened my witchlight. He didn't turn his head toward it or look at me directly. His face was a pulped mass of burn scars down one side, his eyes barely open and, from what I could see, useless. This was Mrs. Pirt's blind man who could see ghosts. Damn!

"I was months on a pirate vessel, halfway between life and death. They only kept me alive for the ransom."

"Lucky for you it was before Mr. Pitt resigned, or Mr. Addington might have left you to rot."

"Ross!"

I raised the witchlight higher. The shadow behind Walsingham resolved itself. Battered and bruised, but still standing, Corwen was caged in a space barely six feet square. The bars glinted silver.

"They've been trying to get me to change into a were-wolf," he said. "Can you believe it?"

I took in the silver bars and the whips and prods hanging close by it. They obviously knew little about wolf shapechangers. They weren't werewolves. Silver wouldn't hold them, and it had less strength than the heavy iron bars in the main hold.

Corwen obviously hadn't changed, If he had, his cuts and bruises would have healed by now, unless they'd been inflicting more, trying to make him angry enough to lose control.

"Mr. Walsingham and I have been having some meaningful conversations," Corwen said. "King George had appointed another Walsingham by the time he got home."

"Sir Edward Walsingham," I said. "Appointed him in your stead, Walsingham, and made him head of the Mysterium."

Walsingham waved a scarred hand at his scarred face. "Maybe it's all to the good. Young chap. Not one of my apprentices, but resolute. Strong."

"I should feel sorry for you," I said. "But—let me see—no, I don't."

"You may be interested to know," Corwen said, "that he blames you for the release of wild magic."

Walsingham wasn't wrong, of course. It had always been there, but I'd removed its restraints.

"How interesting. Does he know the Mysterium witches are out of their depth?"

"Oh, I've known that for a long time," Walsingham said. "A very long time. I knew it even before you found the winterwood box. Mysterium witches are only the visible layer of magic in this country, as you yourself know. Tame. Benevolent. They are all society can cope with. But real magic runs deep, and like an iceberg, most of it is never seen. If we are to continue the analogy, the iceberg has now floated into British waters and is melting."

I pulled the loaded pistol from my sash and clicked back the doghead. Walsingham turned at the slight sound. He had good hearing, even if his sight was gone.

"Do you intend to shoot a helpless blind man, Mrs. Tremayne?"

"I don't doubt that you're blind. I do doubt that you're helpless."

He chuckled, seemingly unafraid of the pistol. "You find me severely disadvantaged since the last time we met."

"Exactly how do you come to be here?"

"It appears I have some value after all, even maimed and blind." He shrugged. "I am here as an adviser."

"You sound very calm for someone who has a pistol pointing between their eyes."

He tutted at me. "You're really not going to use that, are you? You and I have a lot in common." He sounded reasonable. No wonder he'd beguiled my brother Philip to his cause so easily.

"I might not, but Corwen will if you so much as move a muscle."

I edged past him and handed Corwen the pistol while I applied my lockpicks to the problem of opening his cage.

"It might be a good time to consider how many times you advised the new Walsingham to have me beaten," Corwen said. "I think you enjoyed it. You could have turned me into a werewolf again at any time if you wanted to. You've done it before with spellcraft."

"A working like that is delicate. It takes a lot of preparation. I never committed all of it to memory and . . ." He passed a hand across sightless eyes. "It's hard to read notes."

I glanced at Corwen as I worked on the lock. "What he says may be true. He always had the prepared spells on his person in the past. He's not the kind of man to share his notebook with anyone. Besides, if he did, they'd realize he dealt with blood magic. The Mysterium wouldn't stand for that, even from a Walsingham."

Where was Walsingham's notebook? He would probably have kept it about his person, which meant he probably had it with him when I blew him up along with James Mayo's flagship. If it had survived the explosion, would it have survived the sea and the tender attentions of the pirates who pulled him out of the water? Maybe he didn't even have the notebook anymore.

But if it still existed, it was a dangerous artifact.

"I was never under the rule of the Mysterium." Walsingham's words broke my train of thought.

"No, you weren't. My brother told me that. You reported directly to the king and Mr. Pitt, and now Mr. Pitt is no longer in power. I'm guessing Mr. Addington is not such a supporter of the Walsinghams, especially since you failed in your major mission, to prevent the reawakening of the rowankind to magic. That's probably why your successor is now in charge of the Mysterium. It makes him more accountable."

The lock I was working on clicked and the cage door swung open. Corwen stumbled as he came out but recovered quickly.

"Stand up, Mr. Walsingham," I said. "Remove your coat and drop it on the floor."

"And if I don't?"

"Right now I'm on the cusp of deciding whether to leave you dead, or maybe give you to the prisoners in the hold, which amounts to the same thing, but with more pain. Make up your mind."

He took off his coat while Corwen kept the pistol trained on him.

"Now the rest of your clothes. Every last stitch. And if you have any prepared spells tucked away, you won't have the opportunity to use them. Corwen is a very good shot."

When Walsingham stood naked before us, I saw the damage the explosion had done. I'd say he was lucky to be alive, but maybe he wasn't. His coat and the half-light had disguised the fact that his left arm had been lost above the elbow and there were burn scars on his lower torso and hip. His private parts hadn't escaped. I wondered whether he had to squat like a woman to piss.

Corwen drew a sharp breath in sympathy.

"I'd rather have my eyes back," Walsingham said, interpreting the sound correctly. "Even one would do."

"Step to your left, about four paces." I directed

Walsingham to the cage, pushed him in, and kicked it closed behind him, using the lockpick as a key to turn the mechanism and jam it.

Corwen checked Walsingham's clothes. There was nothing concealed in his shirt. He turned to shove it through the bars.

"No, don't. Leave him naked." I wasn't going to give him any garment. "Even the fluff in his pockets could be dangerous."

We left Walsingham shivering in the silver cage and closed the bulkhead door behind us. We'd decide what to do with him later.

◆———◆

As the bulkhead door closed on Walsingham, Corwen pulled me to him and we stood for precious seconds, arms around each other.

"How did you find me?"

"I figured out the cellar, but I couldn't tell where it was. Mr. Tingle helped me make sense of what had happened to you. The cellar was conveniently located close to the Mysterium offices, and it was protected from my searches by some kind of spell. I owe him a favor in return. Unspecified and at a time of his choosing."

Corwen drew air in through his teeth. Making openended promises to magical creatures didn't usually end well.

"Yes, I know, but I was desperate. He confirmed the Mysterium had you. I never thought Old Walsingham still lived."

"They're both as bad as each other, but different. Old Walsingham always relied on spells and his instincts. New Walsingham thinks himself a man of science and aims to discover, scientifically, the root cause of magic. He thinks if he can learn more, he can use it for the benefit of the realm. Whatever he can't make use of, he seeks to eliminate. They thought they'd got a werewolf, and as it was coming up to a full moon, they were trying to get me to change. They were talking about how useful a werewolf could be to Wellington's army. I didn't tell them a real werewolf would be equally as likely to slaughter Wellington's troops as the French."

"Old Walsingham would know that."

"Old Walsingham wasn't there when they started. When he learned who I was, he simply laughed and let them get on with it."

"Are you much hurt?"

"Cuts and bruises. Nothing that won't heal next time I change."

He made light of it, and I knew he would be able to heal himself, but not before the fight that was to come.

"They brought me here and threw me into the cage with Freddie. Even though I'd never seen him in wolf form, I would have recognized him anywhere. He's not well, Ross. It's not just his body, but he's not right in the head. He's been under so much strain I fear he'll break. He hasn't changed back from wolf since he got here according to Olivia. While Freddie stays a wolf, they can't identify him. I think he's trying to protect the family."

"So they were trying to get Freddie to change into a human and you into a wolf."

"They were experimenting on us to see whether they could goad us into it. I only had three days of it, Freddie had weeks."

"But they know who you are?"

"I don't think so. Walsingham never knew me as anything other than Corwen Silverwolf, and the new Walsingham has been more concerned with my magical potential than with my name. We always speculated about what happened to the most powerful witches who registered with the Mysterium. Like Olivia's father, they're conscripted to use their magic for the Crown, either in the army or the navy or, sometimes, to work for the Walsinghams or the Mysterium itself. The magicals are a resource as far as they're concerned. From hints that new Walsingham dropped, I would say any magicals who don't agree to work for the Crown in one capacity or another don't survive very long."

"Bastards." I took his silence for agreement. "But why take Olivia?"

"A mistake, I think. The local Mysterium must have heard about the kelpie. They went sniffing around the reverend, probably because his son registered as a witch. They must have made the connection between Olivia and her father and brought her in for interrogation. I don't think the head office realized how young she was until they got her here. They don't want her. They don't need her."

"So what are they intending to do with her?"

That little muscle in Corwen's jaw jumped as he clenched his teeth. "They threw her in with Freddie to try to tempt him with food."

"They expected Freddie to eat her?"

"So I understand. They didn't expect her to win him over like she has. She and Freddie have become inseparable."

A sick feeling roiled in my guts. "That's horrible—inhuman."

"Magicals aren't considered human. The outbreaks of raw magic have not gone unnoticed. The government is frightened. The Mysterium is at a loss. There's a special committee of Parliament that meets regularly to discuss the matter."

"And the king?"

"Is once more under the heavy control of his doctors, supposedly for his own good, but Walsingham, Old Walsingham, that is, let something slip that was very revealing. They think the king's madness is magically induced. That he's under some kind of spell."

"The Fae are right," I said. "The law needs to change, though I doubt the king can make it happen, and if Parliament has no will—"

"We should kill Walsingham," Corwen said.

"Killing him in a fight when he's trying to kill me is one thing. I'm not sure I could murder him in cold blood."

"He wouldn't hesitate to kill you if he could."

"He said so?"

"He didn't need to."

"Let's think about it later."

He dropped a kiss on my head. "You're a bit too noble for a pirate."

"Privateer." It might be a small distinction, but it was one I wanted to keep. "What about the rest of the rowankind? Why take them? It's not even legal."

"Try arguing that with the Mysterium. They're taking any they can identify as having used magic."

Please let it not be so. Mr. Topping, his family, and the rowankind at the mill were all known to have used magic. Lily's letter would surely have said if they'd had such problems.

"Do they understand that all rowankind have magic now? What about the mill workers?"

"My first thought, too. We need to get back, or at least send Lily a warning."

"I wrote to Lily and warned her she might expect a visit from the Mysterium. I had to be cryptic. I hope she took my meaning."

"She's a clever girl."

"Yes, she is."

"So what next? How many men have you brought?"

"Three." I jerked my head toward Lazy Billy, who was only halfway through picking the locks on the cage doors, and Mr. Rafiq, who was checking on the state of the rowankind prisoners. "Windward's watching the companionway."

"Three won't get us far."

"I thought this was a rescue, not a takeover. You know we're going to have to take the ship, right? There's no other way to free everyone at once. The *Heart*'s acting as a distraction. Her boat's tied up aft."

"Ah, she's the ghost ship everyone suddenly got excited about. Is the light draining you?"

"Not as much as I expected, but I can feel it like a long slow burn in my belly. I don't know how much longer I can keep it up."

"If we take the ship, won't that make us pirates?"

"For sure. The *Heart*'s letters of marque aren't going to cover this. Even I can't claim that I think the *Guillaume Tell* is still under French command."

"Keep the *Heart* out of it," Corwen said. "Send the boat away with as many of the most vulnerable prisoners as we can safely seat. There are plenty of able-bodied magicals, if only we can get them all to agree on a plan. That, of course, might be tantamount to juggling with eels, as they are hardly a unified force."

It was the sensible thing to do, but I would miss Mr. Rafiq and Windward in the coming skirmish. Only Lazy Billy would stay as he was still wrestling with the rest of the locks in the hold.

"What are we up against?" I asked. "Does the new Walsingham have magic?"

"I don't know, but he does have paid witches in his employ. That's why Bulstrode has a flea in his ear."

"Bulstrode?"

"Styles himself a wizard. Has a high opinion of his own capabilities."

"I believe I've met him."

"Indeed his opinion is not entirely without foundation. He is powerful, but three of Walsingham's witches took him down together. He's still smarting from it. One of them is aboard right now."

"How do we stop it turning into a bloodbath? There's a kelpie, for instance . . . and trolls."

"And at least two werewolves," Corwen added. "But the moon is on the wane, so we have a period of grace before they turn again. They can fight, though."

I glanced down the hold. Most of the cages were open now, and magicals were stepping out, stretching their joints and preparing for what would surely come.

"You should go in the boat, too," Corwen said.

"What? No!"

"You're the only link to the *Heart*."

"I'll take the risk. Besides, Old Walsingham recognized me, so it's already too late. I'm staying."

Corwen didn't answer. He knew how stubborn I was.

30

Fight for Freedom

M R. RAFIQ AND WINDWARD didn't like the idea of leaving, but I picked up Olivia and thrust her into Mr. Rafiq's arms. "Get her away safely, please."

Freddie emerged onto the deck and growled, but Olivia touched his head. "Be good. I'll see you soon."

He slunk into the shadow of a hatch and crouched there.

"Take as many of the rowankind as you can," I said. "They'll be better on the *Heart*, not as seasick. Some of them can't last much longer."

With the help of the goblins, we got Olivia and nine of the worst affected rowankind quietly into the *Heart*'s boat while the crew of the *Guillaume Tell* still stared at the ghost ship. Mr. Rafiq shoved off. "We'll be standing close by, captain."

"When we take the ship, we'll run up a distress signal so the *Heart* can come alongside legitimately."

"What if you don't?"

"Look for survivors in the water."

The *Heart* was still giving her light show, attracting attention. I hadn't expected to be able to hold it for this length of time. Anything extra now was a bonus.

—◆———◆—

"We're ready as we'll ever be." One of the goblins stuck his head above the level of the hatch. "Everyone who can fight is free."

He looked too eager, as if he were about to charge forward into the crew all by himself.

"Get everyone on deck. Be ready," Corwen said. "Then it's every man—every person—for him or herself."

There was a murmur of assent.

We crept forward in the shadows. The crew stood silent, their attention still held by the ghost ship. All eyes were turned forward, away from us, except for one pair. I may have imagined the glitter in his eyes—after all I could only see the rest of him as a silhouette against the *Heart*'s light show: the curly head of hair, tall and imposing with a slim outline. Walsingham. I recognized him from the public meeting. He didn't look so much like a dandy now. He appeared to stare right at me, but I crouched into the shadows and squeezed Corwen's arm to warn him to be still and silent. At last Walsingham focused his attention on the shadows on the other side of the ship. It was as if he knew something was amiss, but couldn't justify giving the alarm.

I put my lips to Corwen's ear. "It's now or never. Walsingham's suspicious. Let's go!"

My heart pounded. Was I leading these people to their deaths, outclassed by hoary sailors and Mysterium thugs? Maybe—yet I couldn't leave them imprisoned.

Corwen squeezed my shoulder once. Pistol in hand, he led half the goblins along the starboard side of the ship where they collected marlinspikes and belaying pins and anything else that could be used as a weapon. Bulstrode and the rest of our witches fanned out and took sheltered positions. We'd had a hurried conference about who could do what. The only thing I'd been adamant about was no fire, not real fire, anyway.

The crew would fight, but if they were regular sailors, they'd not know how to fight magic. I was more worried about the contingent of Mysterium thugs whom Mrs. Pirt had described as "muscles for brains." I hoped none of them had their pistols primed, though even without fire-arms and blades they were probably handy with fists and feet.

The rest of the able-bodied followed the goblins. No one held back. They all knew this might be their last chance for survival. The pixies disappeared into the shadows, al-most invisible unless you were looking for creatures that were barely the size of a well-grown rabbit.

When everyone was in place, I let the ghost-lights fade on the *Heart*. I felt a rush of blood to the head. Power I'd been trickle-feeding into the light show suddenly rebounded on me. It was as if my blood was fizzing in my veins.

For a moment there was complete silence except for the normal sounds of a wooden ship on the ocean, the creak of timbers, the flap of canvas and the slosh of water on the hull. Then the *Guillaume Tell*'s crew all began talking at once, speculating wildly about what they'd seen.

That was my cue. I made a yellow light, turning it as or-ange as I could manage and set it to flickering up the for'ard companionway. It looked like fire, but it was cool.

Someone yelled, and there was a general rush and a grab for buckets, with two fire crews manning the pumps. In all the chaos it was easy enough for the goblins to pick off those on the outskirts. I'd hoped to minimize the blood-shed, but we were fighting for our lives and couldn't afford to take able-bodied prisoners. Broken bones and battered heads were the order of the day to even up the numbers.

Lazy Billy stood guard over me while I played flickering orange light up the aft companionway. The ruse worked, maybe as many as thirty or forty crew disappeared below-decks and goblins and witches followed. The pixies, always good at mischief, tripped people on companionways, ran ropes around ankles, and generally caused chaos.

It took longer than I expected for the word to go around, but when it did, it spread faster than the fire warnings.

"Prisoners have escaped!"

I saw a knot form around one man who was still for'ard.

"Walsingham," Corwen said.

"Surrender. You are outmatched!" Bulstrode stalked along the deck, arms outstretched toward Walsingham. A woman jumped forward and met him with some kind of spell. His long stride became jerky, and I saw her shake and him falter. I let the fire-lights go and swept up the air around her, spiraling it upward, leaving her nothing to breathe. She dropped unconscious, but so did Bulstrode. So much for grand gestures.

A small elderly witch, one I'd almost ignored because she'd looked so fragile, had tucked herself beneath the capstan. She cast a spell toward half a dozen of the thugs, to be rewarded with cries of: "Wasps! Get them off me! Get them off!" as the men pounded at their clothing and flapped their arms in front of their faces. Whether there was something there or whether it was illusion, I didn't know, but it worked for long enough for four goblins to relieve them of their swords and pistols.

Sucking up the air worked well; I did it again and again, dropping several sailors where they stood, but not leaving them without air for long enough to suffocate them.

Then something hit me on the back of the head. Light exploded behind my eyes as I dropped to my knees.

Walsingham stepped forward.

The man I'd seen at the meeting in Seven Dials didn't look so composed now. In fact, he looked desperate, which made him dangerous. I still didn't know whether he had any magic of his own, or whether he was first and foremost an administrator. The witch had to be my first concern.

I tried to drop her with my air magic, but she countered with air magic of her own. Damn! She followed with a flaming arrow which I barely deflected. It hit a coil of tarry rope which burst into flames. I used Aunt Rosie's spell to put it to sleep, but that took time and gave the witch an opening. The deck beneath my feet creaked and powdered to dust. I barely flung myself to one side in time.

Lazy Billy grabbed me by the waist and pulled me into the shadows. "Mind yourself, Cap'n."

"Thanks, Billy." I touched my hand to my head. It was sore, but my fingers came away clean. No blood. It had been a spell, then. The witch was powerful. She'd got control over the air, maybe over water as well.

I needed forest magic now.

A fighting ship is a floating forest. Five hundred oak trees go into her making and though, in the case of the *Guillaume Tell*, they were French oak trees, I trusted they'd answer my call. I pulled on that well of power that I'd once used without hesitation. At sea, it was always muted. I needed to be on land now, in a place that was alive to magic. In my heart I called on the Lady of the Forests.

I heard a creak as a twig sprouted from the plank beneath my hand. Yes, that was it. Two saplings snaked up from the deck and wrapped themselves around the witch's shins. She tried to step away, but they held her firm. She lost her center of balance, collapsing backward. I let the saplings weave around her, binding her to the deck.

One down and one to go.

"You. I know who you are." Walsingham's voice still held that sonorous quality even though he had to raise it to be heard over the din of a hundred separate fights. "Rossalinde Tremayne. He said you'd come."

"I don't want to hurt you."

He laughed. "Hurt me? I think not."

I gathered my magic to suck air from Walsingham, but it didn't work. He had some kind of shield.

"I just want the prisoners freed." My voice cracked.

"They're mine."

"You're killing the rowankind."

"Regrettable, but necessary. I need to know what they can do. What all of you can do. How else can I protect this realm from magic?"

"We're not a danger to the realm."

"You can say that? You who freed the rowankind? The single most destructive thing you could have done. You gave them magic."

"I only gave back what had been taken away."

I threw a ball of light, guaranteed to make anyone flinch, but not Walsingham. The light flared and burned out a yard in front of his eyes. He didn't even blink.

He shook his right arm. Something rolled into his hand from his sleeve. He flung it at me. It exploded like glass in midair, shards of magic blasting outward and digging into my flesh wherever they touched, burrowing deeper, searching for my inner being to snuff me out. My face felt as if it was on fire.

"Ross." Corwen dropped to my side. "What can I do?"

This was Walsingham's spell. It wouldn't end until one or the other of us died.

I tried to say kill him, but my mouth wouldn't move.

Walsingham laughed, not an evil maniacal laugh, but the sheer relief that his spell had worked. I wondered how experienced he was in spellcasting and how much he'd had to learn in a short space of time. Old Walsingham had worked at his dark arts for all of his adult life.

Walsingham shook his left arm. Something rolled into his hand. Another spell. I tried to warn Corwen. Walsingham took the time to transfer the spell to his right hand and began to draw his arm back ready for the cast.

Freddie streaked past us and leaped at him with a snarl. Walsingham crashed to the deck under two hundred pounds of wolf.

"Freddie!" Corwen tried to call him off as four-inch fangs met in Walsingham's throat. There was a choked-off scream, a gurgle, and blood sprayed from a severed artery. Freddie tore and tore again. Throat, face, anything he could get at. Rending, gulping, swallowing, until Walsingham's face was a half-eaten bloody pulp.

"Jesus!" Corwen leaped at Freddie.

Pressure and pain gone, I scrambled to my feet to follow him. He threw himself on top of the monstrous brown wolf, heedless of the bloodied maw, and dragged him sideways from his meal. Freddie twisted and snapped, sinking his teeth into Corwen's arm not once or even twice, but again and again. Corwen held fast until Freddie stopped struggling.

I knelt beside Walsingham, shoving my fingers into the ruined meat that used to be his neck, desperately trying to stem the spurting. He was trying to say something, but his tongue lolled out of what used to be his cheek. What came out of his mouth didn't even sound human. I knew it was hopeless. I knew he'd been trying to kill me. He'd thrown a child into a wolf cage, goddammit, so I should rejoice in his death, but he had a family and a fiancée who loved him. Maybe he was trying to say her name. Maybe he was cursing me with his last breath. I had no idea.

I swallowed hard. There was nothing I could do. You can't heal what's no longer there. His eyes were open as I released pressure on his neck. The blood that had been trickling hot between my fingers began to spurt again. His fingers flexed. I grabbed hold of his hand and squeezed.

He stared into my eyes.

"You're not alone," I whispered. "I'll stay with you."

And I did, until his eyes glazed over and the spurting blood slowed to a bare trickle. His last breath rattled out of his ruined throat.

I remembered the vivacious miss at the meeting in Seven Dials and the way they'd looked at each other. She was a widow before she'd had chance to become a wife. Maybe Old Walsingham had been right to eschew family life.

With Walsingham dead, the shipboard struggle was over. The sailors had no more heart for fighting something they couldn't understand. The witch had lost her paymaster, and with everyone else surrendering, there was little she could do even as powerful as she was.

Corwen looked at me over the top of Freddie's blood-matted fur, and I recalled our conversation with the Lady of the Forests after the kelpie incident. Once a magical creature has eaten human flesh they get a taste for it and can never be trusted again. I hoped Freddie hadn't signed, sealed, and delivered his own death warrant.

⟜ 31 ⟜

Rough Justice

I SAW TO CORWEN'S INJURIES FIRST. Twenty-eight separate puncture wounds where Freddie's teeth had ripped into his arm. Luckily, the bites hadn't hit a vital vein.

"I've had worse," he said. "Don't fuss, Ross. It will heal when I change."

"Change, then. It's swollen like a sausage."

"There are other things to deal with first."

With the sailors and the Mysterium bullies locked belowdecks in the cages, and the witch confined to a cabin, having given her parole in exchange for our promise not to set her adrift in an open boat, we were able to put up a distress signal for the *Heart* to come alongside.

We took stock while we were waiting. It hadn't been a bloodless takeover, of course. There were a lot of injuries: broken bones, stab wounds, and seven dead among the ship's crew and the Mysterium hands; three with head injuries from belaying pins, one a victim of his own knife turned against him in a close struggle, and three missing and presumed gone overboard in the chaos. We'd lost one of the goblins, again, missing presumed overboard, and the little old witch who had hidden beneath the capstan and had tormented the sailors with magical wasps was dead with not a mark on her. I suspected she'd overused her power. She looked to be close to a hundred years old. One of the trolls had taken five or six sword cuts to his chest, arm and shoulder, but they didn't seem to be worrying him despite the amount of slimy green blood on the decking. His mate, at least I think he was the male and she the female—it's difficult to tell with trolls—was making a fuss and poking at him, which was probably doing more harm than good. I left them to it.

Suddenly, my hands began to tremble, and I felt near to tears, a reaction that sometimes set in after extreme danger as whatever drove my fight-or-flight response drained away and my mind replayed what had happened and also what might have happened. This was the point at which I usually took myself off to somewhere private until the shakes had passed. When I was captaining the *Heart*, it wasn't appropriate to show weakness. Now it hardly mattered, but old habits die hard. The best I could do in the aftermath of this struggle was to stand by the rail in the waist of the ship and let everything flow around me.

"Are you all right?" Corwen came up behind me.

"I will be." My voice trembled. "Good job I don't get the shakes while the fight is on."

"It's over now."

"Not quite." I pointed to a light out on the ocean traveling toward us. I couldn't see clearly; the spectral figure was still too far away, but I knew who she was. "Mrs. Pirt wants vengeance. She said you would be able to identify the men who took you and killed her and Pirt. I . . . promised her I'd settle the score for her."

Corwen drew a sharp breath of air in through his teeth. "Never make promises to the dead."

"I know, I know . . . but I needed to find you, and I couldn't think of a better way to assess the situation here. Can you?"

"What? Identify them? Yes, I can." He looked unhappy. "What does she want of us?"

"Well, now, that's the question, isn't it?" Mrs. Pirt's figure hovered in the air above the deck rail.

Corwen turned to me. "Did you summon her?"

"Only the first time."

"She showed me the way," Mrs. Pirt said. "And now I'll have my way."

She vanished.

Corwen and I looked at each other and immediately set off for the nearest companionway to the hold.

The familiar stench assaulted my nostrils, though this time the occupants of the cages were the surviving ship's crew and the Mysterium's thugs. Corwen held a lantern, and I brightened it with witchlight. As we passed the first cage, there were a few cries of: "What's happening?" and "What are you going to do with us?" When we got to the second cage, holding half a dozen men, Mrs. Pirt was already there before us.

"Him." She pointed.

I looked at Corwen. "Is she right?"

"Yes, that's one of them."

"I wondered how long it would be before you wanted a little payback." The man rose to his feet and looked at Corwen.

"Payback for rough handling and ill-treatment?" Corwen said. "Yes, I could say that would satisfy me, but it would satisfy her more."

The man obviously couldn't see Mrs. Pirt's ghost. He looked puzzled.

"Do you have a name?" Corwen asked.

"Don't have to tell you."

"No, you don't, but I hate to see a man go to his death without knowing what name to put on his tombstone."

"Now, look . . . we might have roughed you up a bit, but we didn't do more than that."

"Not to me, but what about her?" Corwen said.

I lent Mrs. Pirt's shade some energy and she manifested as she'd died, blood spurting from a deep belly wound and fingers on fire.

The man gave a formless cry and flung himself deeper into the cage, trying to hide himself behind the others.

"And you!" Mrs. Pirt pointed to another of the men.

"It weren't me, missis, honest. It were Lofty."

Five goblins had followed us to the hold, all of them able to see the specter. I hadn't known they had that ability.

"I ain't taking the blame alone. It was you what done for the old cove," Lofty said.

The leader of the goblins drew himself up. "If we goblins were allowed to practice law in this country, the courts would be much more just. Imagine every murder trial where the victim could bear witness and speak for themselves."

"This ain't no trial!" Lofty said.

"I think it is," the goblin responded. "You have condemned yourself out of your own mouth. It only remains to be seen what punishment your victim will seek."

"If the law will hang a man simply for stealing food for his hungry family," one of the other goblins said. "There is only one punishment for murder."

"You can't!"

The goblins looked to me; I nodded.

Lofty and his companion tried to shelter behind the other men in the cage, but they were having none of it. They gave up the two murderers, not wishing to be seen trying to protect them. The goblins swiftly unlocked the door, dragged the two men out, and marched them up the companionway into the clear night.

"How shall it be done, Mrs. Pirt?" I asked her, knowing it was my promise that had caused this trial-by-specter, and it would be up to me to make my word good. I hoped she didn't want a reciprocal death for them. I had no wish to gut them personally. I've killed with sword and knife, but always in the heat of a fight. Tonight had been a sharp and unpleasant reminder that since retiring from my privateering life I had vowed to leave the blood-letting to others.

"Ross, let me," Corwen said.

"I once told you Will had hanged a man for rape, and

you asked if I would have done the same in his place. I said I would. This is no different. If I am, de facto, the captain of this ship, if only for an hour or two, it's my responsibility. And we're all agreed that it was a vile and unjust murder."

"We are agreed," the leader of the goblins said. "To let it go unpunished would be an insult to this sad spirit."

"They are mine," Mrs. Pirt said. "Stand them by the ship's rail."

The goblins did as they were asked, stepping back from the miscreants, but not so far back that they could run.

Mrs. Pirt swirled into the air. She'd been a tall woman with muscular arms used to wielding a meat cleaver. Now she appeared as a blazing spirit with a spectral carving knife in each hand. Growing to twice her size, she swept down upon the pair and thrust a knife into the guts of each one.

Belief is a powerful thing. I knew the only way the dead could harm the living was by the power of suggestion and the simple tool of fear.

As the ghost knives sunk into real flesh, each man doubled over believing this was their end and that their guts had been punctured. They staggered back and fell over the rail into the black ocean. Mrs. Pirt laughed triumphantly and blinked out.

We all rushed to the rail, but they'd sunk with barely a ripple. Not that I would have flung a lifeline if I'd seen them floundering.

There was the echo of a woman's laugh, and I fancied I could see three shades floating over the ocean, diminishing in size until they vanished in the distance.

I felt drained of all energy and sank to the deck, leaning against the mainmast.

"All right?" Corwen asked.

"I'll have to be. Here's the *Heart* come to answer the *Guillaume Tell*'s distress call."

And here she was, within hailing distance.

❖——❖

Hookey could sail the *Heart* with twenty men and the other forty, under Mr. Sharpner, could crew the *Guillaume*

Tell as long as she didn't run into bad weather, so we exchanged crew.

I was right, the rowankind were not as sick on the *Heart*. I'd discovered long ago that my own seasickness abated due to the sliver of magical winterwood spliced into her keel. She was the embodiment of a floating forest. The goblins stayed on the *Guillaume Tell* to keep a guard on our prisoners, getting a certain amount of pleasure from the reversal, though to their credit they refrained from the small cruelties that often happen between jailer and prisoner.

"No bone crunching," their leader agreed, though he looked slightly saddened by it.

As soon as the rowankind had crossed over to the *Heart*, Olivia hurtled across the planks onto the *Guillaume Tell*.

"Where's Brown Boy? I mean Freddie," she asked.

Corwen, right arm swathed in bandages because he hadn't had the opportunity to change to his wolf and begin healing yet, caught the child as she ran across the deck. "He's all right, Olivia, but best to leave him for now. He did a bad thing, and he's upset."

"Where is he?"

A yip and a yowl from the captain's cabin gave it away. Olivia wriggled out of Corwen's weakened grasp and raced for the door beneath the aft castle.

"Olivia, come back. He's dangerous!"

But she paid no heed to the warning. Quick as a flash she drew the bolt and hurtled into the cabin. By the time Corwen and I reached the door, she had her arms firmly clasped around Freddie's neck and the big wolf had his ears pinned to his skull submissively. He growled at us over her shoulder, and she tapped his snout. "Bad dog. Play nicely."

His lips relaxed to cover his fangs.

"I think she'll be all right, don't you?" I said to Corwen. "Get yourself to the *Heart* and change before you get an infection in those bites."

"There's too much to do here."

"Nothing that needs you specifically. I'll come and join

you soon. If we're sailing round to Bur Isle, I'm not going to throw up my guts on the *Guillaume Tell*."

That was the plan. We would sail along the coast to Bur Isle where we had friends in the Reverend Purdy and Olivia's mother, Charlotte. There we'd reunite mother and daughter and bring the freed prisoners ashore. From Bur Isle it was only ten miles to the Okewood. The Lady of the Forests would be willing to take in refugees and guide the rowankind to Iaru if they wanted to go.

It would at least give us a breathing space to decide what to do next.

We'd failed miserably in the Fae's request for us to intercede with the king and Parliament. That was a task for another day. I didn't see how we could do as they'd asked us now. If we showed ourselves anywhere within the capital, we'd likely be clapped in irons once news of our escapade got out. We would have a brief window to go home and set our affairs in order. After that, even Yorkshire wouldn't be safe. It would be the first place the Mysterium would look, and our presence would bring a whole heap of trouble on the family.

Family. I glanced toward the cabin where Olivia and Freddie were happy, for now, in each other's company. What were we going to do with Freddie?

Try as we might, we couldn't get Freddie to change to human and speak to us. Neither could we get him to trust the gangplanks lashed between the *Heart* and the *Guillaume Tell*.

Corwen tried. I tried. Olivia tried.

He remained deaf to pleading and cajoling.

Corwen got him as far as stepping out on to the deck, but as soon as he saw the precarious planks rising and falling between the ships with the gentle swell, he growled and retreated to the shelter of the cabin.

Olivia skipped over the planks secured between the two ships five or six times. Though it was obvious that Freddie was agitated as soon as she crossed over, he couldn't summon the courage to follow her.

It seemed that he was equally afraid of water as a wolf as he had been as a man.

"Come on, old boy." Corwen settled in the captain's cabin, reclining on the narrow cot while Freddie curled up, nose to tail, on the floor. "I know you can understand me. It would be much better if you changed to human again. Then you could cross on two feet, holding the safety rope while you did it. Ross and Olivia skip across as if they're out for a Sunday stroll. I'm no sailor, but if I can do it, you can."

Freddie gave him a baleful look.

"Olivia's waiting for you on the *Heart*. Don't disappoint the child. She's been through a lot. She thinks highly of you, Lord knows why. I think you're a first-rate ass."

Freddie rumbled in the back of his throat.

"Well, what else would you call yourself? You can't deny the wolf. You know what I went through when I first changed. I know you were late, but Lily was there to guide you. Hell, Freddie, you had an address. You could have asked. I would have come."

Freddie grunted and rolled on to his side.

"Don't believe me? Lily wrote, so I went home. First time in six years. I can't believe no one wrote when Jonnie died. You could have done that, Freddie, saved this whole damn mess. You had responsibilities, dammit. What were you thinking? Were you thinking at all?"

Freddie whined.

"Lily's fine. She's running the mill, doing your job. Growing up fast."

Freddie whined again.

"Your family wants to see you, to know you're safe. It's not a vast leap of logic. But in order to get you home, we have to get you to dry land. We can't do that unless you'll cross over that damned plank. We won't be able to pull up to a harbor at Bur Isle. We'll all be going ashore by boat, then Mr. Sharpner will abandon the *Guillaume Tell* to Boney's navy. Do you really want to be left behind and end up shot for a wolf or in a French prison?"

When Freddie didn't respond, Corwen looked at me. "I don't know what to say next."

"Nothing. Freddie's caused enough trouble for now. I've half a mind to leave him behind. I imagine the Mysterium will have something to say about him tearing out the throat of their glorious leader." Freddie shifted uncomfortably. "Yes, I know you can hear me, Freddie, and I know you saved my life and possibly Corwen's by killing Walsingham, but there's killing and killing. Let's not pretend that all's well, because it isn't, but we can't make it better unless you cooperate. Corwen needs to heal. I'm going to take him to the *Heart* and let him change a few times. Otherwise those bite wounds are going to fester, and even a wolf's changes won't beat gangrene. We'll be back before the two ships cast off. Make up your mind. What happens next is up to you."

Corwen opened his mouth to speak, but I shook my head. Let Freddie stew on that for a while.

❖⸺❖

Corwen reached Hookey's cabin on the *Heart*, stripped off his clothes, and sluiced down in half a bucket of water with a wet rag and a bar of hard soap. "Ah, that's better. I needed to change two days ago, but I was damned if I was going to prove to them that they had a wolf man."

I touched the bruises on his chest. "Change now. You're safe. I'll stay with you."

I put my arms around his neck. He winced before he kissed me, but I'll say this for Corwen, he's a good kisser: warm, sincere, not too wet, with just the right amount of lingering, and . . .

"Go change, or I might not be able to leave you alone."

He kissed me again, dropped his forehead to mine, and sighed. "I really do need to heal. I fear I wouldn't acquit myself very well right now. Ouch!" The last word emerged as I squeezed his ribs.

He changed twice before he began to look better. I suspected at least two of his ribs were cracked. The wolf bites on his arm had narrowly missed major blood vessels, and they were ragged and nasty. Even when they healed, they might leave a lattice of white scars.

"They'll fade in time," Corwen said.

I checked him over as if he were a prize horse at Tattersalls. "Your brother has a lot to answer for."

"He does. I fear the Lady of the Forests won't want him to go straight home. She'll want to make sure he's not dangerous. You know what she says about a magical creature tasting human flesh."

"I know. But in your brother's defense, Freddie had been tormented by Walsingham for weeks."

"It hardly matters now." He stretched. "We should go and see if he's changed his mind about the planks."

"I've a mind to net him and have him swung over on a line. We can't waste any more time. The rowankind might be less sick on the *Heart*, but they're far from well."

With that in mind, I explained what I wanted to Windward, the Greek, and Lazy Billy. They prepared a cargo net and spread it, as silently as they could, on the deck outside Freddie's door. With the ropes slack it looked inoffensive enough. Corwen let himself into the cabin.

I didn't go and add my voice to the discussion. If Corwen couldn't persuade his brother, then I wasn't going to be much use. I heard Corwen's voice rise to exasperation levels, more for my benefit than Freddie's I think. "Right, you can stay here and take your chances with the Mysterium!"

The cabin door whipped open, and he stalked out with a reluctant Olivia in tow. The instant he got over the threshold, he shoved the child at me, turned and grabbed Freddie by the scruff of the neck, and dragged him into the center of the cargo net. Lazy Billy gave the signal. Windward and the Greek hauled on the rope, drawing the net around both Corwen and his brother.

"Keep still," Corwen said as Freddie began to struggle. "I'm going to cover your eyes, and if you damn well bite me again, you'll be the only wolf shapechanger without a full set of fangs. Understand me?"

The answer must have been yes because Freddie stopped struggling and the lads swung the net over to the deck of the *Heart*, dropping it as gently as they could amidships. A cheer went up. Olivia and I crossed quickly, Crayfish Jake released the gangplanks and safety line, and the two ships began to drift apart.

"Lay aloft. Loose all sail," Hookey roared, waving a farewell to Mr. Sharpner and the lads on the *Guillaume Tell*.

As I untied the net, Freddie jumped to all fours, front legs braced and snarling at anyone who moved.

"Freddie, don't be such a baby." Olivia walked calmly up to him and encircled his neck with both arms. "This is the quickest way back to land. You don't want to stay on that smelly old ship, do you? We're going home to my house. You can meet my mother."

I wondered how that meeting might go, but Reverend Purdy would give us a lot of leeway, especially when we brought his granddaughter home again for the second time.

Whether we could leave her with her family was another matter altogether. The Mysterium had taken her away once, so they could easily take her away again. She and her mother might be safer in the Okewood. I caught Corwen's glance and suspected he was having the same thought.

32

An Offer

WE STAYED WITHIN SIGHT of the *Guillaume Tell* all the way along the coast, giving the port traffic at Dover and Southampton a wide berth. Corwen and I got to spend some private time together in Hookey's cabin, which was bliss. Freddie preferred to hide out in the little cubby where Mr. Rafiq slept, kept his accounts, and guarded any tangible treasure gained from skirmishes with the French. Since wherever Freddie was, Olivia was sure to follow, Mr. Rafiq finally declared the space too small for three, and slung his hammock in the hold alongside the skeleton crew and the recovering rowankind.

Hookey's seamanship skills guided us deftly along the channel, beating to weather against westerlies. During the day Corwen and I went among the rowankind, hearing their stories, finding out which parts of the country they'd come from, and why they'd been taken by the Mysterium. Each one had a slight variation on the same tale. They'd been fine until they'd begun to use their wind and water magic, and then the local Mysterium had come for them. In some cases they'd gone quietly; in others there had been protests and riots and a few more of the rowankind had been taken because of the unrest.

The Fae weren't going to like this. This was exactly what they'd been worried about and why they'd asked us to make representations to the government and the king.

"I hate to say this," I said to Corwen as we snuggled in Hookey's narrow cot for the second night, "but I think we need to speak to Walsingham."

Corwen raised himself on one elbow, dragging the blankets from my shoulders. I shivered and pulled them back. He didn't seem to notice.

"Walsingham is bad news. Kill him and have done with it."

"There's more we can learn. He probably still has a link to the king, and I think . . ." I screwed up my face because I hardly wanted to admit it. "I think he's lost face. He's lost his position. He's no longer *the* Walsingham. The position as he knew it doesn't even exist anymore. I think we might have something he wants. Being the intermediary between the Fae and the king will give him the whip hand again."

"Would that be a good thing? Blind or not, he's dangerous."

"He is, but at least he's a danger that we know."

"And that's a good thing?" Corwen leaned over and lifted my hair from my ruined ear. "He nearly killed you last year."

"You saw him. He's diminished."

Corwen sat up and wrapped his arms around his knees.

"Physically diminished, maybe, but he's still a force to be reckoned with. I overheard him talking with New Walsingham—he was still pulling strings."

"Did you ever see him use magic?"

"No. I didn't get the impression that he couldn't, though. I overheard him telling New Walsingham to always have prepared spells about his person."

"I can't think of any other way to get to the king like the Fae asked us to."

"Even if we could tempt Walsingham to intercede with the king, the king's intermittently mad. If we get an audience, can the king do anything?"

"He's still the king."

"Yes. Yes, he is." Corwen hugged me to him. "All right. We'll talk to Walsingham before we reach Bur Isle and see if we can reach some accommodation. But if he takes one breath without permission, I swear I'll put a bullet in his brain."

We signaled the *Guillaume Tell* and effected a successful transfer in the boat. Luckily the sea was calm, because the instant I left the *Heart*, seasickness threatened. I managed to fight it down.

Freddie hadn't been happy about our departure, but as usual, Olivia calmed him and Hookey promised to keep an eye on him. Hookey and Freddie had come to an understanding. Freddie had snarled once too often, and Hookey had kicked him in the teeth. After that, they more-or-less ignored each other.

Mr. Sharpner was pleased to see us, and quickly gave us an update on the state of the prisoners. Most of the common sailors, seconded from various vessels currently in dock at Greenwich, hadn't known what their new duty was going to be until they shipped out. They'd been less than charmed to discover they were shepherding a boatload of magicals. Most of them had great respect for witches but preferred not to sail aboard a vessel with one. Many of them had wisely kept out of the fight once they'd realized their opponents were their former prisoners, and now they suffered their captivity stoically as long as there was food and drink. Hot meals and a grog ration appeased them.

The magicals, those not considered dangerous, had the freedom of the ship but were largely restless, especially the goblins, who spent a lot of time pacing the deck and getting in the way of honest sailors going about their business (according to Mr. Sharpner).

The waning moon meant the werewolves were not a threat, but since they knew their rescuers were wary, they wisely agreed to be locked in a cage from dusk until dawn.

The kelpie was permanently caged, but had settled with

good grace once Mr. Sharpner explained to her that we were going to deliver her to the Lady of the Forests so that she could consider her options.

The pixies—well—the less said about them the better. Giving them a little freedom resulted in a whole barrel of salt cod rotting to a glutinous, stinking paste overnight and oozing out of its barrel to contaminate a bushel of oats. Mr. Sharpner had them secured and fed them for the next two days on a porridge of the oats and stinking cod. It may have made him feel better, but I'm not sure it taught the pixies a lesson.

The hobs and the trolls had formed an alliance and spent most of their time together. As scary as they looked, the trolls had caused no trouble at all. They weren't known for their intelligence and reasoning powers, but they'd understood that by waiting they would be given their freedom. Strictly speaking, their freedom would entail permission to join the Lady and her retinue, but they'd grasped that it was a better alternative to whatever the Mysterium had planned for them. The hobs had reassured them they would be comfortable in the Okewood and had even hinted there might be a bridge they could inhabit. Nothing pleased a troll more than being toll keeper at a nice rustic bridge.

"What about the Mysterium's witch?" I asked Mr. Sharpner.

"Knows when she's outnumbered. Eats what she's given. Says nothing. Doesn't show any grief for her former master."

That was probably the best we could hope for.

"We committed him to the sea, very respectfully," Mr. Sharpner said.

"Thank you. And what of Old Walsingham?"

"You left him naked."

"So I did. I was a little preoccupied at the time."

"I didn't want him to freeze to death on my watch, so I gave him some sailors' slops to wear and a couple of wool blankets. He's polite, eats his meals, talks to his jailers, but hasn't tried any tricks. If I hadn't known what he could do, I'd have been fooled into thinking him harmless."

"You think he's still dangerous?"

"I'm damn sure he is, but I can't work out how. I make sure it's never the same man twice takes his meals to him. Anyone with any degree of humanity could easily get taken in."

"A wise decision. Unfortunately, we need to talk to him."

Mr. Sharpner pulled a face. "I wouldn't trust him."

Corwen growled. "Don't worry on that score."

"It's not time for food, or for the slop bucket to be emptied, so have you come to kill me?" Walsingham's head swiveled toward us as we entered the room that Corwen had defined as the interrogation room. As the only occupant, Walsingham had fared well under Mr. Sharpner's care. He'd been given clothes and blankets. That was more than I would have done for him.

"Killing you isn't the top of my list of activities for the day," I said. "But I'm willing to make an exception. You should know that one of us will kill you if you make a wrong move."

"Ah, it's you. I wondered when you would come."

"Yes, it's me."

As if to illustrate the threat, Corwen pulled the doghead back on the primed pistol he carried.

"I suppose it's the wolf holding the pistol, or is it your faithful sea captain?"

"There's no wolf here," I said.

Walsingham snorted softly. "If you say so. But I know the wolf. I know you. We've crossed paths before."

"And look how that ended for you," I said.

"It's true I barely survived the experience. But I'm still here—most of me, anyway." He waved his good hand toward the stump of his arm and to his blind eyes.

"Are you a wiser man, now, Mr. Walsingham?"

"It depends. I'd like to say I've learned not to travel on a ship with a witch who can make fire, but sadly I appear to be doing exactly that."

"I'm not intending to blow up the *Guillaume Tell*," I said. "I am intending to release all the magical creatures."

"There's a kelpie on board, and werewolves."

"We'll take appropriate precautions. We have an ally who can contain them."

"The Fae."

"In this instance, no, but let's talk about the Fae. You understand how powerful they are?"

"I've read all the scant notes left by Martyn the Summoner, and the more extensive notes of Dr. John Dee."

"Two hundred years old," I said. "Besides, Dee had nothing to do with Martyn's actions. He was out of the country when the Armada came, so Martyn was left alone to find a solution for Queen Bess."

"An imperfect solution."

"Perfect insofar as the Armada was defeated by wind and water magic. Imperfect because of what happened to the rowankind afterward. Perhaps if Dr. Dee had spent more time trying to help, and less time writing notes condemning my ancestor, they would have been able to return the weather magic to the rowankind right there and then. The rowankind would have gone home to the Fae, and no one would have been any the wiser. None of this would have happened."

Corwen cleared his throat to remind me that this conversation was getting offtrack. I nodded to show I'd understood.

"Mr. Walsingham, killing you is one option I'm still very fond of, but I might have an alternative."

"I'm listening."

"Let's talk about the Fae. They live in another world, another dimension if you will. They call it Iaru. Other researchers have called it Orbisalius, the Otherworld, and indeed that's what it is."

"You've been there?"

"I have."

He sucked air in through his teeth. I hadn't considered how rare that experience was. Walsingham himself had never crossed over, and I doubted any of the Mysterium's witches had done so either.

"You can speak to the Fae?"

I didn't tell him my half-brother was one. Walsingham knew David only as half-rowankind, and there was no need for him to know more.

"I can, but—more importantly—they can speak to me." I glanced at Corwen, wondering whether to bring him into the discussion, but he waved at me to continue alone. Better not to give Walsingham more than the bare minimum of information.

"The Fae," I continued, "are concerned for the well-being of those rowankind who have chosen not to return to Iaru."

"So that's where they went?"

"You didn't know?"

"Not for sure, though I had my suspicions. Don't forget that at the time all this happened I was the guest of Captain Nicholas Thompson of the *Flamingo*, better known as—"

"Old Nick," I said. "You were lucky he saw your worth for ransom."

Walsingham gave a harsh laugh. "Lucky, yes."

"He has been known to flay men alive if he didn't see their worth."

"That, at least, I was spared."

"Maybe you were spared for a reason," Corwen said.

"Aha! The wolf-man speaks."

I saw Corwen scowl, but he kept the irritation from his voice. "We were talking about the Fae."

"So we were."

"And the status of the rowankind who chose to stay in the world," I said. "You must understand. Though the rowankind have their magic back, a lot has happened in the two centuries since it was ripped from them. Some have taken up trades, made places for themselves, intermarried—even though those marriages are not recognized in law. In fact, the rowankind don't exist in law at all. They have less protection in law than a slave."

"What is your point, Mrs. Tremayne?"

I didn't correct him on the use of my surname. "My point is the rowankind need protection in law, protection from the Mysterium and from any repercussions from the Crown and Parliament. Otherwise, the Fae are not going to take it kindly."

"And what's that to me?"

"You're worried about the current upsurge in magical occurrences, but they're nothing compared to what the Fae can release if they are so minded."

He shrugged. "I spent my life trying to make sure the rowankind were not freed, yet the worst happened. You freed them. I failed." He swiped a knuckle beneath his nose and sniffed. "I failed, Mrs. Tremayne. And here I sit, blind and maimed and a failure before my king. Tell me why I should heed anything you tell me."

I wondered whether the worst was, in his opinion, the freeing of the rowankind or his personal failure.

I heard Corwen growl softly and wondered if, after all his trying, Walsingham wasn't going to induce him to change into his wolf by his self-pity.

I tried again. "You've devoted your life to protecting the realm from magic."

"From wild magic."

"Exactly. You were willing to die to stop me from freeing the rowankind."

"Dying was not part of my plan, though I admit I was willing to take certain risks." His maimed arm twitched. "I feared a magical uprising of empowered slaves against former masters."

"Frankly, so did I. I wasn't without doubts, you know, but I did my best to safeguard against it, and it never happened."

"It still might. You released wild magic. Who knows where it will end?"

"We can help with that. The rowankind can help."

"They are not human!"

Ah, now we were getting to the crux of the matter. "What are they?"

"Creatures. Magical creatures, with the power to do us harm."

"A man with a pistol may do us harm, as may a man with a knife in a dark alley."

"But most men are not murderers."

"Can't you believe that most magical folks are not intent on harm either?"

He sat, rigid.

"You can't, can you?" A cold chill ran down my spine.

"Morals and magic are an ill match," Walsingham said. "Look what your wolf did to my successor. I heard about it, even down here. Tore his throat out."

"That wolf had been tormented for weeks—at your suggestion as I understand it."

"Ate the flesh."

Corwen cleared his throat, uncomfortable with Freddie's actions. "What about the harm you've done to others?"

"Sometimes to fight evil you must harness evil."

"Magic is not inherently evil," Corwen said.

"So you say." Walsingham wiped his mouth with thumb and forefinger, as a fastidious man might do after eating.

"That's an argument for philosophers," I said. "We're here to offer something practical."

"You're making me an offer?"

"In a way yes, though the offer is to the king and Parliament. Change the law, protect the rowankind, disband the Mysterium, or at least give an amnesty to any unregistered witches. We'll work together to contain the wild magic, send it into the shadows it came from. Everyone wins. What you get out of it personally, is that you regain any status you lost when another Walsingham was appointed."

"You think I care about status? I've lived in the shadows all my life."

"On behalf of the king. On behalf of the country. If status isn't important to you, what is? What have you got left in life? Not family, I'll warrant. If you still want to protect Britain from wild magic, this is the way to do it. We may never be friends, but we're both on the same side in this."

He laughed, but there was no mirth in it. "Go hang yourself, woman. I'll not be your conduit to the king and that's an end to it. You can kill me now. I'm no use to you."

I looked at Corwen, and he looked back at me, gray eyes level. If I asked him, he'd pull the trigger and end Walsingham where he sat, but he wouldn't enjoy it. I, on the other hand, would enjoy it very much . . . which was why I couldn't do it.

"Sorry, Walsingham. If you want to find a way to commit suicide, look elsewhere. These magical folks are not going to kill you, and neither am I. Think on that in the dark hours of the night when the ghosts of your dead won't let you sleep."

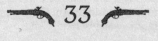 33

Refugees

"**D**AMN! I thought he'd go for it," I said as Corwen and I settled into the *Heart*'s boat for the journey back. Sim let go the mooring and four pairs of oars dipped rhythmically into the gentle ocean swell. "We're going to have to find a different route to the king."

"And Walsingham? We can't let him go."

"No, we can't. I said I wouldn't kill Walsingham. I didn't say I'd see him safe to London. Mr. Sharpner can sail around in circles for a few days so none of the sailors know where we dropped the magicals. Then he can abandon the *Guillaume Tell* and her crew, complete with Walsingham and the Mysterium thugs, under the nose of the French navy to be taken prisoner."

"That sounds like a plan, as long as Mr. Sharpner can do it safely—I mean without any of his own crew being taken by the French."

"I'm confident the *Heart* is fast enough to take all our lads to safety before the French wake up to what's happening."

"That's a plan. So our first task is to get all these magicals

safely into the forest realm." He tapped his foot on the
planks of the boat. "It's going to take a few trips in the boats
to get them all ashore, and we still have to contain the kelpie
and make sure the trolls don't slip away beneath a handy
bridge."

I sighed and touched his fingers. "Ever practical. Did I
ever tell you that's why I love you?"

"And I thought it was my manly charm."

"That, too."

I caught Sim's snigger as he sat at the tiller. Enough of
that kind of talk.

Hookey nosed the *Heart* as close into the bay as he dared.
Bur Isle itself was a hazard to shipping, and there were
sandbars here that shifted with the tides.

I'd thought to take Olivia ashore first, but she wouldn't
come without Freddie, and Freddie obviously didn't want
to abandon the larger boat for a smaller one. I could imagine he was living in a constant state of terror. I told Corwen
to take a turn around the deck with Olivia. Brotherly love
could work both ways. Corwen's exasperation with Freddie
tended to show.

I sat next to the brown wolf and began to speak.

"I was pretty scared when I first ran away to sea, you
know." I thought he was listening. "I didn't have my sea
legs, so every time I slipped with the roll of the waves, I
feared I was going to be pitched overboard. It took me a
while to get over it, and even longer before I became halfway competent enough to be a member of the crew. I'm
not asking you to try any of that. Once we get you to shore,
you need never come anywhere close to the ocean again.
But the plain fact is you're here now, and the only way we
can get you to shore is on the *Heart's* boat. It's a small boat,
but it's seaworthy, and her crew is as sound as any you'll
find. I'm asking you to trust us."

There was a faint rumble of a growl.

"Well, I can see two choices, three actually. One: you can
stay on the *Heart* until you grow old, or until you rub Hookey

the wrong way once too often and he throws you overboard."

The growl intensified.

"All right—you don't like that idea. I can't say I blame you. Hookey wouldn't like it either. Two: we can tie you like a stuffed goose again, wrap you in a blanket and force you into the boat though, to be honest, you'd probably struggle enough to upset it and we'd all drown, Olivia included."

His teeth drew back in an actual snarl now.

"Please, Freddie, Corwen would be upset if you mauled his wife. I don't heal as quickly as you wolves. Look." I lifted my hair to show him my mangled ear.

The snarl abated.

"Good. Three: you can act like an adult and trust us to get you ashore." I paused. "The fourth alternative is me shooting you right now to put you out of your misery, but after all the trouble we've been through to find you, that seems a pity. Besides, I don't know how I'd explain it to your mother and Lily. You have until Corwen and Olivia return to make up your mind. Or you could change to human. I can find a shirt and sailor's slops for you."

Since he didn't change, I assumed he'd rejected that alternative.

Olivia came running and threw her arms around Freddie's neck. "That's where I live." She pointed to the shore. "You can come and live with us, Freddie. I'll look after you like you've looked after me. All you have to do is get in the boat. Please. For me."

Whether it was my talk or Olivia's childlike promise, Freddie stood up, and with lowered head, looked toward where the boat was already waiting.

"Let's do this before he changes his mind," Corwen muttered.

Sim beached the boat on the sandbar closer to the mainland than the island. The tide was rising and would soon submerge the causeway.

A knot of curious fisher folk approached as we landed, and there were exclamations as they recognized Olivia. A couple of boys raced toward the parsonage, each trying to beat the other with the news.

"That's not the same dog as before, is it?" a woman asked. "Wasn't the other one gray?"

"He was. This is his brother."

"They breed 'em big where you come from." She eyed Freddie from a distance but didn't venture closer, possibly because of the growl.

"They do." Corwen stepped forward and flicked Freddie's ear, earning a snap of sharp teeth which missed his hand by a narrow, but deliberate, safety margin. "Behave, Freddie."

Freddie gave his brother a look which was not difficult to interpret and slunk after Olivia as she ran forward to meet her mother and grandfather who came running down the hill.

"You again," Reverend Purdy said, with barely concealed delight, having scooped Olivia into his arms and given her a kiss. She wriggled to reach her mother, and the transfer was accomplished without her feet touching the ground.

His arms now free, Reverend Purdy shook our hands warmly and then stared at Freddie.

"Is he . . . ?"

"He is, but it's a long story. We need your help. You've seen the ships in the bay?"

"Yes, but we never thought they held such treasure." He smiled at Olivia in Charlotte's arms. Charlotte was laughing and crying all at once, cuddling her daughter and patting Freddie who was behaving like a lapdog.

"More treasure than you can imagine," Corwen said. "We have over a hundred magical creatures on board, liberated from the Mysterium: rowankind, goblins, hobs, a couple of trolls, werewolves, and even a kelpie. Don't worry, the kelpie is contained, for now, but we need to get her, and all of them, safely to the Okewood."

"And I think it might be safest to send Charlotte and Olivia with them," I added. "For now, at least. The Mysterium is sweeping up anyone magical. I don't know if those on board the *Guillaume Tell* are the only ones, but they are certainly the ones we can help right now."

"I understand, but Henry . . . how will he find Charlotte when he returns?"

I understood the reverend's concerns, but privately I wondered where Henry was and what he was doing. Conscripted into the army was one thing, but how was the army dealing with its magical recruits? Henry Purdy had very properly registered his magical power with the Mysterium rather than trying to hide it, but it hadn't done him much good.

"Have you heard from your son?" I asked.

The look on his face told me everything I needed to know. We could deal with the missing Henry Purdy later, however. For now, we needed to get the magical creatures safely onto dry land, especially the rowankind who were recovering a little on the *Heart*, but still needed to leave the ocean as soon as possible.

"Will the fisherfolk help?" Corwen asked. "We could unload the magicals onto Bur Isle, keep them there until the tide turns, and then bring them across the causeway."

"It's ten miles to the Okewood," Reverend Purdy said. "Someone is going to see you."

"Can you think of anything better?"

"Keep them on the island? Send them through at night in small groups."

"Then you have too much potential for disaster. What if the Mysterium managed to get here and cut them off at the causeway? We don't want a pitched battle."

The reverend shuddered.

"Better to go as soon as we can, and as swiftly."

The reverend drew the crowd of villagers around him to explain what we needed.

<hr>

Ten small fishing boats put to sea to help with the transfer, some to the *Heart* and some to the *Guillaume Tell*. Corwen went with Walter Pardoe who had some seniority and had been the first to offer his boat. I returned to the *Heart* with

Sim and the lads to supervise. We left Freddie with Charlotte and Olivia, who returned to the house to get ready for the journey, Charlotte having agreed it was probably best to go to the forest, at least for now.

Some of the magicals looked human enough, so we decided they would be the easiest for the fisherfolk to transport. We included the rowankind and also the goblins who were all able to summon enough of a glamour to pass for human. Even the werewolves, at this phase of the moon, were not a problem. We didn't want to scare the fisherfolk with the kelpie, the hobs, the trolls, or the pixies, however; so we asked for volunteers from among the *Heart*'s crew to row them ashore. Some of the lads were easier with magic than others. Those members of the crew who had been with the *Heart* for some years had, at least, learned to turn a blind eye to magical goings on, though sensibly they still regarded it with some caution.

The pixies, in particular, would be a nightmare to transport. Barely as tall as my knee, they got into mischief wherever you put them, whether it was rendering food inedible by trampling it underfoot and pissing on it gleefully, or unwinding the wool from a sailor's sweater as he was wearing it, or tying his bootlaces together while he worked. They weren't deadly dangerous in and of themselves, except they could inflict a nasty bite that had a tendency to get infected, but they could cause accidents by untying a rope, or tying one in the wrong place, or guiding a careless hand toward a sharp implement. They were caged aboard the *Guillaume Tell* after Mr. Sharpner had discovered a pixie's promise was, in fact, a statement that it would do exactly the opposite. I'd heard about the frantic search to get them all contained again after we'd taken the ship, and even now Mr. Sharpner wasn't sure he'd got them all. I hoped Corwen could come up with an ingenious way of transporting them and wondered how on earth we were going to keep them in line on the ten-mile march to the Okewood.

In the meantime, I had to marshal the rowankind from the *Heart* onto the fishing boats. My volunteers worked steadily. For a bunch of barely reformed pirates, some of my crewmembers could be as soft as butter when required. Lazy Billy had been cooking food for the recovering rowankind that was light on sea-sickened stomachs. He fed them on broth and bread, and used all the eggs he'd taken on board in London, intending to pickle them. Windward and the Greek had swabbed belowdecks without complaint, offering no recrimination for the mess. Sailors may laugh at seasickness, but they know there's a point beyond which it becomes no laughing matter. Now they all helped the sickness-weakened rowankind down the rope ladders into the waiting boats.

I saw them off, heading for the island, and boarded the *Heart*'s boat to help Corwen on the *Guillaume Tell*. Climbing aboard and hopping over the deck rail, I thought he'd achieved the impossible. Five boatloads of witches and goblins had already departed and the pixie population was significantly reduced.

He reached for my hand and kissed me swiftly on the cheek before returning to the job at hand, which was to bind each pixie individually and give it directly into the hands of the most dangerous magical creature he could recruit.

The kelpie, licking her lips, clutched one to her. "Is it tasty?" she asked.

The pixie shuddered noticeably.

"Probably not very," Corwen answered, "but if it gives you any trouble, you're welcome to try a leg."

"Please not give me to this." The pixie whimpered. "She eats me."

"Only if you misbehave."

"I no mis-bee-hay."

"That's what worries me. We have a long journey, and while I want to see you safe from the Mysterium, I also want to see people safe from you."

"Horse-lady not safe."

"She's safe while I'm here," one of the trolls said behind us, his voice a deep rumble.

I turned to see that he had a pixie of his own firmly trussed and tucked under his arm as if it were nothing more than a roll of blanket. It was quiet, its eyes closed. I wondered about the soporific property of a troll's armpit and decided I didn't ever want to experience it for myself.

"All right," a hob said. "The uglies and the scaries are ready for the boats."

"Am I truly ugly?" the kelpie asked, tossing back her mane of white hair which grew down her spine and disappeared inside the neck of her shirt.

"You, my dear, are the most beautiful of us all," a second hob said, "but also the most lethal."

"Don't worry, I know when to curb my appetite. I heard what happened to my sister on this island. She was stupid and paid the price. I am not stupid. But I am hungry."

"The Lady of the Forests will have enough food for all," Corwen said.

"Is that true?" I asked him softly.

"I hope so. She's never let me down yet."

"You've never delivered over a hundred refugees all at one time."

"True." He grinned at me.

We loaded the uglies and the scaries into boats crewed by our own men. It took three hours to get everyone to the island. The island folk themselves had congregated close to the causeway.

"We don't much like it," the innkeeper said, "but you got rid of the kelpie for us, so we'll put up with it for one night. Only one, mind you."

"They'll be gone as soon as the tide clears the causeway in the morning." Reverend Purdy bustled through the crowd of rowankind. "In the meantime, think of them as shipwrecked folk that need saving from the sea, for that they surely are. And no one would refuse their hospitality in such a case." He beamed at the innkeeper as if it were all settled. "If you could see your way to giving some of these sickly folk your help, it would be a Christian kindness. I myself will stay here with them."

By setting a good example he shamed or cajoled the island people to offer blankets and shelter to the more normal looking magicals while the rest we housed in the inn's cellar, under guard. Though whether the guard was to protect the island people from the magicals or the magicals from the island people was a moot point. Bulstrode, the self-styled wizard, wrinkled his nose at the humble cottages and settled between the kelpie and the hobs.

As the sun dipped below the horizon and the tide rose to cover the causeway, I watched the *Guillaume Tell* set sail. Mr. Sharpner would spend the next few days at sea, sailing a random course to confuse the occupants who were all locked belowdecks. It was important no one knew where we'd disembarked. We didn't want to bring trouble on Reverend Purdy and his flock if word got back. Mr. Sharpner would rendezvous with the *Heart* and abandon the *Guillaume Tell* to the French fleet with everyone on board, trussed like turkeys. I felt bad for the common sailors, delivered to the French through no fault of their own, but I couldn't trust that they wouldn't spill their stories to the nearest Mysterium office if we let them go ashore.

I worried about letting Walsingham go, but I'd made my decision and Corwen had backed me. This Walsingham had lost his power, and the new one was dead. They'd appoint another, in time, I was sure, but hopefully we would have a breathing space.

❖─❖

"You can't expect them to walk ten miles," Reverend Purdy said, looking at one rowankind family as a young woman led them away to one of the island's tiny cottages.

"I know it will be difficult," I said, "but what choice do we have?"

"Take my carriage. It will carry six and another two on the box. I'll drive it myself. You can use the governess cart, too. Charlotte's perfectly capable of driving that, and the pony is docile. I have two riding horses as well. That's twelve taken care of. If I ask the villagers—"

"They've already risked enough for us. If the Mysterium finds out what we've done, it will be hard for them."

"What can the Mysterium do to them? They aren't magical themselves."

"There are laws to cover those who help unregistered witches."

"But no laws about unregistered kelpies or trolls or hobs or goblins. Not even pixies."

"Only because the law didn't know about kelpies, trolls, hobs, goblins, and pixies. It does now. Things may change."

"Until they do, let me help. If I'm going to lose Charlotte and Olivia to the forest at least let me make sure they are safely transported."

"I hope it won't be forever."

"I wouldn't want to leave my parishioners here, but I could seek a parish closer to the Okewood for when Henry returns."

It would be a miracle if Henry ever returned, but I didn't tell him that. When there were less pressing matters to attend to, Corwen and I would go in search of Henry Purdy.

"Take the reverend's offer, Ross," Corwen said. "And a couple of carts for the hobs and the trolls would hide them from view. As soon as the causeway is clear, I'll make a run for the forest and bring help. Hopefully, we'll meet you halfway—Modbury, maybe."

The narrow lanes of South Devon wound in an alarmingly indirect manner from village to village, cutting deep tracks through fields. Hiding a cavalcade of magicals would not be easy.

We grabbed a few hours' sleep in the inn's cellar, a space dug out of the rocky hillside which had an outside door that opened right onto the beach. The pixies chittered from inside their bindings, but so far none of the creatures had damaged their small, but annoying burdens. Even the kelpie's pixie still had both its legs, though every time it noticed me checking on it, it gave me a baleful look which caused the kelpie to bare her teeth at it as a reminder. Despite my former experience with the black kelpie, I was beginning to respect, if not exactly like this one.

The causeway began to emerge from the sea before dawn. Corwen stripped off his clothes in the dark, pulled me to him for a kiss—brief, but heartfelt—and dropped to all fours as a wolf.

"Go swift and safe, my love." I touched his head in farewell.

With one yip he raced across the wet sand toward the mainland.

As the first fingers of dawn streaked the sky with violet, I roused the magicals to get ready for the trek. The causeway was exposed enough now to accommodate our cavalcade. The reverend went ahead to organize what wagons he could, but by the time we all reached the mainland, all that was waiting for us was his own coach and pair, two riding horses, and a small, tub-shaped governess cart with a rotund pony harnessed between the shafts. Charlotte had the reins, and Olivia sat by her side with Freddie at her feet.

"You can walk," I said to him. "We can make room for two more people in here who need to ride more than you do."

Obediently he jumped down.

"Your brother has gone ahead to alert the Lady of the Forests. You would be doing us all a great favor if you would range along the lanes and make sure we're not walking into trouble."

I didn't know whether Freddie was biddable, but I could only do my best.

"Grandfather says he's arranging for farm wagons," Olivia said.

I gave the riding horses to two elderly goblins, loaded the sickest of the rowankind into the coach, and two elderly women, both witches, into the governess cart with Charlotte and Olivia.

The villagers of Bigbury on Sea had roused from their homes on our arrival and were exclaiming at the trolls in particular, whose bulk and the greenish cast to their lumpy, open-pored skin made them stand out even above the hobs who were shorter than most humans and squarish in appearance. Their prominent features and jutting foreheads gave the impression of them having a single eyebrow. A couple of village children giggled at them, and the hobs began to fade from view, becoming invisible in the cool dawn. I hadn't known they could do that. The pixies each one of them still carried didn't become invisible with them, but appeared to float in the air. The children shrieked and skittered behind their parents.

"I could make this journey better on four hooves." The kelpie came up behind me, making me jump at her proximity.

"I'm sure you could," I said, "but what would stop you from sweeping up one of the fisher-folk and taking to the sea?"

"I have given my word. Isn't that worth something?"

"I hope so."

"Have I not proved myself?"

"So far, but you must be hungry."

She licked her lips. "More than you know."

"When do we leave?" Bulstrode marched up to us and interrupted the conversation.

"Now him I could eat, though he might be tough," the kelpie said.

"I'm almost tempted to let you," I muttered under my breath.

Bulstrode set me on edge. Everything about him from his overly-loud voice to the way he looked down his nose at me, made me instantly dislike the man. Now he glared at me. "You need a driver for that rig." He gestured toward the reverend's carriage, with the reverend's man holding the horses to calm them as everyone milled about.

"We have one," I said as he made to mount the box. "Reverend Purdy will be taking the reins. I'm afraid you'll have to walk like the rest of us, Mr. Bulstrode."

He harrumphed at me, but turned away.

We didn't have long to wait before the rattle of wheels along the track announced the arrival of Reverend Purdy with a high-sided wain pulled by two sturdy farm horses, and a flatbed hay wagon pulled by a team of four, led by a gnarly older man with a face like a pickled walnut. A boy of about twelve guided the team pulling the wain by riding the nearside animal. The boy looked askance at the two trolls, but one of them touched his forehead politely and gave his thanks in words that rumbled from his belly. The boy gawped, eyes round as saucers, and ran a hand through his lank hair.

"Don't worry," I said to him. "They won't hurt you." I noticed the wain dipped slightly after the trolls had settled themselves and saw that the two invisible hobs had climbed on board, too. The floating pixies gave them away.

"Is it true they're all magical folks?" the boy asked.

"It is, but they aren't dangerous."

"I ain't worried about that. I'm going to register with the Mysterium when I'm eighteen. I can move things with the power of thought."

"Yes? Like what?"

"I knocked a cup to the floor, an' I cracked three of my ma's best plates."

"Did you mean to do it?"

"Nah, it just kind of 'appened."

I wondered whether the boy was simply making an excuse for carelessness. "Maybe you should try moving things without breaking them in future."

"My ma said something like that."

"I'm sure she did."

While the trolls settled into the wain, the remaining rowankind scrambled onto the hay wagon, and Reverend Purdy mounted onto the driver's box of his coach. "Shall we go?" he asked.

"Lead the way, Reverend. We're in your hands."

34

The Battle of Modbury

THE JOURNEY TO THE FOREST was slow. The roads wound endlessly between high hedges, appearing to change direction at random and we crawled at the pace of the slowest walker. Some of the lanes were barely wide enough to allow the carts to pass through, and there were places where the rowankind had to pull their legs away from the sides of the cart they rode on. Trees clung to the side of the high banking with their roots exposed and shook hands with each other across the road, making some lanes seem more like tunnels.

"I don't like it." One of the elderly goblins whose name I'd discovered was Irving Twomax rode beside me. "I was brought up in the city of London, in the sewer tunnels. This reminds me of my youth." He jerked his head toward the high hedges. "Tunnels have their advantages, but they have their dangers, too. Have you thought what a killing ground this would make if anyone were setting a trap for us?"

I had.

I looked around uneasily. The column was moving too slowly. News of our passing could have outstripped us. I hoped Corwen had made it to the Okewood and that we'd soon get help from the Lady. I wasn't sure what form her help could take, but right now anything was better than this snail's pace we were managing through constricted lanes that were looking more and more like a trap every minute.

"I've sent the brown wolf ahead," I said to Mr. Twomax. "Do you think some of your goblins, the younger and fitter ones, might be willing to walk behind and let us know if anyone follows?"

He turned to wave at a bunch of young goblins. They'd let their glamour slip since we'd left the villagers behind, and now sported the pale, slitty-nosed faces that I'd ceased to think of as being unusual. He said something to them in a guttural language that was beyond my comprehension, and the group split up. Four dropped behind and one shinnied up the bank to the left and one to the right, agile as cats, disappearing over the top. The level of the fields on the other side was considerably higher than the roadbed, and they immediately shouted to Mr. Twomax in their goblin tongue.

"Everything's clear for now," he translated.

I hoped it would stay that way.

And it did, until we approached Modbury.

The first sign of anything wrong was when Freddie came racing toward us as we climbed a long straight hill on the outskirts of the small town. He was obviously agitated but refused to change to human to tell us in words. All the information we had was that something was wrong.

"Freddie, for goodness sake." I knelt by his side. "You need to change and give me some details."

He whined.

"Change, Freddie."

He whined again, his ears flat against his skull, then bounded over to where Olivia sat in the little governess cart and pushed his way between the occupants to bury his head in Olivia's lap. For the first time I wondered whether he'd suffered so much that he'd lost the ability to be human. Whether he couldn't or wouldn't change, there would be no more information coming from that direction. I called to Mr. Twomax. "There's something ahead."

He whistled, and the two youngsters flanking us on the bank popped into view. "Anything?" he asked. "The wolf thinks there's danger ahead."

"There's a village," one of them said, "but it's quiet. I'll go and see."

"Wear your glamour," Twomax called after him. He looked at me. "Children," he said. "Always reckless. Think they know everything."

Goblin concerns were not all that different from human ones.

"Get ready. There may be trouble ahead." I warned the reverend, and I passed the word along the column to be prepared.

The young goblin slithered down the bank, breathless. "Kingsmen," he gasped. "Up ahead at the crossroads. There are redcoats, too."

"Can we take another route?" I asked Reverend Purdy, wondering if we could actually manage to turn the wain and the wagon in this narrow lane.

One of Mr. Twomax's goblins came running up the lane, panting. "Behind us," he gasped. "Redcoats. Twenty of them, with muskets at the ready."

"God's ballocks!" One of Hookey's favorite curses was out of my mouth before I thought about it. Kingsmen: the bastards who were responsible for carrying out much of the Mysterium's dirty work. Apprehending unregistered witches was their usual line of business, but I guessed they'd had their hands full with more dangerous magical incursions over the last few months. Maybe that's why they'd developed the capability for rapid response. Someone must have sent word to them.

However it had happened, they knew, they were here, and we had to deal with the consequences. Flight was out of the question; it was fight or surrender.

"I'm not going back to that ship." Bullstrode came up behind me. I saw the tension in his eyes, heard it in his voice. The veneer of bombastic confidence had truly cracked. It was the first time I'd had any sympathy for him.

"Neither are we." One of the rowankind spoke up. "We'd all have died on the ocean. Better to die here, clean and quick."

I wondered if they had any idea of what a clean, quick death looked like in the context of a pitched battle. Sometimes it was quick, but it was rarely clean.

"Anyone who wants to make a run for it can try and no hard feelings." I raised my voice. "There's going to be some confusion. You might make it through."

The pixies all began to thrash about in their bindings.

"Let them loose," I said. "If anyone stands a chance of slipping away, it's them."

But, once released, the pixies lined up as if under the orders of some fierce drill sergeant. The one who appeared to be their leader squinted at me. "Run and they come after. Finish it now."

"Goblins?" I asked Mr. Twomax.

"My cousin Tingle makes those red coats for the army. Once we get close enough, we can cast a glamour to look like redcoats. That will confuse matters even more."

"You're Mr. Tingle's cousin?"

"On my mother's side."

"I owe him a debt, unspecified and at a time of his choosing."

"And you're wondering whether he will accept my rescue as payment?"

I raised one eyebrow.

"My cousin makes shrewd deals, but if we both survive this, I will ask him. Whether he counts it as paying off your debt or not, my family and I are beholden to you." He grinned, and I saw now how alike Twomax and Tingle were. "And I don't say that lightly."

"Then we'd better both survive," I said, grinning back despite our impending predicament.

"We're not built for running." The trolls lumbered out of the wain, the hobs at their side.

"Now can I change?" the kelpie asked.

"Protect yourself in any way you can," I said. "Though for your own sake, don't eat anyone."

She gave me a sideways look. "I will carry you into battle," she said. "Climb on my back, but watch what you do with your heels."

"And afterward?" Oh, hell, there might not be an afterward. "All right."

She peeled off the skirt and blouse Charlotte had found for her, causing a couple of the younger goblins to snigger until she dropped to all fours and swiftly changed to a creamy white mare, upward of fifteen hands with fair eyelashes and a pink velvet nose.

"Oh, pretty horse." One of the witches in the governess cart reached a hand toward her, but Olivia rapped her across the knuckles.

"Kelpie, do not touch," Olivia said.

I might regret it, but I grabbed a handful of the kelpie's mane and swung myself onto her back.

We moved forward cautiously. Around the second bend, where the lane widened to accommodate a crossroads, we came face-to-face with half a dozen Kingsmen, backed by a line of redcoats.

"Does it have to come to a fight?" Reverend Purdy said. "Let me talk to them."

"You can try," I said.

The reverend climbed down from the box and left two rowankind standing at the horses' heads. He walked forward with both hands in the air.

"Give us time to talk," I told Mr. Twomax, "but if it all goes to hell, send in the pixies to cause confusion and use the rowankind to call the wind, then try to drive the column forward out of this killing ground.

"Freddie, stay with Charlotte and Olivia. Look after them."

"Follow the reverend," I told the kelpie, taking care to keep my heels from her side.

Corwen, where are you? I let my mind rove out and I

summoned him as hard as I'd ever summoned anyone in my life.

❖———❖

"It's Hampson." Reverend Purdy scowled. There was one non-uniformed man, mounted on a sturdy farm cob, close behind the Kingsmen, flanked by at least twenty redcoats.

"Hampson?" I didn't recognize the name.

"Uncle of the boy the kelpie killed. That's who informed against us. I should have guessed the Hampson family might take against us helping magicals."

"You couldn't have known."

"I should have thought. They lost a child."

Hampson wasn't our problem, now. We got to within hailing distance of the line of dark-coated Kingsmen. Behind them, the redcoats had muskets at the ready.

"That's far enough." The Kingsman officer, mounted on a dark bay horse, was dressed in midnight colors with gold-braided epaulets and a sword already out of its scabbard — a curved cavalry blade, for slashing, not stabbing.

My primed pistol was in my sash and my own sword, still sheathed, hung heavy at my side. That sword and I had been through many a skirmish together.

"We only want to pass peacefully," Reverend Purdy said. "Let us through. We don't want anyone to get hurt."

"There is no peace with creatures like them on the loose," the officer said, jerking his head toward our cavalcade.

"They won't be on the loose," I said. "Once they're safe in the Okewood, you'll never hear from them again. I promise."

One of the mounted soldiers by the officer's side crossed himself at mention of the Okewood.

"Promises from heathens." The officer didn't quite spit, but his meaning was clear.

"We have women and children, elderly and sick. These people have been badly treated for no good reason," Reverend Purdy said.

"Incorrect assumption, Reverend. They are not people, and we have a job to do. Stand aside." He looked at me. "Tell your creatures to surrender, and there need be no harm done to them this day."

"Maybe not by you," I said, "but what about tomorrow when the Mysterium has them in its power?"

"That's not for me to say."

"Will you stand by and see them tortured and abused?"

"Before I will see human beings attacked by magicals—yes, I will."

There was no more to say.

"Let's go back." I said it to the kelpie as much as to the reverend, but as she turned, a brown shape hurtled past us, heading straight for the Kingsman officer.

"Freddie! Stop!"

But he didn't falter.

Several of the red-coated musketeers had enough sense to fire a round, but they were wild shots. Freddie leaped for the officer's throat and only the man's quick thinking and the upward angle of Freddie's trajectory saved his life. He managed to protect his throat with his arm, but Freddie still unhorsed him, and the pair fell into the dusty roadway.

I heard the word, "Charge!" yelled by the officer's second in command.

The mounted Kingsmen directly between us and the redcoats saved us from a musket volley that would surely have done for those of us in front. There was no barrier, however, between us and the redcoats closing in from behind. They would try to outflank us. I heard the command, "Fire!" a moment before the roar of discharging muskets, but at the same time I was aware of a great rushing of air. I snapped my head around to see the rearmost redcoats in the middle of a fierce windstorm. They could hardly stand, let alone aim. Some tumbled backward out of sight. Four were set upon by pixies.

I've been in battles before, though usually on a rolling deck. The same principles apply, however. The surge of fighting spirit pushes you to react faster than you can think. Either that, or it slows down time.

The Kingsmen sprang forward at a gallop, blades drawn and leveled. The reverend, on foot and unarmed, didn't stand a chance. I grabbed him and, thanks to the kelpie's magic, swung him onto her back behind me.

I drew my sword to meet the oncoming rush.

"Hold on, Reverend." I didn't really need to tell him to hold on. You couldn't dismount or even fall off a kelpie unless she released you. This kelpie wasn't releasing either of us. She met the Kingsmen with flailing hooves, making it almost impossible for me to get a swing with my sword. I saw a line of red open up across her shoulder as the point of a saber sliced across skin.

The kelpie whirled beneath me, spraying blood droplets in an arc. The Kingsmen were past us now, or we had passed through them. I wasn't sure which. Redcoats surrounded us, but some of them were our own—goblins glamoured to look like soldiers. The goblins were laying about them with whatever they could snatch for weapons. A few had blades of one kind or another that they'd liberated from the *Guillaume Tell*, but most had nothing more than stout sticks and the will to wield them. The redcoats faltered, unsure of who was friend and who was enemy.

Some rowankind had rushed forward with the goblins. Two were tackling a muscular sergeant with sticks against a sword and pistol. I drew my own pistol and put a ball into the shoulder of another redcoat as he raised his musket to fire at a troll standing head and shoulders above three assailants.

Bullstrode hurled something at the mounted Kingsmen and three horses fell, pitching their riders to the ground where two hobs and a brownie took advantage.

A high-pitched keening asserted itself over the chaos: men yelling, trolls roaring, weapons clashing, horses screaming in terror. I looked around wildly. Pixies! Thank goodness they were on our side for once. Too small to do much damage singly, they were attacking knees and feet, swarming up horses and setting them rearing and bucking, and generally causing mayhem.

"Look to the lane!" I shouted to the rowankind, pointing

wildly as a group of redcoats, rallied by a sergeant, took aim.
I sent my own whirlwind through them, scattering bodies
and weapons before they could aim and fire. I saw Charlotte,
standing in the governess cart with Olivia crouching behind,
follow my lead and direct some of the rowankind to split
their efforts, blasting swirling gales at our enemies on all
sides. I didn't see what had happened to the witches who had
been riding with her. They'd entered the fray, no doubt.

Then the horses pulling the coach spooked, pulled loose
from the boys holding them and charged forward wildly,
knocking aside anyone in their way, friend or foe. It was all
too much for the stolid little pony pulling Charlotte's cart.
He half-reared and lunged after the fleeing coach. Charlotte toppled out of the cart and Olivia was carried forward
into the thick of the skirmish.

"Charlotte!" The reverend, clinging on behind me, saw
her fall. "Olivia!"

"Quick! After them!" I hauled on the kelpie's mane and
forgot about not using my heels, but she turned with a will,
saw what I was about, and leaped over two redcoats, or
maybe one redcoat and one goblin, wrestling on the
ground.

A bayonet blade flashed toward me and was gone as we
shouldered another redcoat out of the way. The coach
plowed its way across the battlefield, miraculously not tipping as it bounced across ruts at the crossroads, cleared the
last fighters, and rattled up the lane. The little, two-wheeled
cart was not so lucky. The pony balked at a fallen man, and
a redcoat grabbed its reins while another aimed his musket
at Olivia.

Everything slowed again. I saw what was happening, but
I couldn't get there in time. It was like one of those night-
mares where the faster you try to run, the slower you go . . .
except . . . everything was slowing and the sounds of the
scrap were fading.

Then a silver-gray wolf leaped at the pointing musket in
real time, knocking it to the ground, and an ethereal female
voice echoed through the air: "You will stop. Now!"

And stop we did.

The whole scene froze.

Even the wind died away, but the soldiers caught in its embrace hovered where they were, some defying gravity, held mid-fall. I saw one of the trolls stilled in the act of trying to wrench the head off a Kingsman, and a wild-eyed horse rearing over backward at an impossible angle with three pixies clinging to its rein.

The silence was utterly eerie.

Then into that silence came the sweet trilling chirp of a dunnock and the harsh cry of a gull, followed by the clip-clop of hooves as the carriage which had disappeared up the lane, came into view, its horses walking calmly, led by Hartington.

The Lady of the Forests, mounted on a sturdy roan pony with a single horn growing from its forehead, occupied the center of the crossroads as if she'd been there all along. She surveyed the scene.

"Stand down," she ordered without raising her voice, but I swear everyone flinched, no matter which side they were on.

❖──────────❖

It took a while to extricate everyone from their positions. When time began again and the laws of nature took over from magic, those who were falling continued to fall, the rearing horse plunged over backward, scattering pixies like water droplets and throwing its rider into the hedge.

The Lady didn't allow it to happen all at once, but by degrees. A small army of sprites removed every weapon to a pile at the Lady's feet before movement returned and blood began to flow. A hob, who might have been crushed by the falling horse, was released to scramble to safety before the animal crashed to the ground.

My thigh was suddenly hot and wet with blood, and a stinging pain washed over me. I hadn't even felt the bayonet that sliced it open.

"You're hurt, Ross." Corwen was at my side in human form, dressed in buckskins and linen. "Let your riders go, kelpie. You've done well."

She groaned as if releasing us from her back was the most difficult thing she'd ever had to do, going against her nature completely, which I supposed it was.

The reverend slithered down, muttered something to me which I didn't catch, and rushed off to Olivia. I thanked the kelpie and checked her wound which had already sealed itself, before sliding to the ground and into Corwen's waiting arms.

"It's a scratch," I said, knowing it wasn't as I began to shake.

He carried me over to the roadside, one more among the wounded. A sprite, barely three feet tall, but slender and perfectly proportioned, brought me an acorn cup of something bitter and a pad of some kind of moss to press to my wound.

"I'm all right. I can manage," I said to Corwen. "Go and help someone else. Find Freddie." I didn't tell him I'd last seen Freddie trying to kill the officer in charge. Either he'd succeeded or he hadn't, but the intent had been there, which was what counted.

Corwen dropped a kiss on my head. "Shout if you need me. I'll hear."

"I know you will. Go."

On one side of me a redcoat groaned and held a broken arm protectively to his chest. He glanced sideways at me.

"The battle's over," I said. "Look to your injuries."

"Who is she?"

I didn't need to ask which *she* he referred to.

"The Lady of the Forests, ruler of the Okewood," I said. "Mind your manners and do as she tells you."

"I wouldn't dare do otherwise. I'm Elsworth, by the way. Elsworth Smith."

"Pleased to meet you. Elsworth Smith, though I'm sorry for the circumstances."

"Me, too, sir . . . er . . . Miss."

I'd almost forgotten which set of clothes I was wearing. My garments didn't fool the magicals for one moment. It must have looked odd to Mr. Smith to see Corwen kissing me.

"Can't fool you, Elsworth Smith, though I'd be obliged if you'd keep it to yourself. How's your arm?"

"Not hurting near as bad as it should be."

"That's the Lady's bounty. The little acorn cup of elixir eased your pain." I could feel the warmth of it in my own veins, and lifting the pad of moss from my thigh I saw that the bleeding had almost stopped, though it was going to need a stitch or ten.

A troll lumbered across to us carrying a Kingsman. Elsworth flinched away.

"It's all right," I told him, and turned my attention to the troll. "Who have you got there?"

He laid the unconscious figure next to me. "Didn't ask his name. Don't think him dead. Head still fixed."

"That's good," I said. "Leave him here. Are you all right?"

"Not a scratch. Takes a bit to scratch a troll, though." He laughed as if it was the biggest joke in the world. Maybe if you were a troll, it was.

Gradually the wounded were lined up by the roadside and the sprites attended to everyone according to their needs, not according to which side they'd fought on. Everyone was subdued, even the uninjured. They spoke in low, quiet voices and cast occasional glances toward the Lady and her retinue.

Corwen staggered toward me with the blood-matted furry shape of Freddie in his arms. A broken blade protruded from Freddie's side.

"I haven't dared try to remove it," Corwen said. "I think the blade is the only thing plugging the wound."

He waved to a sprite who came over and frowned at the damage. It gave Corwen a tiny cup of elixir and indicated he should get Freddie to take it. Then it sprinkled some kind of powder around the edges of where the blade was embedded in flesh. Freddie growled, but swallowed. The sprite grasped the end of the metal and placed Corwen's hand on Freddie's side, giving him a fresh pad of moss and miming pulling out the blade and pressing on the pad.

"Don't they speak?" Elsworth leaned over to watch.

"They can, but I don't think they do it often. At least I've never heard one, though I believe they talk to each other."

We watched as the sprite drew out three inches of bloody steel from Freddie's side and Corwen pressed the moss to the wound as fresh blood welled out of it.

"Change, Freddie," he whispered. "Change and heal."

Whether Freddie was too stubborn, or too weak, he remained resolutely wolf. Corwen looked at me over Freddie's body. I knew that look of pure helplessness. Unless Freddie changed, he was likely to die.

A rogue thought crept into my mind. Perhaps it would be better if he did, but what would that do to Corwen?

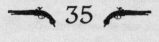

35

The Okewood

I'M NOT SURE HOW LONG we sat helpless as the life ebbed out of Freddie. Maybe it was hours, maybe it was only minutes, but suddenly the Lady was there.

"I can't get him to change," Corwen said as she leaned over to look.

"It's not only the wound," she said. "He's heartsick, deeply ashamed, and very frightened."

"The officer, did he . . . ?" I asked.

"He lives, though he'll carry the scars for the rest of his life. That's his blade." Her eyes rested on the broken end of the sword the sprite had removed. "The officer was not the first, was he?"

Corwen told her about Freddie killing Walsingham on board the *Guillaume Tell*.

"Ah, I understand now. He believes he doesn't deserve to live. I can make him change, which will give him the chance to heal, but I'm not sure if I should."

"Please," Corwen said. "He's my brother. I'll return to your service. Anything. Help him."

"I may not be doing him a favor, Silverwolf. He's tasted

human flesh, reveled in it. He'll want more. That's a difficult place to return from."

"And yet you've accepted the kelpie into your service."

"I have." She looked thoughtful and sighed. "All right. Your brother will change whether he wants to or not, but he may not thank you."

"I understand."

"I don't think you do now, but you will, and I am sorry for it."

She moved on down the line to check the neck of the Kingsman whom the troll had tried to decapitate.

Under Corwen's hand, Freddie began to groan. He stretched and writhed.

"Come on, Freddie," Corwen said. "Change. You can do it. You must do it."

Freddie's long snout began to shrink into his head and the fur on his face melted away into a fuzz of beard and straggly hair, much in want of tending. I looked on the human face of my brother-in-law for the first time. Gaunt and pale, he looked little like the young man in the portrait hanging at Denby Hall.

"Jesus bleeding Christ," Elsworth Smith said over my shoulder.

"That's it, Freddie. You're nearly there." Corwen still held the moss to Freddie's side. As fur turned to naked flesh he checked beneath the pad and told me the bleeding had stopped. He glanced at me. "Ideally, he should change and change again to be sure, but I'm afraid I'll lose him again once he reverts to wolf."

"How is his breathing?"

"Shallow, but there's no bubbling, and he's not bleeding from the mouth."

"Leave him, then," I said. "Give him time. Is he conscious?"

"I think he's aware."

"Then you've done all you can."

"Freddie! Where's Freddie?" Olivia came running up the line of wounded with Charlotte following more slowly, sporting a cut on her forehead and a purpling eye.

"He's here." Corwen indicated the naked man.

"That's not Freddie." Olivia backed away. "Where's the real Freddie?" She ran off calling his name.

"I'll speak to her," Charlotte said, dropping her knitted shawl over Freddie's torso to cover him up. "Try to make her understand."

She hurried off, limping slightly.

"Corwen!" Freddie's eyes flickered open, unfocused. His voice was barely there, but even in his weakened state there was no denying his anger. "You should have let me die in peace."

He closed his eyes again, but I didn't know whether he slept or whether he simply wanted to shut out reality.

I was left with a deep sense of foreboding.

❖──────❖

Once the injuries on both sides had been tended, the Lady clapped her hands and a procession of small, open carts appeared, each pulled by a shaggy pony such as could normally be found roaming the Darkmoor. There was a place for everyone. Corwen and I rode on the flat farm wagon with Freddie stretched out between us. The Lady directed a sprite to drive each of our vehicles, leaving behind the gnarly man and the boy who had survived the battle without a scratch. The ponies drawing her carts seemed to know where they were going.

We pulled away from the scene of our battle, with the smaller vehicles going first and ours at the rear of the line. Thus it was that we witnessed the Lady draw together the Kingsmen and the redcoats, the hale and the injured. Miraculously, it appeared no one had died here today, on either side.

"Gentlemen . . ." She addressed them quietly, but her words carried to all. "This was ill-done today and may have further consequences when news reaches the Fae. For my part, I urge you to go home and heal your hurts. In the deep of the night you may remember how you came by them. For now, you will forget. You were set upon by ruffians with a pack of dogs. Do you understand me?"

Something like a cloud swept over them and passed, leaving the day bright.

"I said, do you understand me?"

"Yes, ma'am." They answered in unison, like a school class repeating rote learning.

"Good, then we are done here."

She gave us the briefest nod as she passed us on her way to the head of the cavalcade. We began to move, not the lumbering motion of a heavy farm wagon, but the sensation of flying as we swept through the lanes at a speed faster than I could ever imagine, traveling without a jolt or a bump, taking curves so smoothly that Freddie lay undisturbed.

Corwen sat by his brother, concern evident in his expression.

"It will be all right," I said. "We'll get through this somehow."

"How?"

I didn't know. The hopelessness in Freddie's voice had truly frightened me.

"Together," I said.

⊰⊱

The journey to the Okewood took no time at all. The Lady directed her sprites to help the injured out of the carts into the woodland glade so typical of her favorite places. The ponies took away all but the human-owned vehicles. Reverend Purdy looked around him in wonder. I smiled to myself. The sprites had only been the beginning. Here were shape-changers, dryads, semi-sentient woodland animals obedient to the Lady's commands, and the Lady's consort, the Green Man himself, as slow and deliberate as his trees, but also as strong.

The Lady clapped her hands. "First we will finish tending your wounds, and then you must eat and drink with us. After that we shall decide what's to be done."

The sprites did their job as well as any surgeon, dealing with the badly injured first. My leg had stopped bleeding beneath its pad of moss, but I confess I flinched when a sprite came at me with a needle that looked more like a long, slender blackthorn than an actual surgical needle. It did the job well enough, though, and soon I had a line of a dozen neat horsehair stitches to close the wound. The fresh pad of cool moss that followed did much to ease the sting, and a linen bandage held it in place.

When Corwen handed me my breeches, he'd magically joined the ripped cloth. Pity his talent didn't extend to bones and flesh.

The sprites brought us each a tiny serving of something which might have been a mushroom, and an acorn cup of liquor which tasted like mead. Small as it looked, the meal was more than enough to sustain if you let it. I'd eaten the Lady's bounty before and nibbled it slowly and with pleasure. Some of the others regarded it suspiciously, but once they tried it, they sat back, replete and smiling, even the kelpie.

Only Freddie would not eat.

Two sprites had brought him a linen shirt and buckskins, and grudgingly he'd allowed Corwen to dress him. I could see that every movement pained him, but eventually they left him in reasonable comfort, leaning against the stout trunk of an oak.

"Freddie—" Corwen began, but Freddie closed his eyes to shut him out and feigned sleep.

"Come, walk with me." The Lady appeared in that disconcerting way she had; not there one second, there the next, so it always seemed as if she'd been there all along. She beckoned to both of us.

"Freddie—" Corwen began.

"He will sleep."

If the Lady commanded sleep, I doubted Freddie had much to say about the matter.

"So, Silverwolf, you bring me refugees."

"Should we have left them behind?" Corwen asked.

"No, you did the right thing. It seems Britain regards her magical folk as a problem."

"That's always been the case," I said. "Only now there are so many more of them, and the Mysterium finds it has more to deal with than a few unregistered witches." I bit my bottom lip. "It's my fault, isn't it? I freed the rowankind."

"Yes, you did, but it's not your fault the rowankind were enslaved in the first place. Besides it was not your freeing of the rowankind that allowed wild magic to break its bounds, not directly. You can blame us for that . . . us and the Fae in equal measure."

That was something I'd not heard before.

"Your leg pains you," the Lady said. "Sit."

In truth it did, though I hadn't wanted to say anything. Gratefully, I sat on a fallen tree trunk. Corwen perched next to me.

The Lady continued, "When you freed the rowankind, Rossalinde, the Fae wanted them to return to Iaru, and we agreed to open the earthly forests as a conduit—gateways to Iaru for all those rowankind who wished to go." She sighed. "But gates can be traversed from either side, and both Iaru and our deep forests hold secrets. Now some of those secrets have manifested in the world of men. That is truly not your responsibility."

Was she trying to make me feel better?

"So I have called a meeting with the Fae Lords, and I ask you to attend with me."

"The Fae asked us to approach the king," Corwen said. "They wanted us to deliver an ultimatum. Treat the rowankind better or else."

The Lady frowned. "Much has happened in Britain since the Fae last dealt with the monarchy. Even a king can't snap his fingers and make things happen—especially a king who dips in and out of madness and now has a first minister in Parliament who is not especially sympathetic."

"You follow politics?" I asked.

"I have my informants." She smiled a close-mouthed smile. "It's a pity the Fae take little interest in humans or they would already know this. We must all talk. We will cross into Iaru; prepare yourselves."

We found ourselves in the Lady's retinue, processing on foot through the forest which turned from an English spring into the deep green of Iaru's permanent summer within a few paces.

The Lady's favorite kind of habitat was a balmy woodland glade, but it was always, first and foremost, woodland. It had seasons and weather. The Fae, similarly, made their homes from trees, but their trees had become living cities. Tall trunks swept upward into vaulted canopies; nature as both art and architecture. Furniture, rustic but elegant, appeared and disappeared as it was needed.

"Ross." David greeted me at the entrance to the Fae's cathedral-like meeting hall and pulled me aside as the Lady led the way in. Most of the Fae were standoffish, but David hugged me as he used to do before we knew he was anything other than my bastard, half-rowankind brother. "You are injured."

"It's taken care of. Another scar to add to my collection. How goes it with you?"

"Well . . . mostly. I attend my father and stand at his shoulder in meetings. I'm expected to learn Fae history and lore."

"Law?"

"Lore, though with the Fae it's almost the same thing. It's all about precedent and tradition . . . and honor, of course."

I knew about Fae honor, sometimes taken to literal extremes.

"How's Annie?"

"She's well."

Corwen cleared his throat to grab my attention as seven high-backed chairs materialized in a semicircle in the center of the hall and a procession of seven Fae lords entered, each one attended by a youngster. David strode away to take his place behind Larien, to stand at his shoulder.

I recognized the seven Fae lords from our encounter the previous year, but the only two I knew by name were Larien and his half-brother, Dantin. I believed Larien to be sympathetic to humankind, but Dantin was not, even though he'd taken my Aunt Rosie to his bed for a number of years and they had a daughter, Margann, who now attended Dantin as David attended Larien.

The Fae had lifespans that made them almost immortal. One of the youngsters I recognized as Galan whom I knew to be at least two hundred years old, even though he looked about my age. I couldn't even begin to guess the age of the most senior lord whose skin was puckered and wrinkled. If he'd been human, I'd have guessed eighty, but as a Fae he could be eight hundred or even eight thousand years old. The others deferred to him as he settled himself in the chair on the left and waved his hand. Five more chairs sprang into being to complete the circle. The Green Man and his Lady sat, Hartington on the Green Man's right and Corwen and I on the Lady's left, which put me next to the Fae elder.

David winked at me over Larien's shoulder and it was such an un-Fae-like gesture that I almost laughed out loud. I thought I heard the elder Fae chuckle deep in his throat, though it could just as easily have been a cough or a belly rumble, if the Fae ever did anything so undignified.

"We have a problem," the elder Fae said.

"That which we did to welcome the rowankind . . ." the Fae on the elder's left said.

"Has released wild creatures . . ." Dantin took up the sentence.

"Into the world of the humans." Larien finished.

I'd seen them pass around a sentence like this before, so it was no surprise when the last three Fae in the circle said: "So we meet here . . ."

"To find a solution . . ."

"With our brother and sister of the Okewood."

"Welcome," they all said together.

Having stated the case in such a way as to involve each one personally, Larien looked to Corwen and me. "We asked you to speak to the king. Has that not been done?"

I counted backward. "That was only eleven days ago. We've had a few problems with the Mysterium in the meantime, but in any case, ordinary people can't simply get an audience with the king. Even if they could, the king can't simply snap his fingers and make something happen."

"Excuses!" Dantin frowned.

The Lady held up her hand. "It's many years since you involved yourselves in the world of men. Once, maybe, a king was an absolute ruler, but in this age a king does not simply issue orders. Since you last visited the English court, the king of Scotland became the king of England, there has been a civil war, another king was beheaded by his people, and Parliament held sway for a time before the monarchy was restored, but restored only to rule through Parliament. Then, to save England from a Catholic monarchy, a new king was invited from Germany. Parliament governs now. The days of god-kings are long over." She went on to explain the workings of Parliament much better than I ever could have.

David leaned forward and whispered in Larien's ear.

Larien nodded. "My son reminds me that the human called Walsingham reports directly to the king."

"That's changed in the last few months," Corwen said. "The Walsingham who was so set against Ross restoring magic and freeing the rowankind was not, as we thought, killed at sea last autumn, but he was badly injured. In the many months it took for him to recover and return to London, the political situation changed. Mr. Pitt resigned as Prime Minister, and Mr. Addington took his place. Mr. Addington saw no need for the secret organization that the Walsinghams had run for over two hundred years to protect the realm from magical threats. He merged its resources with the Mysterium, appointing a new Walsingham in charge of the whole. The old Walsingham, maimed and reduced to blindness, and much out of favor, no longer has access to the king, but has made it clear that, even if he did, he would not plead our case."

"You got close enough to speak to him and he still lives?" Dantin asked.

"I wouldn't stoop to murder a blind man in cold blood," I said. "Though I did send him to be a prisoner of the French. We won. He lost."

"A decision you may come to regret," Dantin said.

I hoped not, but I feared he might be right.

"We have much to discuss." The elder's voice carried without apparent effort. "The refugees waiting in the Oke-wood, the closing of the gates, the retrieval of the magical creatures who have crossed into the human world. It be-comes obvious that we must once more involve ourselves in the affairs of men. We must find a way to deal with this Parliament, and with the cooperation of our friends from the Okewood, we must effect a solution."

The discussion was long and intricate, but by the time we'd finished, there was an agreement in place to leave some of the gates open for the rowankind although these entries would be guarded. The Lady offered to send her people to hunt and retrieve those magical creatures who could be safely contained, and to put an end to those who were a danger to themselves and others. The Fae pledged a contingent of young warriors to help. Given that the Fae were not familiar with the human world, it meant teaming them with those more experienced. I suspected that might be an interesting experiment.

I caught David's eye as he leaned forward to whisper in Larien's ear again. I thought he might have been volun-teering for that particular duty.

Our refugees would be allowed to come to Iaru if they wished, particularly the rowankind, as there was already a thriving rowankind community here.

The troll problem was simply solved by making one of the gates into a bridge and employing the trolls as keepers, allowing magicals to cross in one direction only. I thought the hobs might decide to work with them.

The goblins had already expressed a desire to return to their own communities. Many were from London, but there was a small group from Bath, one lone goblin from Birmingham and two from Sheffield where their family had set up as cutlers.

The Lady of the Forests said she would take charge of the kelpie, the werewolves, and the shapechanger, dismiss-ing Freddie as quickly as that. I thought she'd done it deliberately, without giving the Fae much say in the matter, which, given that these magical creatures were all killers and that the Fae's version of justice was somewhat simplistic, seemed like a good thing for Freddie, providing he could be rehabilitated.

"What about the pixies?" Hartington asked.

"You can deal with those." The Lady and Larien spoke at the same time and then raised their eyebrows at each other.

"One of us has to," the Lady said.

"Where did they come from in the first place?" the elder asked.

"Ah, all right . . ." The Lady sighed. "I will take responsibility for them."

"They did stand with us in the fight," I said.

"Of course," she said. "There's nothing they like better than a good rumpus. I'll find something to keep them busy and out of mischief."

"I'll come and see you tomorrow." David caught up with me as we left. "You may need help getting to Yorkshire with some of the gates closed—if Yorkshire is your destination."

Was it? I looked at Corwen. His shoulders twitched.

"We have to take Freddie back."

It was a risk. We didn't want to bring trouble on the family or to the rowankind at the mill, and we certainly didn't want to bring suspicion on Lily, yet the business with Mr. Kaye, Thatcher, and the breaking of the sluice gates had still not been settled. Even though Thatcher had gone to ground somewhere in London, we could hardly leave Lily to deal with the aftermath alone.

We had to go to Yorkshire, even if only for a short visit. Better we do it while the prisoners aboard the *Guillaume Tell* were in French hands. We had a period of grace before news of what had happened reached England.

My eyes were gritty and my leg ached fiercely. Decisions about our long-term future would have to wait until another day. I reached for Corwen's hand as we returned to the Okewood.

36

Casualty

FREDDIE WAS STILL SLEEPING when we arrived back at the glade, so Corwen and I curled close by, sharing a blanket made from some kind of woven leaves. It kept us warmer than any woolen blanket, while the bed of moss beneath it was as soft as any feather bed.

"How is it so comfortable?" I asked, easing my injured leg.

"I don't know, it just is," Corwen murmured in my ear, already half asleep.

I listened to the sounds around me gradually diminish until even the chatter of the pixies subsided. Corwen's breathing settled into a steady pattern as sleep claimed him. I had no right to feel so peaceful with the future still uncertain; yet here we were, together in a warm embrace. Only a few days ago I feared I'd lost him forever. Whatever happened, we two would be all right. Once we left Yorkshire, we could stay in the Okewood or return to Aunt Rosie's cottage since that was protected from the outside world by a Fae glamour. We could even call the *Heart* and sail to Bacalao where the Mysterium had no influence or power.

First, however, Corwen had a duty to his family. I mustn't drag him from that; it was too keenly felt. He'd taken responsibility for Freddie, and until Freddie could take responsibility for himself—and for the Deverell family fortune—Corwen would not wish to leave them unprotected. I drifted to sleep wondering if Freddie would ever come to terms with his wolf and step up to his responsibilities.

Screams woke me in the middle of the night. To be fair, they woke everyone in the grove.

"Freddie!" Corwen pushed aside the blanket which dissolved into a pile of leaves, floating to the ground around us.

He was at Freddie's side in less time than it takes to draw breath.

Freddie wasn't awake. He was locked in a nightmare. The single scream had mutated into wolflike yips and howls, and he was thrashing about. The wound in his side had opened and begun to bleed into a spreading stain on the linen of his shirt, black and slick in the semidarkness of the waning moon.

"It's all right, Freddie. You're all right. You're safe now." Corwen grasped Freddie's hand and murmired a string of reassurances. "You're all right. All right."

Freddie gasped and sat bolt upright, his eyes wide open, but I wasn't sure what was behind them. "It's not all right." He managed to make himself understood between heaving sobs and gulps. "It'll never be all right."

He gave an inhuman growl and launched himself at Corwen, but weak as he was, Corwen was able to catch and hold him.

"Freddie." Corwen hugged his brother. "It's all right. I'll take you home. Mother will look after you—and Lily. You are loved."

"Get off me!" Freddie shook him off. "Monster! We're all monsters. Walsingham should have put us down like the mad dogs we are." He said more, but the rest of it was hidden in the spasms that wracked his body.

A sprite hurried across and sprinkled drops of liquid

over his contorted face and into his eyes. Gradually, the tears subsided, and Freddie fell into a troubled sleep.

"You get some rest. I'll sit with him," Corwen said.

"I'll stay," I said. "He's my brother, too, now."

◆————◆

"Are you sure you want to do this?" the Lady asked Corwen over Freddie's sleeping form.

"I don't think we have much choice," Corwen said. "Freddie needs to be with his family, to rest and to heal."

"It's not only his body," she said. "His mind is troubled. There's a sickness in his spirit."

"I know."

"He deserves a chance. One chance," she said. "But only one. If he proves a danger to himself or others, you must bring him back."

"I'll not let you hurt him."

"I haven't hurt the kelpie, have I?"

Corwen shook his head.

"He may not be able to control his wolf." There was sympathy in the Lady's eyes, but also a hardness.

"I've bitten humans, too," Corwen said.

"You've never enjoyed it. You've never preyed on humans."

I was relieved to hear that, because I'd seen what Corwen's teeth could do.

"I will lend you a cart. Travel through Iaru." She held out a small crystal flask, seemingly undecided about which one of us should take charge of it. In the end she swung her hand toward me. "Tears of Oblivion," she said. "They will make Freddie forget and calm him, but only for a short while. The effects are temporary. If he loses control, you shouldn't hesitate. That's why I've given them to Ross, Corwen. You'll always want to give him another chance. Trust Ross on this. If you have to use the drops, you must bring him back to me, and I will do what I can." She turned to me. "Ross, you need to keep reading your Aunt Rosie's notebooks and learning. What is in there may yet be your salvation." Another of the Lady's semi-cryptic comments.

As she departed, Charlotte and Reverend Purdy approached with Olivia between them, holding their hands.

"Olivia understands, now, that Freddie is not only her big furry friend," the reverend said. "Don't you, my sweeting?"

Olivia nodded, shy as she'd never been before.

"She heard you were taking Freddie home," Charlotte said. "We thought we should bring her to say good-bye, and thank you."

"What will you do?" I asked. "A lot of the rowankind are going to Iaru."

"We couldn't," she said. "Henry . . ." She looked at the reverend. "And Papa."

I didn't want to make any promises about finding Henry Purdy that we couldn't keep.

"The Lady of the Forests says we can stay here with her," Charlotte said. "I'm sure I can find something useful to do, and Father . . ." She blushed slightly to call the reverend this. "Father says he'll look for a parish near the Okewood."

"It shouldn't be too difficult to find one," Reverend Purdy said. "There's a lot of superstition about the place. Clergy don't tend to stay long. If I'm close, we can visit."

"Good for you." Corwen shook hands.

Olivia let go of her mother's and grandfather's hands and tiptoed cautiously to where Freddie lay.

"Little Livvy." Freddie's eyes were clear for once. "We made a fine pair, didn't we?"

"Is it really you?"

"It is. Don't be frightened, I can't bite you now."

"You would never have bitten me."

He smiled weakly but said nothing.

Suddenly Olivia dropped to her knees and flung her arms around his neck. He winced as she caught his side, but didn't flinch. He patted her shoulder awkwardly.

"Come, Olivia, Freddie is tired now." Charlotte scooped up her daughter and, with a dip of her head toward Freddie, took her away, speaking in low, gentle tones.

"We will see you again, won't we?" The reverend asked.

"God willing, Reverend," I said. "As long as the Mysterium doesn't catch us first."

By the time David arrived, we had Freddie wrapped in a blanket and sitting in the small open tub-cart. He seemed calm after Olivia's visit, so we took advantage of the period of grace.

The cart looked too wide to pass between the dense tree trunks, but somehow it did, and the pony drawing it appeared to float over the ground. Corwen rode with Freddie while I doubled up on David's Fae-bred mount, swapping news as we rode.

With David as our guide, we passed through Iaru without the need to emerge for overnight stops. The whole journey condensed into a few hours, though we had to take a detour around an area where the blight of industry bled through.

"Sheffield," David said. "Birmingham and London are the same. We have our wisest minds working on the problem of the flow between your world and Iaru. We've never seen anything like this since London's great fire, and even then the damage healed itself within a decade. This new blight is worsening and might mean sealing off the affected areas completely."

"Is Iaru in danger?" I asked.

"Not yet, but it's troubling."

We emerged into the little wood between Deverell's Mill and Denby Hall where no permanent gate to Iaru had ever existed.

Freddie became agitated when he realized where we were, but Corwen calmed him and we continued to the Hall. As we gently lifted Freddie from the cart, David said goodbye and departed. The pony followed him as docile as a dog.

◆———◆

I'd known on some instinctive level what an effect Freddie's return would have on the household. Corwen's mother fell on her son, tears streaming down her face, not knowing whether to hold Freddie or scold him. She was so taken with the prodigal that she didn't even glance at my breeches, let alone comment on them. It was only when she saw how badly Freddie was injured that she stood back. Stephen Yeardley, vastly experienced at manhandling Mr. Deverell up and down stairs and in and out of his wheeled chair, took charge of getting Freddie into his bedroom, kept in a permanent state of readiness in the hope he would return one day as if nothing was wrong. Poppy, noticeably more round, waddled ahead to open doors and turn down sheets. Mrs. Deverell followed.

"Is he dying?" Mrs. Deverell studied his complexion, as ashen as any rowankind, but without the grain marks. "We should send for Dr. Boucher." She dabbed at the unhealthy sheen of sweat on Freddie's forehead with a cool cloth.

"He's tired, Mama," I said. "And hurt, but he's far from dying."

I was pretty sure the Lady wouldn't have allowed us to move him if he'd been on the brink of departing this earth, but the journey had exhausted him, and I had to admit that he didn't look good. The dried bloodstains on his shirt didn't help.

"He's already been seen by a good physician, Mother," Corwen said. "He needs time and some tender care, which I'm sure you can supply. Where's Lily?"

"At the mill where she is every day. I don't know why she doesn't simply have a bed made up in the office. I've sent one of the stable lads for her."

Lily must have pushed Brock to gallop all the way from the mill, for she arrived sooner than we expected. It should have been a joyous reunion of siblings, but Freddie, though taking hold of her hand as if he would never let it go, refused to answer any of her questions. By this time Mrs. Deverell had recovered from her shock and was taking charge of the sick room, redoing everything Poppy had already done perfectly adequately. I might have taken exception to this at one time, but now I saw it for what it was, a sign of the fierce love she held for all her children. At least keeping busy prevented her from panicking and made her feel useful, though I could have wished she'd left the Lady's moss in place.

Yeardley brought Mr. Deverell to see his son, and I

detected as much of a smile as the old man could give on the good side of his face.

Freddie remained quiet through it all, but I could see tension in his clenched jaw and white knuckles. I had the feeling he was barely holding on to sanity.

"We need to get everyone out," I whispered to Corwen. "Freddie needs to change. I'm not happy his wound is bleeding again."

"I'm not sure he can change," Corwen said. "And if he does, I'm not sure I can get him to change back."

"I don't think we have much choice," I said.

"Mother." Corwen tapped her on the shoulder. "Freddie needs to rest and heal."

"Like Lily did when she hurt her head," I said, raising one eyebrow. "Privately."

"Oh, of course." She bundled everyone out except Lily, Corwen, and me, but then she hovered in the doorway.

"It'll be all right," I said, hoping it would be.

She nodded once and left.

"It's not going to be simple, is it?" Lily asked.

"I don't think so," Corwen said. "He's frightened of his wolf and equally frightened about what's in his head when he's human."

Corwen told her briefly about Freddie killing Walsingham and trying to kill the Kingsman officer.

"Oh, poor Freddie." Lily's sympathy was immediately for her brother.

"Why don't you publish it in the newspaper?" Freddie asked. "Talking about me as though I'm not here. Well, I'm not, am I? I'm not Freddie Deverell anymore. I'm just a thing, a monster. I'm not even that. I shouldn't exist. It would be better if I died." He punched himself on the side and gasped in pain.

Lily grabbed his hand, and he snarled pretty convincingly to say he was still human.

"Don't say that, Freddie," Lily said. "This family has suffered enough. Mama and Papa have suffered enough. You must get better."

"Must?"

"Yes, must. I'm giving you an order, damn you."

"When did my little sister learn language like that?"

"When she took charge of your mill. Now grow up and do as Corwen says. Change. And when you've changed, change again. If you won't do it for Corwen, do it for me and for Mama."

"You don't understand, Lily. I'm not worth it. If you knew . . ."

"Why don't you tell me?"

He closed his eyes for a moment and took a deep breath.

"I . . . You wouldn't understand."

"Try me," Lily said.

"I've never been able to be myself at home. I knew for a long time that I was unusual—even before I changed into the damned wolf. At school and university it was different. I had . . . friends, one particular friend who was . . . like me."

"You're not talking about the wolf, are you?" she asked.

"I'm not."

"You're trying to tell me you don't like girls."

He pressed his lips together and looked to see how Corwen and I were taking the news. Corwen shrugged. "I've known for some time, brother."

"And I'm not so missish that I don't know what you mean," Lily said.

"Does Mother know?"

"I doubt it," Lily said, "or she wouldn't have spent so much time trying to pair you with Dorothea Kaye. I think the Kayes were trying to marry into the business. They must see us as an opportunity, or maybe a threat. At least you don't have to worry about that now Mr. Kaye has shown his true colors." She quickly told him how Kaye's agent, Thatcher, had almost ruined the mill.

"So you have a particular friend," Corwen said. "Is he in London?"

"He was. He went to the country—Gloucestershire—to undertake some family business. We didn't part well. I was unkind—upset that he was leaving. That's when . . ."

"When you went running as a wolf on Hampstead Heath," Corwen said.

"It was foolish of me, I know," Freddie said, "but I'd held the wolf in check for so long, and I felt as if I'd burst if I didn't do something."

"Your mistake was going to the same place time and again. Rumors drew the Mysterium."

"I know that now. I never wanted the wolf, but in the end I couldn't deny it. And once I'd changed, it felt so good to run. The night was alive with scents. After so long without changing, everything was intensified. It was like nothing I'd ever experienced before. Then, one night, there was a net and I knew it was all over. I didn't know what to do, but I reasoned that if I could stay a wolf, no one could ever find out who I was."

He looked at Lily. "If they discovered my identity, they might have come looking for you."

"Oh, Freddie, you dear, sweet man." Lily took his hand and held it to her cheek. "My big brother still looking out for me, but you know that the longer you stay in wolf form the harder it is to remember you're human."

"So I found out. When they starved me for days and threw the child into my cage, I wanted to eat her, but I didn't. I didn't."

"Olivia," I explained to Lily. "A rowankind child. Freddie protected her." Or perhaps she'd protected him.

"She kept me sane. Then Corwen arrived, and I knew if I changed to human, they'd realize we were brothers and the family would suffer."

"I guessed that was why you were refusing to change," Corwen said. "Sound thinking, brother."

"It was hard. When freedom came I still couldn't change. By that time, I wasn't sure I wanted to. I saw that hateful man, the man who'd tortured me and had callously thrown Olivia into my cage to be my supper. I saw him hurl the spell at Ross and turn his aim to you. It was as if my vision was suffused with blood. And once I'd sunk my teeth into him, he tasted so good, and I was so hungry . . ."

Freddie's voice had shrunk to a whisper now. I held a glass of water to his lips, and he sipped before carrying on.

"I felt so ashamed afterward that I knew I didn't

deserve to be human again. I was an animal—a monster—
and it was my fate and my punishment to stay that way.
Once I started to think of myself as an animal, it became
easier to accept. The Kingsman at Modbury—he was an
enemy. I didn't hesitate."

Corwen put his hand on his brother's shoulder. "We all
do what we must to protect those we love."

"I'm not sure I can control it."

"You need to spend more time as a man, Freddie. It's
been difficult, but it's over now. There's plenty of time. You
can rest and recuperate and get the wolf out of your head.
When you let him back in, do it on your own terms. But
first you need to heal, and to do that you need to change."

"Into a wolf."

"Only briefly, and then to human again."

"Don't let me out of here while the wolf is on me. Lock
the door. I don't want to hurt anyone."

"If you wish. Will you change now?"

Freddie lapsed into silence, which we took for assent.

We stripped the clothes and the bandages from him and
laid him as comfortably as we could on his uninjured side,
then Lily held his hands and urged him into the first change.
It was a long time coming. His hands sprouted fur between
his fingers, and his nails curved into claws; he lay there for
minutes before the fur appeared on his forearms. The
whole change must have taken at least an hour, but finally
a shaggy brown wolf lay on the bed.

"It'll be a few hours before he has the strength to change
again," I said to Corwen. "You tell Lily what happened
while we were away, and I'll go and see what's in the larder.
I don't know about you two, but I'm famished."

By the time I returned to Freddie's room with half a
cold meat pie, a loaf of bread, and a bottle of claret, Corwen was telling the tale of Mr. Tingle the goblin tailor.

"He's already been in touch about a cloth order," Lily
said. "And there will be another order after that if we can
deliver by August. Is he a real goblin? I mean, really real? I
thought they were fairy stories."

"He's real."

"Well, I'm glad of it. His order came when I was at my wit's end. It's gone a long way toward saving the mill."

"And our friend Mr. Kaye?" Corwen asked.

"Quiet for now. I suppose without Thatcher we can't prove anything against Kaye, but I have watchmen posted at night. I'll be ready for him if there's a next time."

I thought Lily would. She seemed totally comfortable managing the mill. It would be a talent wasted if Freddie recovered and stripped her of that responsibility.

Corwen finished his story, and I continued by telling her about taking the *Guillaume Tell* and our battle at Modbury crossroads.

"So are you both on the run from the Mysterium, now?" Lily asked.

I shrugged. "It depends on what news gets back to London. Walsingham, the Mysterium thugs, and the sailors should end up in a French prison. I feel bad about the sailors. Boney will be pleased to regain the *Guillaume Tell* from the British Navy, I'm sure, but not pleased enough to let her crew go free. We're safe for the time being, but we shouldn't take safety for granted."

"Has the Mysterium man been sniffing around?" Corwen asked.

"Mr. Pomeroy?" Lily laughed. "He has, but not in the way you might expect. I think he's taken with me."

Corwen's chin nearly hit the floor.

"Your baby sister is not such a baby anymore," I said.

"Are you . . . I mean is that all right with you?" Corwen asked.

"He's handsome, don't you think, Ross?"

"I suppose he is, but he's Mysterium."

"Who was it who said about keeping your friends close and your enemies closer? Besides, we've talked. He's quite progressive."

"You haven't told him anything?" Corwen asked.

"Credit me with more sense than that. Of course I haven't. Our conversations have been much more wide-ranging."

"Conversations?"

"He may have called to pay his respects a few times." She grinned mischievously.

Corwen's mouth closed with a snap, and he gave me a perplexed look. It was my turn to laugh.

◆━━━◆

Sometime in the early hours of the morning, Freddie began to get restless.

"I think he's ready to try another change." Corwen crossed to Freddie's bedside and barely pulled his hand away in time from snapping teeth.

"Let me." Lily took Freddie's paws in her hands, eliciting a soft growl but no bared teeth.

The change was no easier, but at least Freddie showed himself willing. Human once more, he flopped back on the bed, naked and sweating but not as ashen as he had been. The wound had stopped bleeding.

He glared at all of us. "Can't a man get some rest? Get out, the lot of you, and leave me be."

We got out.

"He sounds as though he's feeling better," Corwen said as we closed his bedroom door behind us. I should say *our* bedroom door because this was the first night we'd spent at Denby Hall as man and wife. A fire burned red in the grate, and a single candle flickered on the nightstand.

I looked at the bed. "So many times I wanted your mother to turn a blind eye so that I could slip under the covers with you, and now all I want to do is sleep."

He laughed and held his arms wide. "Come on, m'lady, I'll help you get out of those clothes."

Sash and waistcoat first, then breeches followed by boots and stockings, freeing my long shirt to drape around my thighs. He ran his hands over my legs, carefully avoiding my bandage and continued along my flanks, over my breast binding and up my arms, neatly drawing my shirt over my head in one movement.

"Ah, Ross, my lovely Ross."

He unlaced my breast binding, an adapted pair of short stays that stopped me jiggling in unmanly fashion, though

I'm not well-endowed with bosom, so jiggling is relative. He cupped my breasts and kissed each one in turn, sending a thrill through my body despite my aches and exhaustion.

"Come, love, lay with me and rest." He pulled aside the coverlet and I scrambled into the bed, the clean sheets cool against my body. In less than a minute he'd divested himself of clothes and slipped in next to me, bare skin to bare skin. He slid one arm beneath my shoulders and held me close.

I turned to him and touched the firm muscle of his arms and reacquainted myself with his chest, his narrowing waist and what was below.

"Ah . . ." He sucked air sharply between his teeth. "I thought you were tired."

"I am. My body doesn't know when to give in."

"It's a lovely body."

"It's a sore one. Mind my leg."

He gently lifted my bandaged leg to lie across the curve of his waist and cupped my buttock, pulling me close and closer still until we were one being.

"I love you, Mr. Deverell."

"And I love you, Mrs. Deverell."

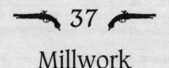

37

Millwork

POPPY NOW WADDLED instead of walking, her belly making itself felt.

"You need to rest more, Poppy," I said to her as she bustled into our room the following morning with a bucket of coals. "I know how to dress myself, and Sarah can see to the fires. I never had a maid on board ship."

"You never had stays and a bib-front dress to deal with, or your hair to dress respectably on board ship," she said. "But I'm not dressing Mr. Corwen."

I laughed. Corwen had dressed himself and gone to Freddie's room at first light.

"How's your leg? Does the bandage need changing?"

I shook my head. "I'm supposed to let the moss do its job for three days. It's sore, but as long as I don't try and do too much, it's bearable."

"Don't tell Mrs. Deverell you've got moss on it. She thinks it's nasty, dirty stuff."

"Well, she doesn't know the Lady and her sprites."

I explained to Poppy how the rowankind had been imprisoned on the *Guillaume Tell*. She shuddered at the idea of suffering the sea, and then grasped the wider implications. "They're locking up rowankind for their magic?"

"Those they catch using it."

"What about the rowankind at the mill, Mr. Topping and the weavers? That Pomeroy man from the Mysterium knows about the water magic when the sluice got smashed and . . ."

"What?"

"Since then, they've been using magic to lift water from the tailrace to the header pond to keep the waterwheel turning. Stephen—Mr. Yeardley—heard Miss Lily telling her father. She seemed proud of it. Said it couldn't be against the law because the rowankind were doing it at Styal Mill with impunity."

"God's ballocks! We were so absorbed with Freddie yesterday that we hardly discussed the mill. It isn't against the law, but that's not stopping the Mysterium from snatching rowankind. We need to tell her to stop. Where is she?"

"Gone to the mill already."

"I've slept too long. Quickly, I need to go there. I'll finish my hair. Send young Robin to the stables to ask Thomas to saddle Dancer. Not the sidesaddle."

"Your leg—"

"I'll manage."

Corwen met me on the landing with a kiss. "Going somewhere?"

"The mill." I explained quickly.

"I'll come with you."

"No, you should stay with Freddie. Does he need to change again?"

"He does, but he won't let me help him."

"You need to guard him."

Whether Corwen was guarding Freddie from the household, or the household from Freddie was a moot point.

"Don't go alone."

"I'll be fine."

"Take your pistol."

I wasn't going to argue. "I will."

Rather than take my navy pistol, I primed the pair of

small pistols made by Mr. Bunney of London. They were small enough to fit in the hidden pockets in my dress and my redingote covered the bulges adequately.

In lieu of breakfast, I grabbed a russet apple from the dining room, one that had been in store for too long and had lost some of its sweetness and crisp texture, but it would have to do. Four hearty bites took care of most of the slightly fluffy flesh. I hobbled across to the stable yard where Dancer was tied to a ring in the wall, already saddled. He whinnied as I crossed the yard and whickered more softly as I approached him.

"Did you miss me? Have you been good?"

I gave him the apple core, and he tossed his head in what might have been a nod.

"Mrs. Deverell, would you like a hand?" Thomas emerged from the tack room as he heard my voice.

"Things are going to get awfully complicated with two Mrs. Deverells, Thomas. You can call me Ross."

"How about Mrs. Rossalinde?"

"That's a good compromise."

Under normal circumstances I could mount Dancer without difficulty, but I didn't want to pop my stitches, so I led him over to the mounting block. Thomas scurried to hold his head while I mounted. My thigh protested, and a pain shot through it as I straddled the saddle, but once my feet were in the stirrups it settled to a manageable sting.

"Thomas, I'm going to the mill. I should be home by noon. If I'm not I'd be obliged if you would send John Mallinson to check on me."

"Should I tell Mr. Corwen you're going?"

"He knows. He's with Freddie."

"Right you are."

As soon as we were safely out of the stable yard, I sat well down in my saddle, touched Dancer's sides with my heels, and gave him his head. He needed no more urging, but sprang into a ground-eating gallop, only slowing to collect himself before swinging around twisty bends on the uphill road, and that, I suspect, was only to avoid flinging me off.

A pain stabbed through my thigh as he rounded a sharp bend. I transferred my reins into one hand and pressed on the wound gently.

Unexpectedly, Dancer slowed. Ahead, through a screen of trees still dressed in spring buds, I glimpsed a flash of red. I knew that shade, dammit. Redcoats on the road, heading for the mill.

I needed to get past them, but this stretch of road ran along the steep valley side. I could either head to the right through a stand of trees and up onto the rough moorland where I might be seen, or plunge to the left and slither down to the river below. On any other horse I wouldn't have tried it, but I swallowed the lump in my throat and put Dancer at the steep descent, where gnarled trees clung to perilously thin soil. Clumps of grass hid twisting, exposed roots. Whippy saplings and brambles waited for the unwary. My brave horse didn't hesitate. He tucked his hindquarters beneath him and began the perilous descent while I tried to maintain balance, keeping my center over his to be as little hindrance to him as possible.

Terror of the drop drove away all thoughts of my leg, but gripping his sides firmly turned the dull ache into a sharp jab. I felt Dancer slide. My instinct was to yank on the reins to stop him, which would be useless since he couldn't stop himself. Instead, I grabbed the front of the saddle and tried to steady myself while my horse almost disappeared from underneath me. One false move would be a broken leg for him and a broken neck for me. He regained his footing, checked, and started down again. I daren't look back to see how far we'd come or whether the redcoats had spotted us. I kept my eyes on the ground ahead, dizzyingly steep with the river churning through the valley bottom, neither wide nor deep, I knew, but swift and broken by rocks and rills. The river loomed quickly. At the last minute I saw the water had undercut the sloping bank, leaving a six-foot drop. From his barely controlled slither, Dancer launched himself outward into the river. I came clean out of the saddle, but by some miracle landed back in it as Dancer scrambled for purchase on the riverbed, the water almost up to his chest.

"Brave boy," I told him, my voice trembling. "All right?"

As if in answer he plunged upstream, now knee-deep, now chest-deep in water as he encountered sink holes. There was a weir ahead, with a gush of water flowing toward us over a drop of maybe three feet, not a huge jump to make on level ground, but from the riverbed to uncertain footing above was more than I wanted to risk. The bank rose even more steeply here where the enterprising weir builders had quarried stone for their endeavor. The water gushed over the weir's horizontal lip, and for a moment I thought I was seeing double. Then I saw that the second horizontal line was a clapper bridge built right above the lip of the weir, its stone slabs balanced on submerged pillars. The whole thing was barely a foot above the level of the water. When the river was high, it would be under water completely, so it was likely to be slick with weed and moss.

"What do you think, Dancer? Jump clean over or land on top?"

On top would take us to a narrow track, and we could exit the river on the opposite side to the redcoats.

"On top." I told him following the old horseman's adage that if you throw your heart over an obstacle, your horse will surely follow. In this case I threw my heart on to a slippery three-foot–wide slab of Yorkshire sandstone.

Dancer gathered his haunches beneath him, bounced almost on the spot, and leaped, landing with a clatter on the stone and twisting so his forward momentum carried him along the bridge and to the far bank. I pitched toward his shoulder and felt something tear in my leg, but managed to right myself.

"Magnificent beast." I patted his shoulder heartily. He snorted at me, and with solid ground beneath his feet again scrambled up the narrow track. My dress and redingote were soaked to mid-thigh, but luckily my pistols were still dry in my pockets. My leg, bandage now thoroughly soaked, had begun to go numb. I should be thankful for small mercies. We arrived at the mill across the field behind the tenter croft—thank goodness, before the redcoats did—but we didn't have long. I slithered off Dancer and clung to his saddle while I tested to see if my leg would hold me up. It would. I threw my reins to a surprised boy in the yard. "Cool him off and rub him down well," I said as I limped toward the office, wet skirts slapping against my legs.

"Lily!" I shouted as I mounted the stairs. "Lily! We have to get the rowankind out of here. There's a troop of red-coats on the road."

"I know," Lily said.

The man standing with his back to me turned. Mr. Pomeroy.

<hr/>

I stared at the Mysterium man, my jaw slack. Condemned out of my own mouth by my own stupidity. I felt the weight of my pistols in the hidden pockets beneath my dress. Could I actually shoot Mr. Pomeroy in cold blood, even to protect myself, the Deverells, and the rowankind?

My hand went to the metallic lump, but I was wearing a redingote on top of my dress and couldn't reach into my pocket surreptitiously. I felt the shape of the pistol. Was it possible to draw the doghead and squeeze the trigger through three layers of fabric? I'd have to fire from the hip and could hit Lily as easily as Pomeroy.

All these thoughts flashed through my brain in an instant.

I touched my hip where I had been so used to wearing a knife. I saw Pomeroy's eyes widen because he recognized the gesture even though nothing else about my appearance alerted him to potential danger. Of course, he'd been a navy man, used to defending himself. Maybe I simply had murder in my eyes.

"Ross. Ross!"

It was the second time Lily said it that got through to me.

"George has ridden ahead to warn me," she said.

I took one thing from that other than the obvious. She called him George. His interest in Lily ran both ways.

I breathed again. The moment for murder was over.

I staggered sideways into Lily's desk and banged my leg. "Oww! How much does he know?"

"Ross, your leg. Sit before you fall."

I flopped into Lily's chair. "How much does he know?"

"I told him the rowankind have been helping out with their water magic, but we haven't been paying them to do it."

Pomeroy relaxed his stance. "Unfortunately, the matter of payment is irrelevant now. The Sheffield office has received new orders from London, and I have received my orders from Sheffield. All known magic users are to be detained." He grimaced. "I'm sorry. I blame myself for sanctioning magic use. This is not what I expected." He rubbed his forehead with the heel of his hand. "Some of us in the organization are seeking reform."

"Reform?" I was still recovering from the shock of seeing Mr. Pomeroy apparently on friendly terms with Lily.

"George was just telling me . . ." Lily said.

Pomeroy looked earnest. "Things have changed, and we have to change with them. I know your rowankind saved many lives by their action when your sluice gate was smashed. They shouldn't be punished for it. Why should we suppress magic when it can be used for good?"

"The redcoats?"

"Under direct orders from Sheffield."

"Damn!"

"What are we to do?" Lily asked.

"Mr. Pomeroy, do you have orders to take all our rowankind?" There were at least forty of them.

"My orders are to take those who have been actively using magic."

"You told your superiors in Sheffield about that?"

"Only of the night when their actions saved the valley from a flood. The rest came from an informant."

"Let me guess, someone from Kaye's Mill."

"I couldn't say." He spread his hands wide. "I'm not being coy. I honestly don't know."

"How do you intend to identify the magic users?"

"I have a list of names."

Lily waved a sheet at me. "Twenty names, including Tommy Topping, but not his father."

"What if your redcoats find all those on their list gone, will they take others?"

He hesitated. "No, they won't. I can prevent that, but how can you hide twenty men?"

"Leave that to me."

Over George Pomeroy's shoulder Lily mouthed *Iaru*, and I nodded.

"Lily, get those named on the list together, I'll be down in a moment. Mr. Pomeroy, you know how sick the rowan-kind are on the ocean?"

"I've seen the unfortunates."

"The Mysterium is sending their captives to sea, rowan-kind as well as magicals."

"I didn't know."

"Now you do."

"I need to get back to the troop. I may be able to delay them. How long do you need?"

"As long as you can give me."

He turned to leave.

"Mr. Pomeroy . . ." He halted at the top of the stair. "Thank you."

He nodded once and headed into the yard with Lily close behind.

They left me in the office, surrounded by wooden-lined walls and bare floorboards. I wondered . . . would this do? I remembered Corwen patting the wooden headboard of the bed we slept in at the inn in Bath and saying: *It depends on your definition of woodland.*

I concentrated hard and *summoned* David.

It felt as though I was hanging upside down and all the blood was rushing to my head. My eyes felt too large for their sockets, as if any slight increase in pressure could pop them out, and my fingers and toes tingled. Dizziness threatened to claim me.

"Whoa, Ross, what's so important?"

I leaped out of my chair, whirled around and almost stumbled into my brother's arms.

"David! Thank goodness ... quickly ... you've got to help." I explained the problem. "I need a gate to Iaru, right now. Right here. Can you do it?"

"Here?"

"The wood. Isn't that how I called you?"

"One person may slip through, but twenty? Where are the nearest living trees?"

"Beyond the tenter croft. Two fields away."

"That will have to do."

"I'm not sure we have time."

We clattered down the stairs one after the other. Well, I clattered—still limping—David's footsteps made no sound. I'm not even sure he would have left footprints in the dust.

There were already half a dozen rowankind in the yard. Lily was scowling at the paper, ticking off names.

"Where are the others?" I asked.

She stared at David.

"You remember my brother?"

"I do." She curtsied, which was something humans tended to do when faced with a Fae. Even a fifteen-year-old one was impressive. David's clothes bore no relation to human fashions. He wore a flowing outer robe of deep azure blue over close fitting dark trousers and boots. On his head was a suggestion of a gold circlet, light enough to be an illusion but obvious enough to show his rank. A Fae prince.

David waved away her curtsey. "Sister."

"Where are the others?" I repeated.

"Mr. Topping has sent to the dam for them," Lily said.

I could hear feet on the road, marching in step. My hearing is witch-acute, so probably no one else except David could hear yet, but it wouldn't be long before the redcoats rounded the bend and crossed the bridge.

Three more rowankind came across the yard at a run.

"What's up, Miss Lily?" one of them asked.

"Redcoats are coming for magic users," one of the others said. "We're making a run for it."

"I can't leave our lass," one said. "She's due in less than a month."

"We'll take care of your families," I said. "Better that they know you're safe, not floating out to sea in a prison ship from Hull."

"Ship?" One of the others said. "I ain't going on no ship."

"Where are we going, missis?" one of the others asked.

"Iaru," David said.

It was as if he'd materialized all of a sudden. The men dropped to one knee before him.

"Run," he said. "You have to do the first bit for yourself. That grove of trees across the tenter croft is where the gate will be. Don't stop to gather your things or say good-bye to anyone. There isn't time. Run now. The others will follow."

I could see some of them still had questions, but the footsteps on the road were drawing closer.

Four more rowankind came across the yard at a brisk walk.

"Run, damn you!" I shouted.

They broke into a trot and lengthened their stride as Lily waved them on.

"Thirteen down. Where the hell are the other seven?" Lily said, ticking off names.

As the redcoats rounded the bend and came within sight of the yard, the last seven, with Tommy Topping bringing up the rear, ran from the direction of the dam.

Mr. Topping followed behind at a slower pace and waved his son onward.

"Thank the Lord." Lily finished ticking off her list. "Follow the others if you don't want to be shipped off to sea," she shouted. "We'll explain later."

There was a shout from the redcoats, but Mr. Pomeroy, riding at their head, said something to the sergeant in charge and the troop didn't break formation.

I heard the sergeant say, "But, sir, they're getting away."

Pomeroy's hesitation gave our rowankind a head start, but he couldn't stay the redcoats forever.

David kissed me on the cheek, inclined his head to Lily, and trotted after the fleeing rowankind, not hurrying, but covering the ground faster than any of them. They had a lead, but it wasn't enough, so when the sergeant called for the redcoats to load their muskets and take positions, they were still well within range. Muskets were not particularly accurate, but a volley could easily kill or injure at that distance.

The last group of rowankind pounded across the field, Tommy Topping now in the lead, urging them on. My heart nearly stopped beating as one of the laggards tripped and spread his length on the ground.

"Hold your fire, sergeant." Mr. Pomeroy still had the command voice of a naval lieutenant. "Our orders are to apprehend them, not slaughter them."

"My orders are not to let them get away, sir, and I shall carry out my orders. First rank, take aim!"

Tommy Topping slithered to a halt and whirled around. He didn't hesitate to go back for the fallen man, dragging him to his feet and hauling him forward by one hand.

David caught up with them, stopped and turned, putting himself between the redcoats and the rowankind. A wall of flame sprang up with a wave of one hand.

"Fire!" yelled the sergeant.

Muskets barked. Smoke and the acrid smell of black powder engulfed us. Lily began to cough. Mill hands who'd run into the yard to see what was going on began to shout their disapproval. Mr. Topping, thoroughly out of breath, panted up to join us. The grain marks on his face stood out dark against his ash-gray skin even paler than usual. "Tell me they're not trying to kill my boy."

I reached out and grabbed his arm. "David won't let them hurt anyone."

David stepped forward through the wall of flame. He glowed with power, the fire crackling around him without so much as disturbing the azure robe.

"Put away your weapons." He didn't shout, but though he was a hundred yards away, his voice was clear. "Tell your masters the rowankind are protected!"

He turned and walked into the flames.

The sergeant tried again. "Second rank, step forward. Take aim. Fire!"

I saw the sparkles in the wall of flame as each musket ball vaporized.

"Hold your fire, sergeant. You can't shoot the Fae." Mr. Pomeroy said.

"Fae, sir, don't exist, sir. No, they don't."

The flames winked out of existence. There was no sign of any rowankind or my azure-coated brother.

"I believe we've had a demonstration that they do." Pomeroy gave both me and Lily a measuring glance. "If you wish to make absolutely sure, take your men and search that woodland. I'm pretty sure you'll find nothing. There's not even a scorch mark on the grass."

The sergeant marshaled his men. Muskets in hand, they trotted toward the wood.

"What happened here?" Pomeroy asked.

Lily shook her head. "I don't know."

"Do you know?" he asked me.

I pressed my lips together.

"You?" he asked Topping.

"I don't know how and I don't know why, but that was a Fae lord, and unless I'm very much mistook, the boys are gone to Iaru."

"Where?"

"The home of the Fae where you can't hurt them."

38

The Silver and the Brown

WE SETTLED THE REMAINING ROWANKIND with as much reassurance as we could give them. Lily insisted on checking my leg in the privacy of her office. I'd ripped a couple of stitches, but the damage wasn't bad enough to need a new dressing. I pressed the Lady's moss over the wound, and Lily retied my bandage.

"You know George will have to tell the Mysterium what happened," Lily said.

"I would expect nothing less."

"Though I know he'll deflect suspicion that anyone at the mill knew anything about the Fae."

"It may be good for the Mysterium to know what they're up against, as long as they realize they can't fight the Fae."

"Will they know that?"

"If they try, they'll soon find out."

The sound of hooves in the yard announced the arrival of John Mallinson. We met him at the door. The look of relief on his face when he saw us was palpable.

"Thomas sent me to see if you needed anything," he

said. "I saw the redcoats on the road and Mr. Pomeroy with them."

"They return empty-handed," Lily said. "Though it was a close-run thing."

"I'm glad of it," he said. He boosted me into Dancer's saddle while Lily took Brock from the stable boy and stepped up from the mounting block in the yard. Turning his big brown gelding, Mallinson fell into step behind us as we headed for home.

"How goes it at the house, John?" I asked him.

"I'm not sure, Mrs. Rossalinde. There was some kind of fuss this morning after you left, but I don't know any more than that."

I glanced sideways at Lily. "Shall we pick up the pace?"

"I think we should."

We pushed Dancer and Brock into a smart trot.

Mallinson took the horses to the stable, and we entered the house to find Sarah carrying a bowl of bloodied water across the entrance hall. Her face was pink from crying.

"Mother, sit and let us take care of you." Corwen's disembodied voice drifted into the hallway.

"Don't fuss so, Corwen. It's not deep."

"Mama?" Lily rushed forward, following the voices into the small parlor where Corwen loomed over his mother's chair. She had a bloodied napkin tied around her left forearm, and despite her words, her face was pale and drained. Poppy knelt by her side, ministering to her. As I moved closer, I could see the wound was a swollen mess with several puncture wounds the size of a wolf's incisors. I assumed Corwen hadn't bitten his mother, so that left only Freddie.

"What happened?" Lily asked.

"Freddie." Corwen's anger was barely controlled. "If he were a dog, I'd shoot him for this."

"It was my fault. When he didn't answer my knock, I unlocked the door and went into his room. I didn't know he was changed. I startled him," Mama said. "It's not as bad as it looks."

Poppy made a face. It was easily as bad as it looked.

Sarah brought a bowl of fresh water, and Poppy continued to clean the wounds. "I think a few stitches might help," she said. "The bites on the wrist are deep. Luckily, it didn't hit a vital blood vessel."

I looked from Corwen to his mother. "Where's Freddie now?"

"In his room," Corwen said through his teeth. "Don't worry. The door's locked. Leave him to cool off for a while."

We sat while Poppy cleaned and stitched and bandaged.

"I'll need to check the dressings tomorrow, Mrs. Deverell," she said. "In the meantime, don't try to do too much and keep your hand folded on your chest, not dangling by your side. I recommend putting your feet up for the rest of the day, though I can fashion you a sling if you wish."

"No, it's all right, Poppy dear. You're a marvel. I'll take your advice and sit on the chaise for a short while."

"I'll bring you a blanket, Mother," Corwen said.

"And ask Sarah to bring some tea, Corwen," I said. "We could all use some. I need to tell you what happened at the mill this morning."

Mama waved her thickly bandaged hand. "How on earth am I going to pour tea like this?"

After explanations, we left Corwen's mother sleeping on the chaise longue and walked out into the garden. Robin kicked clods of grass by the lake, hands in pockets. He perked up as Poppy came clumping down the slope to meet him. There was little spring in her step these days, and I thought it would not be long before her baby was born.

"Are you all right?" Corwen asked. He asked that a lot lately. I'd dearly like to be living a less exciting life.

"Yes, I'm fine."

"Leg?"

"It's smarting like the devil, I admit, but it's still packed with moss, and I don't think I did much damage."

He sighed. "We should go and see if Freddie has calmed down."

"You need to talk to him."

"If he'll talk to me."

We went back inside. Corwen slowed as we climbed the stairs to Freddie's room. As he took the key from his pocket, his mouth compressed to a thin line.

"Freddie? It's me. How do you feel?"

No answer. Corwen pushed open the door.

The room was a wreck. The bed had been dismembered, the coverlet and mattress shredded. Feathers had settled on upended furniture. Smashed porcelain from the jug and basin on the washstand lay in the hearth with candle holders and a broken mirror. There were deep indents in the candles from fangs.

The room stank of shit.

My stomach roiled. It was daubed over the walls.

At first glance I thought Freddie's wolf had rampaged around the room, and maybe he had at the beginning, but a wolf didn't smear shit up the walls to a height of over six feet and a wolf didn't open a casement window and climb out.

Freddie had gone.

"His clothes are still here." Corwen leaned out of the wiindow. "He's climbed out naked, and run off as a wolf. I should have . . ." He turned back to me and smacked himself on the forehead with the heel of his hand. "I've been crediting Freddie with more rationality than he has. When he opened up to us yesterday, I thought he'd begun the healing process, mentally as well as physically. Do you still have the Tears of Oblivion?"

"Of course." I patted my pocket where the small crystal flask rattled against my pistol.

"Bring them. Follow as fast as you can."

He ran out of the door.

Corwen's discarded shirt lay at the bottom of the stairs, his boots and his buckskins by the side door. Of course he would be able to track Freddie much better in wolf form. His nose was a remarkable instrument.

He didn't need his nose this time, however. A sharp scream was enough.

Poppy and Robin.

With a pounding heart, I ran around the side of the house.

The frozen tableau by the lake seared itself into my memory.

Poppy had pushed Robin behind her and was facing off against the big brown wolf, shouting at him and waving her arms in his direction to make herself appear big and fierce. Half crouched, the wolf was ready to pounce. His demeanor said he'd prefer the easy target, the human cub, but he'd take the bigger one if she was all that was on offer. A silver-gray shape bounded toward him, but Corwen was still a hundred yards away.

Then Robin's nerve broke. He bolted toward the house, shrieking, and the wolf sprang to follow, streaking past Poppy. With great presence of mind, but little thought for herself, Poppy flung herself at Freddie, almost missing but managing to catch his hindquarters and grab onto his tail. Freddie yelped and squirmed around, jaws snapping, but Poppy flung herself back and twisted. Freddie howled.

It was enough of a delay.

Corwen barged into Freddie. Poppy let go, scrambling backward, but I could see she was hurt. She didn't even try to get to her feet, but curled around her belly on the ground. I picked up my skirts and ran, calling for assistance as I went.

The two wolves, silver and brown, snarled and snapped, blood-flecked foam flying from their jaws. Corwen fought ferociously, silent except for the snapping of teeth. Freddie yelped and growled, darting in for any exposed fur he could reach.

As I got to Poppy the two wolves broke apart and began to circle each other warily. I still had the pair of pistols in my pockets, one shot in each. Could I shoot Corwen's brother?

No. This fight was by no means over. I had to leave it to Corwen.

"Poppy, I'm here. What's wrong?" I dropped to my knees by her side. Her skirt was wet.

"Baby," she gasped.

"All right. Hold on." I could see Yeardley, Thomas, and John Mallinson running across the grass, no doubt alerted by Robin. "We'll get you back to the house. Are you bitten?"

"No, just—" She gasped and curled around her belly again. I grabbed her hand and let her squeeze mine.

Contractions didn't usually start this hard or this suddenly. I wondered if Freddie had torn something loose inside. There was no blood, just fluid. That was good, wasn't it?

With a snarl, Freddie leaped for Corwen's throat, only to meet empty air as Corwen whipped around and shouldered him to the ground.

The men arrived. Oblivious to the fight, Yeardley's first concern was Poppy.

"Carry her to the house, Stephen. Her baby's on the way."

He lifted her carefully in his arms and set off at a brisk pace.

Thomas and Mallinson hesitated as the fighting wolves bowled toward them. Thomas carried a twitch, a loop of leather on a stout pole, designed to keep even a heavy horse as still as a statue by twisting its lip and applying pressure. Not kind, but sometimes necessary. Mallinson had a long coaching whip.

"The lake," I yelled. "Drive them into it. Freddie's terrified of water."

"Which is which?" Mallinson asked.

"The silver one is Mr. Corwen," Thomas said.

The three of us stood shoulder to shoulder and took a pace forward, Mallinson poking the fighting pair with the end of his whip and Thomas jabbing with the twitch if they came too close.

Corwen must have guessed what we were about because he, too, began to push Freddie to the lakeside.

Freddie was too frantic with rage to notice anything, so the shock of cold water locked him rigid. Corwen took advantage and dived in after him, turning from wolf to naked man in mid-dive. There was blood on his shoulder, flank, and leg, but I couldn't tell if it was his or Freddie's.

Wolves are ungainly in water. After a brief moment of shocked stillness, Freddie began to panic and thrash about.

"Your twitch, Thomas." Corwen held up his hand and deftly caught the handle as Thomas tossed it. He got purchase on the lake bed, secured the twitch around Freddie's snout, and twisted until the loop tightened. The fight melted out of Freddie and as Corwen manhandled him to the shore, he began to turn from wolf to man. I was sure Thomas knew the family secret, but thought this might be new to Mallinson. If it was, the coachman was made of stern stuff. He got his hands beneath Freddie's arms and heaved him out of the water as if what he'd just observed happened every day. Corwen followed, running his hands through his hair to squeeze out the excess water.

"Leave me. Leave me." Freddie muttered. "Throw me back in and let me drown. What have I done?"

"We'll sort it out, Freddie," Corwen said, kneeling by his brother. "I'm here."

"Where were you when I needed you most?"

"You know why I left."

"So when you left Father took it out on me instead. Freddie, do this, Freddie, do that. Freddie, finish your studies. Freddie, become a cloth merchant. Freddie, marry Dorothea Kaye. Freddie, don't turn into a wolf. Freddie, you are the ultimate disappointment to me in my old age."

"How can any of this be my fault?"

"We're twins—supposed to share—you left me to bear it alone."

"You could have followed, or at least sent a message. I would have come home if I'd known."

"Like hell, you would. You didn't even write when Jonnie died."

"I already told you that I didn't know—not for months. When I found out, I came back straightaway to sort out the mess. Your mess, Freddie, boy. Then I came to find you in London."

"Too bloody late."

"Stop feeling sorry for yourself. You were stupid. Got caught. Did you want to be exposed?"

"I thought it might be easier if it was all over."

"Suicide by Mysterium. Neat."

"But it wasn't suicide, was it? It was the sea. My worst nightmare."

Sentence by sentence their voices rose until they were shouting into each other's faces, then Corwen dropped his voice to a controlled whisper. "Yes, your worst nightmare, but it's over now."

Freddie glared at the lake. "That's where it started. You took to swimming like you were made for the water. I was nervous. One day Father brought me down here, threw me in, and walked away. Swim or drown, he said. It was the only way to learn. I was drowning. You pulled me out."

"You were never in any danger. It was Father's ploy. He'd told me to hide by the lakeshore, just in case, but he believed when you had no choice, you'd swim. He was wrong. I was wrong for not warning you."

Freddie was crying now, silent tears streaming down his face.

"Freddie—"

"It's too late for me. What I've done . . ."

"You can change."

"Can I? That little boy . . . He smelled like food. There, I've said it. Walsingham, the Kingsman, even Mother. Food."

Corwen paled and stepped away. "Give me the Tears of Oblivion." He held out his hand to me. "It's time to use them."

◆———◆

By the time we got Freddie to the house, Corwen and Freddie's nakedness aroused no interest. Everyone was focused on Poppy, giving birth on the chaise in the parlor. Corwen's mother, bandaged hand still folded upward across her chest, sat in a chair at Poppy's head murmuring encouragement while Lottie, the cook, mother of three and grandmother of seven, attended the business end.

Yeardley paced the hallway as if it was his own child about to be delivered and Sarah and Mary ran back and forth with hot water and clean linens.

Despite the bad start, it seemed as though everything was going the way it should go.

"Ross!" Poppy saw me peek around the door and called me in. "Stay with me, please."

And so I was pulled into one of the most natural, painful, exhausting, and joyful processes on earth.

When, four hours later, Poppy's half-rowankind daughter gave her first cry, we were all weeping and laughing at the same time.

"She's beautiful, Poppy." I handed the squalling pink thing to her proud mother. "What are you going to call her?"

"Alice," Stephen Yeardley said from behind me. I hadn't even heard him come in. "It was the name of my mother and the last ship I sailed on. We can call her Alice Yeardley, Poppy. Now will you marry me?"

"Of course I will, you great clown. Alice is a good name." She winked at me. "And Alice Yeardley is even better."

Corwen cleared his throat in the doorway. "May I come in?"

"Everyone else has." Lottie was drying her hands on a clean towel.

"A gift for the newborn." Corwen placed a golden guinea in Alice's tiny hand and her fingers flexed around it instinctively.

"She'll never want for anything," Lottie said. "Now, how about Stephen takes Poppy upstairs, and I can get on with preparing tonight's dinner."

I saw Corwen bend and whisper in his mother's ear. She looked startled. "Good-bye?" she said, her voice rising to a wail. "But he's only just come home."

The door swung open to reveal Freddie, dressed in breeches, shirt and frock coat, and wearing Corwen's second-best boots. Thomas and John Mallinson flanked him, but all the fight had vanished. His face was set in a bland half-smile, and his eyes appeared slightly glazed. The Tears of Oblivion had done their job.

"We're taking him to the Okewood," I said. A statement not a question.

"You don't have to come," Corwen told me.

"Yes, I do. I'll change and tell Poppy while your mother is saying good-bye. Do you think he'll ever be able to come home again?"

"I don't know. Physically he's fine, but his mind's a mess."

"The Lady will help."

"She tried to tell me, didn't she?"

"She did, but in the end she had to give him a chance."

"And let me find out for myself."

"That, too."

I ran upstairs to change into my breeches and jacket, already losing sight of my resolution to be a proper lady. I did, however, throw some linen shifts and a couple of my Fae-made gowns into my bag just in case. I returned to the hallway in time to hear Freddie apologizing to his mother for her wounds, though he didn't sound convincing to my ears. He probably couldn't even recall doing it.

Lily drew us to one side. "How long will you be away?"

"We don't know," I said. "It depends on the Lady, and whether there's a price on our heads when the dust settles. We don't want to bring trouble to your doorstep. But we'll let you know what's happening."

"No disappearing for another six years, brother," she said to Corwen.

"I promise." Corwen dropped a kiss on her forehead. "You'll be all right, won't you? With the mill and Mother? You have loyal servants and the rowankind."

"I've got Topping to help with the mill, and now that I know about Kaye's duplicity, I won't get fooled again."

"The Mysterium?"

"George—Mr. Pomeroy—is a moderate gentleman. I believe I have a friend."

"I believe you have a conquest," I declared, earning a questioning look from Corwen. "I'll tell you while we ride." I put my arm through his.

Dancer, Timpani, and Brock were waiting for us by the door with Robin holding Brock's head.

"Are you all right, young man?" I asked him. "You did well to raise the alarm."

"Yes, ma'am. Thank you, ma'am. Can I see Poppy?"

"When she's had a little rest."

"Is it true I've got a new sister?"

"She's called Alice."

"That's pretty."

"Yes, it is."

Corwen's mother came to the door. She swiftly embraced us, both together, and let us go.

"We will come back, Mother," Corwen said. "When we can. Right now you're safer without us."

"Where will you go?"

"To the Lady of the Forests. She can help Freddie. The Mysterium will never find us in the Okewood."

"You'll let us know how you are?"

"Of course. Lily knows how to get a message to us."

With Freddie mounted on Brock, we three rode away from our settled life, not knowing when or even whether we would be able to return. Freddie would have a long journey to recovery, but if anyone could help him, the Lady could. If he truly wanted redemption, he would find it with her.

The breeze swirled around us, bringing the first breath of summer to Yorkshire's hills. I would miss this place, but the family would be safe, and Poppy would be happy with Yeardley.

Corwen and I would be all right, too. Whatever the future had in store for us we'd face it together.

Jacey Bedford
The Psi-Tech Novels

"Space opera isn't dead; instead, delightfully, it has grown up."   —Jaine Fenn,
author of *Principles of Angels*

"A well-defined and intriguing tale set in the not-too-distant future.... Everything is undeniably creative and colorful, from the technology to foreign planets to the human (and humanoid) characters."
—*RT Book Reviews*

"Bedford mixes romance and intrigue in this promising debut.... Readers who crave high adventure and tense plots will enjoy this voyage into the future."
—*Publishers Weekly*

Empire of Dust
978-0-7564-1016-2

Crossways
978-0-7564-1017-9

To Order Call: 1-800-788-6262
www.dawbooks.com